A Free Man
Lewis Warsh

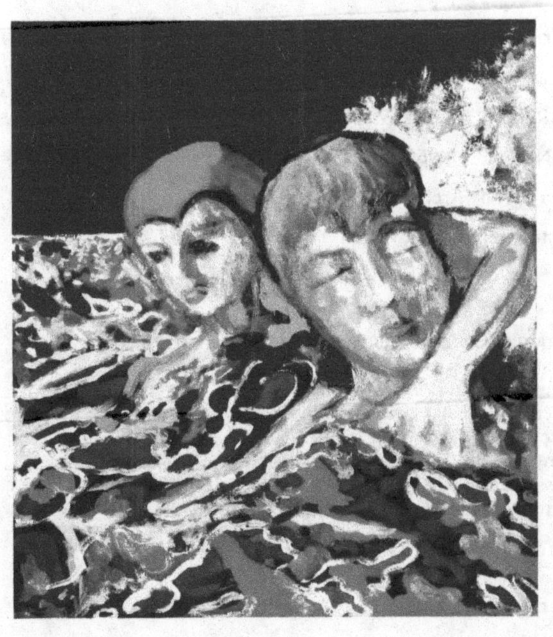

SPUYTEN DUYVIL
NEW YORK CITY

Thanks to Bernadette Mayer, Joanne Kyger,
Robert Creeley, Douglas Messerli, Tod Thilleman.

A Free Man was originally published by Sun & Moon Press in 1991.

ISBN 978-1-949966-19-0

Cover art by Archie Rand

Photograph by Max Warsh

Library of Congress Cataloging-in-Publication Data

Names: Warsh, Lewis, author.
Title: A free man / Lewis Warsh.
Description: New York City : Spuyten Duyvil, 2019.
Identifiers: LCCN 2019006716 | ISBN 9781949966190
Classification: LCC PS3573.A782 F74 2019 | DDC 813/.54--dc23
LC record available at https://lccn.loc.gov/2019006716

for Bill Berkson

1

The woman in apartment 1-C was old enough to be Frank's mother. Old enough to be the grandmother of his children, if he had any. Frank's own mother was always badgering Gina about when she and Frank were going to have kids, but this woman lying dead under a white cotton sheet on the kitchen floor of her modest ground level apartment didn't resemble Frank's mother, not at first glance anyway. Both women had passed from middle to old age; now they were young old people at best. Frank had just turned thirty, but felt old as well. Lucky was the person who could grow old gracefully and still retain the memory of what it felt like to be young.

Unlike Frank's mother, who dutifully went to the beauty parlor every Saturday at 10 a.m., this woman had made no attempt to disguise her age; her hair, chopped at the nape of her neck, was the color of copper, an alloy of pearl and copper, and looked like it had been cut by someone drunk or deranged. Frank couldn't remember what his mother had looked like when she was younger; she wore so much makeup now to mask her wrinkles, and the color of her hair, as well as "the look," was never the same from week to week. He was jealous of the attention his parents gave to his brother and sister and their families, as if having children was the only measure of success they respected. He was jealous of Angelo, the man who worked on his mother's hair every Saturday morning, and to whom she confided her intimate secrets. Angelo had graduated with Frank in the same class from

Erasmus High School in Brooklyn; now, thirteen years later, he was owner of "Angies," a unisex hair salon in Park Slope. Angelo's boyfriend was a painter, they'd traveled in South America, Spain and North Africa together, and the walls of the salon were covered with murky canvases of anacondas and piranhas, interspersed with portraits of people suffering through the last stages of malaria. At least, from their tortured expressions, that's how they looked. This woman was dead, and Frank didn't know anything about her; whether she'd been married or had kids or why anyone would want to harm her. His own mother was alive; at that very moment probably lounging around in the blue terrycloth robe Frank had bought for her last birthday. Sitting at the window of her apartment, painting her nails.

Everyone in high school knew Frank was going to become a cop; his father, uncle, and brother were cops too. There were probably some gay cops, but Frank didn't know any; or didn't know any who'd admit they were queer. Angelo lived in a condominium apartment with his boyfriend in Brooklyn Heights, Frank and Gina in a private house in the Pelham Parkway section of the Bronx. (Where one lived, and whether one owned one's own house or not, was probably a measure of success as well.) They'd been married two years but hadn't slept together since the night a month before when he returned from work and Gina confronted him with the mysterious news she'd been having an affair ("I can't tell you who with"). The next time Frank's mother asked him when they planned to have kids Frank felt like telling her, point blank, that not only weren't they going to have kids, it was unlikely their marriage would survive the summer. How could she get pregnant if they didn't sleep together (pregnant by him, that is)? If a month ago he could return home and she could tell him, without warning, that she was sleeping with someone else, it was inevitable—if he stuck around—he'd return home another evening and she'd be sitting on the living room couch with her legs folded beneath her, "I'm pregnant, Frank," she'd say, as she sipped her drink, "what should I do?" If nothing else, this new piece of information (implying that she no longer saw him as her husband, but rather as her confidant or best friend) would give him a reason to leave; he was tired of sleeping on the couch, if what he did at night could be called sleeping, tired of getting up at dawn too helpless to even fix himself a cup of coffee, tired of going through the motions of his day as if nothing were wrong. Tired of sitting alone at the kitchen table, late at night or early in the morning, staring into space while Gina slept upstairs. If only he could condition himself to the idea marriage wasn't something that necessarily went on forever—that people who'd bothered to ritualize a momentary feeling (or the illusion of a feeling) paid hundreds of dollars every day to lawyers so the memory of that feeling could be erased—he'd understand what had happened to him and Gina ("we made a mistake") wasn't unusual. Most of all, though, he dreaded telling his parents the news. Not having children was bad enough. "You know, I never really liked that girl," his mother would say, not realizing she was making things worse but secretly pleased she'd never have to set eyes on her daughter-in-law again, this person who ("I knew it all along") wasn't worthy of her son.

Frank went to the window and parted the curtain, standing a few inches to one side so anyone looking in could see only his hand. Maybe the murderer, just to be playful, had written his or her name in the dust on the glass. It was his job to look for clues, and eventually he'd begin to sift through the possessions of this woman who only yesterday, or even earlier today, was probably standing at this same window, innocently watching the world wander by. A uniformed policeman was positioned outside the building, swinging his nightstick at his side as he chatted with a man who might have been the building's super, while a woman who might have been Frank's sister-in-law wheeled a stroller past the front stoop, oblivious to the fact that someone resembling her own mother (or anyone's mother) was lying dead on the kitchen floor. But this younger woman with child, whose husband was probably at work, and whose own job was to stay home and take care of the kid (that was how they divided their lives: "He works—I stay at home") wasn't connected, as far as Frank knew, to what had happened in apartment 1-C that morning. There wasn't even any dust on the window, which was unusual, and possibly a clue in itself. Maybe this old woman had hired someone to clean the windows, maybe this had happened recently, and just maybe this person—unlicensed, itinerant—had returned with the excuse he'd left some object, a mop or pail, in the apartment. So the innocent woman let him in, much in the same way Frank's own mother, so absorbed in the article she was reading in the *National Enquirer* about how to lose 40 pounds in 3 days written by a famous female movie star, might absentmindedly open the door of her apartment without even asking, "Who's there?" Frank's mother always told him he needed a haircut and suggested he make an appointment with Angelo, remember him? You went to high school together. The first year after they were married Gina had cut his hair; she liked it long and wouldn't trust anyone else with her baby, which is what she called him. "Did you have a hard day, baby? Let me fix you a drink." Soon an ambulance would arrive and take the body of this woman away. Her relatives (if she had any)—children, sisters and brothers—would be informed. Morning light dusted the linoleum squares. Who found the body? What was the cause of death?

It was 10 a.m., but it wasn't Saturday, and Frank's mother was undoubtedly home, painting her nails. A cup of Sanka cooling on the arm of her chair. What set Angelo apart from other hairdressers was his ability to put people like Frank's mother (to whom "unisex" meant something risque) at their ease. "It's going to be a hot one," Frank's father, a retired cop, was saying, referring to the summer up ahead, as Frank and his brother and sister and their kids took their places at the dining room table. One Sunday a month they all gathered together in the apartment where Frank's parents had lived for twenty years. "I suppose Gina's visiting her family today." But there must be something else they could talk about besides the weather; they were his parents, after all, he was their son, and it seemed, if they only saw each other once a month, the least they could all do was rise to the occasion. If a dead body is discovered at 9:15 a.m....

Frank turned from the window to the interior of the

apartment, avoiding the body of the dead woman; took a pipe from his jacket pocket and rubbed the warm bowl against his cheek. "Hi Mom, it smells good in here." Another Sunday afternoon around the table with the family. "I meant to tell you all that Gina and I are getting a divorce." The woman was murdered some time early this morning. Her name was Bette Eckstein and she was the landlady of the building. She owned the building in a partnership with her brother Morris, and had lived in the same apartment for twenty-two years. Her husband died of a heart attack the night the Yankees lost the playoffs in three straight games to Kansas City. (It was the night the television cameras caught George Steinbrenner, the owner of the Yankees, rushing from his seat in disgust after the final out.) He was sitting in the armchair with the springs pushing through the cushion in the living room of his four-room apartment watching the game on TV. (There was the armchair, there was the television.) Only a few hours ago, or less, someone had entered this apartment and strangled the woman who hadn't even bothered to say who is it?, but who had permitted whoever was knocking to come in, no questions asked. At least that was one possible scenario. There were a few unwashed dishes in the sink, breakfast dishes that this fastidious old woman was about to clean before her life was interrupted; strips of white paint peeling from the kitchen ceiling. Frank felt like doing something—this was his job, after all—but all he could do was think and wait. It was his job to poke around with the hope of uncovering a few obvious clues but all he could do was move a few inches at a time and then stop and look around at whatever was directly in front of him. It had been weeks since he'd been able to concentrate on what he was doing, think clearly, act purposefully, and though the people he worked with—"the guys"—knew something was bothering him, there was no one among them, not even his partner, Joe Hopper, whom he could talk with openly. He wanted to remember how right after he and Gina got together her presence in his life had created an aura around everything he was doing so even the most trivial activities seemed meaningful and filled with urgency, but it was like trying to enter the skin of another person, sift through the debris of memory till he recognized himself: this is me.

Now an ambulance would come and take the body away and he'd be left, finally, with the pieces of a puzzle, which with luck he'd be able to fit together in some kind of symmetrical way that would allow him to at least pretend to himself that what he'd discovered was true, the truth, "the whole truth," this person's the murderer. But the level at which "finding the murderer" was important didn't matter anymore. He was no longer the person who'd made fun of Angelo Donatio in the hallways of Erasmus High School because Angelo was queer and Frank knew he was going to be a cop and this knowledge made him feel superior, not only to Angelo but to everyone else; he knew what he wanted to do with his life, and they didn't. He'd wanted that identity and now he had it, but it was just a label he could pin to himself so he wouldn't have to worry about anything else. Knowing who you are might be better than not knowing but if you know and you don't like what you know then maybe it's better not to know anything. He wasn't the self-satisfied person who drove home from work every day with a smug expression on his face: "Can I get you anything, baby?" Maybe she was a virgin when they got married, maybe not, did it matter?

The woman under the sheet wasn't Frank's mother. She was sitting at the window in the blue bathrobe Frank had bought for her 60th birthday, painting her nails, lost in thought, unaware of the shadow of the man with the cord of rope or nylon stocking who had entered the apartment (she'd left the door unlocked by mistake). She didn't make a sound. It wouldn't be a case where her cries for help were ignored by her neighbors. There were no signs of struggle. When Gina told him she'd been unfaithful, that night in mid-April when he returned from work, he'd felt like strangling her, too. It's possible your sympathies lie as much with the murderer as with the victim. Whether it was his mother or someone he didn't know, what was the difference? His sense of himself as a protector of the people—put that in quotes—along. with the label he'd pinned to himself ("I'm a cop") had faded away. Maybe if we'd had a few kids things would have been different, but we were only married two years, what can you expect? It had been his idea to sleep on the couch. He couldn't imagine sleeping in the same bed with her if she were sleeping with someone else. Everything he did left a trail of thoughts, but the person having these thoughts was no one he knew. This person he'd been able to identify so clearly had been murdered too, and the thoughts and feelings, like the torn articles of clothing the rapist leaves dangling from the branches of a tree as he escapes, were clues to the memory. And if the analogy could be made, it was probably easier to track down the murderer of this old woman than to find himself. In the latter case, who knew where to begin?

2

Frank took a spiral notebook from the inside pocket of his jacket, unclipped a ballpoint from his shirt pocket, and placed both objects on a corner of the table, averting his eyes while the young woman poured his coffee.

"Do you take sugar?"

There was a bowl of sugar and a milk container on the table. On the side of the container an ad for a local New York radio station ("We play Jimi, we play Janis, we play The Beatles, we play Elvis, we play Frank") which Frank read as the woman replaced the coffee pot on the stove. Part of him wanted to think he wasn't here on business, but instead that he'd met this woman in some other context and for other reasons—in a bar or at a party given by mutual friends, after which she'd invited him back to her apartment ("would you like some coffee?") Just this morning he'd been sitting alone in his own kitchen, last night's dinner dishes piled high in the sink. If Gina wasn't going to do the dishes, and she'd been neglectful of her household chores recently—they were thought of as *her* chores only because he was the one who went out and worked—he wished she'd tell him just when or what she intended to do so he could take care of things like dirty dishes and dirty laundry himself. Conversations dealing with the practical aspects of life had become rare; they never, for instance, talked about "having children," which at one time—and it didn't seem to Frank so long ago—had felt like an inevitable possibility. It had been a while since Frank had gone anywhere with the purpose of meeting someone ("picking someone up") and he'd lost any sense of what to say or do if the object of the encounter was to end up in bed with the other person. As a single person he'd never been very adept at meeting people in this way, which is why getting married had been such a relief: now I don't have to think about that anymore. Telling people you were a detective usually put them off, especially women, though there were probably a few who were attracted and titillated by the idea of being with someone who was carrying a gun, or the knowledge that his occupation ("I'm a cop") involved more than the average amount of risk. That if you were married to such a person you might one day receive a phone call informing you that your husband had been killed or wounded in the line of duty. Would this appeal to anyone?

There was always the possibility that he and this woman, whom he'd just met, could end up in bed together, but it was necessary to resist that train of thought if he ever expected to accomplish anything. She'd permitted him to enter her apartment so he could ask her a few questions. He was working, this was his job. The pen and the notebook were there for a reason. If she said something he thought was important he'd write it down. The coffee was just regular American coffee that she'd brewed by heating water and then pouring the coffee grounds into the pot, cowboy style. He'd been in her apartment maybe three minutes and all he'd told her was his name—flashing his badge—and that he wanted to ask her a few questions, was that all right? She'd consented—"of course it's all right"— and had offered him a cup of coffee, "no trouble, it's already made." At home, when he felt up to it, he made coffee for himself in an electric coffeepot someone had given them for a wedding present (them, the newlyweds, Frank and Gina). Every morning for almost two years Gina had fixed him breakfast while he was in the bathroom getting dressed for work. What does she do all day while I'm gone?

When he kissed her goodbye she was still wearing her nightgown, the one with the small beige flowers embroidered on the sleeves and along the collar. He couldn't imagine her just sitting around all day, talking to her mother on the phone or visiting with friends she'd known since high school and who also still lived in the Bronx, all of them married, mostly to men they'd known since high school, all of them housewives, some with babies, with nothing to do while their husbands went off to work, though comparing notes over the phone about what their so-called husbands were like in bed was the equivalent of holding a full-time job or of going to school. "I think I'm going back to school." While Frank ate his breakfast—two scrambled eggs, well-done, and a slice of toast with jam—Gina, the waitress, the wife, the mother-to-be, sipped her coffee. "Goodbye, baby, have a good day." They embraced on the threshold, and Frank drove away.

From where he sat at the kitchen table he could see the entire apartment. It was more like one medium-sized room divided into three tiny ones, except that there were no walls or doors between rooms. Even the bathroom, just a water closet containing sink and toilet, had no door. Space between objects or furniture could be measured in inches; i.e., a few inches to Frank's right there was a bathtub covered with a wooden board, on top of the board a stack of white plates and an old coffee tin containing knives and forks. The door of the apartment opened into the kitchen. In what passed for a living room there was a couch, an extremely narrow floor-to-ceiling bookcase, and a brick wall covered with posters and photographs. The third room contained a desk (another wooden board, possibly a door, propped up on crates) with a manual typewriter, a chair and a bed. There were no closets. A laundry bag overflowed at the foot of the bed, spilling over what looked like an old fan and an assortment of wire coat hangers and screens. No "feminine" touches, so to speak. Not the dwelling of a human being who was obsessive about order, or keeping things tidy. Blouses and sweaters hung from hooks on the bedroom wall. A cat peeked out from beneath the bed. (Frank liked cats but Gina was allergic so they didn't have any.) A.TV set on a wooden crate in the living room facing the couch; on top of the set a copy of TV Guide. The only windows in the apartment were in the bedroom.

Lying in this woman's bed, if it came to that, head propped on pillows, one could see the trunk and branches of a tree in the courtyard behind the building, and in spring and summer listen to the birds. When the birds alighted on the fire escape the cat went crazy. When the cat was in heat she went down the fire escape into the courtyard. At the sound of a siren or a car backfiring or a firecracker the birds disappeared, out of their element except for the quiet hours before dawn when they could make the pavement and the tree and the fire escape their home. The woman in the apartment downstairs didn't have a fire escape; if there were ever a fire she could just walk out the front door. Plaster was peeling on every wall. The apartment was so empty Frank wondered if this woman had just moved in, though instinct told him it was as possible she had lived here many years. Some people, like the woman downstairs and like Frank's mother, saved everything. Shoeboxes filled with bank statements and electric bills dated 1950. Every letter that they ever received. It's only when you move around a lot from place to place that you think of discarding the documents of the past. Toss the letter into the fire, you'll never see that person again. The older you get the more you like to be reminded, though, of what happened in the past; and the objects that related to your past serve to remind you that your memory is more than a dream. It's not necessary to search out the detritus at the bottom of someone's closet to find out what they' re like; all you have to do is look them in the eye.

The woman wore a light-blue long-sleeved wool sweater, the same sweater she'd worn all winter, and jeans with patches on the knees. The patches were a different shade of blue from the pants. As soon as she had some extra money she was planning to buy a new pair. The sweater, like most of her other clothing, was a gift from a friend, and made her breasts seem larger than they were. When she was younger she'd been embarrassed about the size of her breasts and would have purposely worn clothing to make them look larger. (When Gina—in the old days— kissed him goodbye in the morning, Frank could feel the pressure of her breasts beneath her nightgown, and for the moment it made the idea of going to work more ludicrous than it already was.) She perched on a stool across the table, sipping her coffee. Though Gina still occasionally made coffee for him in the morning ("since we still live together we might as well be friends") and when they were home together, at dinner time, prepared a meal, which they ate, often, in silence, Frank couldn't help feeling grateful for this minimum display of hospitality (most people were reluctant, even after he identified himself—"it's the police"—to open their door). It was the way so-called civilized people acted and the way everyone should act, not naively, not cynically, but free of the thought that this strange person, whoever he or she was, would bite your head off or say something outrageous or impertinent or do something hideous that would make you think twice the next time someone knocked. A cup of coffee was the least anyone could offer.

Frank had never been very successful at going to bars and picking up women; he'd rather spend the night alone than put himself through the ordeal of trying to explain "who he was" to another person. (It never occurred to him that conversation of this kind wasn't necessary, that you could go to bed with someone without knowing more than his or her name, if even that.) Once, drunk, he'd made a pass at a woman in a bar, she'd slapped his face, and the bartender ("but I'm a cop!") had escorted him out the door. If he'd met this woman in other circumstances—at a bar, or a party—and if it were eleven at night or later, not eleven in the morning—he would probably be tempted to reach across the table.... "Why did you invite me into your apartment if you didn't want to go to bed with me?"

There were dark circles under the woman's eyes, as if she'd been awake most of the night: six empty beer cans (Rheingolds) and an empty fifth of Jack Daniels littered the floor near the refrigerator. Though he'd interrogated many people over the years, sitting across the table from this woman in her apartment was, for Frank, a kind of education, since despite her slovenliness and utter disregard for physical appearances, he felt attracted to her anyway, attracted to the whole mess and disorder of her life. And it didn't surprise him either. Why not be attracted to the opposite of what he'd been taught women should be? Gina had fit that earlier image, and look what happened. ("It's just me, I'm a person like everyone else, you've seen women naked before, what's the big deal?")

When he was first courting Gina he used to bring her flowers, roses—when they were in season and he could afford them—but most often daisies and chrysanthemums ("my favorites!"); on the day they were married, at St. Bridget's church in the Bronx, not far from where Gina's family lived, he wore a carnation in the button of his suit jacket, a flower he might have saved, if he were truly sentimental, preserved between the pages of an old book. All the men at the wedding, relatives and friends who were also his co-workers, wore carnations. The night before the ceremony his best man and partner, Joe Hopper, had organized a bachelor party. Gina spent the night at her parents', even though they'd already been living together for two months. Joe showed home movies featuring his wife Irene and their two sons, taken the previous summer on a camping trip in the Adirondacks, and a pornographic movie he had rented for the occasion. Frank sipped his drink and realized that except for Joe he didn't think of any of the other men at the party as his close friends. Being together with a group of men, socially, made him uncomfortable, even more so since these particular men, whom he saw every day and with whom he got along well in a superficial way, in the context of his job, seemed to regard him as the center of attention and couldn't understand why he preferred to sit back and watch everyone else enjoy themselves, or try to; if the party was being given in his honor he should at least be allowed to do that. "Are you drunk yet, Frank?" They all had some preconceived idea about what he, as a person about to get married, was supposed to feel like, and part of the image involved getting drunk and falling down and passing out and even being sick, so sick he had to be helped home and put to bed and ministered to so that he'd be able to function ("here, drink this coffee, it'll make you feel better") the next day. He and Gina had considered the possibility of getting married at City Hall, maybe go to a restaurant afterwards, get up in the morning and go to sleep at night as if nothing particularly momentous had happened in between. As Frank watched the tangle of bodies on the screen, the preoccupied faces of the women as they lay on their backs or on their stomachs and spread their legs (Frank had once taken part in a raid on a hotel room where a porno movie was being made and he remembered how young all the women looked in the hot arc of the kleig lights, as if they'd just stepped off the bus from Cedar Rapids or Sioux Falls) it occurred to him maybe he and Gina had made a big mistake. All he could think about at the bachelor party, as he nursed his drink, was that tonight, of all nights, he was going to sleep alone.

"Do you think we should have a baby?" They would lie in bed, holding hands, and plan their future. Gina was only twenty-three and wanted to wait awhile, understandably, before having kids, which was fine with Frank, everything Gina wanted was okay with him. Even when she decided, a year into their marriage, to return to school and study art history so she could go out and work too—teaching art in high school was a realistic ambition and something she'd always wanted to do—he didn't discourage her, even though it meant she might not be at home when he returned from work (though his hours were erratic, especially if he was on an important assignment, he liked the idea that she'd be there, waiting up for him, or even asleep with the bedside lamp turned on, when he came home late).

He had lived alone for eight years before meeting Gina and looking back at that time from the vantage of being a married person with a house and a job made him wonder what part of himself had given his whole self the license to accept the solitude that went along with being a bachelor, returning home every night to an empty apartment, waking every morning alone in bed. During that time his married friends acted as if he were the lucky one among them, they projected their own fantasies about life as a single person onto him, what they read about the single life in newspapers and magazines or saw in the movies, while they were stuck with wives and babies and mortgages and the prospect of living with just this one person for what seemed to them like forever while he was free, free to go out and sleep with a different person every night. "I'm afraid it isn't that simple." If only he could convince his friends it wasn't that simple ("at least not for me") and how much he envied them, they should count their blessings, he thought, as he stood around their houses and in their backyards on weekend afternoons when they invited him over and he could see first-hand the amount of energy and stimulation and distraction having a wife and kids generated. It presented him with the illusion that with a family there was never a chance to lapse into some mood that you couldn't express because no one was there. Frank had always assumed he'd eventually meet someone he'd fall in love with and want to live with but that didn't mean his life with this other person had to resemble the lives of his friends. No one he knew—not his father, or brother, or even Joe Hopper—could even pretend to be a model of what he imagined his life as a married person would be. Meanwhile he would wait, he would wait nervously, he'd be patient.

On nights when Gina was at school and he returned home from work it was hard for him not to slip back into those pre-marriage feelings: the empty house, the silence, eating alone over the sports pages, playing the radio just to fill the house with sound. But then, and this was the difference, this was what made it all possible, an hour or two later she'd be back, and they'd sit on the couch with their arms around each other, her legs thrown over his, his hand resting casually at the open collar of her blouse, they would share a beer and tell each other the story of their separate days.

Now he was asking this strange woman a question

and—trying to concentrate—he was writing down the answer. Not word for word, but in a kind of shorthand legible only to himself. She's too relaxed, Frank thought, for someone who only that morning had discovered the dead body of someone she knew, the landlady of the building, an old lady who lives in a shoe, it isn't every day you stumble across a dead body, is it? ("My name is Rosemary. What's yours?" They were sitting at a bar and he was telling her, drunkenly, and with his hand on her thigh, about the time he was waiting on line in the bank and the guy in front of him pulled a gun on the teller, "do you know what happened then? do you know what I did then?"—when the man she was with came up behind her and took her arm—"She's with me, buddy"—and led her away.)

"I was going down to pay the rent, I always try to pay the rent by the end of the first week of every month if not before but this time I was late. Mrs. Eckstein, Bette, never minded—she didn't care if I was a few days late, or even a few weeks. She knew I had a steady job and I've been living here almost two years so she knows I'm going to pay. She wasn't the type of landlady who'd threatened to throw you out if you didn't pay the rent on time. If there was ever any problem with the apartment, if the walls or ceilings needed plastering or if the pipes in the bathroom leaked, I would tell her—and usually all I had to do was tell her once—and she'd get it fixed, the super who lives in the building down the street would come either the same day or a day or two later. You should talk to him, Mr. Rosario, at 110, just down the street. He might know something. I don't know anyone in the building very well. I mean I nod and say hello to people when I pass them going into the building but I've never been in anyone else's apartment. I didn't know Mrs. Eckstein very well. Usually, on days when I'd go pay the rent we'd have a cup of coffee together if I had the time. She liked to talk about her family and show me pictures of her son. He lives in California, I think."

"We've already spoken to him."

"Sometimes she talked about selling the building and moving to California so she could be near her son. He visited once a while back but I didn't get to meet him. I saw Bette almost every day, sitting at the window of her apartment, looking out at the street, she was usually there when I left the house in the morning. I work in the library near the park so I see her a lot. Warm days she sat on a folding chair on the sidewalk. She seemed to know everyone in the neighborhood, all the storeowners, she's been around here a long time. I don't know if she had any enemies or if there was anyone who disliked her; you should talk to the other people in the building, but I can't imagine she didn't treat them the same way she treated me—as long as they paid the rent, eventually, there was never any trouble. But I don't think it matters how many friends or enemies she had; if you ask me the person who did it had never set eyes on her before, that's just my opinion, though it was probably—could have been—somebody who lives in the neighborhood who knew she was the landlady of the building. I don't know if she ever kept any money in the apartment but from the look—you saw it yourself—someone obviously thought she kept something there. And maybe she did. Am I being helpful? Is there anything else you want to know?"

"Tell me exactly what you saw when you came in to her apartment."

"Well, first of all, the door was open—maybe three inches—and that's unusual. No one ever keeps their door open, not around here. Everyone has some kind of special lock and Bette was no exception. She'd never open the door to someone she didn't know. So I was surprised when I saw the door open and didn't hear anyone talking. I knocked on the door, once, and called her name. Maybe she'd gone out for a second and left the door unlocked. Maybe she'd gone to get the mail but it was too early for that. The mailman usually comes at around eleven, around now. I waited a few moments, called her name again, and then I pushed the door open all the way. And there she was. The door opens into the kitchen, just like this apartment, as you saw, even though her apartment is twice the size of this one, and there she was, stretched out, just like you found her. She was probably standing at the sink when whoever it was entered the apartment, unless whoever did it dragged the body to the sink, though why would they do that? Someone, the killer, crept up behind her when she was standing at the sink. At least that's what I thought—that was my first thought—when I saw it all. And then I saw the bag of groceries on the floor and noticed she was wearing a sweater over her dress. Which meant that she'd been out shopping and the person who killed her followed her into the apartment. You don't have to be a detective to figure that one out. Some people like to go shopping early in the morning before the stores get crowded. Bette wasn't the type of person who went shopping just as an excuse to get out of the house. She wasn't a lonely person. I don't know how old she was but she didn't act like an old person. When you talked to her you realized there was a part of her that was still young. Anyway, I'm not sure what I did at that exact moment. I think I screamed but I don't know how loud or if anyone heard me. I knew it was Bette. I didn't have to look at her face to know it was her. Who else could it be? She always wears the same dress around the house, she's been wearing it ever since I've known her. She'd sit at the window facing the street wearing that housedress. It seems like she must have had a few housedresses in the same style since I can't remember her ever not wearing it and I'm sure she must have taken it off to wash it some time. She'd even wear it when she was going to the store. She wasn't the type of person who cared very much about the way she looked which is odd for people her age who are usually concerned with their appearance. She didn't try to fake her age by trying to make herself look younger, like she never went to the beauty parlor—maybe once a year on special occasions—but she didn't go regularly like a lot of older women do. And I don't think she ever went out at night. She liked to stay home, watch television, read the paper. Once she told me that before she went to sleep she listened to some talk show on the radio, and that she often fell asleep with the radio on; you know, the type of show where people phone in, cranks usually, and express their—opinions—if that's what you want to call them. People who live alone and need someone to talk to—that's what those shows are all about, right? That's why they're so popular. Though as I said

I don't think Bette was particularly lonely, less so than a lot of people her age I know, she just used the radio as a kind of sedative—the way some people take sleeping pills before getting into bed. Is there anything else?"

The trouble began a few months after Gina started going to school, and if Frank had been quicker and more attentive to her, less involved in his job, he might have realized that her desire to get out of the house and have a life of her own was a symptom of something that had more to do with their marriage than with some practical idea about what they could do if both of them were working. Having more money wasn't the issue. At least it never occurred to Frank that she envied other people for having things—objects, clothing—which she couldn't afford; on the contrary, she seemed to enjoy living within her means, it was a source of satisfaction not to sit around and complain about money, which is what everyone they knew seemed to do.

Frank had gone through periods when he questioned whether he was truly suited for his job, whether he enjoyed what he was doing, whether enjoying what you were doing was a criterion for continuing to do it, whether he was just wasting his life or biding time till he could retire and live off his pension. It was amazing to him that no one he worked with ever expressed similar feelings of self-doubt; everyone accepted the level at which their life was taking place, as if they had no choice. It was a matter of reaching the point where you merged with the mirror image of yourself; there was the "you" looking at an "I"—standing back, distancing yourself, wondering who that person might be. Unfortunately, there were no answers; no matter how long you questioned yourself, there were still two people—the person who asked the question and the person who went through life as if there were no questions to ask. Gina's feeling that she could change her life, or widen her horizons, as they say, by being more than just a housewife, a policeman's wife, the future mother of Frank's kids, had inspired Frank to think he could make his own life different as well. He didn't particularly want to get up every morning at the same time, shave, eat breakfast ("Have a good day, baby"), and navigate his car through the morning traffic from the Bronx down the East River Drive to the precinct on Pitt Street; didn't enjoy prowling around strange apartmentbuildings, knocking on doors, staring at charred corpses, riding around in an unmarked car with a false mustache pretending he was someone else. He had learned how to do something once and he was still young enough to learn how to do something else, even if he was no better off—in the sense of knowing what he wanted to do—than he'd been ten years previous.

She was gone, she was off on her own. When he came home from work the house was empty. Hours passed. The trouble began then. She was supposed to be home at a certain time. He worried about the walk from the subway stop to their house. This neighborhood was no better or worse than anywhere else. She could be raped, mugged, whatever—and no one would be surprised. Especially in winter when it got dark early and the streets were empty—everyone hidden in their houses, brooding over the newspaper or watching TV—the branches of the trees made one continuous insinuating shadow on the sidewalk: if something happened—and Frank, as a cop, was conditioned to think something could happen—and she called out for help, no one would hear. Maybe she stopped off at her parents' house, they lived within walking distance, but he didn't want to call them and worry them if she wasn't there. He'd told her always to call if she were ever going to be late—it was the same thing he'd tell his teenage daughter if he had one—but what reason could she possibly have for being late? If she came home and he was there, waiting for her, it was up to her—or so Frank thought—to make him forget that she hadn't been there when he wanted to be with her, make it up to him somehow, as if that were part of the job of being his wife, but instead, when she did return home, hours after he'd expected her, she was more distant than ever, no need to even begin to explain where she'd been or what she'd been doing all the time since class had ended, not even to him, me, her husband.

"Would you like a beer?"

They sat in silence at opposite ends of the couch. All the easy intimacy of those first nights, when she'd return home from school and they'd practically fall into one another's arms, had vanished. If he asked whether something was bothering her she'd shrug and complain about being tired or indicate, without saying anything, that she didn't want to talk about it, "it," whatever.

"Have you ever slept with anyone else, Frank? I mean, since we've been married. Have you ever thought of it?"

The trouble began then. Frank, suddenly overly conscious of the angle of his arm in relation to the arm of the couch and the way the light from the table lamp seemed to be burning a grotesque hole in the orange upholstery, began to wonder if there was any difference between the lit part and the part enveloped in shade, and whether possibly he should change the position of the lamp, move it an inch to the left—or to the right—so the beam would fall somewhere else. The couch was falling apart anyway; it had been given to him when he was still living alone, about a year before he and Gina met. The couple next door were moving out; he met them one evening in the hallway and they told him they were leaving the couch and that he was welcome to it. Frank couldn't believe they were going to give it to him for free; he'd been brought up to believe that everything cost something. Was there anything wrong with this couch? Did it have bugs? This couple, whom he didn't know well, and had never seen again since the day they packed all their things into a big van and drove off, helped him carry the couch down the hall into his apartment. "There's nothing wrong with it," the woman, who was three months pregnant, assured him. When Gina and Frank decided to move into the house in the Bronx, Gina was adamant about taking as much as possible with them. It seemed foolish, and a waste of money, to replace perfectly good pieces of furniture, things that were still functional, with objects that were new, badly made, and could just as easily fall apart as the things they already had. As Gina delivered her speech in defense of the couch, Frank focused on the word "functional": that seemed like the key word, the bottom line, so to speak, in terms of whether an object was salvageable: if it wasn't functional then you might as well get rid of it, right?

"I bet you never thought I was so practical."

It was true, he hadn't seen that side of her before. "What about a new bed?"

"I think this one's fine, I'm getting attached to it in fact."

"I think we could afford a new one, don't you? They make bigger beds than this one, you know."

"I know about beds, I mean I know they make bigger beds but do you really think we need a bigger bed?"

They were actually lying in bed when this conversation took place, but as Frank, months later, studied the lamplight on the couch, he couldn't remember how they'd evolved from that moment to the one he was experiencing now where in order to answer or to continue the train of conversation he would have to become another person, anyone but himself. Waiting for his response Gina paced the floor, smoking. Obviously, if he wasn't going to answer she'd have to fill the silence by telling him what she really meant ("I don't know what you mean" was a possible response Frank had vetoed). One moment her back was to him and then she was facing him and then she was throwing her hands in the air and laughing nervously as if to say: "You're impossible, we can never talk about anything!", stomping out of the room only to return a moment later with a drink in her hand. The shrillness in her voice, when she did say something, was what startled him. Maybe he should just answer the question direct, deadpan, as if asking such a question was something he could fit, casually, into the repertoire of possible things a husband or wife could say to one another. "Oh shit, I might as well tell you what's on my mind." He started to relight his pipe and then stopped; the temptation, now, was to fling it at her—if not at her, then through the living room window into the night. Equilibrium, the feeling that everything was all right, the feeling of complacency—which equaled joy—wasn't something you could buy at the corner store.. Maybe the night when they lay in bed in his old apartment, discussing what they'd take with them, had been a kind of peak; certainly a signpost from which Frank could step back and realize the difference between his life with someone and his life alone. And then the flicker of anxiety when she didn't come home from school on time, when she wasn't there when he came home from work, when instead of doing anything he found himself staring into space—waiting— and then, when she did come in, instead of greeting him with open arms, perching on his knee and opening a beer which they'd then share, she would act as if it wasn't his right to even question what she'd been doing.

"I'm tired, Frank, we'll talk in the morning."

Or "Not now, Frank" when he tried to embrace her— maybe she was tired—and she'd step back, as if she want- ed to get away from him, a glass of orange juice in her hand.

It was odd how contrary feelings like peace of mind and anxiety could coexist in the same organism; no won- der people went crazy. Every instance of disharmony, ev- ery argument or fight, was like one additional crack in a terrible mirror that reflected only surfaces—the arm bending into the light, the lampshade with its delicate fringe and which had once been perfect, a source of lu- minosity and real pleasure. When he finally answered her question with a simple "No"—since it was the truth, he hadn't slept with anyone since they'd met, hadn't even considered it—the knowledge that he was telling the truth, that she'd know by his tone he was telling the truth, the whole truth and nothing but etc. made the venom underlying her response all the more surprising: "Well I have. Every Tuesday and Thursday for the last month. Do you think I just walk around by myself after class? Do you think—" Frank caught her as she burst into tears, head buried in his right shoulder.

"You must hate me."

"No, I don't hate you. I just want to know what you want me to do."

"Aren't you hurt? Don't you feel like you want to kill me?"

"Who is he? I think I feel like killing him." (I'm a cop, I can kill anyone.)

"But why him? You'd probably like him if you ever met. *I'm* the one who's been unfaithful to you."

Two years! Only yesterday they were lying in bed in his old apartment arguing over the pieces of furniture they should or shouldn't take with them. At least it seemed like yesterday. There weren't enough memories between then and now for Frank to fall back on, like buffers against the storm. The whole scene made him think he must be an extremely dull person (something he occasionally felt about himself anyway) for her to have lost interest in him so quickly. He remembered lying in bed with her, watching her sleep, and wondering—they'd only been married a month—whether it was true they'd remain faithful to each other forever. Wasn't that the whole point of getting married? It seemed unimaginable, at the same time, that Gina—who was seven years younger and had only slept with two or three men before him (at least that's what she said)—would be able to sustain indefinitely whatever feelings of satisfaction she received from him. If, in fact, she received any satisfaction at all. The way you expressed what you were feeling when you were in bed with someone was one of life's great mysteries, especially when there were so many other feelings involved. If you were going to share a bed with someone every night of your life there was no ultimate way of feeling, one night passed into the next, every night was different. What mattered was that you had chosen to be in bed with this person to begin with. No arguments or fights or lengthy discussions ever ensued from whatever passed between them when they turned out the lights. Neither of them felt self-conscious about undressing in front of the other; sometimes she waited for him, other nights he got into bed first. He made a point of going to bed when she wanted to, even if he wasn't tired. If there was some ultimate knowledge about what was to proceed from whatever did take place in bed.... Gina folded her nightgown, the one with the beige flowers, over the back of a chair. Frank was so lost in his sense of well being he didn't stop to think about what she was feeling. He didn't want to think that anything could ever go wrong.

"Listen," she was saying, "I love you, I don't love him. That's the truth. I won't blame you if you go away and leave me. I want you to stay, I think things will get back to normal after awhile. I'm sorry"—Frank could no longer recognize her—"I don't know what I'm doing."

And then, when they'd gotten into bed: "I can't sleep"—this was Frank speaking—"I'm going downstairs."

He put on his bathrobe and descended the steps to the kitchen, filled a shot glass with bourbon and leaned back against the sink. The idea of lying beside a woman (which was only an idea, after all), his wife no less, when she'd been unfaithful to him a few hours before, made him doubt whether he'd ever sleep again, though part of him knew that the best cure for the way he was feeling was to shrug his shoulders and pretend he didn't care. Like a child throwing a tantrum will stop if you ignore what he or she is doing. He didn't know how long he'd been in the dark, in the corner of the couch where he'd been sitting when she first told him ("I didn't really mean any of that, I just wanted to see what you'd say"), when he heard her footsteps circling behind him.

"Are you coming to bed? You're going to feel horrible tomorrow"—she was trying to be nice—"if you don't get some sleep."

And when he didn't answer: "I can't sleep alone."

"Well, you better get used to it."

"What does that mean?"

And then it was her turn to go into the kitchen, light a cigarette, fix a drink—these were the props, and anyone looking in from the street (and anyone could look in, the curtains were wide open) would see these two characters, actor and actress, playing out their scene—perched on the edge of the couch, the folds of her robe falling open around her knees and thighs as if she were trying to tell him: I can love you too, nothing has to change. I can love two people at once (in this case love means "fuck"), anything's possible.

Frank felt bombarded by any number of things he might say that could cause her pain, and in this way restore some kind of negative balance to their lives. Yet he felt innocent, too—he was still in love with her, after all; anything he said could only make things worse. It would be impossible for them to talk sanely without him delivering some final ultimatum: If you don't stop sleeping with him—whoever he is—I'm going to leave. And then what would she say? By telling him she was being unfaithful she was inviting him to leave. She'd even said: I don't blame you if you go. If I were you I'd probably do the same thing. At the same time she seemed to be saying: If you love me enough then try to understand what I'm feeling. I don't want to leave you for anyone else. Something happened and I'm trying to deal with it the best I can. Do you think I didn't think twice before telling you? Why do you insist on making me feel guilty?

Frank knew if he drank enough the tension would eventually dissolve; he'd forget whatever he was angry about and collapse, fully dressed, into his own bed, oblivious of whether Gina—who'd never seen him so blasted—was there or not. But what made it hard for him to really lose himself this time was the thought that when he woke tomorrow the whole situation—if you could call it that—which was really his life, a real soap opera, wouldn't be any different, the sadness and the anger and all the confused feelings and mixed signals he didn't even understand would still be there, sliding off the top of his mind into some steep ravine. How could he go to work tomorrow and pretend to function without showing what he was feeling to the people he worked with, his so-called friends (if they were truly his friends wouldn't they be able to sense something was wrong just by looking at him?), didn't Joe Hopper, the best man at his wedding, brag about girlfriends of his own and hadn't Joe said—when Frank told him he was planning to get married—that no matter what anyone said a man needed to sleep with other women, there was no one person who could do it all for any other person, not forever certainly, and that in the context of a marriage (not the phrase Joe used) you had to give the other person room, otherwise marriage was just torture, the pits, absolute hell?

"Whenever I sleep with someone it makes me feel real close to Irene," Joe had told him. "I mean it makes me want to sleep with her even more."

"But does Irene sleep with other people?"

Joe lifted his glass, signaled to the waitress: another pitcher.

"Yeah, she slept with a guy once. It just happened once. Remember the time you and Gina came over and Irene had a black eye? You asked how it happened and she said she'd walked into a door? Well, she told me about this fucker she'd been with the night before—(swallow)—and that's what happened."

It was still dark at 6 a.m. when Frank backed the car, a Ford station wagon he'd bought used from a friend of his father, out of the driveway ("no need for all this room now that we're not going to have any kids"), not even waiting as he did most mornings to warm up the battery, but just taking off, flicking the brights as he dipped from the curb to the street. Since Gina had gone to bed—sighing, she swept her robe over her knees and touched his shoulder ("can't we be friends?") as she walked by him—the voices in his brain had been issuing frightened signals, as garbled, but less mellifluous, as the voices of the birds in the trees. All the logical tracks led nowhere. He could rewind the tape and play back the conversation in the hope that something she said would make him feel different. The only thing to do—and this is what the voices in his head eventually informed him—was to move, physically, from his position on the couch to some other place, any other place, in this case where didn't matter as long as he could get up the strength to move. As long as he sat in one place staring into space, occasionally lifting a glass to his lips or lighting a cigarette, the shadows on the walls of the impenetrable dungeon he was creating for himself would grow more forboding. If he could move his whole physical structure then the thoughts in his head would change too. And possibly in order to really implement some kind of change that would make a difference he'd have to keep moving for an indefinite period of time.

The morning air, as he rolled down the window, was certainly an antidote to something, but what he really needed was the presence of another person. The only person he could think of visiting was Joe Hopper, who lived with his wife and kids about a mile away. Joe often chided Frank for not visiting more frequently, or as often as he did before he and Gina were married, "I mean it's not like you live in Staten Island or something," and it was true, since meeting Gina Frank felt less inclined to socialize with anyone. Maybe it was because he'd spent so many years living alone, wondering what he could do to get himself out and with other people. Now that he was with someone he just wanted to stay home and bask in the glow. The memory of how he'd felt on weekend afternoons when he had nothing to do was still too vivid in his mind, and every afternoon he spent alone with Gina was another step in obliterating that person. It didn't matter what streets he took to get from his house to Joe's as long as he drove in the general direction (Gun Hill Road, Williamsburg Road, etc.) he'd get there, and he was in no big rush.

"Frank! You look awful. What are you doing up so early? Do you want some coffee?"

It was Irene, still in her nightgown, which was blue and almost transparent, with small bows on the shoulders and a larger bow that resembled a corsage at the V of the neckline, who greeted him at the door.

"Is something the matter?"

She held the screen door open wide so he could brush past her into the kitchen. For a moment their bodies connected, and Frank was tempted to lean forward and kiss the crease in her neck. Though he'd known Joe and Irene almost eight years he'd rarely seen Irene without make-up—he'd never had reason to visit them at six in the morning before—and he was stunned by her beauty (she was a woman, after all, not a girl), the way the waves of her brown hair rolled across her back and shoulders and still seemed to glow under the dismal circle of fluorescence emanating from the kitchen ceiling. All the time he lived alone he had used Irene as the model of the person he might someday fall in love with and marry; when Joe recounted his infidelities Frank felt he was being unfaithful to Irene as well. If it were he who were married to her he couldn't imagine wanting to sleep with someone else. Seeing Irene now, he realized it was she whom he was anxious to talk to, not Joe, and that he'd known all along, since it first occurred to him to visit, that it would be Irene who'd be awake, drinking coffee at the kitchen table, getting breakfast for her husband and kids. And there she was, just as he imagined her, drinking the day's first cup and smoking the day's first cigarette, as if she were waiting for him—or if not him then for someone (anyone) to come by and confide in her. Since Joe made it a habit of telling Frank the details of his married life, Frank felt a deep sense of empathy towards Irene, and this feeling was heightened, now, by the fact they were both in the same boat, as people say, each with a husband and wife who, well. ... "I don't want to talk about it."

She poured him a cup of coffee and sat down in a chair facing him, so close that their knees touched. An unfaithful spouse wasn't the half of Irene's problems, but she'd learned how to temper her emotions in a way that allowed her to stop thinking about herself when necessary. She hadn't been born to lie awake in a bed all night, a man she no longer loved sleeping beside her, but it seemed, after awhile (and after going over the same ground in her head so many times), too selfish to be so completely self-involved. So she welcomed the chance to listen to someone else, even though she might have guessed what was wrong—"would you like some sugar?"—from the expression on Frank's face (it was as if she were seeing herself) when he walked through the door.

Once, at a party she and Joe had given at a time

when Frank was a single person, she had drunk more than usual and had taken Frank out to the backyard and cried on his shoulder, briefly; well, not really cried, but as a way of making a pass at him or of introducing the idea into Frank's mind that if he wanted her she was available, if not right at that moment (it was after 1 a.m. and the party inside the house was getting out of hand; Joe had taken off his shirt and was dancing with the 18-year-old cousin of a friend) then the next day or some other time. She'd taken Frank's hands in her own and placed them—stepping toward him, the tears in her eyes—down the front of her dress. Frank wasn't Joe's best friend, but he was his friend, they were partners, and Frank wasn't drunk enough to think of anything to do but let his hands rest momentarily on her bare skin, before withdrawing them like an idiot and saying something like, "Don't you think we better go back in?" He couldn't admit that he wasn't attracted to Irene, or that since that night he'd spent hours lying in bed wondering what might have happened had he acted differently, since when they returned to the house the living room was practically dark and Joe and the friend's 18-year old cousin were sitting on the couch; or rather, the living room was empty except for Joe and the friend's cousin, who was sitting on Joe's lap; Joe's hand had disappeared under the girl's blouse or rather the friend of the cousin had gone home with someone else's wife leaving the cousin who had just flown in from Minneapolis or Indianapolis to fend for herself; "I like younger girls," Joe admitted afterwards to Frank, who had taken Irene into the kitchen, not certain she'd seen what he had seen, even though he knew that in the kitchen all he could offer Irene was another drink and that was the last thing she needed. Joe wouldn't have even cared (or known) if they'd stayed out in the backyard ("Don't tell Joe, okay?," Irene might have said, adjusting her dress), he would have been happier if they had stayed out there. Frank's fantasy about what might have happened had he actually taken the cue from Irene (even though he thought he'd learned his lesson that night in the bar when the woman he was sitting next to put her hand on his knee and her boyfriend or husband suddenly appeared; what if Joe had discovered them rolling around on the ground in the backyard?) kept backtracking to some point in time which involved Irene taking his hands and placing them on the tops of her breasts, but it was confused, as well, with the sight of the breasts of the girl on the couch with Joe, the cousin from Indianapolis, who had turned around suddenly, since she wasn't drunk and was quite aware of what she was doing, when Frank and Irene entered the living room (it was as if—with her hand down the front of Joe's pants—she was taunting Irene for being so hopeless), she was the person whom Frank—and this is where the fantasy dissolved, completely—they, she and Frank, were the people who were supposed to have met at the party, that was the whole purpose of inviting the girl since everyone including Joe and Irene and the girl's cousin and his wife knew that Frank would be the only unattached male at the party, everyone else there was married and it was assumed they'd all go home with their respective husbands and wives, the only excitement involved vicariously contemplating the possibility that

Frank and this girl would get together, leave together, it was what made parties like this worth the trouble: "She's only in town for a few weeks—why don't you show her a good time?"

Frank told Irene everything. He didn't have to say much—she knew, she nodded her head, she understood, she tightened her grip on his hands (once again she'd taken his hands between her own and placed them, unselfconsciously, on her lap, so Frank could feel the warm folds of her nightgown, and beneath the nightgown her bare skin), she lit a cigarette, she would have let him cry on her shoulder, literally cry, if he wanted. The way she was moving her hands made it hard for Frank not to calculate how much time they'd have to fuck before Joe and the kids came down for breakfast. Irene had her own problems, but she could be a saint, at times, if she wanted. Most days she waited till Joe and her two sons, ages 6 and 8, were out of the house, before she even attempted to go back to bed and get some sleep. And that was the only time, most days, she could sleep. "I have pills but I don't like to take them—they put me to sleep but I feel awful when I wake up, worse than I feel when I don't sleep at all. Worse than a hangover without the pleasure of getting drunk. Maybe I need different pills, or maybe what I need is something to do to keep my mind off all the things I think about that keep me awake."

"If I called in sick"—that had been Irene's suggestion—"what would I do all day? Just think about it some more. Maybe if I do something else I'll forget about it all for awhile." He was going to say "Well, I'm not the first person this has happened to," but then he remembered that, indeed, Irene knew all too well he wasn't the first person who was experiencing these feelings. He wondered what Joe would say if he told him about Gina. The coffee tasted good. Irene noticed he'd finished the cup and poured him another. (He had chatted briefly with the girl from Indianapolis but all she'd said was "Oh, gee" or "Is that so?" in response to whatever he was saying in an attempt to engage her in some kind of real conversation, she'd never said anything that would have made him, in turn, say something that would have, in turn, made him feel he wasn't *trying* to have this conversation, in other words forget the feeling of self-consciousness he was experiencing knowing that this encounter was supposed to lead to his eventually leaving the party with this girl and that it was obvious everyone was waiting and watching to see what would happen, i.e., if they did leave together would he take her back to his place—it was a subject for post-party gossip, *he* was the subject—and if Frank didn't suddenly sneak out with this girl when the party wasn't even half over what was wrong with him anyway? Didn't he like women?)

Irene left the table and went upstairs to help her two sons, Joe Jr. and Patrick, get ready for school. "I'll be right back," she said, but both she and Frank knew their moment had passed. He thought of Gina sleeping alone in the bed they'd shared for two years. The same bed he'd slept in alone before they met. A mattress, box springs, clean linen, cool sheets. She liked to sleep with the window open, even on nights when it was zero degrees and the wind chill factor, so-called, made it seem twenty degrees colder. They'd lie under the blankets and huddle together for warmth. Possibly they'd make love, in some innocent way, with her back facing him, though most often they'd just doze off in each other's arms. He could spend whole days looking forward to this moment; it was quintessential, and made everything about the rest of the day bearable. He felt like he was paddling a small boat through a mythological lake or stream. He could hear her heart beating beneath his hand. He never remembered who fell asleep first.

The two kids stared wide-eyed at Frank as they took their places at the kitchen table. It wasn't every day they had a guest for breakfast. Irene had changed out of her nightgown into jeans and a maroon short-sleeved blouse. Questions and demands filled the air. What kind of cereal do you want? I want a banana with my lunch. How about some breakfast, Frank? None for me, mom. I burnt the toast, can I have another piece? Joe just hit me. Where's the paper towels? Did you do your homework? Get it yourself. If you don't eat fast you'll be late. Etc.

Frank realized the difference between himself and Irene was these kids: that's why she was so docile, at least on the surface, and why Joe felt no need to disguise his infidelities. Without children there was virtually nothing to keep the marriage (any marriage) together, at least a marriage both parties thought of as "unhappy," and in this case Frank had the feeling things would have to get a lot worse than they were before Joe and Irene split up.

Footsteps on the staircase. Irene caught Frank's eye and smiled. Frank wasn't her type, really, but she couldn't deny that when they first met she'd entertained the thought that someday they'd end up in bed together. She could tell that Frank was the type who needed someone who'd make the first move; acting aggressively, in this way, wasn't something Joe ever permitted, if you could call acting out of a feeling of desire for someone "aggressiveness." The alternative to acting aggressively was playing games as a way of disguising what you were feeling. She knew that Frank would never make an advance and that it would be necessary for Irene to grant Frank permission so he wouldn't feel guilty or question himself afterwards, but even then she wasn't certain he'd follow her lead, even though she sensed desire and even love from his side.

Sometimes, when Joe wasn't home and she was trying to fall asleep, she had fantasies about what it might be like to make love to Frank. Once, fucking Joe, she'd thought of Frank as well. They were out in the backyard, it was the night of the party when she'd drunkenly taken Frank's hands and put them down the front of her dress, but in the fantasy she was lying on her back in the grass while Frank hovered over her, "hurry up, Frank," she was saying, careful not to say it out loud because there was no denying the fact that no matter how far away she could go in her head it was Joe—"don't stop!"—who was inside her.

Fantasies kept her awake, and defeated the purpose of trying to fall asleep: put on the light and smoke another smoke. It upset her that life had reached the point where she could actually imagine going out and finding someone else to sleep with. Imagining and doing were two different things. "There must be more to life than this" was the endless refrain. She imagined a million women, husbands at work, sitting at kitchen tables, midday, like waitresses in an empty diner. Refrigerator music droning in the background. Alone, and lost, lost in a space in her head.

Joe patted the place under his jacket where his gun was strapped and ran his hand over the edges of his chin. He wanted his presence in the room to mean something, for everyone's attention to focus on him. It wasn't necessary for him to say or do anything. It was his kitchen, after all, Irene was his wife and there were his kids, though they might grow up into people he wouldn't recognize as his own. They would bear his name; their children would be his grandchildren. Frank was his partner, as well; the idea of possessiveness could extend beyond the immediate family. He'd had other partners but he and Frank had worked together for three years now and that was as long as some marriages lasted. Joe didn't worry about whether he was happy or not, or whether what he did gave pleasure to the people around him. That wasn't the point. After shaving, which he did every morning, he slapped aftershave lotion onto his skin and glared at himself in the mirror (like in the commercials). But Joe wasn't the type who'd ever be picked out of an anonymous crowd to advertise anything, much less shaving cream or lotion, not unless the company was intent on bankruptcy. The flesh on his cheeks was chalky and soft. He wanted his presence to command authority; Joe Jr. and Patrick were frightened of him, his outbursts of anger. Sometimes Irene tried to superimpose her memory of the person she'd married ten years before onto this person who to her mind no longer had the capacity for human feelings, if by human she meant feelings that were supposedly common to everyone: thoughtfulness, commiseration, compassion. He wanted to be taller than everyone else though actually he was only 5 feet 8 or 9. Average height. In the last year he'd taken his doctor's advice and gone on a diet. Stopped smoking, then started again. He had more than the average amount of hair on his chest and legs. His father had gone bald before he'd turned forty and Joe worried about that. He ran his hand through his hair every two minutes as if to check that it was still there. He forced himself to exercise, lift weights, swim a few laps. He wanted someone to say "you're the best" but no one did. Irene had been attracted to his dark eyebrows and sideburns, his hazel eyes, the knot at the base of the spine which felt like a stone embedded beneath his skin. After making love, in the old days, she'd run her fingers along his back until she found the place; as she eased back into reality it was her way of identifying herself, and him. The idea of being the wife of the person who commanded so much attention when he entered a room appealed to her since it meant she didn't have to do anything but be there, basking in his shadow. An ornament, a doll. Some men like to dominate women because they attribute to women a secret power—like the ability to give birth—which they lack. At least that's one theory. Joe could have benefited from a week on the beach somewhere; his skin lacked color, he didn't tan well, lying on a beach (and vacations in general) made him nervous. His skin was white. He was the gift to all women, or so he thought, and couldn't understand what someone like Gina was doing with a guy like Frank, which isn't to say he didn't like Frank.

"You look horrible," he said.

His wife, his kids, his partner, his kitchen.

"I felt horrible," nodding towards Irene, "but I'm feeling better now."

"You still look pretty bad. Donahue isn't going to like it if you show up looking like you spent the night on a park bench. You and Irene should form a club—Insomniacs Anonymous. You could get together every morning at 6 a.m. and tell each other your problems. I'll bet you'd start sleeping better if you knew there was someone else who couldn't sleep at the other end of the line. There's probably at least one person in every household in the Bronx who has trouble sleeping: you could all get together every morning, you could meet each morning in each other's houses, you could sit around in a group and tell each other your problems. Shit, Frank, I didn't know you had trouble sleeping. You always seem so wide awake and alert. You taking speed or something? My wife here can't even take sleeping pills. I tell her that maybe if she didn't drink about two pots of black coffee every day she'd have an easier time but she doesn't believe me."

"It's not the coffee, Joe, it's you."

"You see, Frank, it's me. I'm the problem. You should come over one morning and just stand outside the window and watch us. There's Irene, sitting at the kitchen table, drinking coffee and smoking a cigarette, waiting for me to finish getting dressed. There're the kids fighting about something. I have a wife who can't sleep and two kids who hate each other. Who hate me, probably. Here I am innocently getting dressed so I can go out and greet the world feeling good and the first people I have to deal with are the inmates of this loony bin some other people might call my happy home. I have problems too but I don't lie awake chainsmoking and grinding my teeth and going to the bathroom every five minutes."

"Oh, shut up. Frank doesn't have insomnia. He just couldn't sleep, that happens sometimes to you ordinary people too, you know. He's here on a friendly visit, he's our neighbor, remember? If he can't sleep and he feels like driving over here at 6 a.m., he's welcome."

"Who says?" Joe winked at Frank. "I happen to like a little peace and quiet when I get up. I don't want the house filled with people I see everyday all day anyway. I like to eat breakfast in silence. When was the last time that happened? I like to eat my breakfast and read yesterday's paper and relax a little before leaving the house. Frank, you're not welcome here at six in the morning. Gina isn't welcome here. No one's welcome here. Speaking of breakfast, I don't smell any bacon. I certainly don't smell any eggs. All I can smell is the goddamn cigarette smoke and coffee which I can smell in my sleep by now."

"I guess I'll go. Thanks for the coffee, Irene."

"Hey, Frank, aren't we going to drive downtown together? What's your big hurry? I was only joking." .

He caught Irene around the waist and buried his face in her neck, but she pushed him away. It was difficult for Frank to tell whether Joe was being playful or whether he'd been serious about what he'd said. He felt like someone was rattling a pair of castanets in his head. He stood at the door and stared at a patch of light on the linoleum and tried to imagine Irene alone in the kitchen, on afternoons when Joe was at work. What did she do all day by herself? Maybe Irene was right and he should call in sick, but it was hard (everything was "hard") to face the prospects of either spending the day by himself or confronting Gina again and continuing from where they left off. He wanted to sit at that table with Irene, holding hands forever. Moist palms, lifelines merging. "Let me tell you your fortune." Joe Jr. and Patrick, taking their cue from their parents' voices, kids are smarter than you think, had fled from the room, and as Frank opened the screen door he turned and saw Irene's hand raised in mid-air as if she were going to rake her nails down the side of Joe's face as they struggled and shouted at each other in some kind of imitation of how Frank imagined people he didn't know acted (and he didn't want to know them, these people weren't his friends, were they?). Maybe the neighbors would eventually call the police and complain about all the noise from the Hopper house and two patrolmen much like Joe and Frank had been when they first joined the force would get out of their car and climb the front steps.

"Are you all right, miss?"

"Oh, officer. You shouldn't have bothered." (She was holding an icepack against her right eye and her night gown was torn around her shoulders and breasts.) "It's just my husband. He got drunk last night and we had a small argument. I'm sorry if we...." And at this point she broke down and collapsed in the patrolman's arms.

"That son of a bitch! *He tried to kill me.*"

3

It was 9 a.m. California time when the call came from New York. Max, still in bed, a white sheet draped over the lower half of his naked body, was reading a battered hardcovered copy of *A Moon For The Misbegotten*, Eugene O'Neill's last play, which he'd found in a used bookstore in Berkeley. (A first edition; if it wasn't in such bad shape it would be worth some money.) The book was open flat on the bed alongside a black sketchpad he used as a journal and which he was now using to record his ideas about directing the play. Reading any book is slow going if every few lines something prompts you to stop reading and stare into space, and thoughts about directing the play (which was only a fantasy on Max's part) could easily turn into thoughts about his relationship with Caroline or what he was doing in a place as alien to him as California. It was as if a voice inside him had to emerge from the wings and demand that he concentrate on nothing except what he was doing. "If I can't concentrate on what I'm doing it means I'm not happy where I am."

He remembered a time when concentrating on reading a book didn't require so much energy, but it was too easy to blame his distractedness on life in California, or life with Caroline. Too easy to lie back and contemplate the patterns of light dovetailing through the curtains onto the sheet, prop himself on one elbow and stare out the window at the horses grazing in the pasture behind the house. Before coming to California he'd spent his entire life enclosed in tiny sunless apartments, where a room bathed in natural light for a few hours a day made you feel you were a privileged person, and it was hard—though he'd been here a year and Caroline laughed when he tried to explain this to her—to take simple pleasures (like sunlight, clean air and trees) for granted. If his wide-eyedness at all these things struck Caroline as naive, too bad for her.

Thinking a lot about anything was always a bad sign, and keeping a journal was a way of rebelling against the emphasis on "doing nothing," which was all that the people he'd met since arriving in California seemed to encourage. It was a continual source of amazement that a place so beautiful could harbor such lethargy. For the last month or two he'd been trying to organize a small drama group—using The Provincetown Players, which produced O'Neill's early plays, as a model—but every time he scheduled a meeting someone called up sick or with an excuse Max translated to mean the person wasn't truly interested. So the meeting would be postponed, re-scheduled, postponed again. Max was beginning to wonder whether he was the only one who was really serious, and whether it was his seriousness that scared people off. It was all right to have ideas or intentions or even ambi-tions, but to do something about them was another story.

He was wishing Caroline would come in from the patio where she was doing her early morning yoga exercises and bring him a cup of coffee, black coffee, espresso, not in a mug, but in a cup on a tray; that would make the moment perfect. (The thought of preparing the coffee for himself made him nostalgic for all the mornings in the past when he woke alone and there was no possibility of anyone getting him anything.) If he lingered long enough maybe Caroline would finish her exercises and they could drink coffee together in bed. They could lie in bed writing in their respective journals (or use their journals as surfaces on which they could write letters to their friends), they could make love and take showers and with their bodies still wet return to the bed and (if they had any energy) make love again. Afterwards they could fix themselves sandwiches, lettuce and tomatoes (the reddest tomatoes Max had ever seen) from someone's garden and strips of bacon pressed between slices of homemade bread. They could lie in bed, listening to the radio or the rain, nibbling the crumbs from their plates, and stare out the window; commenting about the weather and whether there was anything either of them might want to do (though wanting to do anything other than what they were already doing was a form of heresy: there were enough things one *had* to do, why make life more complicated?)

Whenever Max complained about the pain in his lower back, attributing it to the depression, a small valley, really, in the center of the mattress, and suggested to Caroline they buy a wooden board to fit under the present mattress, or even better, a new bed, she gave him one of her sideways glances and told him he was turning into an old man. (Referring to one's partner as "my old man" or "my old lady"—as opposed to "husband" or "wife"— indicated that one had become a person so settled into complicity one might as well forget or forfeit the possibility of ever making a change.) The longer he stayed in California the easier it became to lose sight of what he was going to do with his life (even the phrasing, "doing something with my life," had an old-fashioned sound), and the feeling he was drifting aimlessly through a vacuum made him unhappy, and worried, like hearing an old song makes you remember the face of a person to whom you'd been married a short time. If he acted like someone's grandparent possibly it was because he was getting bored with the drowsy pace of life in California. "You're not bored with me, are you?" He permitted Caroline, ten years older, to play the role of big sister, in a way that was the paradigm of some kind of vaguely incestuous scene. There was no logical way of articulating what he might want to happen to make his or their life better or different, and most days she doubted his sanity for imagining there was more to life than what was now being offered. (Instead of lying in bed, naked, sipping coffee and writing in his notebook, instead of making love whenever either of them felt like it, he could—"you could"—be sitting in an office somewhere, like most of the rest of the people in the world, going through the motions of being alive.)

The phone was in the kitchen. No one he knew would call him this early; that was enough reason to let it ring. (If it were important, whoever was calling would try again. If it wasn't important, why were they bothering to call at such an hour?) Maybe, hopefully, it would be a wrong number. It would most likely be for Caroline, still on the patio doing her exercises.

He caught the phone on the sixth ring, held the receiver against his ear. The voice at the other end—no one he knew—sounded like a recorded announcement.

It was the voice of the telephone operator ("the number you dialed has been disconnected"), the voice of the person hired by the radio station to hover in a helicopter over the major arteries leading away from the center of a city, whose job was to inform the people in the cars below of delays caused by accidents. "There's a tie-up on the FDR Drive, heading north" such a voice might say. There was no way of interpreting the gravity of the message from the person's tone. The words sounded like they were coming from a machine at the end of a dark tunnel, a tunnel where natural daylight never penetrated. "Who am I talking to?" Max said in disbelief. He switched the receiver to his other ear so he could write down the person's name but the pen slipped out of his hands. He was about to say, "How do you spell that?" when he heard the click that meant the person at the other end had hung up.

When he told Caroline what the man on the phone had said she began crying. She'd never met Max's mother and the only image that came to mind was the one she knew from the photographs Max had shown her, grainy snapshots of father, mother, and son, together and separately, taken years ago when they were all young. Her own father had died when she was still in college; her mother, remarried, lived in Los Angeles, but they saw each other only once a year. Sometimes she felt guilty about seeing her mother so infrequently, but at the moment this arrangement seemed sanest for everyone. (The first time Caroline had visited her mother and her new husband, she'd encountered Hank, her stepfather, in the hallway of their small mansion, late one night after a drunken party, and he's made a pass at her—"tried to rape me," as she described the scene to Max, was more accurate—a few feet from the bedroom where her mother was sleeping (she'd managed to escape, not without first inflicting a permanent scar on the side of his face); after that incident, though, she thought it wisest to keep her distance.)

Until Max's father died his mother had never been very interested in cooking, somehow defying the stereotype of the Jewish mother whose goal in life was to feed everyone. His father had preferred his food prepared simply, not for dietary or religious reasons but because he was a moderate person by nature and frowned suspiciously upon anything hinting of the exotic. Eating food that was familiar, the same food every day with tiny variations, was a form of security, his own parents had been moderate (one hesitates to say "repressed") people as well, and Max's mother had learned early on in their marriage to underplay her natural instincts (of which devotion to food was one) as a way of insuring her own security, even if it meant denying herself something she loved to do. Her husband's lack of interest in food was consistent with his ideas about pleasure in general. If you thought of yourself as a failure, as Max's father did, though he was hardly that in the eyes of the people who knew him, there was no possibility of giving yourself a reward at the end of the day, even if all that meant was a good meal cooked by someone you loved and who loved you in return. A well-cooked meal might be an expression of that love.

Max's mother didn't think her husband was a failure and cooking a meal was just one way of expressing one's feelings, though maybe it wasn't necessary to express one's feelings at all. Nonetheless, Bette—which was what Max called his mother—felt trapped by her husband's sense of caution, his xenophobic attitude towards anything that didn't fit into his vision of how things should be (a vision the size of a stamp). Max's mother had tempered her more adventuresome feelings to conform with those of her husband; when he died it was as if a stone had melted away. She realized that Max, her only child, had learned more about the world once he'd left home than he'd ever learned from herself or her husband. Though this isn't unusual, most parents can't accept that it's true. The foods you prepared and ate were symbols of the possible varieties of human experience, or the widening of those experiences, and it was something mother and son could now share, since for Max's mother the possibility of preparing something different for her son when he visited was a way of widening her own experience as well as a way of pleasing him. When they got together they talked about food as if it were the most important thing in the world. It seemed possible that if they truly devoted themselves to the pleasures of eating they could erase all the thousands of bland meals that punctuated the days of their past, Max's father sitting between them, the memory of which was their secret.

Max hadn't seen his mother since the night before he left New York. The last time he talked to her had been the afternoon of March 1 when he called long distance to wish her happy birthday. The last communication of any kind he'd received was a postcard with a picture of the World Trade Center on the back, thanking him for the roses he'd wired to her, flowers, again, like food, a secret pleasure, the love of anything beautiful and alive. ("What a waste of money," he could hear his father say.) Max knew his presence in New York added excitement to her life and felt guilty: he hadn't planned to stay in California this long. She'd never been west—it was the first time for Max, as well—so there was always a lot to write home about. Once a week he composed a letter whether she answered or not: no one could criticize him for not being a dutiful son. She'd always encouraged him to tell her about his girlfriends ("Are you seeing any-one?")—this was true even when his father was alive, though his father was never included, or showed inter-est, in these conversations—but Max wasn't certain how much she really wanted to hear. In his last letter he'd told her he was living with Caroline, but neglected to say she was ten years older, at 35 hardly "a girlfriend." Max had been contemplating a return to New York with Caroline, if she wanted to come, either for a visit or to live per-manently, but he'd never mentioned his intentions to his mother since he didn't want her to anticipate something that might not happen immediately. Caroline had left her husband to live with Max; when he arrived in California she was married and her husband still lived in a house in the same town, and seeing her husband every day while she was living with Max made everyone's lives compli-cated; all the more reason—if they were truly serious about one another—that they start a new life together somewhere else.

At least that's what had been on their minds when the call came from the detective in New York saying his mother had been killed. Killed, murdered—all words sounded too harsh, like headlines in a tabloid: Mental Patient Rapes Nun. There was no question he'd have to return to New York immediately, what else could he do? He wanted to cry, felt numb, as if a roulette wheel had stopped spinning on a number, not his. ("Sorry," the croupier said, "you lost again.") Caroline held his hands tightly between her own and they sat at the table in silence. The kitchen smelled of the chili (1 1/2 cups fresh tomatoes, 3 to 4 cups kidney beans, 1/2 cup chopped onion, 1/2 bay leaf, etc.) Max had made the night before. Caroline wasn't his mother, but both of them enjoyed cooking. He reached out to flick an inch-long ash from the tip of his cigarette into the ashtray but missed the mark and the ash dissolved onto the surface of the table, which was wooden and like the rest of the furniture came with the house. The person who owned the house lived in Berkeley with his family. If they moved somewhere else—New York, or anywhere they, he and Caroline, would have to buy new furniture. New curtains, a new coffee cup. (Max liked to attribute magical qualities to objects—in this sense, he had more in common than he thought with the people in the town—and the cup from which he drank his coffee was one. The dailiness of the ritual, the memory of what he was doing when the cup entered his life, who gave it to him or the place where he bought it, his state of mind when he bought it, the combination of all these things was what gave the object its glow. He had brought a coffee cup with him from New York but it had broken and he'd never replaced it. The cup he drank coffee from these days belonged to the owner of the house. Max didn't feel any great attachment to it, and somehow that lessened the pleasure of the ritual. "You should drink tea," Caroline suggested, missing the point. Secretly he was hoping she would buy him a new cup.) Max had come to California with a single suitcase: in a year, all he'd accumulated was a carton of books. Most people in the town owned their own houses; Caroline's husband had been in the process of building a house when they split up. Renting created a feeling of transience—you could pack up and leave whenever you wanted—counter to the general feeling of loyalty to place, about which there was much idealistic talk. Max couldn't help think all the talk about commitment was just a way for people to rationalize their guilt about having money: enough money, anyway, to buy at least a modest-sized lot, build a fence around it, post *no trespassing* signs on the trees.

It was the end of the rainy season, a time when everyone who could afford it left Northern California for the warmer weather down the coast. This particular town, an hour north of San Francisco, was filled with people who had money to take long vacations. Even those who didn't have much money managed to escape for a while. For Max it had been his first winter out of New York City, so he didn't mind the perpetual fog, the thunderstorms that lasted all night and into the next day, flooding the roads and causing electrical outages, high tension wires slithering around the trunks of the eucalyptus trees like baby pythons. Caroline, who'd lived in the town for ten years, taught him how to build a fire, and in general initiated him into the pleasures of California life, at least one version of it. Whenever Max experienced anything new he felt a physical sensation that he interpreted as the residue of the initial feeling of breaking loose from his father's sense of disapproval and narrowness. He even had a fantasy about his mother moving to California, but knew she'd never leave the apartment, much less New York, where she'd lived all her life. After so many years of marriage part of her had grown accustomed to the feeling of rigidity, her husband's legacy; cooking a meal with condiments was one thing, actually leaving the city of one's birth for points unknown was too much to ask.

"I'll drive you to the airport," Caroline said. There was no question of going with him, not this time around. She was on the phone, negotiating with a friend to borrow a car. Maybe if it were necessary for him to stay in New York longer than expected she'd be able to join him, even though moving to New York wasn't something she really wanted to do. "If it's a choice between you and living in New York...." From time to time they argued about where to go, what to do; if anything, the future ("should. we have children?") was their main problem.

Max felt like an outsider in this town where everyone knew everything about everyone else and where every time he went to the store he met Caroline's husband or a person who had been a friend of both Caroline and her husband when they were together and who now felt a confused allegiance to one or the other. Most people who didn't know any better had thought Caroline and her husband were happy together; Max was the interloper who'd come along and ruined everything. Max never doubted Caroline and her husband would have split up whether he'd come to California or not. His presence on the scene just speeded things along. Caroline's wasn't the only marriage that had dissolved since he'd been there; how come everyone was so shocked?

Caroline wished he would cry or she could say something to console him. The difference in their ages bothered her more than it did him. She assumed she loved him more than he loved her because she needed him more, needed some sense of permanence, a feeling of stability, couldn't imagine getting involved with someone else so soon after she and her husband separated and then breaking up all over again. The older you are the more difficult it is to set up a household with someone, then watch it collapse, for whatever reasons.

Max went into the bedroom, took his suitcase from the back of the closet, placed it on the bed where an hour ago he'd been sleeping peacefully in Caroline's arms, and snapped open the lid. The night before they'd stayed up late, drinking wine and watching *White Heat*, a gangster movie with James Cagney and Edmund O'Brien. There was the TV, an old black-and-white portable, on a chair at the foot of the bed. He wondered what he'd be feeling if someone had called to tell him his mother had died of natural causes, as O'Neill's mother had died, in California, with her son Jamie at her side, while Eugene was in Cape Cod. He was living his own movie now, watching himself ("now I have to get dressed") from a distance. He was playing with his friends on the street and he could hear his mother's voice calling him from the window of the ground floor apartment. It was dinner time, time to wash up, help his mother set the table. Caroline folded his shirts, much as his mother might have done, and stacked them neatly in the bottom of the suitcase. "Are you all right?" He wanted to return to bed, pretend nothing had hap pened. His mother zipped up his coat and handed him a brown paper bag containing his lunch. A sandwich, an apple. Some cookies. "Take this," Caroline said. He sipped from the glass and swallowed the pill without looking at it. The man at the other end of the line might have been anyone; there was no way of knowing what he'd said was the truth. What if someone—a friend of Caroline's former husband, perhaps—was playing a joke? Back in the kitchen, the smoke from another cigarette stinging his eyes, he dialed his mother's number in New York, counted the rings: eight, nine, ten—then hung up, consulted the list of numbers tacked to the wall above the phone, and dialed the number of his mother's brother who lived in Brooklyn. Uncle Morris. "Oh Max," the man said, "when are you coming home?" He recognized his mother's voice inside the voice of his uncle, and his own voice as well. A bad connection, they were back in the tunnel again.

Max couldn't remember why he'd ever come to California. It was a matter of trying to relate to the inside of the mind of a person who had existed a year ago. He had sat in the kitchen of his small apartment on the Upper West Side with a map of the United States unfolded on the table. "I'm sorry," Uncle Morris said, as if he were apologizing for something that wasn't his fault but for which he felt responsible, "they'll find the person who did it," as if that mattered, "don't worry."

Some mornings Max would join Caroline on the patio

while she performed her exercises. It was a performance in the sense that she was both aware and ohliviou of his presence at the same time. "You can talk to me, but don't expect me to answer. I can't carry on a conversation and do yoga at the same time." She'd sit at one end of the exercise mat with her head between her knees and breathe deeply. Then she'd draw her legs toward her chest and rock backwards and forwards, her hands beneath her knees. Watching her made Max think he should do some pushups or situps since most days his only exercise was to walk into town for groceries, a mile each way, and even then, if he were alone, he usually managed to get a ride. Someone was always driving by whom he knew, and people in cars and vans tended to stop when they saw someone they recognized on the side of the road, whether that person had his or her thumb out or not. Even if he wanted to walk, Max thought the driver would be insulted if he declined. (On one of these trips Max was picked up by Caroline's best friend, Laura, who suggested they stop off at her house before going into town. "My old man isn't home," she said, putting her hand on his knee and winking.) After the rocking exercises Caroline lay on her back and rested. Then, breathing in, she lifted her right leg till it was at right angles to the rest of her body. Then the left leg. Count: one, two, three. Then both legs at once. Another exercise involved lying on her stomach with her chin touching the edge of the mat, Breathing deeply again, she raised her head, then her shoulders and the upper part of her body, while the lower half ("this is The Cobra") remained on the mat.

He watched her spine curve like a cat as she bent forward to clasp her right ankle with her hands (simultaneously placing the sole of her left foot along the top of her right thigh), all the while breathing invisibly like a contorted tree or flower. Mornings would begin and end with some variation of the act of drinking coffee and exercising and sometimes (after the exercises and the coffee) returning to bed. When they first met Caroline wore her long brown hair loose, or in braids, but a month after they began living together Laura had cut it all off (what are best friends for, anyway?), even though, in Max's eyes, she now looked like a recent inductee into a branch of the American army which permitted women to work as nutrition experts or clerks (seeing duty "in the line of action" was out of the question), but only if they repressed their feminine characteristics and showed willingness to act and look as much like a man as possible. In the course of doing her exercises Caroline was ultimately exposing every part of herself to him and some of the exercise positions were similar to positions one might assume while making love.

"Laura's very attracted to you, you know," Caroline had once said. There was some implication that the three of them—Caroline, Max, and Laura—might all go to bed together if Max showed any interest, why else would Caroline, normally jealous of women who showed interest in Max, say such a thing, or even imply it? And should Max, in turn, tell her that Laura had already propositioned him? Maybe Caroline already knew, and Laura, for her part, was just testing him to see whether a momentary infidelity was part of the repertoire of possibilities that might have occurred to either of them now that they'd lived together all of eight months.

Max never worried that Caroline might be sleeping with other people but it did occur to him, as they rode to the airport, that if it were necessary for him to stay in New York for more than a week he'd have no reason to expect her to remain faithful until he returned. Maybe she'd even go back to her husband in the interim? Before walking out the door he had the thought that they should make love one last time, as a way of securing some kind of feeling or memory that would make it more difficult for either of them to forget each other. He thought of the character in *The Stranger*, by Camus, who had made love to his girlfriend a few days or hours after hearing that his mother had died, and how heartless everyone thought he'd been, or the character in *Moon For The Misbegotten*, Jim Tyrone, who spent the days immediately following his mother's death in the company of a prostitute, on a train carrying his mother's body from California to New York. O'Neill was notorious for cannibalizing people he knew to create characters (Charles Marsden, in *Strange Interlude*, was a combination, at least in name, of the painters Charles Demuth and Marsden Hartley), but all writers use their own experiences or the experiences of others to a certain degree, though some—as a way of protecting the so-called sanctity of the creative act— would deny that the people and events they created were anything but the products of their warped imaginations. Warped, like a record that repeats the same notes, again and again.

At moments, Caroline reminded Max of Nina in *Strange Interlude*, except that Caroline's hair wasn't "straw blond" (as O'Neill described his character when she made her entrance in her father's study, act one), nor did she have "broad square shoulders, slim strong hips and long beautifully developed legs"—the resemblance had nothing to do with physical appearances. Whenever he read a play Max cast it with people he knew. "You'd be perfect for the part." Maybe, if it were necessary for him to spend more than a few days in New York, Caroline would fly south to visit her own mother, in the big mansion in the Hollywood Hills with the big picture windows from which you could see all of Los Angeles and the blinking lights, like fire flies, of the cars on the freeways, even though, the last time she'd gone, her stepfather—in a scene O'Neill might have appreciated—had tried to rape her.

As they approached the airport Max felt a twinge of regret for all the things he hadn't done in California. He always wanted to travel south, to Mexico City and the Yucatan. He wanted to go north as well, to the Sierras. Caroline had a friend who lived in a town in the foothills; wherever Max wanted to go Caroline had a friend at whose place they could stay. Though they had enough money to live without working (yet another friend who worked for a publishing company in San Francisco occasionally sent them manuscripts of books to copy-edit) they never had enough to take a trip, whatever "enough" meant.

They were sitting together at the end of a row of blue and orange plastic chairs, in a large open area, waiting for the plane to depart. An airline official in a dark blue uniform was standing behind a wooden lectern filling out forms and answering questions. Beyond the windows, men in silver jumpsuits and striped caps were loading tiers of luggage through a small opening m the tail of the plane. Max wet his lips with the tip of his tongue. His mouth was dry but he didn't have the strength to stand up and navigate the corridors of the terminal in search of something to drink. Nor did he want Caroline to go off, even for a moment. Whenever she was unhappy or worried she looked at least five years older than she was; at the moment her face was a mask of lines and furrows.

"When I get back," Max said reassuringly, taking her hand, "we'll go off by ourselves for awhile."

It was the least he could say to assuage her fear—and it wasn't necessary for her to even say it, he knew what she was thinking—that he had no intention of ever returning.

4

There was a basketball game on the color TV above the bar, but no one was watching. People didn't go to bars to watch television, they could do that at home, but the television did serve a function. If you found yourself between conversations you could always pretend you were watching, drink in hand, so as not to appear stranded, or unpopular, too boring to talk to. It wasn't a singles bar, either, or didn't have that reputation, but it wasn't unusual for people to meet one another here for the first time and go home together: "Your place or mine?" Mostly groups of friends or married couples stopping for a beer after a movie ("what time did we tell the babysitter we'd be home?") or single people on their way somewhere else, an occasional "older" Ukrainian person already drunk when he or she came in.

Rosemary slipped a quarter into the jukebox and was meditating on the names of the songs, surprised that she'd never heard of so many of them, when Richard, whom she'd met here a year ago and gone home with, came up behind her.

"I didn't mean to scare you," he said when she jumped. He kissed her on the back of the neck, encircled her in his arms, placed his hands alongside hers on the front of the jukebox. Rosemary responded by pressing back against him slightly—it was possible to sleep with some one once and still be friends with them afterwards. (It was possible, as well, to sleep with someone and never see the person again.)

The music was too loud and she missed most of what Richard was trying to tell her. She nodded at what she thought were the right moments and let him guide her to the bar so that they were at a point that made a tri-angle with the TV and the jukebox. Whenever she said anything it was necessary for him to bend forward so her lips were practically touching his ear. Part of her wished he would kiss her again. He'd been in love with her once, at least that's what he'd said the night they'd spent togeth-er, and as she absent-mindedly fingered the buttons on his shirt she realized she had to be careful not to let him misinterpret her affection as a sign they might go home together again. (Who knows, he might still be in love with me.) At the same time it seemed odd to rule out the possibility that anything could happen. She wondered what he'd think if she told him he was the last man she'd slept with.

That night, a year ago, Maureen had gone to visit her parents in Maine, and Rosemary had come to the bar just to be around other people, not intending to go home with anyone particular. On the contrary, she'd been looking forward to going home alone, sleeping alone and waking in bed alone with her cat curled on her stomach—poor cat, Rosemary had been spending too much time at Mau-reen's, and Taffy, sullen and underfed, was withdraw-ing into herself, destroying books and overturning the catbox out of spite. It was only after Maureen confessed to sleeping with an old high school friend during the visit to her parents that Rosemary told her about going to bed with Richard. He reminded her of Fred, her first boyfriend in high school. (At least that's the reason she gave to herself for wanting to sleep with him.) Whenever Rosemary visited her family in Brooklyn she always took time to walk around her old neighborhood, usually in the evening, or right before dinner, in the hope of meeting some of her high school friends who still lived there. Fred still lived there; he was married now, with two kids. The neighborhood was like a small town (women still swept the pavement outside their attached houses) and all the shopkeepers recognized her, said hello, asked jokingly when she was going to get married. How could she not be married? If there were any possibilities other than getting married and having children they didn't want to hear about them. She wondered what she and Fred would talk about if they ever met. She saw herself in the role of wife, his wife, walking hand in hand with their kids, pushing a stroller over the cracks in the familiar streets, past the steps of all the houses where they used to neck after high school dances. "Be home by midnight," Rosemary's father said. Everyone had their histories, though people's memories worked differently; regardless, just as a fact, she'd been Fred's first lover too and she assumed that counted for something.

Rosemary didn't know whether Maureen had seen her come into the bar and wished she could pretend that she didn't care. Even talking to Richard, trying to focus on the conversation while listening to the music and drinking beer, wasn't enough to distract her from the pinpricks of jealousy that penetrated her skin. At least they were pinpricks, not stabs; she didn't feel wounded or bereft, just hurt, in a way that made her feel passionless and somewhat dumb. (If I had any brains, I wouldn't have come here to begin with.) Eventually, if she and Maureen didn't make contact, someone in the bar who knew both of them would ask whether or not she and Maureen were talking to one another, had they had a fight? And it would be easy to shake her head, respond curtly, in anger: "It's none of your business," even though it was more in her nature to confide openly to anyone, even a complete stranger (assuming she was drunk enough) who seemed genuinely interested. Richard would be more tactful, that was his manner; he'd avoid the subject, talk about anything but Maureen. He'd put his own feelings aside, like a good social worker, which is what he did to earn a living, and try to be helpful. Rosemary knew she was asking for trouble by coming to the bar, but following the logic of her thoughts when the thoughts involved her emotions was a form of self-flagellation she wanted to avoid. If she didn't go to the bar there was no telling when they'd see each other again; being in the same room with Maureen, whether they talked to one another or not, was better than not seeing her at all.

After the visit from the detective she'd gone off to work, as usual. He'd call her later—even wrote her phone number down in his black book—if he needed to talk with her again. When a boy in high school asked you for your number it was usually an indication that he'd eventually ask you out on a date, though some boys just liked to fill their address books with as many numbers as possible as a way of impressing their friends. To give a boy your phone number was a signal of at least a partial willingness to see him again. Fred and his family lived down the street from the house where Rosemary had grown up; they'd played together, every day, as kids. "Goodnight, Fred." In between kisses they'd sit on the steps smoking, not inhaling, a strand of tobacco caught on her tongue. They didn't kiss with their tongues, that would come later: all the intensity of the kiss occurred in the pressure of their lips gnashing together.

The detective was probably married and had kids too. She told him where she worked and the hours, 12 to 5, Monday through Thursday, even gave him her work number in case something important came up. The library, at the southeast corner of Seward Park, was only a five minute walk from her apartment. Walking to work was convenient but often she wished she worked uptown so she'd have a reason to leave the neighborhood. She wondered whether she'd been naive to treat the detective like she would anyone else, offer him coffee. The idea of sitting at her kitchen table across from a stranger, a strange man no less, a man who carried a gun but who otherwise might have been anyone, was almost as unnerving as finding the body of the dead woman.

"If you can think of anything else," he'd told her, "let us know."

He gave her the number of the precinct where he worked and when she stood up to write the number on the pad she kept near the phone she felt his eyes follow her as she crossed the small room. For a moment Rosemary felt tempted to move her body in a way that might suggest a willingness to go to bed with him—anything can happen when you're alone with another person—just to see what he would do. But by the time she finished writing down the number he was standing at the door, waiting for her to turn around and face him so he could say goodbye.

After he left it occurred to her she could use the murder as an excuse not to go to work. It wasn't as if someone in her own family had died—though on previous jobs she'd actually used the death of an imaginary relative as a pretense not to go in. But it wasn't every day you were the person who discovered the body of a person who'd been murdered. Where was Maureen? She dialed her friend's number, and when she heard the voice on the answering machine she felt like shouting "Fuck you" into the phone—that would be her message. "This is Rosemary," calmly, "if you have time call me at work." There was no point staying home if she couldn't meet or talk with Maureen. The murderer could be anyone—the faces of all the other tenants in the building flashed though her head—and the need to be in a place where she could talk to someone ("you should see a psychiatrist") got her moving at last.

She wasn't surprised that everyone at work already knew about the murder. Her involvement made her, momentarily, the center of attention, since whatever they knew she knew more, could supply one more detail which they in turn could use to embellish the story when they told it to someone else ("I know the person who found the body"), bring them one step nearer the actual scene of the crime. Violence was titillating as long as you didn't know the people involved. Maureen never returned her call, of course she wouldn't, and Rosemary knew she was feeling desperate when it occurred to her ("I have to talk to you") that she might call her again. She stood at the main desk checking out books, accepting fines for overdue books, trying to keep up appearances. People in libraries didn't require much attention—she wasn't trying to seduce them into buying something they didn't want, that wasn't her job. There was a purity about the environment that made thinking about sex an inevitable preoccupation. Some afternoons she sat behind the desk and watched the bodies of the people moving from shelf to shelf, incorporating them into her fantasies. If she were attracted, for instance, to the young black man with the dreadlocks who was studying a manual about how to fix foreign cars, she could imagine them alone in the library together, it was night, the strings of fluorescent tubes scaling the ceiling had burned out, she was lying on her stomach on the floor near the biography section, waiting while he unfastened his trousers (again, the scenarios were endless). Then a voice "Could you tell me where I might find books about Jewish history?"—would interrupt her. On the verge of blacking out, she'd wake from her daydream and adjust her sweater, momentarily fearing that this man who might have been her father's father and who leaned on a cane as if he were about to topple over knew everything she was thinking or feeling. When the object of her fantasy passed in front of her, and she accepted the library card from his or her hands, it was hard to prevent herself from blushing; instead, she made a point of avoiding eye contact, photographing the card and placing the computer card in the pocket of the book and pushing it across the desk with a show of indifference.

Everyone needs a friend to confide in, someone with

whom they can trust their secrets. But as soon as you tell a person something you realize there's still another layer you can never reveal. It's as if the articulation of one thought allows another, deeper thought to take its place, deeper as in oceanic, boundless, possessing infinite depth.

The job at the library paid $4.50 an hour, no wonder she never had any money. She owed Maureen $200—they kept their finances separate—Richard $100, and other people smaller sums: $5 here, $10 there. On more than one occasion she'd found it necessary to cross the street or bide her time nursing a cup of coffee at the counter in a restaurant or hide in the stall of the ladies' room in a theatre in order to avoid someone to whom she owed money. Her apartment was in a state of perpetual disarray (it was pointless, if you had no money, to even pretend that things mattered, it would be too frustrating otherwise), though there were times she wished she had enough money to buy, say, new curtains—velvet curtains would be her choice if she had a choice—anything to make this place where she slept and ate and lived her life feel truly like home.

She wondered if the state of her apartment (as seen through the detective's eyes) coincided with the possible profile of an apartment in which someone who might commit a murder could live, whether she herself fit the profile. It was only the second apartment she'd lived in since leaving home; now, even if she wanted to move, rents were too high, there was nowhere to go, everyone she knew paid twice or three times the amount she did, she was doomed to this hole-in-the-wall forever. In between apartments (she'd been evicted from the first) she returned to Brooklyn, thinking—if it was all right with them—she could live with her parents for a month or two, save enough money to find a decent place. But too much time had passed and going to sleep every night in her old room had made her feel she was regressing back to some preadolescent state of being—the monolithic volumes of the Britannica coated with dust (didn't anyone ever open them?) on the shelf above her old desk— and after a week ("I don't know, mother" "I'm not sure, mother") she borrowed money from a friend and rented the first apartment she saw, had been there since.

Not long afterwards she met Maureen and her life changed again. If they pooled their resources they could find a halfway-decent apartment together—this was Maureen's fantasy—but it had never materialized. There were too many reasons why one or the other of them imagined it wouldn't work out, though Rosemary acknowledged it was she who'd been most diffident about making the move. Maureen, five years older, had had other girlfriends; for her, if you loved someone it made no sense not to live with that person, or at least try. If it didn't work out it wouldn't be the end of the world (easy for her to say) but if you didn't make the attempt you'd never know whether it was possible. Maureen was the first person Rosemary had met whom she could imagine living with. At the same time (and this, when she thought about it, was her main "reason") being with another woman so intensely was a new experience; she didn't want "faithfulness" (if they did live together) to become an issue.

And it was an issue, whether they lived together or not. Maureen didn't mind—or so she said—whether Rosemary went to bed with a man, but made it clear that seeing other women—or even expressing interest in another woman—wouldn't be tolerated. "Yet you sleep with other women...." It made no difference. Rosemary knew if she felt attracted to someone and went to bed with that person she could do it without involving her feelings; most of the time—as with Richard—her desire to be with another person came more out of a half-drunken state of empathy for the person, and a feeling of loneliness on her own part, than anything malevolent.

Until she met Maureen, Rosemary had slept only with men; starting in her senior year in high school, she could see their faces, she could name them all. (Fred was the first. Everything began with Fred. Her first instinct, when he took her hand and placed it down the front of his pants, was to pull away. They were sitting in the balcony of a movie theatre in a neighborhood where they didn't know anyone and Fred had draped his coat over his knees. It was a weekday night, the theater half-empty. Fred instructed her how to move her hand, slowly at first, her head resting on his shoulder, her face turned toward the screen. After a few minutes he began breathing heavily, a signal, she later learned, that if she kept moving her hand in a certain way he'd come. When it was over she wiped her hands on his coat. Jerking him off became the focal point of all their dates together. (How could they regress to merely necking and petting after this?) It didn't take long for her to learn that the more time it took him to come the more pleasure accrued, as if there were a form of pleasure that equaled frustration, and as soon as she heard him breathing, the telltale sign, she'd slow the pace till his breathing became regular again.

It was a perverse source of pleasure to wake from a dream of an old (male) lover and realize the person lying in bed beside her was a woman, though Maureen—if Rosemary dared tell her these dreams—would interpret them as a sign that she herself was at fault, and what they didn't need (I better keep my mouth shut) was something to fight about, another big scene. What happened in bed when you were with a man and what you were feeling when you were with a man seemed to exist on two levels running alongside one another, while with a woman—or at least with Maureen—love and sex flowed together as part of the same convoluted stream. Knowing this, however, didn't prevent Rosemary from feeling attracted to men in some random way Maureen claimed was just habitual or vestigial, she'd get over it in time. It was a pleasure to look at men as sex objects, much in the same way Rosemary imagined they looked at her (and similar to the way Maureen regarded other women). A relief, in fact, not to want men to love you, or expect that they could, and then be disappointed for whatever reasons.

Rosemary preferred to think she hadn't made a choice between men and women, but had chosen Maureen, a person, and that her feelings went beyond the sense of choice. The pressure to turn your sexual preference into a political cause seemed to devalue the feelings that were the source of the choice in the first place. Sleeping with a member of your own sex didn't seem any more political than getting married and having children, and Rosemary didn't feel any strong antagonism towards men, refused to be convinced by Maureen or anyone else that in her past dealings with men she'd been used or oppressed. She was skeptical of anyone who thought their sexual preference, publicly stated, was something radical or enlightened, just by definition. The only thing that mattered was your ability to love another person; thinking about the gender of the person you were with just got in the way.

If she drank one more beer she'd get up enough nerve to approach the booth where Maureen and her new girlfriend were sitting. Drinking, if nothing else, diffused her feelings of stubbornness, which informed her that Maureen should be the person who made the first move. Playing games of any kind was humiliating and demeaning, especially if you knew there was a higher place to be, free of cynicism and the fear of acting like a fool. "If you want to end it all why don't you just say so?" It hadn't come to that yet, or so Rosemary hoped. (She didn't know for a fact that this other woman was really Maureen's new girlfriend, or whether they were even sleeping together.) It was tempting to order another beer and babble endlessly to whomever was sitting next to her at the bar. Not Richard, who was really Fred, but preferably someone she didn't know. If she put her head on the bar and burst into tears—which is what she really wanted to do—Maureen would think she was crying to get her attention. She was past the point where she could bother to feel self-conscious about the way she looked or how she was acting. Did anyone really care? Maureen used to criticize her for drinking too much; if she approached the booth now she was risking the possibility that Maureen would see how drunk she was and ignore her completely. If Maureen and Sally laughed together over something and she was sitting in the booth with them there was no way of knowing they weren't laughing at her. A private joke, schoolgirl laughter, a form of intimacy. Women who went to bed with other women just to see "what it was like" were all fools. Women who treated other women as sex objects were as stupid as the men on the street who whistled as you walked by, or made comments about your anatomy.

"Why don't you join us?" the voice said. "We've been waiting for you."

Rosemary lowered her beer bottle to the surface of the bar and focused on the eyes, then the mouth, of a woman whom she didn't know. They were so close that if either moved a few inches toward the other their bodies would merge and melt together. She looked over her shoulder toward Maureen, who was still sitting in the booth, smiling in their direction, then stepped down off the stool without losing her balance and let Sally, Maureen's new friend, guide her across the floor of the bar (Rosemary didn't know whether she should push the woman aside or allow this stranger the familiarity of physical contact), her fingers making small indentations in the sleeves of her blouse. There was the hint that something was being offered, but what was it? When they reached the booth Rosemary realized she was drunker than she'd thought, swayed slightly and leaned back against Sally to keep from falling. "I found this dead body on the floor," she wanted to sing, as Maureen (who'd never answered her call and consequently knew nothing about what had happened that day) made a space in the booth so she could sit down beside her. It wasn't I, it wasn't me. They sat so close together their shoulders touched; joy and pleasure, like undersea flowers, floated to the surface. The "I" was this person who was thinking, who had thoughts, but there was another "I" who, when she was with you, became another person, a shadow of her true self.

More important to feel included than to feel the burden of oneself, alone, no matter how much strength and comfort one derived from the feeling of loneliness. To be with another person one had to turn slightly from that self, or give it up completely, if necessary, become the person who was both object and subject of another person's love. Either way was frightening. Life permitted you to wallow in a kind of fear that was a rationalization for assuming you could do what you wanted, disregarding the consequences. The only solution was to become so helpless, so dependent on other people, that it was impossible to be alone, to function in the simplest of ways, call a cab, find the key that opened the door to the place you called "home." And even so, there were people lying in doorways right now with no money and no place to go. People who had listened to the voices in their heads which had told them, "It's better to go get drunk and forget it all." It wasn't necessary for you to manipulate me into thinking a certain way; all I ever wanted ("last call," the bartender shouted) was your trust. The problem with history was that people kept making the same mistakes. They made the mistakes because they forgot what went wrong to begin with. Forgiveness was a form of forgetting the mistakes you made in the past. Poison fills the wounds that heal with time.

5

Frank stood on the corner across from the building on Henry Street, the scene of the so-called crime, leaning against the wire fence bordering a small concrete park where three middle-aged black men sat on a bench passing a bottle. Despite the warm weather the men all wore long overcoats, caught in a time warp that had less to do with the air temperature than the images they had of themselves: it was as if the concrete at their feet were a mirror, or body of water. One of the men wore a woolen cap, a fringe of gray showing above his ears. Though he hadn't reached the point where he could identify with them, Frank felt like he was trapped in a time warp as well. It seemed, for instance, that more than twenty-four hours had passed since he'd discovered the body of the old woman. Or to be more accurate: twenty-four hours had expired since the woman who lived upstairs had discovered the body of her landlady, twenty-four hours since Frank had sat across from this younger woman in her tiny apartment, drinking coffee, undressing her in his mind as he took notes in his black book. Time—not the kind of time you learn about in school—was something that couldn't be measured in hours or minutes, but rather in terms of the intensity of the thoughts in his head. (Later that night, lying on his living room couch, Frank tried to imagine what it would be like to wake up in that woman's bed. Did she snore, as Gina did? Did she talk in her sleep?) If Joe Hopper, or one of his other colleagues, drove by, they'd think it odd he was standing there, hands in the pockets of his jacket and the sun on his face, as if a murder (or any crime) could be solved by doing nothing. He could say he was waiting for someone (Joe would probably think he was playing around, and wink in a way that implied Frank was finally shaping up after all, the wink Joe's version of the Good Housekeeping Seal of Masculine Approval) and at least that would be half-true. (If the opposite of all truth was falsehood, one could also say that everything true was also false, and that consequently everything was both half-true and half-false.) A team of men in green jumpsuits hauling cases of Molson Ale down a ladder leading to the basement of a nearby bodega diverted Frank's thoughts from all his usual problems, mainly Gina, and how much he was beginning to hate his life as a cop. The men hauling beer were black or Spanish, all in their early twenties. They didn't have the luxury of wondering whether they liked their jobs or not; instead they were happy just to be working at all. To think too much about the future was pointless. Once they'd been fooled into imagining that if they stayed in school long enough to get diplomas they'd be entitled to do something that might require them to take a modicum of responsibility for their actions. These guys hadn't worked long enough at their job to feel bitter; give them a few more years. At least now that the warm weather was here, they could take pleasure standing out on the sidewalk in the early afternoon, eating enormous tongue-shaped sandwiches and drinking beer while admiring the bodies of the young women as they paraded by, most of them in what seemed like a state of near undress. It had been a long winter.

The men passing the bottle had nothing better to do than sit on a bench in a playground strewn with broken glass, a playground that, like themselves, had seen better days. When they accosted people on the street it was to tell them about these better days. Elaborate on some moment in the past when things had been different. There were slides and swings in the playground, a sandbox, but no children. Not the place you'd want to take your kid, if you had a kid. There were no women with strollers or baby carriages sitting on the benches, gossiping about their various ailments, the ailments of their kids, and whether one of them, or any of them, would ever want to get pregnant again. It was one of the warmest days on record for the middle of May.

In his mind Frank was back in the upstairs bedroom of his house in the Bronx. He turned on the bedside lamp, kicked off his shoes, and lay down on his back in the center of the bed. He could hear Gina singing in the shower and smiled because he knew she thought he couldn't hear. She was singing "Fever," the old Peggy Lee version. It was from a record she had of Peggy Lee's Greatest Hits. Then the water in the shower stopped and Gina stopped singing. She stood in the doorway, holding an orange towel around her breasts and thighs. Frank could see the drops of water glistening on her thighs. Her hair was wild and seemed to have been poured from a vat onto her back and shoulders. She stood at the side of the bed—not the side where she normally slept, but his side with her legs slightly apart.

"Turn off the light."

When the bottle in the brown paper bag was empty

the three men would return to the men's shelter on East Third Street for lunch: soup and rice, white bread coated with margarine. Either that or they'd resume their posts at the intersections along Houston Street. Every time the cars cruising east along Houston stopped for the light they'd rush into the street with a can of Windex and a rag and wipe the grime from the windshield, whether the driver wanted them to or not. Once the work was done it was difficult for the driver, with good conscience, not to roll down his or her window and hand the man a dime or quarter. After an hour or two the three men would meet in front of the liquor store on Second Avenue and Third Street and pool the money, adding it up as they stood in a circle on the street. On good days it was usually more than enough to purchase a bottle of Thunderbird. The big red "T" on the label of the bottle had the same effect upon the men as the pendulous object a doctor in the early days of psychoanalysis might sway in front of a patient in an attempt to induce hypnosis. If necessary they'd get down on their knees and pray on the sidewalk to the red letter. All fear of the hereafter vanished at the sight of the "T" on the label of the bottle the man behind the counter at the liquor store passed beneath the glass enclosure in return for the money: the nickels, dimes, and quarters (the man in the liquor store was used to small denominations) given to them by the people in the big cars.

Frank saw her as soon as she turned the corner. She was walking slowly, one arm swinging at her side. She didn't carry a pocketbook or purse like most women (Frank couldn't imagine Gina ever leaving the house without taking with her an enormous shoulder bag—of which there were about ten in her closet—stuffed with a million useless objects), only a jacket, a man's sport jacket, which she'd been wearing, no doubt, the night before, and which she carried over her shoulder like a sailor. Frank couldn't help feeling a twinge of jealousy—he wasn't her lover, after all, or her father—at the thought that she'd stayed out all night, and what that implied.

The men down the block drove away in their truck. A Concorde jet dipped beneath the white sky. Frank didn't want her to think he was spying on her. Wanted to make it seem that meeting her again was coincidental. It was logical that he'd be prowling around the building looking for clues. There was no reason for her, or anyone, to think he was motivated by anything more than a desire to find out who killed the old woman. If he told her he had some more questions to ask she might even invite him up to her apartment again for a cup of coffee. It was a pleasure just to follow the movement of her body as she climbed the steps to the door of her building. Watching her walk down the street was like seeing someone in a dream, someone in real life whom you dreamt about the night before. (In the old days Gina used to tell him her dreams. She'd make breakfast and they'd sit together at the dining room table. She wearing the low cut nightgown with the blue flowers, Frank fully dressed, a revolver strapped to his side.)

"Oh shit, not him again," Rosemary said to herself, as she saw Frank cross the street. She hadn't slept more than a few hours the night before and had a hangover as well. She'd folded her jacket over her arm and was fumbling in the pocket of her pants for her keys when she heard this man's voice calling her name.

The events of the previous day had yet to filter into the present. Yesterday didn't mean the day before, in this case, but was part of everything that had ever taken place in the past. Just because it was something that had happened recently didn't mean it was fresher or more distinct than something that had taken place years ago. All the events crowded together: this person, this body, this room, this bed. The fact that the detective had chosen to call her by her first name, implying a level of intimacy that didn't exist, and would probably never exist, was what confused her most.

"Oh, it's you," she said, trying to smile, as if making him think she was glad to see him again was the appropriate way of acting. She took the ring of keys from her pocket and dangled them in front of him, hoping he'd get the message and go away. If he insisted on asking more questions she'd be late for work; all she wanted was to get upstairs, take a quick bath, change her clothes. Her initial impulse, when it appeared he wasn't going to say anything or explain why he was waiting for her, if in fact he was waiting for her, was to ask him, as she had the day before, if he wanted a cup of coffee—he looked like he could use some, didn't cops ever sleep?—but she held off saying anything, deciding it was up to him to take the initiative. His diffidence, since he didn't say anything at first, reminded her of boys she'd known in high school, too shy to even take her hand or put their arm around her shoulders when they walked down the street or sat side by side in the movies. (She remembered how the nervousness of the person beside her made it impossible to concentrate on the movie, and the sense of relief when she—feeling desperate, the movie was almost over—lowered her head onto the person's shoulder, and he, in turn, and with great fanfare, as if everyone in the theatre were watching, took his cue from her gesture and let his arm drift across the back of her seat, the tips of his fingers at the V of her open blouse.)

And Frank, in turn, felt the same rush of nervousness (which was truly a fear of rejection) that he'd experienced when he first began asking girls out on dates. Often the fear of rejection had been so strong he'd avoided the situation entirely, despite the potential pleasure ("aren't you going to kiss me?") if the particular girl consented. It was important for him to learn that being rejected wasn't the worst thing in the world, and that asking a person for a date was a form of flattery, a way of showing another human being you were interested, even though it gave the object of your feelings the power to say no. It was only if the girl had a streak of cruelty (she'd been rejected in the past herself and was now taking it out on you), or was basically tactless (in which case she wasn't worth asking out to begin with), that you would walk away feeling rejected. There were ways of saying no that didn't make you feel more repulsive than you already might. "Can I buy you lunch?"

"I have to make a phone call"—it was pointless to argue—"I'll be right down."

She turned her back on him, inserted her key into the front door of the building, and disappeared. Frank lowered his weight onto the fender of a parked car and stared at the ground floor window where the old woman had lived (until yesterday a neighborhood fixture—"nice day, Mrs. Eckstein"—her arm resting on the windowsill) then let his eyes wander to the window directly above. If nothing else, the fact that she'd consented to have lunch with him was a small triumph amid a string of zeros.

Rosemary was in her apartment by now, calling the library to tell the people she worked with she'd be late —"this cop, the guy who talked to me yesterday, wants to question me some more"—unbuttoning her blouse and tossing it on the pile of dirty laundry at the foot of her bed, then realizing she had no more clean blouses, which meant picking the one she'd worn the day before out of the pile—cleaner and less wrinkled than the one she'd discarded—splashing cold water from the kitchen faucet onto her face. No way to hide the lines beneath her eyes, deep grooves at this point, what difference did it make? The people at work were accustomed to seeing her semi-hungover and unlike most places where she'd worked before no one admonished her if she walked in late or called in sick every few weeks. Everyone at the library assumed everyone else who worked there had a personal life that was possibly as erratic as their own: the boss, a middle-aged gay man, was especially tolerant, though Rosemary didn't know whether he knew she was gay as well. Rosemary emptied what was left of a cardboard box of cat food into the plastic tray near the icebox; no milk in the icebox, no sign of the cat who was usually waiting for her at the door when she came home after spending the night out.

Walking down the street to her house she'd been trying to tie together all the events of the night before: going to the bar, talking to Richard, the smile on the bartender's face as he placed the chilled bottle of beer in her hand. Maureen and Sally sitting in the booth. All the clusters of people she didn't know. She'd been trying to remember it all when the man named Frank called her name. (The way he said "Rosemary" made her think it must be someone she knew well.) She remembered leaving the bar, arm in arm with Maureen and Sally. Another beer in Maureen's apartment, but she hadn't finished it; there it was, a full can, warm, at the foot of the bed when she woke up. Another dead beer. Sally and Maureen were still asleep. She'd managed to find her clothing, get dressed, and extract a five dollar bill from Maureen's purse without waking them. Sally slept on her stomach and was breathing heavily into her pillow, as if she were suffocating. Maureen's familiar body was turned on its side, one arm flung over the edge of the bed. (By the time she was a senior in high school, and had begun going out with Fred, everything was different. Who cared what the people sitting around them thought? Who cared about the movie? Often, before the movie began, she would go to the john and remove her underpants and bra, so Fred wouldn't have to waste any time fumbling around.)

She remembered lying back on the bed in Maureen's apartment, the open beer propped on her chest. She could hear the two women talking in low voices in another room. It was no longer necessary for her to remind herself that these women—Sally especially—were friends, not strangers or adversaries. All afternoon she'd been wondering whether she and Maureen would ever sleep together again, and it was comforting to be back in the familiar bed (the framed photos of Maureen, taken at various times in her life, stared down at her from the opposite wall) where she'd spent so much time during the past year. She was just about to close her eyes when the two women appeared, naked, on either side of the bed, and began undressing her.

It was Frank's job to question everyone who lived in the building. He'd written the names and phone numbers of all the present tenants in his notebook—Olga Pozo, Brooke and Gerald Malone, Estaban Lopez, Benjamin Cherry, Frank LaMott, Hector and Angelica Bravo, David Cherubini, Norman Godfrey, Lee Tim Chung—as well as the names and forwarding addresses of everyone who'd lived in the building for the last five years. He'd talked to most of the people in the building yesterday— for each name there was a face ("what were you doing yesterday at 9 a.m.?"), a voice—but he'd missed a few and ostensibly that's what he was doing today. After he interrogated the tenants he'd interview the local storekeepers and call a few people listed in the woman's address book. Joe Hopper, his partner, was busy canvassing the winos and junkies, some of whom were informers and knew everything that was going on in the neighborhood, who hung out along the railings and benches in Seward Park. They'd meet later, back at the precinct on Pitt Street, and compare notes.

If Rosemary didn't go to work she didn't get paid, and she was already behind on May's rent. But who was she paying rent to now? Her most recent utility bill, as well as her phone bill, were also past due; any day she'd get a shut off notice for one or the other, and go around borrowing money from friends. The utility companies had become more impatient in recent years. The moment they sensed you were falling behind they threatened you with a disconnect. At her worst moments, she'd managed without a phone; if people wanted to get in touch they'd call her at work, or at Maureen's. What she needed more than anything, or almost anything, was a large sum of money so she could settle her past debts and start anew.

Here, Kitty!

While Rosemary was in the bar downtown with Maureen and Sally, Frank was having a late dinner in a combination restaurant and bar on the Upper West Side. Ever since Gina returned to school he felt an affinity for college hangouts, as if being around kids ten years younger than himself would bring him closer to her world. When he did get home, around midnight, the house was dark, Gina asleep or in bed upstairs, at least he assumed she was home (it was to her credit that whatever else she did these days, she was always home when he returned from work), he didn't even bother to check whether she was there but just poured himself a drink, unlaced his shoes and kicked them under the coffee table, lit a smoke, and stretched out on the couch, propping a cushion beneath his head. "Is that you Frank?" It was she, his wife, at the top of the stairs. He inhaled, coughed, unbuttoned his shirt, set the drink on the floor. He couldn't see her but imagined her standing in the shadows, wearing a nightgown fringed with lace or a blue terrycloth robe or possibly—since it was so warm—nothing at all, heard the sound of water running in the sink of the upstairs bathroom, then her voice again: "Why don't you come to bed?" A lot had changed in the month since she'd confessed—if that's the right word—her infidelity, and this wasn't the first time they'd played this scene. Once, she'd actually come downstairs and sat on the arm of the couch, and when he persisted in not saying anything or answering her questions—he couldn't really believe she wanted him to act as if nothing were wrong, as if he had no reason to feel angry—she told him what he'd already secretly guessed. "It's all over, Frank, I'm no longer seeing him." She regretted it ever happened, she'd made a mistake, it's you I love, I married you, doesn't that mean anything? I want your babies, she said, leaning over him. He was frightened that if they made physical contact some part of him he didn't know about might react to what he was thinking and he'd do something he'd later regret ("I didn't mean to hit you"). There was no way to pretend that nothing had changed. Who could say—if he did forgive her—the same thing wouldn't happen again? Babies or no babies there'd always be the thought that there was someone else and he knew if it did happen again she'd be smart enough not to tell him: he'd return from work and find the butt of a Pall Mall in the ashtray in the kitchen and know someone had been in bed with her—no matter what she said to defend herself. "I'll do anything, Frank," they were like characters in a soap opera, she didn't even need a script, his mother was a soap opera addict but what would she think if she knew her daughter-in-law had been unfaithful? "I never liked her anyway," she'd say, and what help was that?

He lay on the couch with his ankles crossed, heard

Gina sigh, the sound of her footsteps as she returned to the bedroom. For a moment he felt empathy for her—it was the last remnant of real feeling—and that maybe she was truly repentant for the suffering she'd brought on hoth of them. All he had to do was climb the stairs and get into bed like he'd done every night of their marriage before all this had started. Advice to the lovelorn: forgive and forget. It wasn't so difficult, things like this happened every day. He tried to direct his thoughts elsewhere: the dead woman, his job, Rosemary, whether they'd ever find the murderer. Maybe the old woman's son, arriving from California, would know something. Whenever a car passed, the beams of the headlights rippled across the walls and ceiling. Love was like a kind of disease and the only cure was more love but beyond a point it was necessary for one's sanity to build a moat around oneself and not let anyone near for fear that whatever happened before to make you suffer was no one's fault but your own and that if it happened once it'll happen again and maybe if you can't deal with it you're better off avoiding it completely.

Irene. Rosemary. Someone to talk to. He wondered if everyone at work knew his marriage was falling apart. He tried to imagine what it would be like living alone, turning the key in the lock as he opened the door of the small apartment, eating alone, going to bars where no one knew he was a cop. If the woman he'd met that morning could fend for herself, why couldn't he? "Irene's cousin is in town, why don't you come over?" Joe's strategy, using sex as a form of retaliation, would be to go out and fuck anybody, it didn't matter who.

The clientele of the restaurant where Frank and Rosemary went for lunch were mostly older men and women, retired people who'd been born in the neighborhood and had moved away, to upper Manhattan or Riverdale, somewhere on the fringe of the city where you could actually see the veins of a leaf as it changed color, where you could stand under a tree and bathe in the rays of sunlight passing through the spaces between the branches. There weren't many restaurants in the neighborhood to choose from, but even Frank, once inside, was amazed at how dismal it was. All the old people sat at separate tables, staring morosely into their bowls of borscht. There was a sign that read: Special Today—Egg and Mushroom Sandwich. It sounded horrible. The restaurant was the kind of place where you took your tray, loaded it with silverware and napkins, and waited on line. It was more like the lobby of a nursing home or a funeral parlor than a restaurant, and Frank instantly regretted taking her here.

"What would you like?"

On the wall there were lists of cold sandwiches, salads, soups, appetizers, dairy dishes, desserts. The overhead lighting, tinted fluorescent beams offset by fake wooden panels, created an eerie pre-storm feeling: the meal you ate here, for all you knew, might be your last. The old men behind the counter, in white aprons and yarmulkes, played out their Alphonse-Gaston routine: "Did you take their order?" "No, did *you* take their order?", each of them winking, in turn, at Frank and Rosemary, just in case they didn't realize that this little skit was being performed for their benefit. (Rudeness creates its own ambience; it's possible people might be drawn to a restaurant as much for the psychotic behavior of the waiters and waitresses as for the food.)

Frank waited till Rosemary had ordered—"mushroom & barley"—"what kind of bread?" "challah"—before making his choice (he was tempted just to say "I'll have the same"), a bagel with cream cheese and lox and a cup of coffee. (Lox was one of Gina's favorite foods, or so she said, but Frank, who'd eaten it only once before, couldn't remember whether he liked it or not. "You should try something new once in awhile," Gina would admonish him whenever they went out to eat.) They carried their trays to a table near the windows and sat down under a sign that read Aid To Choking Victims, with a lot of diagrams and instructions about what to do in case the person you were with fell forward into his or her soup, a not uncommon occurrence considering the temperature of the restaurant was about 100 degrees.

Rosemary had passed the restaurant every day but had never eaten here. When she did go out to eat in the neighborhood she usually went to one of the cheap Chinese restaurants on East Broadway, just west of the Manhattan Bridge. There was a special place where she and Maureen used to go when they were first seeing one another. It was during their most idyllic phase, both of them between jobs. In those days they'd stay up till dawn, sleep till mid-afternoon, relax over coffee, their feet propped on the kitchen table, smoking cigarettes and listening to the disco station on the radio, immersed in the rare pleasure—no need to say anything—of just being.

There was no reason why that feeling couldn't last,

but it never did. Some people spent a good deal of time mourning the loss of that feeling, while others tried to recapture it, forsaking the pleasures of long-term relationships in the hope of recreating that feeling, every few months or years, with a new person. There was always someone new, and in a sense it was the newness or unfamiliarity that mattered, especially as far as sex was concerned. Some people took the lessening of interest in sex as a signal that from this point the relationship was all downhill. If it were possible to take the concept of "love" down from its pedestal, so that "falling in love" was synonymous with "physical attraction," i.e., if you want to go to bed with me that means you're in love with me, then maybe it would be possible to fall in love so frequently that promiscuity—sleeping with a different person each night—would seem like the ideal state.

One needs a lot of leisure to lie around and recreate the crystalline moment of first falling in love with another person, and something as mundane as the need to earn money is often enough to limit the amount of time and energy one can spend finding or giving love. There was no question that the repressive nature of making a living had a direct relationship to one's sexual feelings. It was true (at least Freud thought it true) that at a certain age you had to compromise your ideas of ultimate pleasure and begin to channel your energies down a path that was more practical and realistic, taking into account the exigencies of, say, supporting a family, not only the person you live with but all the other creatures who had evolved out of that initial feeling.

One way to start a conversation is to ask the other

person a question. "How long have you been a cop?" "Are you married?" "Have you ever killed anyone?" While a psychiatrist might sit passively behind his or her desk, a policeman would aggressively attempt to get information from a suspect, threatening violence if the person he was interrogating acted dumb or like he or she didn't know anything about a crime in which this person was obviously involved. The longer they sat together at the table in the restaurant the more it became obvious to Rosemary that Frank wasn't interested in questioning her further about Bette Eckstein. (Bette Eckstein, remember, the woman who was murdered yesterday?) On the contrary, it was she who finally asked him, after a long silence, whether they had any ideas about who did it. Were there any clues? She was tempted to just tell him what she was thinking but it was a matter of phrasing the question so he didn't feel hurt, though why she should care about his feelings was a whole other question. Instead she said, "What part of Brooklyn are you from?" and this question keyed a discussion about the various neighborhoods they both knew. She'd known a few people who'd attended Erasmus, he didn't know anyone who'd gone to her high school, St. Saviour, and given their age difference the chance that they knew any of the same people was unlikely. It began to feel very much like being on a blind date where all you know about the other person is what the person who arranged the date told you though in some cases the less you know the more there is to talk about, and even if you do know something it's better to play dumb.

Being in a room with so many old people made Rosemary nervous; she sipped her coffee and craved a beer. She needed a space in time so she could replay everything that had happened the night before, think about Sally and what it felt like to be in heaven. She resented Frank for presuming that just because he was a cop he could take up her time for reasons that had nothing to do with "business," taking advantage of the authority that went with being a cop to get close to her personally, make a move. (Doesn't he know I like women?) She didn't think of him as "Frank"—there was no reason to address him as anything—just as this guy who was sitting across from her who seemed like he wanted to talk about himself, presuming, again, she was interested in the humdrum details of why he'd become a cop and what growing up in Brooklyn was like—though she knew as much as he did about all that—and ultimately, how much he hated his job (he didn't even have to say he hated it, you could tell by the way he talked), he was only thirty and it seemed he still had time to learn how to do something else, when he said this she could actually see his eyes grow wide like a small boy suddenly aware of the possibility of something horrible or beautiful, it was like being trapped in a tunnel under a river at rush hour and then finally, after what seemed like forever, spying the light up ahead at the end.

"My father and uncle were both cops and everyone in the family just assumed I'd be a cop too. It was too hard to fight back, even if I'd wanted to, and I must admit, and I know it sounds stupid, I can't remember ever wanting to be anything else. I can remember seeing my father in his uniform, and my uncle, the gun in the holster hanging in the closet. 'Don't ever touch,' my parents would say. Instead they'd give me toy guns for my birthday. Cap pistols and imitation tommy guns and six-shooters. My problem is I never wanted to be anything, never had the chance to even consider I might want to do something else. So I became a cop, it was easy, I'm a good cop...."

You can't order people to make love to one another as if they were machines, but you can act as the catalyst for a situation where people who don't know one another come together in such a way they might eventually end up in bed.

"Listen," she was tempted to say, "all this is very interesting," but she didn't say anything, patience was a form of strength, the gift of attention a kind of miracle, it was too easy to say something nasty or cruel, harder to wait it out—"do you have the time?"—until he was finished. If, when it was time for her to leave, and she was already late for work, he asked her if he could see her again, and by "seeing" he meant "going out together," in the old sense, she'd be forced to make a little speech about her sexual proclivities with the hope that, if nothing else, this would deter him from whatever fantasy image he was concocting about her, he would be shocked, possibly, that he could be so off target, excusing himself, "but all I meant was... ," as if you couldn't read everything he was feeling on his face. She'd offered him a cup of coffee—it was no big deal—and now he was returning the favor. The soup was good. She could say, "Thanks for buying me lunch" and make it sound like she meant it. Cops had the potential to be as psychotic as anyone else, even more so, and the way he was acting made her feel that if she did or said something there was the possibility he might think it meant something she hadn't intended, a person who goes around wearing a gun under his jacket has to be a little crazy. To his credit, she had to admit he wasn't coming on to her in a way she could consider offensive, but that only confused the issue.

What was he doing waiting outside my house?

It occurred to her that for reasons she couldn't imagine (all right, I found the body, so what?) the cops were watching her. If you thought too much about something it was easy to become paranoid. One could take one's most far out notion to the limit, draw a circle around it till the last glimpse of truth faded away. Maybe someone—one of Frank's colleagues—had followed her from the bar to Maureen's apartment; if so, they probably knew more about what had happened than she did. (If Frank himself had been at the bar last night she was certain she would have recognized him.) Maybe the cops had somehow planted a tape recorder in Maureen's apartment and at this very moment were sitting around some dingy basement listening to the sounds of the three women making love. Is that how they worked? It was a free country, but anything was possible. She took a pair of dark glasses from her jacket pocket, wiped them on the sleeve of her blouse, and stared out the window, just as three middle-aged black men in winter coats staggered by. If I want to get drunk, she felt like overturning her tray and shouting, and go home with my girlfriend, my ex-girlfriend, it's nobody's goddamned business but my own.

6

Only a few hours before Max had been lying in Caroline's arms. Now—as if he'd fallen back to sleep and had slipped off the edge into a bad dream—he was sitting in an airplane above the clouds, a blonde woman in her mid-twenties wearing a red dress with a belt made of tiny gold loops (the buttons along the front of her dress were gold too, as were her earrings) sitting beside him, a woman he'd never seen before but who seemed anxious to tell her life story to whoever was sitting next to her as people on planes, trains, and long-distance bus rides like to do. The idea of sitting in such close proximity to another person for so many hours without saying anything was as anxiety-provoking as being on the plane itself; one talked, incontinently, like a small child, to relieve the tension. You had to be so completely lost in your own thoughts to be unaware of the presence of this other body, and the intimacy created by the physical closeness (when she crossed her long legs the tip of her high-heeled sandals grazed the leg of his pants) permitted a kind of openness other one-to-one situations rarely inspired. So at the end of a long trip you might find yourself discussing your sexual preferences—"I've slept with a few women, but men are more interesting"—secure in the knowledge that when the trip was over you could say goodbye—"nice talking to you"—and never see the person again.

It wasn't until he'd taken his seat on the plane that Max realized how sequestered he'd been the last year, immersed in the intrigues of his life with Caroline, and with small town life in general, reading the newspaper only when it was thrust in front of him (the San Francisco papers were more involved with the vicissitudes of provincial society and gossip about people he'd never heard of before, what so-and-so wore to what party, than with what was happening in the world). Back in a world where people's concerns were potentially as various as the number of people themselves made him feel self-conscious. Most of the men around him were wearing suits and ties; engrossed in the contents of the looseleaf binders and instruction manuals and whatever else they kept hidden away in the attache cases at their sides, this trip across country was nothing more than a commute from one point to another, a chance to catch up on the minutes of the last meeting. Max, unshaved, in dungarees with patches on the knees and a blue workshirt, was surprised when the woman beside him appeared so eager to make conversation, though perhaps, like himself, she just needed someone to distract her from something she didn't want to think about. He had planned to take another tranquilizer for the trip. He didn't know what was going to happen when he arrived in New York and wanted to be at full strength, well rested, ready for anything. Cops, codicils, relatives, funeral arrangements, lawyers. He thought of Caroline, driving back along the coast road, back to their empty house and the unmade bed, the patio with the view of the ocean, the horses grazing in the pasture out back, and wondered when they'd see each other again, if ever. Living with one other person was like creating an island immune from the disequilibrium that results when a few billion people attempt to coexist in the same space. He'd never spent so much time alone with anyone, and part of the anxiety he felt now—though he hated to admit it—was because she wasn't there.

The woman in red opened a fashion magazine and pointed to a photograph of herself in a single-piece bathing suit. She was leaning back against a big rock with the ocean in the distance, blonde hair flying in her eyes. He barely listened as she rattled on about her career, her apartment in New York, her family in Michigan (she'd attended college in Michigan as well, but never finished), the friends she'd been visiting in San Francisco. Whenever one of the men in suits and ties wandered by they made a point of staring at her, probably wondering what she was doing talking to a person like Max when she could be talking to one of them.

"Modeling is fun. I've been doing it since I was fifteen. What I really want to do, though, is act, get into movies. Just a few days ago I was introduced to a guy who asked me to be in a film but when I got to his studio—he was a sleazy bastard, I must admit, and I don't even know why I went—he wanted me to take part in some big orgy scene, it was one of *those* movies." For emphasis, she placed her hand on Max's arm (her fingernails long and manicured but unpolished) as if to say: You know what I mean, don't you?

You're alive aren't you?

Her story (what she chose to tell) took about an hour. When she was finished, possibly just stopping for a rest, she stared questioningly at Max, and he assumed that it was his turn to tell her about himself. He told her about the town in the country where he'd been living and which she'd actually visited once, not on her most recent stay in California but a few years before Max had moved there; he talked a little about growing up in New York, how he was returning to the city to see his family, knowing it didn't really matter what he said and that for all he knew she could just as well have been telling him a lot of lies. After he'd given her enough perfunctory information to make her feel they were true allies (even though they had almost nothing in common), they sat back in their respective seats, tipped as far back as they could go, sipped their drinks and stared into space.

When she talked again it was with the purpose of steering the conversation back to herself.

"Next week I'm going to fly down to Barbados. Have you ever been there? The best thing about modeling is the traveling. Last year I was in Paris and Munich for a month. Someday, though, I'd like to move to the country and have a lot of kids, not a lot but maybe one or two, but there's time for that. I don't know what I'd do now if I got pregnant. The idea of having an abortion horrifies me. I hear too many stories about women who have abortions, something goes wrong, and they can never have kids. I'm not so stupid to think this kind of life can go on forever. So it's important to make contacts with other kinds of people, nothing ever happens if you don't go out and let people know you're available, show yourself off. My roommate just started doing TV commercials, like for Ivory soap and things, and she's going to introduce me to someone...."

A stewardess with synthetic blue eyes and a sexless blue uniform brought them their food. Max hadn't eaten since late the night before when he and Caroline had shared a ham and cheese sandwich and a bloody mary in bed before going to sleep. Sitting naked on top of the blankets with the crumbs falling around them, watching TV: eating, then, had been a function, not so much of hunger, but of simple pleasure, something two people could do together. Living together was synonymous with sharing: space, food, emotions, private thoughts. Sometimes you went off into your own world—hid behind the pages of a book or fell asleep—but it was only knowing someone else was nearby that made this kind of separateness possible. Max was concerned the woman beside him would think something was wrong if he didn't even make an attempt to eat but as he lifted a forkful of dry white rice to his mouth he noticed his hand was trembling, maneuvered his body behind the tray so he could reach the vial of Valium in his pants pocket, swallowed one down with a sip of black coffee, and wiped his lips.

Anxiety isn't related to intelligence. You can't wash away your feelings by thinking about them. Internal security, self-value, independence, *amour-propre*—these are the states of being you're supposed to strive toward. After so many moments of time, like links on a gold chain, you grow up to become this person. If you feel anxiety in the present maybe you can try to link the feeling to something that happened in your past. This was the person you'd become! Some people can learn how to use their intelligence to direct their feelings away from the source of anxiety. Avoid, from past experience, situations that create tension. Other people purposefully court situations fraught with anxiety and tension, not masochistically, but—like Rimbaud—as a way of testing their strength. "Je suis un autre" is one way of saying "I can do anything." At a certain point one discovers one's limits. A caterpillar crawling up a window might be a signal to stop what you're doing. Depending on when you were born, the conjunction of planets and stars might have some significance. There's always someone or something outside yourself who will tell you you've gone too far. My intelligence (though intelligence has its limits) tells me if I do that I'll go crazy, or be ostracized. No more internal security, no more self-esteem, no more independence. Different shades of gray fill the spectrum. Awake in the middle of the night listening to the trucks and the sirens. An empty bed. "Maybe I should get up and take a pill."

In a seat across the aisle a child was crying. The plane was passing through a storm and the trays of food were bouncing erratically. Being in an airplane was like being a child, powerless, a victim, dependent on others. A stewardess patrolling the aisles lost her balance momentarily and clutched the back of Max's seat to keep from falling. "Don't cry, everything's all right," the parents of the child were consoling their daughter. Max had never been on an airplane with his parents. The few times they traveled anywhere—usually to Miami, where they stayed in a motel on the beach for a week—they took trains, though one winter, during the Christmas holidays, they rented a car and all drove south together, Max alone in the backseat, his father behind the wheel, his mother up front with a map and a basket of food. And a red thermos: Max's father drank coffee as he drove.

The woman next to him cursed as a speck of food fell on her dress. "Can I borrow your napkin?" If they had met in a bar he—or she—would have suggested by now that they go home together. "My apartment's right around the corner." Posing on a rock with the ocean in the distance, a closeup of her shoulder, water dripping from bare skin. She wanted to be in the movies but that didn't mean she'd go so far as to fuck someone she didn't know while the cameras were rolling. A friend had been offered a lot of money to pose in the nude for a magazine but she couldn't imagine doing that either, "not that anyone would ever ask me."

Max thought of his father, that taciturn man who took so little pleasure in life. Even on vacation he preferred staying in his air-conditioned motel room, while Max and his mother sat around the pool or went to the beach. A year after he died, during one of their Sunday dinners together, his mother confessed that she'd almost married someone else, changing her mind at the last minute and returning the ring. (Soon afterwards she'd met Max's father and had married him immediately. "He was different then. He changed. I don't know what happened.") Their post dinner conversations often involved her telling him stories about the past (a single glass of wine and her eyes began to glow), but Max always left thinking she hadn't told him what was most important. Had she been in love with his father? Did his father ever express his feelings in a way that made her feel he was in love with her? Did she regret not marrying her first suitor?

He couldn't imagine his parents lying in bed together except with a lot of space between them—a year before his father died they began sleeping in separate beds—but it was equally difficult to imagine what it was like to he married to the same person for twenty-five years. (It was no wonder children spent half their lives, most often unsuccessfully, trying to distance themselves from the images of "marriage" their parents created.)

"Would you like some ice cream?" the mother asked her child.

Towards the end of the trip the woman in red fell asleep. She didn't announce that she was tired or that she was going to take a nap; she didn't even sigh, just closed her eyes and dozed off. Max reached beneath his seat for his shoulder bag and took out the black sketch-pad he used as a journal. He wrote in it only infrequently and often wondered if Caroline read it when he wasn't at home. (Despite his almost daily reassurances—"you know I still love you"—he knew that she still felt insecure about their life together.) He'd kept journals when he was younger but they always embarrassed him when he looked at them afterwards—"afterwards" could mean as little as a month—and the feeling that he no longer recognized the person who had been doing the writing discouraged him from continuing; the person who put his thoughts and feelings into words was only a fragment of who he really was. When he left New York he'd stored most of his possessions (except for the furniture which he'd sold to help finance the trip) in his mother's apartment, in a closet in his old room, including a carton containing all the notebooks he'd kept for a few weeks, then stopped.

Beginning something enthusiastically and then stopping: was this a problem? In order for anything to change—and by "anything" (or "anyone") Max included himself, as well as "the world"—it was necessary to devote a long period of attention and concentration to one thing. (Max sometimes wondered whether he was fooling himself about being a director. In his journal he'd berate himself constantly for being too self-indulgent: no matter how much work he did he never felt he was making full use of his time. Caroline saw his ambitions as a threat, and that was no help, especially since what she wanted, at age thirty-five, was to have a child. Each day brought with it new distractions, and Max could slowly see his dreams fading away.) He was frightened that he was the type of person who became disinterested too easily once the initial flush of feeling or excitement began to change, or became absorbed into something "other." (Similarly, in your relations with people, nothing could ever evolve if it didn't exist over a period of time.) Change seemed to involve a process of disintegration, and rather than be a participant in a situation where the feelings would eventually disappear, wasn't it better to cut it off suddenly and start all over again with something different or someone different as soon as possible, with as little time in between the one thing or the other thing so you didn't have to think about why, or how, or what you could have done to make the initial situation last forever, if that were possible.

Yet always desiring to start something new was a way of denying yourself the knowledge of what happens when something continues. It was like diving beneath the surface and then coming up for air without ever touching bottom, without even considering the possibility that one could go farther, truly extend oneself to some place where one had never been before. Not changing, doing one thing, being with one person, was harder than changing, doing many things for short periods of time, seeing many people simultaneously. At a certain point in one's life one grew weary of the repetition that comes from starting over—as the song goes—again and again. The need to be secure and comfortable and loved by one other person begins to dominate whatever vestiges of restlessness still remain. Caroline had reached the place where she wanted one thing, and one person—though her marriage had been a mess she hadn't given up hope that it was still possible to make a commitment, that it was worth it despite the potential turmoil—and Max, after a year of living with her, had seen the advantages of such a relationship. He'd experienced, for the first time, what it meant to be "settled," even if he couldn't imagine thinking of California as his home. He'd always disdained the idea of home, preferring to think he could be anywhere, live anywhere; he couldn't understand that "constraint" and "limitation" meant something positive; he'd thought—when he was too young, perhaps, not even twenty—that he'd arrived at a way of thinking and feeling that was synonymous with a self he knew, never even questioning that the whole idea of "self" might be an illusion. He'd never dreamt, before coming to California, that he'd meet someone and that they'd set up a household together, much less that the person (Caroline) would be married, and ten years older. That there was such a person and that they could connect so positively was reassuring.

Other than the notes he'd made in his journal that morning, he hadn't written anything in over a week. The best time to write in a journal was late at night, when it was possible to get some kind of perspective on everything that had happened during the day. I woke up, I had breakfast, I did this, I saw so and so. If one stayed on the surface in this way it was less likely that one felt embarrassed at some later date. For Max, writing in his journal depended more on his mood than on any specific time of day. Living with Caroline had inhibited his writing; he didn't want to go too deeply into his feelings for her for fear—well, if I were her, I'd be tempted to read it too. The last entry, which he turned to as the "No Smoking" and "Fasten Your Seatbelts " signs flashed on, a signal they were nearing the end of the trip (if only in terms of distance since who knows how long they'd have to spend circling the airport waiting clearance before landing), had been written on the beach, facing the Pacific, a five-minute walk from their house across the area of town known as The Mesa. It was the part of town that could be most thought of as a tourist attraction, the place people driving up on weekends from San Francisco went to, there was even a parking lot adjoining the beach (empty on weekdays) to accommodate the visitors. Most of the residents knew enough to stick close to their homes on weekends, so as not to feel invaded by strangers who secretly envied you for having the perspicacity to live in such a beautiful place. On weekdays, when the beach was deserted, Max and Caroline, and occasionally each separately or with other people, would go down in the early evening when the sun was sinking into the ocean to walk along the reefs looking for agates or just sit back and watch the clouds as thev followed the sun across the horizon, disappearing over the edge like a herd of buffalo or sheep. Max had found a special place where he went when he was alone, a kind of alcove where the mesa jutted out above the sand. On this particular evening Caroline was off in the city with friends. He remembered it all clearly because they'd argued that morning, she wanting him to go with her into the city (they didn't own a car so whenever one of their neighbors was driving to the city it was always tempting to invent an excuse and go along), knowing that the real reason he didn't want to accompany her was because once they got there they'd be spending time with people who were her friends. Max was weary of trying to prove himself as a replacement for Caroline's former husband, tired of being identified in the minds of her friends as "Caroline's new boyfriend," tired of his own lack of identity apart from her. What was the point of thinking about all that? Caroline feared that if he didn't accompany her, her friends would think he didn't like them. The more places they went together the more they'd be taken seriously as "a couple." Max countered by saying it wasn't necessary for them to prove anything to anyone. "We might as well move to New York if we want to play these games." He didn't want to think about what other people were thinking; didn't want to go somewhere he didn't want to be. Living in what seemed to him the closest thing to paradise required, to his mind, a new way of thinking about other people. Caroline was always seeking ways to accommodate her past—"You don't understand," she would say, "these people are my friends"—and didn't want to feel she had to forfeit anything for Max.

"It's not that you don't like these people, you don't like anyone," she would say, knowing this was only half-true, and that a good part of his dissatisfaction had to do with feeling frustrated about his work. He, in turn, criticized her for drinking too much, and for gossiping heartily and into the night about people he didn't even know. He couldn't understand how people's lives could be so empty they had nothing better to think about than what their neighbors were doing. In the city—New York—he didn't know most of his neighbors. Here, it was impossible to go to the general store in the center of town for a container of milk or a loaf of bread or to the liquor store for a six-pack of beer without meeting at least ten people whose houses he had frequented socially, for dinner or a party, and with whom he felt obliged to chat and make conversation.

There was an undercurrent of tension and competitiveness amid many of the middle-aged married women, most of whose husbands commuted to San Francisco each day, for the attention of the few younger men who lived in the town. It was almost as if the women were daring their husbands—who, to their credit, had girlfriends of their own in the city—to leave them alone during the day. Many of the women, after their husbands left in the morning, didn't even bother getting dressed, but just lounged around on their various patios in nightgowns or bathrobes, an early morning pitcher of vodka and orange juice close at hand. Every few weeks Caroline would tell him about another marriage that had dissolved. The husband had moved in with his girlfriend in the city. The wife, whose children were away at school, would open her house to her new lover and his friends. Often this state of affairs would last a few months; then husband and wife would reconcile their differences, fly off to Hawaii or Mexico for a two week vacation. There was so much drama and electricity in the air at all times—it was no wonder Max had a hard time getting people interested in performing a play.

The woman in red shifted toward him in her sleep, bare knees brushing his thighs, her head slipping unselfconsciously onto his shoulder. Asleep, she was assuming the position she might take in bed with her lover, curled on her side like a young girl. Max studied the strands of blonde hair a few inches from his eyes, hair combed to appear "wild" and "tame" at the same time, and tried to stop the progression of pictures as they flashed like tinted movie stills across his mind: his mother, an apron knotted at her waist, preparing dinner in the kitchen; Caroline kneeling on the patio performing a yoga exercise known as the Ustrasana—head thrown back, spine arched, small breasts pointed straight out under her black leotard; his father sinking deeper and deeper into the big easy chair in front of the TV—home from the job in the garment district he hated; the arms and legs of all the women he'd ever slept with (his first lover, Sonia, a Japanese woman, had lived in an apartment on the top floor of his mother's building—on warm nights they'd make love on a narrow mattress on the roof—but had been forced to move when Max's mother found out)—if he stared long enough into the face of the stranger sitting beside him, and beyond her to the animated reefs of clouds drifting off the wing, it might occur to him that being in transit between all these points in his mind, the subtle interstices between past and future, was as valid ("maybe I should take another pill?") as being anywhere. He uncapped his fountain pen and turned to the first blank page in his journal. (On the inside cover he'd pasted a photo of O'Neill, the famous photo taken after he learned he'd won the Pulitzer for *Beyond the Horizon*, running, arms outstretched, from the ocean at Cape Cod.)

"On the plane," he wrote. "Going home to see my mother." The woman moved again, mumbling something in her sleep, her head almost directly beneath Max's chin.

And then, as an aside to Caroline, "Missing you."

The less you know someone the easier it is to become the person they want you to be. Lover, friend, parent—I'll be whatever you like. If everything is thought of as having meaning, then there are no real accidents, and who you meet at a particular moment in your life takes on the burden of whatever you might anticipate in the future. (In the same sense, every new person you meet acts as a kind of door opening into the future.)

As he wrote he noticed his hands were no longer trembling; the result, he assumed, of taking the pill.

"Fasten your seatbelt," the stewardess with the fake eyelashes admonished, and Max pretended he was complying, not wanting to move so suddenly that the woman beside him would wake up. As long as she stayed asleep he could admire or study her body without feeling secretive, or feeling that the way he was looking at her suggested something that was merely sexual—he didn't want to think on that level, the way her reflection in the eyes of the world had altered her sense of beauty (since she knew she was beautiful, how many men or women had told her that?) It was a rare chance to see a person so closely and not be in bed.

A minute before the plane touched ground she woke, rubbed her eyes, grinned. Stretched her arms and yawned. "How long have I been asleep?" She made no attempt to adjust her dress over her knees, no concession to being decorous or prim. To fall asleep with your head on the shoulder of a stranger wasn't abnormal, or something that should be noted or talked about, though some women might blush at the thought they'd placed themselves in such close proximity to another person, the so-called "compromising position," both literally and figuratively, leading the man to believe—"well, she must want to make love to me"—granting him the permission to encroach even further on her space.

At the door of the plane the stewardesses and the captain said goodbye—this was part of their job—and Max and the woman followed the other passengers through a long funnel-like hallway into the body of the airport. It was early evening, just beginning to get dark. Max was aware that all the men they passed turned around to stare at the woman walking beside him and couldn't understand how they could act so overtly when she was obviously with someone who might be her husband or lover. Whenever he passed someone on the street who

attracted him and this person was accompanied by someone else he made a point of dropping his eyes or looking
away. It was always hard to differentiate, even to oneself,
between the pleasure one was taking in a person's physical self and the feeling of sheer beauty the person ema-
nated, which had little or nothing to do with sex.

Though they were no longer on the plane, they were
still "together" in some undefined way. Maybe she needed him to help her with her luggage or just as a form
of protection from the men (the men in suits and ties)
who if she were alone would probably be swarming (like
cattle, like flies) around her, offering her rides to the
city in the limousines their companies provided or—as
if she had nothing better to do—drinks and dinner in
the restaurant of the big hotel near the airport, during
which time a proposition would be articulated {money
itself might be mentioned), an attempt would be made to
place a hand on her knee and if she didn't push it aside
it would mean that after one more drink she would accompany him (whoever) to the suite of rooms on the top
floor, which he was sharing with a few other vice-pres-
idents who were probably already lounging around in
various states of undress and waiting for her, some of
them drunk and so eager they felt ashamed, afterwards,
and burst into tears.

They passed through the glass doors of the terminal
and stood on the sidewalk—it had been her suggestion
that they travel together into the city—waiting for a cab.
Like Max, she only carried a single suitcase; she'd been
on vacation, after all, which meant freedom from thinking about clothes. While waiting she slipped her arms

through the sleeves of a short suede jacket, tied a white silk scarf around her throat. Though it was warmer here than in San Francisco there was something ominous about the vibration in the air that made one feel self-protective. Even Max had forgotten the intensity and sense of self-importance with which people here went about their lives, as if each person was the center of a private world. He felt a rush of adrenaline just being back, and patted his pants pocket where he kept his pills, as a form of reassurance, knowing he'd need them during the next few hours.

A cab stopped (he remembered Caroline asking him whether it was true taxi drivers in New York charged unsuspecting foreigners exorbitant sums for driving them around the block), and the driver—a foreigner himself—deposited their suitcases in the trunk. Max held the door open so the woman, an inch taller than he was in her high heels, could maneuver her long legs into the tight space, then followed her, slamming the door—"It's still open," the driver, an Israeli, shouted back at him—slamming it a second time, pressing down the button for emphasis. The cab was so narrow their legs pressed up against the back of the driver's seat. "What's your address?", and when she told him ("33rd Street between Third & Second"), he conveyed this information to the driver. It seemed possible that they could make love in the cab without touching or even kissing or that resisting the temptation was as intense as doing anything (the opposite of resisting was succumbing; in the middle of making love one could either laugh or cry). They sank as far down as possible (so the driver, looking for them in his rear-view mirror, would spy only the tops of their heads), and for a moment it occurred to Max—as he lit her cigarette and one for himself—to tell her the real reason he was returning to New York, since it was hard for him to imagine she didn't sense something was wrong (and possibly it was that sense which had attracted her to begin with). "I knew it," she would say, and take his hand (which she'd done, anyway), "I knew something was bothering you, why didn't you tell me before?"

7

Morris and Sylvia's son, Jeff, drove him home from the cemetery. Jeff's wife Flora sat in the front seat, nervously biting her thumb. Max wanted nothing more than to take a drive around the city and stare passively out the window but under the circumstances it was equally tempting to close his eyes and nod off. Occasionally Sylvia patted him on the knee—this in the middle of a long silence—as a way of reassuring him she understood how he was feeling, how he must be feeling, since what difference did it make if someone you love died from natural causes or was "murdered" (it was a word everyone hesitated to say), the person was gone, what did forever mean anyway?

Of all his relatives, Morris and Sylvia were the only ones he kept in touch with in a way that wasn't merely obligatory. When they traveled to Mexico or Hawaii or Canada in the summer they sent him postcards, and on his birthday, a check for $20 which he acknowledged, in turn, with a postcard or letter of his own, keeping them up to date on what he was doing. Once every few months his mother invited them for dinner, a Sunday afternoon when she knew Max would be visiting. More than his parents ever had, they encouraged his interest in the theatre, didn't treat it as if it were something he'd grow out of eventually, but assumed—with no real reason—that one day he'd be a success. Dinner-table conversation revolved around the plays and concerts they'd seen, and Max would notice how his mother, who rarely went anywhere, would withdraw into herself, and grow silent for long moments of time. When he was living in New York they'd make a point of calling him—"we're not bothering you, are we?"—not to pry into his life in any way that made him uncomfortable (they were too tactful to do that) but to let him know there were people out there who cared, fulfilling their own need for human contact, as people who are generous often do.

Jeff, as far as Max knew, worked in some nebulous capacity for an advertising agency. Possibly because they'd spent so much time together as kids (born a few months apart, they were both only children) there was a feeling of competitiveness built into their relationship, not to mention hostility, which had made it difficult for them ever to be friends. There was no law that said just because they were first cousins they had to be friends. You can acknowledge another person's existence by respecting the differences between yourself and him, and perhaps the best way of doing that is to avoid the person totally. The last time they'd seen each other had been at Max's father's funeral. A few months before leaving for California Max had received an engraved invitation to Jeff and Flora's wedding, but had chosen not to attend, despite pressure from his mother. The reception had taken place in a restaurant in New Jersey, and Max wasn't about to spend a day and night of his life fulfilling an obligation to someone he disliked, though he did admit to feeling curious about the person Jeff had married. He sat at the kitchen table in the familiar apartment while his mother described the scene: Flora (her dress, her hair), Flora's family, the food in the restaurant—hinting, in her judgmental way, at her scorn for people who indulged themselves so ostentatiously ("it must have cost thousands")—though Max knew she was secretly jealous. "Everyone asked about you," she said, but Max assumed that was a lie. Who was everyone? As he stepped out of the subway, flattening his tie against the front of his shirt, he wondered if Jeff and Flora were the type of people who'd hold it against him for not coming to their wedding.

The funeral parlor was on Queens Boulevard, a large white modern building. Morris knew someone who worked there and had arranged everything. "It's the same place," he told Max on the phone, giving him directions, meaning the same place they'd held the service when his father had died. The same cemetery, too. When he was alive, Max's father had been very conscientious about making certain "everything would be taken care of" when he and Max's mother died. Salesmen from various cemeteries would periodically call him at home, hoping (so it seemed) to take advantage of the weakness of incipient old age ("you're still alive, aren't you?") by convincing him of the advantages of different types of coffins, headstones, and gravesites. They'd follow up the phone calls by sending brochures, which Max's father would study before filing them away in his bureau drawer.

Bette wasn't a religious person, and the rabbi who presided over the service wasn't someone she'd ever known. If Max had been in the city he might have insisted the service be held in the neighborhood where his mother lived, if only to make it easier for her friends to attend. He wished that he, or at least Morris, someone who knew her well, could stand up and deliver a simple unadorned speech describing what his mother was really like, rather than permitting this stranger to ramble on in his impersonal way. "The loving mother," "the devoted sister," all this was true. Still, no matter how much dignity he brought to the occasion there was something hypocritical about what he was saying. How could you deliver a eulogy if you didn't know the person? There was something more important than a ritual that condoned superficiality, and occurred for its own sake and for no other reason, i.e., this is the way things are done.

Max lowered his head, locked his hands in front of him, and whispered—along with everyone else—the words of the 23rd Psalm. A prayer, at least, was like music and you could get lost in the rhythm and the sound of the words—its purpose, if it worked, was to make you transcend wherever you were. Max wanted to escape to a place where the layers of self-consciousness melted away, and you could express what you felt without diffidence or fear and without assuming, cynically, that other people thought you were a fool ("I never know what you're feeling," Caroline often told him) if you spoke about something with conviction. When it was all finally over, Sylvia took his arm and they walked up the aisle to the back of the chapel, much in the same way they might leave their theatre seats at intermission ("what did you think of the play?") and where Max, wanting most of all to smoke a cigarette, accepted the condolences of people he hadn't seen in years, who seemed to be eyeing him peripherally as if they didn't know what to expect.

There was Goldie Berkowitz, his father's sister, her

husband Ray, and their daughter Adrienne; there was Judith Stein ("my best friend" Max's mother described her) who lived in one of the cooperative apartment buildings on the other side of Seward Park, and whose husband had died a few months after Max's father; there were Libby and Michael (Max couldn't remember their last names), his mother's first cousins, and their father, Albert, Max's mother's uncle, who was in his late eighties and seemed about to topple over into Max's arms; there was a black man named Howard, Max remembered Howard, he'd been the super for the building when Max was a child, he'd lived in an apartment in another building for which he was also the super and Max's mother and the landlord of the other building shared his services, Howard, whom Max remembered because this older black man had offered him candy and had performed magic tricks with rubber bands while discussing with his mother the plumbing problems in apartment 3-B; there were the Cohens who'd also lived in the building when Max was younger, and who, like Howard, now lived somewhere else; there were his mother's other cousins and even some of their children and all of his father's family, people whom Max's mother, when alive, saw maybe once a year; there was a woman named Elvira with bright red lipstick who owned a clothing store on East Broadway and who insisted on kissing Max on the lips, leaving what felt like a permanent imprint, or death itself; there was even a person who'd gone to high school with Max's mother, so she said, and who began telling Max about a play she'd been in with his mother, "my friend Bette," more than forty years ago at Julia Richmond; there was

Flora, a blue band constraining brown shoulder-length hair, who touched his arm as a way of expressing a kind of concern that was almost too real to be true ("I'm Flora, Jeff's wife") considering they'd never met before; and there, leaning up against a marble pillar outside the funeral home, a cigarette dangling from his lips, was a man whom Max decided at first glance was the murderer. Either that or a cop checking out the scene. Eyeing the storm clouds with their dark centers massing on the horizon. Staring at the faces of everyone who attended the service and taking everything in with a trained and experienced eye so he could report on what he'd seen to his superior or his accomplices.

A man from the funeral parlor opened the door of a black car and as Max got in he looked behind him but the person leaning back against the pillar was no longer there. An hour later, though, as they stood around the open grave, he thought he saw him lurking behind a tree as the rain began falling onto the newly uncovered dark brown earth and the same rabbi from the funeral parlor turned the pages of the prayer book while the gravediggers, like the chorus in a minor Greek tragedy, leaned on their shovels and stared blankly into space. It was only when Morris handed Max one of the shovels and he sifted the pile of dirt in front of him and walked toward the grave, tilting the shovel so the dirt spilled on the top of the coffin, that he felt—for the first time since he'd received the phone call in California—like bursting into tears. It was as if the burden of silence that made all those dinners together seem so interminable suddenly burst through his memory to reveal the pointlessness of his parents' lives, and his own life as well, all the things they'd neglected to tell one another, or him, gone forever.

"I'm Flora, Jeff's wife." Ultimately, that was the only real voice he had heard all day. He handed the shovel back to Morris and turned from the grave, but the man behind the tree was gone. "It all happens so quick," he thought, but in this instance speed was a kind of blessing; no one would want a funeral to drag on too long.

They were parked in a line of traffic, wedged between two trailer trucks, at the entrance to the Lincoln tunnel.

"There's only one lane. What a waste of time!" Jeff's disembodied voice floated above their heads like a puff of smoke.

"What's that?" It was a typical dialogue between Morris, who pretended he was hard of hearing, and his son.

"There's only one lane. What do you think we're sitting here for?"

"That's no reason to be rude, Jeff," noting the anger in his son's voice.

"You must be exhausted." Sylvia patted Max's knee again with her gloved hand, sensing it was a good moment to change the subject. "Sometime soon you have to visit and tell us all about California. You're not going back immediately, are you?"

Max stared at the back of Jeff's head, the fringe of black as it touched the collar of his jacket. The curve of his shoulders as he relaxed at the wheel, foot on the brake, the car moving forward a few inches, then stopping. He wondered what Caroline was doing: drinking tea on the patio with one of her friends, possibly, or walking alone on the beach with a big piece of driftwood in her arms.

He focused on Flora's profile; the way she took a last puff on her cigarette, rolled down the window and tossed it onto the embankment. The way she always seemed on the verge of speaking—in this sense she was just like his mother—parting her lips slightly and turning her shoulders in Jeff's direction, then stopping in mid-gesture and resuming her cold stare. Like all of them, she had no idea what to say at this moment. She didn't realize that what they all wanted, and Max especially, was a feeling of levity and brilliance which only she, as the outsider, could provide. Not liking Jeff, while feeling curious about his wife, drawn to her because of everyone at the service she had seemed human in a way he could recognize, and feeling gratitude for her touch of warmth outside the funeral parlor, Max couldn't help but wonder why she'd ever married his cousin in the first place. A supercilious thought, but one familiar to him. He had the impression, as their eyes connected briefly in the rear-view mirror, that Flora was looking ahead to a time in the future when they'd meet again, not the whole family, not even Jeff, just she and Max, a happier moment when, if they felt inclined, they'd sit down, talk, get to know one another, become friends. It was presumptuous of him to assume they weren't in love. He'd spent a lot of time with married couples, that's how he'd first met Caroline, and could usually tell, after a few dinners together, whether the marriage was working or not. He wondered what Jeff had told her about him; no doubt, at one time, they'd compared notes about the various members of their families. Ticking off that list of names, which almost everyone has, of people one sees only at funerals or weddings. He tried to imagine her in bed, alone, the curve of her body beneath the sheet, her hair spread out behind her on the pillow. Smoking a cigarette, staring pensively or petulantly at the ceiling. What was Jeff doing at that moment? Why didn't he come to bed?

Possibly that very morning they'd had an argument about something, the same chronic argument they'd been having for years. When they were with other people they tried to pretend nothing was wrong but as soon as they were alone they began bickering again. Fighting about problems didn't solve them; it was easier to pretend there was no problem, carry on some ridiculous charade, as if the rest of the world were that easily fooled. If Max decided to stay in New York, which was unlikely (but who can say?), it was inevitable that he'd see Morris and Sylvia more frequently—in a way, Max thought, they're like my parents now—not just talk on the phone intermittently as they had in the past. He would travel to Brooklyn dutifully by subway for Sunday dinner and on one of these occasions Jeff and Flora would be present. He'd sit in the living room with Morris and Jeff while Flora helped her mother in-law in the kitchen. He'd try to be polite, ask Jeff about his job, reminisce about when they were kids. "No, I don't remember ever doing that," Jeff would say. Morris would bring out his photo albums and show Max pictures of Max's mother when she was young. Photos of Jeff and Max playing ball in a park. At dinner he'd sit facing Flora and Jeff while Sylvia and Morris occupied opposite ends of the table. What's for dinner? "A nice brisket," Sylvia would say. Her collection of miniature porcelain statues, mementos of her various excursions, lined the bookcases. Max remembered dropping one—a horse and rider—on purpose, as a child, and his father scolding him afterwards. "Oh, it's nothing," Sylvia had said. He idealized Sylvia and Morris; at least from a distance they were perfect parents. It seemed that if one of them had a thought about something he or she would instantly relate it to the other. What more could one ask of anyone but the revelation of thoughts as they were happening? Morris took a book from the shelf in the living room, a volume of plays, and handed it to Max: "I think you'll like this." They were schoolteachers, radicals, writers of letters to the Times, petition signers, demonstrators, marchers, former Communists. The girl in the painting on the living room wall resembled Flora. "It *is* Flora," Morris said, in response to Max's query, and the woman sitting opposite him blushed.

For a few minutes, after dinner, they were alone on the couch. Months had passed since his mother's funeral. "Are you going back to California?" she wanted to know. There was a tremor in her voice that indicated the question meant something to her, and Max, surprised at her interest, felt like reaching out and taking her hand. He was tempted to tell her that she was the reason he had stayed all this time, but knew he couldn't control his voice in a way that would make it sound true. He didn't trust the truth, felt blinded by it, preferred a state of uncertainty where there was no possibility of making a commitment.

Once, on the phone, he asked Sylvia how Jeff and Flora were doing, thinking that if he showed interest in them it might prompt her to invite them all to dinner, and she had hesitated in a way that made Max realize she and Morris sensed something was wrong. Jeff seemed to be locked in a tiny alcove in his mind. He could barely complete a sentence without questioning the purpose of what he was saying. His job—inventing images and slogans to entice people to consume objects they didn't need—was frowned upon by his parents. His goal, unlike theirs, was to make as much money as possible. When Flora spoke her arms floated away and made shadows on the ceiling. Her skirt, when she crossed her legs, folded into a tapestry of plants and flowers. Morris refilled their glasses with white wine: it was the middle of summer and everyone was getting high except Jeff, who wasn't drinking. "We better go now," he said, spoiling the fun. They drove Max home, "it's no trouble," continuing uptown to their apartment on the Upper East Side. Flora played with the dials of the radio and hummed along with the music. She lowered the window and rested her bare arm on the ledge.

The next morning, 9 a.m., the doorbell rang, "it's me, Flora." She peeled off her skirt and blouse and they made love on the kitchen floor. When it was over her head rested a few inches from the leg of the table. "Is this where your mother died?" she wanted to know. Not perversely, but with a kind of dark humor that gave the idea of "death" new meaning. Death and sex, her heart beating beneath his fingers, these were words, and what were words but objects lost in space? They—the police—had found the murderer, it was a man or a woman. He, she, had confessed everything and had been sent off to prison. Every weekday morning Flora arrived at his apartment. He had an extra key made so she could let herself in. She'd wait till Jeff left for work, didn't care—as she put it—whether he found out what she was doing or not. She told Max that she was going to get a divorce and find her own place but months passed and every afternoon she returned to the apartment on York Avenue. Whenever she said "I'm going to move out," it was with the hope that Max would suggest that she move in with him, but he never did. She lifted her legs, balanced them on Max's shoulders, and drew him toward her. When they kissed her hair fell over her eyes and mouth and she laughed, brushed the strands to one side, kissed him again.

Months or years went by, Sylvia and Morris were both dead. Flora was pregnant. "I'm three months late," she said. "I've been to a doctor. I've had tests." She couldn't believe Max doubted that he was the father. It was true she was still living with Jeff and that occasionally they slept together, how could they not? "You mean you're jealous of Jeff?" The night she told him she was pregnant he called Caroline in California. "Are you still alone?" he demanded. She'd never given up hope that one day he'd come back, and when he told her he'd be arriving the next morning she laughed—"I'll meet you at the airport"—as if he'd only been gone a few hours. He felt like he'd just scaled the face of a mountain in his mind, and now he was descending, while all the voices of all the people he'd ever made love to echoed in the cavernous space beneath the clouds. When Flora called him the next morning he acted distant. "I'm coming over now," she said. He tried to picture her in the apartment uptown, the apartment she shared with Jeff and where he'd never been, sitting on the edge of the bed. "No, you can't do it," he shouted into the phone, and hung up.

At twenty-five the scenarios for the future were endless. "You have your whole life ahead of you," Morris had said. It was possible to chart your life as a logical progression of events, as Jeff, or the men Max had seen on the airplane seemed to have done. The alternative was to drive with your eyes closed, 100 miles an hour, crash into a brick wall, and still keep going.

This apartment building was his now, he could do whatever he wanted. Sell it to a real estate agent who would renovate, go co-op, triple the rents, sell it for a profit to someone else. Morris said he would contact Max's mother's lawyer. "Just tell me what you want to do. I'll handle it." How much was a building like this worth? He could take the money, fly to California, travel across India, North Africa, Scotland and Sweden. Caroline could have her baby, if that's what she wanted, and they could travel together around the world. They could hire an *au pair* girl to look after the child at night. He could buy a house in Cape Cod or Maine and convert an old barn into a theatre. "Produced and directed by Max Eckstein." The words burned brightly on a marquee in the back of his mind.

Sylvia, Morris, Jeff and Flora were going out for dinner. Max declined their invitation to join them. "I want to be alone for awhile," he said, though it wasn't really true. They stood on the sidewalk in front of the building on Henry Street. Max kissed his aunt, embraced Morris, and shook Jeff's hand. "We'll see you again," Flora said, touching his arm.

Back in the apartment he took off his suit jacket, loosened his tie. There was the chair in the living room where his father had died. There was the kitchen floor, where his mother's body had fallen. There was his old room, the heavy mahogany bureau where, after doing his laundry, his mother had stacked his clothing, all the shirts with starched collars, neatly folding everything away. (It wasn't until he left home and found his own apartment that Max realized you could wash shirts along with your other clothing in a washing machine, and that starched collars weren't exactly a necessity of life.) That bureau, and a matching piece in his mother's room, had been part of the household since before Max was born, a testimony to a period of time when objects were built to last forever. A knob had come loose from the lower drawer of his old bureau and was resting on the floor in a patch of sunlight. The entire apartment was stamped by a moment of time—this was the way it was the morning his mother had died. The police had gone over the rooms for fingerprints but had been careful not to rearrange anything. Max's mother was a compulsive tidier, taking out the garbage as soon as the single bag under the sink filled up, washing every dish as soon as the meal ended, sponging the table and sweeping under it till every crumb had vanished. Except for a stack of newspapers and magazines on a table in his mother's bedroom—*Good Housekeeping, The New Yorker, The New Republic, The Nation*, the magazine and real estate sections of *The Sunday Times*, an occasional issue of *The National Enquirer*—and a similar stack on the coffee table in the living room, the apartment had an unlived-in quality, the reflection of an inhuman sense of order. Directing her energies toward keeping the apartment neat had been one way of staying sane as she drifted off into old age. There was the living room, which Max had always thought of as his father's room, and where he'd spent less time than any other room in the apartment. The kitchen, which served as the dining room as well, and the living room, were the two largest rooms in the apartment. Max's room was the smallest; big enough for a bed, a desk, a bureau and bookcase, not much more. Often, when his father was at work, he did his homework at the dining room table. His favorite times were those evenings his father called to say he'd be working late and he and his mother ate dinner alone. He'd even dare to sit in the living room and watch television, not in his father's chair but on the small sofa with the ugly orange upholstery. Working late usually meant his father would return home in a bad mood, the sound of the key in the lock signaling an end to peace and tranquillity. It was as if someone had purposefully taken the needle of a phonograph and scratched it across the surface of the record. *The Pastoral Symphony* by Beethoven. Debussy's String Quartet. A concerto by Vivaldi for strings, trumpet, and oboe. "Turn off the television now," Max's mother would say. He'd linger at the door of his room or sit at his desk with the door open and try to hear what his parents were saying. If they rarely argued in his presence, it was also true that they never talked intimately about anything either.

He remembered interminable summer afternoons playing in the park across the street. There was his mother, sitting at the windowsill, or on the front stoop of the building, talking with her friends. Occasionally he'd stop what he was doing and wave at her until she waved back. He remembered trips on the Staten Island ferry, a subway ride to Coney Island, the dinosaur room at the Museum of Natural History, *The Nutcracker* at City Center. Sometimes, on weekends, his father joined them, and they'd go uptown to the Central Park Zoo. Max would ride around a dirt track, with other children, in the back of a cart pulled by a bedraggled pony, and when he passed his parents, standing behind the gate, he'd wave and smile at them and try to catch their attention. He remembered the distracted expressions on their faces when the ride was over and the man in the gypsy outfit who rode on the back of the cart and kept the pony in line helped him down: "I think we better go home now," his mother would say, though they'd only been there an hour. Pleasure was portioned out in small doses. Sitting in the back of the cart with the other kids was a first glimpse of freedom. He wanted to get his parents' attention so they could share in his pleasure but they weren't looking at him and as the cart passed the gate where they were standing it seemed they were both talking rapidly at once, his father leaning forward so his face was only an inch or two from the face of his mother who for once in her life wasn't backing away—Max was her son, after all, and there was a limit to everything—but was holding her ground, like an angel at the door of a cave. Max remembered the streak of white between the ears of the pony as the cart went into its final turn. The black smudge on the forehead of the gypsy as he helped him down from the cart. There were clouds in the sky and all the light had vanished from his mother's eyes. She took his hand, his father off to one side, and they began the long walk to the entrance of the park.

The closet in his room was filled with cartons of books, records, letters, a few articles of clothing, everything he wanted to save before going to California. And they were still there, untouched, but he had no inclination to go through them, books of plays by Ibsen and Artaud, letters from every woman he'd ever slept with, he could count his lovers on the fingers of one hand, two hands, three hands. When he visited his mother for Sunday dinner she always asked him about his latest girlfriend, "latest" implying he had a new girlfriend every week and as a consequence wasn't very serious about anyone. He'd never brought any of his girlfriends home for dinner, and it was true, he'd never reached the point in any of his relationships where he could imagine introducing her—whoever—to his mother. It seemed like the ultimate commitment. "Mom, I'd like you to meet...." The person he had in mind was a composite of Caroline, Flora, the woman he'd met on the plane. Animated conversation around the dining room table. Max uncorked a bottle of wine. "This calls for a toast." Each of them would be nervous in their own way. "This is the room where I used to sleep," Max said, giving the woman a tour of the apartment, almost apologizing for its modesty while his mother looked on in awe. They'd take out the old photograph album and Max and the woman, his future wife, perhaps, would sit on the edge of his narrow bed, while his mother retreated to the kitchen or stood in the bathroom and stared at herself in the mirror. "Who's the fairest of them all?" It wasn't a question that had to be asked. "This is the summer we drove to Miami." "You look more like your father in this one than your mother." She placed her arm around Max's shoulders, secretly hoping his mother would at that very moment enter the room.

Max had an appointment to meet the cops who were working on the case. He changed into the clothing he'd worn on the airplane the day before, dungarees, a maroon turtleneck, the blue workshirt, and hung his black suit jacket on a hanger in his old closet. He'd never been inside the local precinct on Pitt Street. "Do you know where we are?" the cop who called had asked. He couldn't tell whether it was the same cop who'd called him in California. "Just tell the person at the front desk you want to see DeLauria or Hopper."

There was a Buddhist temple two doors down from the building on Henry Street, a Catholic church with gothic towers on the corner. It was 4 p.m. by the clock on the church, bells ringing, sweet Saint Teresa. Two women in high heels and tight sweaters, one in a short leather skirt and swinging a large purse, stood a few feet off the curb at the entrance to Seward Parle It was Friday afternoon. A barge hauling trash inched across a blue rectangle of water. If you stood on the corner of Henry and Rutgers Streets you could see the water, a calm surface, the waves no more than tiny indentations, like the creases in a recently ironed blouse. "Take off your blouse." The two women leaned back against a parked car, eyes scanning the faces of the approaching drivers. All the shops on Essex Street, selling yarmulkes and tfillins and all the prayer books and paraphernalia essential to the Jewish ceremonies, closed early Friday afternoons. Not much had changed in the year he'd been gone. All the young winos and junkies still congregated around the small fountain in the park. The playground and sandbox were empty as usual. No parent in his or her right mind would take their child to a park strewn with broken glass.

A car stopped and one of the women, the one with the gold chevron stitched into the back pocket of her tight jeans, opened the front door and ducked inside. A bald monk in an organdy robe was sweeping the steps of the Buddhist temple. After a year of breathing fresh air Max felt like he was walking through an invisible cloud. (If air itself was a kind of impediment to clear thinking, no wonder everyone on the streets looked slightly insane.) "Don't go near the park," his mother had warned him. People he'd gone to school with had ended up spending their days dealing pills in a corner of the park, but he didn't recognize anyone there now; maybe the people he once knew were now unrecognizable, as no doubt he was to them. People passing on the street eyed one another suspiciously, as if the sidewalk consisted of invisible corridors and if you weren't careful and attentive to where you were walking you might collide.

He walked along East Broadway until it intersected Pitt Street then turned north, past the huge middle income housing developments and a nursing home where a group of men and women sat on benches and in wheelchairs in the shade of a tree with white blossoms. As he passed, a slight breeze sent the blossoms drifting through the air to the ground. His mother had taught him to call policemen "sir." "Excuse me, sir, could you give me directions to the precinct on Pitt Street?" Above the sound of the radios and the traffic he could hear his mother's voice. After his father had died he'd tried to convince her to move, possibly to Brooklyn so she could be closer to her brother. It was too dangerous, he argued, to live alone in this neighborhood. Returning to the place where you were born and walking the streets was like putting on an old coat. "I thought you threw that coat away." It was threadbare, and needed new buttons.

Across Delancey Street there was a steep hill with deserted lots on either side. The lots were filled mostly with trash and sprouts of grass, an occasional tree with a charred trunk and one live branch. Bricks and lumber, the detritus of the tenement that had once been there, and which no one had bothered to cart away. The street was wide and the cars were parked at angles to the curb, stickers visible in each windshield indicating that the vehicles belonged to members of the police department. There were no other pedestrians on the street. A dog ran out of one of the lots looking frightened, and darted between the parked cars to avoid Max, who suddenly realized he felt safer now that the police precinct was in sight. He'd never been mugged or robbed in New York, but it was only because his mother, at an early age, had made him wary of all the dangers. There was nothing wrong with going out of your way to avoid a possible confrontation. If the person approaching you on a deserted avenue looked out of control you could always cross over to the other side. Some streets were safer than others. More pedestrians, more traffic, better lighting.

He couldn't imagine his mother, so cautious, opening the door for a stranger.

Sonia had been his first lover. She lived on the top floor of the building on Henry Street. In warm weather they'd go up on the roof and watch the lights blinking across the river. They'd spread a blanket over an old mattress and stare up at the sky. It was like being in another world, alone amid the lights of the helicopters and planes, the clusters of stars, bright Venus, formidable Mars.

"She's too old for you," Bette said, when she found out they were seeing one another. Every time he went out she looked at him suspiciously. He would have to pretend he was truly leaving the building, not just going upstairs to visit Sonia. There was a way of entering the building through the basement, and his mother knew that even if he made a pretense of leaving the house from the front he could always circle back and enter the building by this alternate method. When she moved out (her lease was up and Bette was threatening to raise her rent beyond the legal limit as a way of coercing her to leave) it was with the understanding that they wouldn't see each other for awhile. He was a freshman in college. She'd been married and divorced. Max knew it was only a matter of time before he moved out as well and found a place of his own even if it meant dropping out of school so he could earn money and support himself. But as long as he lived at home he sensed his mother's anxiety whenever he left the house at night. For months after Sonia was gone, he'd go up to the roof alone, as if he were in mourning, and stare at the dull glow of the decaying industrial plants across the river. He'd walk past the door of her apartment—a Spanish couple and their two children lived there now—and tried to superimpose her figure in the doorway. A ghost, with a rose in her hair, fading into the shadows.

Every sound was a message, but unless the person who was speaking was whispering in your ear you couldn't hear a word ("Beg your pardon?") that was being said. And it didn't matter whether you heard every word, or every other word; if what was being said was important the voice in your head could fill in the blanks. In the course of making love a man or woman might say "I love you" and not really mean it. Or in the course of an argument one might say things with the single purpose of hurting the other person. Emotions are easy to express if you forget about risk: the fear that if you express your feelings the object of your feelings (in this case "object" means "person") will betray you, cast you aside, give you a look as if to say: But I don't even know who you are, get lost! A woman on a street corner selling snakeskin belts, a man hawking umbrellas in the middle of a storm. Emotions were that cheap, if you thought about things cynically. Two for a dollar. Three for fifty cents. Feelings weren't subject to the trends of inflation. It's easy to say "I love you, too" when someone says "I love you." Words impersonated feelings, like fake flowers. When you make love to someone it might be necessary to assume that the person you're with knows exactly what you're thinking.

"I'm Detective Hopper," extending his hand, "have a seat."

The room he'd been sent to contained a desk, a filing cabinet, and two chairs. On top of the scarred wooden surface of the desk was a white manila folder. The walls were bare except for a black and white photograph, under a glass frame, of a middle-aged man wearing a suit and striped tie, whom Max assumed was a former chief of police but who could have been anyone.

The second detective ("I'm DeLauria, we spoke before") asked him if he wanted a cup of coffee, disappeared and returned a moment later with a white styrofoam cup from the communal coffeemaker that served the entire precinct. There was too much cream and sugar, Max took his coffee black, but after the first sip he realized it would have tasted worse undiluted. But we're not here to talk about coffee, are we?

"We're here to ask you some questions regarding, uh, your mother's death.

"We know this is probably a bad time for you so we'll try to be brief.

"Let me tell you that we're doing everything we can. There are a lot of unsolved murders but we're not going to file this one away. We have our informers—contacts—people on the street who owe us favors, and we expect a break in the case any day. We've already talked to everyone who lives in the building. As a landlady it would seem likely your mother would have some enemies. But your mother, I'm happy to say, seems to have been a very unusual person in that regard. We've checked the records and there's only been one eviction petition served on anyone in the building in the last ten years, and that case—maybe you know about it—never even got into court, the person your mother was trying to evict, a woman named Sonia Wong, moved out before that happened. We've tried to locate Miss Wong but haven't had much luck; she could be anywhere, she could be married and living under a different name. Everyone who lives in the building now thinks your mother was a very special person. Any time they needed anything fixed she called in the janitor the same day. Manny Rosario, you must know him, we've questioned him as well, and he's given us the names of all the handymen in the neighborhood who might have worked for your mother during the last year. Maybe there was an argument that had to do with repairing the building, though your mother doesn't seem like the kind of person who would hassle anyone about money.

"As you probably noticed we haven't touched anything in your mother's apartment.

"If in the course of going through her things you find anything that might be relevant we'd appreciate it if you contacted us immediately. What I mean by relevant is something that seems suspicious or out of the ordinary. A name and a phone number on a scrap of paper. We know you've been out of the city for a year and that the person who killed your mother might have been someone she met since then but regardless, if you can think of anyone who held a grudge against her, for any reason, in the past, let us know. Think about it. Call us up any time. There's always the possibility that the murderer had no reason at all to kill your mother, no specific reason that involved her directly. But if we thought like that we might as well pack it in and go home. We' re not gods, by any stretch, but we know our jobs. Between us we have twenty-two years of experience. This doesn't mean we can't use all the help we can get.

"That's why, and I know this is difficult for you, I want you to try to remember any conversation you ever had with your mother in which she showed the slightest trace of anger towards someone. After all, she was an elderly woman living alone in a dangerous neighborhood. You must have had moments when you worried about her safety as well. Everyone worries about something. There are a lot of guys with plaques on their walls who make $100 every forty-five minutes so people like you and me, every day people, normal people, people who wouldn't harm a fly, can have the chance to tell another person, someone uninvolved emotionally with their lives, what's on their minds.

"There are a lot of crazy fuckers out there, let me tell you."

Max lit a cigarette to kill the taste of the coffee and the detective who called himself DeLauria found an ashtray in the drawer of the desk (it occurred to Max that maybe he wasn't a real detective at all but someone who hung around police stations and tried to ingratiate himself to the cops by running errands) and skidded it across the surface in Max's direction. A person who had argued with his mother? He thought of Sonia Wong standing at the door of her apartment. Only a few minutes before they'd been lying in bed, in the aftermath of making love for the second or third time, she lying on top of him, her straight hair curving like the sides of a silo around his face, both of them knowing it was time for Max to go. And when he was finally dressed she would escort him to the door, wearing a white kimono, a white sash knotted at the waist. She'd adjust the flower in her hair and stand in front of the full length mirror on her closet door, smoothing the folds of the kimono over her breasts and thighs, as if she were preparing herself for another lover who was waiting in the hall. The last Max had heard she'd been living in a loft on Spring Street, but he wasn't about to volunteer that bit of information to the police. He saw a flash of starlight above the rooftops. A chain of lights as the cars streamed over the bridge. The ghostly figure in the white kimono standing in the doorway. "Just lie back and relax," she would say, unlacing his shoes and slipping the cuffs of his pants over his ankles. "Does that feel good?"

Hopper took a handkerchief from his pants pocket and wiped the sweat from his face, starting with his forehead, gingerly passing over the scar on the edge of his double chin.

"I told Irene I needed a new handkerchief."

The two detectives stared at one another, shrugged, and Hopper extended his hand a second time, a signal—since Max, obviously, had nothing to offer—that their little conference was over. Frank held the door of the office open (indicating, again, that his main purpose was to provide the most menial services) and as Max brushed past him said, in a voice lacking any authority whatsoever, "We'll be in touch."

It was the voice of the person who had called him in California to tell him his mother had died, but Max didn't care. He was thinking of Sonia's tiny hands and whether they had the power to strangle an old woman.

8

Gina closed her eyes, leaned her head back against the sofa, and placed her hand gently on the top of his head. She could feel his fingers under her blouse, his face buried in the side of her neck. It was only when, with his free hand, he tried, awkwardly, to unfasten the silver button on the top of her pants, that she pushed him away, grabbing the hand buried inside her blouse and digging her nails into his wrist. She stood up, her breasts still partially exposed, turned her back to him just as he leaned forward from his place on the sofa in an attempt to pull her down on top of him, and left the room.

Shoulders hunched forward, her fingers splayed on the formica surface, she bent over the kitchen counter, trying to regain her composure. Dirty dishes from last night's dinner—plates, silverware, cups and saucers—littered the counter, along with tiny boxes of spices (sage, rosemary, marjoram, allspice, and thyme), a cellophane bag containing fresh chives, and an uncapped jar of honey. Even though Frank rarely came home for dinner she still went through the motions of preparing a meal for herself, with a little extra, just in case he did come, and was hungry. (Though in his present state if he were hungry he'd never admit it, he'd wait till she'd gone upstairs before entering the kitchen to fix a meal—usually no more than a bowl of soup and a sandwich—on his own). Often, by the time dinner was ready she would have lost her appetite, would push her plate aside without touching it, light a cigarette, turn on the radio, and stare out the window. She'd had a drink before dinner and another preparing dinner, a third drink she took with her upstairs after clearing away the dishes. It was a simple matter to get drunk when you didn't eat much all day, and in the process of carrying the dishes from one room to another a plate or cup would slip from her hands and smash into a thousand pieces. More than once, returning home late at night, Frank had discovered the broken shards she'd neglected to sweep away. A minute ticked off on the kitchen clock. The refrigerator purred. On the cabinet above her head there was a color snapshot taken last summer at Central Park. Sunday at the zoo. Feeding time. His arm around her shoulder, both of them staring peacefully into the eye of the camera. The person who took the photo hadn't said anything to make them laugh; if they were smiling it was simply because they were happy being together. The fact that Frank hadn't ripped it into pieces seemed, to Gina, like a good omen, a sign that if she were patient, someday, somehow, things would return to normal.

Still, when Joe closed the front door behind him she couldn't help but feel a wave of disappointment. She knew that if he had followed her into the kitchen and set his hands firmly on her shoulders and spun her around, she would have had a hard time resisting. She was surprised after everything Frank had told her about his partner that Joe hadn't been more persistent. He might have assumed, and with good reason, that she was just playing hard to get. From what Frank said he sounded like the type of person who wanted women to fight back since it provided him with an excuse to display his strength, overpowering whomever he was with in an attempt to prove, once and for all, that as a man he was stronger than they were. And he *was* stronger; obviously, what Gina needed was a good smack. (He'd thought, once, of advising Frank along these lines, since he'd already assessed Gina as an oversexed female who wasn't "getting enough.") When a woman's resistance was broken—this was Joe's advice—you could make her do anything.

"Where did you get that bruise?" Frank would say when he came home. It was the first time he'd commented about her appearance in weeks, or even looked at her. She wondered what he'd think if he knew his best friend came to his house when he was at work and tried to make love to (rape would be the better word) his wife. ("I have something to tell you, Frank. I've been sleeping with Joe Hopper. We're in love with one another. Irene knows all about it, she's known for months. He's filed for a divorce. We're going to live together. I want his babies.")

He'd arrived, uninvited, knowing Frank wouldn't be home. It was his day off. Irene was upstairs sleeping and wasn't even aware that he'd left the house.

Gina had flirted with Joe at parties and knew that he was attracted to her. The fact that he was her husband's best friend made it inconceivable that he would ever entertain the thought of going to bed with her, or that such a thing was possible, even though Irene ("that bitch!"), given the chance, wouldn't think twice about sleeping with Frank. (If Joe had been smart he might have told Gina that Frank and his wife had slept together, just in case "feeling guilty" was what was preventing her from sleeping with him.) There was no question in Gina's mind that Joe knew she'd been unfaithful to Frank and that as a consequence she and Frank had stopped sleeping together. Now that the affair she'd been having was over she felt stupid for ever telling Frank. She couldn't understand how she'd been so naive as to think that sleeping with someone else wouldn't be a threat to their marriage. Maybe a different type of person might have been more understanding, but not Frank. In any case, whatever Joe knew, he sensed the possibility of seizing the moment when it would appear that Gina would be most vulnerable: what did she do all day, anyway? He'd been right up to a point: she *was* vulnerable, also confused, frustrated, and most of all in need of company, someone to talk to or distract her or make her laugh.

"It's good to see you," had been her first words when he came in. And then: "Frank's not here," as if he didn't already know. It wasn't as if she were throwing herself at him, or doing anything to make him think that—since they were alone together, and the possibility existed— she wanted to make love to him. Still, she couldn't help feeling self-conscious as she led him into the living room. If he had arrived fifteen minutes earlier she would have answered the door in her nightgown—the one with the blue flowers which she often "modeled" for Frank before getting into bed, playing the role of the tart to excite him—and who knows what might have happened then.

She awoke that morning, hungover as usual, thinking about Frank and what she could do, if anything, to gain his forgiveness. She could acknowledge his reasons for feeling hurt, but still, it didn't seem that what she'd done was the end of the world. All she saw now was his unremitting stubbornness: didn't he understand how childish he was being? The last thing she wanted was for him to leave, walk out on her, but sometimes his false presence was worse than not having him there at all. If he was planning to move out she wished he'd get it over with. She wondered what he did on nights when he didn't come home till one or two in the morning. She knew—and remembered being shocked when she found out—that his experiences with women had been limited before they met. The fact that he wasn't a ladies' man somehow contradicted her image of a cop. Maybe it would be all for the better if he had a few girlfriends; at least it would take the burden off her. He could return home, satisfied that by sleeping with someone else he had balanced her infidelity with one of his own, settled the score (so to speak).

When they first met, Gina had been living with her parents in a house in the Bronx, not far from where she and Frank eventually decided to live. She'd gone to Catholic schools and then to Hunter College at night, working during the day first in an art supply store and then a woman's clothing store on Fordham Road. During high school she stayed close to her family, going out occasionally on weekends to school dances or with groups of friends. Her parents went to Mass every Sunday and she did too; she followed along. Somehow she'd been given the impression that she wasn't very attractive; she was small, her posture was awful, and as a form of self-deprecation she would use the word "dumpy" to describe herself. That is, when she stared at herself in the mirror, she'd use that word to describe to herself the way she looked. Her main goal during high school was to do well enough to get into college, since her only other choice was to work as a secretary or a salesclerk, until, as her parents imagined, she'd meet someone and get married. A nice Catholic boy. And that's all she'd known—nice Catholic boys, who were anything but nice, if her parents only knew. "Gina the Hyena" is what those nice Catholic boys called her.

"Why don't you go out more?" her mother would ask, as a form of encouragement.

When she told her parents that she wanted to go to college they greeted her announcement with a wall of silence, frightened that for all their good intentions they'd created a monster. Her only true friend was her brother Ted, who was equally reclusive and who also dreamed of attending college: Fordham, Holy Cross, Notre Dame, the farther away the better. All he wanted to do was get out of the Bronx.

"Dumpy? You're not dumpy, Gina. But there's something about you"—this was Ted talking—"that makes people think you don't care about yourself. It's your attitude."

The first Christmas, after he'd been away at school for a few months, he came home with a friend, Dick Miller, and there was a big family reunion, the kind of celebration you'd expect a prisoner of war to receive, with Ted as the star attraction. Gina, lurking in the shadows, felt happy for her brother, but jealous of all the attention she felt should somehow equally be apportioned to herself, wasn't she going to school as well? The other kids in high school called her "The Hyena" because she talked up so often in class, and because she stuttered, because her voice and her body seemed ill-matched, and for awhile she felt nervous about ever saying anything. Life was completely dismal. If Dick Miller wanted to put his hand between her legs—they were necking in the front seat of his car—well, she'd let him.

"Do you have a thing?"

Pleasure was pleasure, but she couldn't go that far. She wanted him to be happy just to be with her for no reason; didn't want him to get the impression that because she was a year older, his best friend's older sister, she knew something he didn't, when in fact she knew nothing at all. And it was almost a miracle that when she pushed his hand away he didn't mind. They'd see each other again, and not in the back seat of a a car. Things would be different someday; there'd be other holidays. It was almost as if he were asking her to wait for him, in some capacity, as if going away to school was truly a return to the battlefield (and who knows if he'd return wounded or maimed?) "I'll call you as soon as I get back to Worcester." She was his best friend's sister, she reminded him of his sister. And besides, it was too cold in the car, even with the motor going and the heater on, how could they do it? It was too complicated to begin with but for a moment, if she'd sensed any solution, she would have let him do anything. He was different from all the nice Catholic boys she had known, he came from some other part of the world, he'd never even been in the Bronx before, he owned a car, he didn't smoke cigarettes, he wanted to be a lawyer, he thought it was great that she was going to college too and he even asked to see her water colors and drawings, he was the first person who had ever expressed any interest in that part of her other than Ted from whom, till now, anyway, she had kept no secrets, but his bringing Dick home only made her love Ted more. She wondered what Dick would tell her brother about what had happened in the car.

"Why don't you give me a tour of the Bronx," Dick had said.

The world was spinning too fast and it seemed to actually have edges; if you didn't watch your step you could fall off, and no one would care. The world might well be flat, after all, and it was possible just to sail out into the distance where horizon met sky and drop into the arms of the demons and trolls who were waiting for you. And now she was supposed to go to confession, Sunday morning, just like always, a good daughter, and tell someone she didn't know what had taken place between her and Dick. It was the first time she'd have something worth confessing and she couldn't do it.

"I have cramps, mother. I want to stay in bed."

A small part of her had always known, even at the bleakest moments, that it was possible to change, but what she hadn't realized was that once the changes began there was no way of preventing them. No way of backtracking or reversing speeds. There was only the desire to reinforce the change by way of repetition before it faded into one's memory, like everything else. The phone was ringing but it wasn't Dick calling from Worcester. It was him, but it didn't have to be him, she would always love him for being kind to her that night in the car, but there would be others as well. There was no way she could go on being the person she was before she'd met Dick, and as part of the change what her brother Ted described as her "attitude" began to change as well. She was blossoming—everyone noticed it, an aura encircled her as she moved through life as this new person, and it was a revelation to no longer be the old person, the old Gina, it was as if she'd taken some drug that permitted her to abandon all preconceived notions about whatever she thought she'd once been, even her parents noticed the change and even though she was still going to college and didn't seem on the verge of getting married they no longer felt the need to criticize her as they'd done before, she was beyond criticism in a way; she'd become her own person.

The first person outside her family to notice her in this new way was her boss, the owner of the art supply store where she worked, Mr. Adano, but as a married man with children he had no other solution as to how they could be together than to suggest, as Dick had, without saying it, that they do it there, in the backseat of his car; they'd been to the movies after work and he was driving her home, and again, given the circumstances, Gina allowed herself only to go so far. But Mr. Adano was less understanding than Dick, there was no turning back after he'd reached a certain point. (Gina was certain that Dick, like herself, was a virgin, or had been a virgin when they were together in the car, though by the time they saw each other again it was unlikely this would be the case, one or both of them would have slept with someone in the interim, Gina could tell by the way Dick treated her that sleeping with her now—even necking with her in the car—meant he was being unfaithful to someone else, which didn't mean, on the contrary, that he didn't want to sleep with her, but that he was embarrassed for having committed himself innocently to her on his first visit, and again, it was the fact that he had these thoughts at all, that he cared enough about her to think he might be hurting her, which made her love him in a way that lessened the importance of whether he was still a virgin—or whether she was—what did it matter?) Mr. Adano, on the other hand, made it clear that whatever happened in the back seat of the car, or didn't happen, would somehow affect what went on between them during the day; the girl Gina replaced at the store could have warned her about what was now happening, it was a common experience—if you don't come across there'll be hell to pay. It was only when Gina felt the bare skin of her upper thigh on the rough upholstery that she realized—with a sense of awe—her own naivete for thinking that people might be interchangeable. Mr. Adano and Dick may as well have been members of different species, and being men (having a penis?) was possibly the only thing they had in common. If she actually went through with this she'd hate men forever, and what difference would it make then if he fired her or not?

The same thing would happen next week, he'd expect it to happen, and if it happened once (they would go to a restaurant or to a movie after work, he would remind her that it was getting late and they should start for home, but on the way home he would detour the car down an empty street, and it would seem, now, that everything that had happened earlier in the evening had been a kind of subterfuge leading up to this moment when he would turn off the ignition, extinguish the headlights, reach across the seat and draw her toward him) there was no way she could prevent it from happening again. What would her brother Ted think of her if she allowed this to happen? What would the person she eventually fell in love with think when she had to describe, in answer to his questions, how she lost her virginity with someone she hated in the front seat of his car?

Meeting Frank was a revelation. He'd come into the clothing store where she'd found a job as salesclerk after being fired from her job at the art supply store and when he left the store with the package under his arm she thought, well, I'll never see this person again. But two days later he returned, the same package under his arm, a present for his mother which didn't fit correctly— it was a housecoat she'd helped him pick out, misjudging his mother's size from the description he gave her— and which he wanted to exchange for another, identical housecoat, two sizes smaller. She turned from him and scanned the shelves behind the counter, aware that he was watching her. (Later, Frank told her that when she turned her back to him he'd had the impulse—"and I must admit I never felt this way before"—to reach across the counter, vault the counter if necessary, and put his arms around her, and that something about the way she acted and spoke and moved her body had given him the feeling that if he'd followed his instinct and had made a move— they were alone in the store at the time—she wouldn't have stopped him, not for a second.) Not only was Frank unmarried, but he had an apartment of his own, he lived alone, he had a job ("I never thought I'd marry a cop!"), he even had a car but having the apartment made the car superfluous as a place where they could be alone, and it was she who suggested, after their first date (restaurant, movie, etc.) that they return to his place, who cares if it's late. (Again, after they'd been living together awhile, he confessed that he'd planned to take her directly home— her home, not his—after the first date, both as a way of winning her parents' favor and to prove to her, as well, that he was interested in something other than sex, that in a million years he'd never dreamed of asking her to come home with him—"you mean you didn't want to sleep with me?"—and spend the night.)

After Joe left she wandered around the living room, rearranging the copies of *Vogue* and *Mademoiselle* that had fallen from the coffee table in front of the sofa, picking up the contents of an ashtray that had overturned. Though she tried to focus on what she was doing she felt like she was walking in circles. With every step the circle widened, like the ripples when you toss a stone into a lake. She was combing the shoreline in search of the smoothest stone. The lake was wide, the surface a sheet of glass reflecting trees and sky. The houses on the opposite side of the lake, with their private beaches, were empty, it was the end of the season. If she wanted to she could take off her clothes and wade in.

She sat on the side of her bed in the room upstairs, legs crossed, drawing a brush through her hair, staring at a small circle of light on the bedroom floor. If Joe hadn't left, if he'd truly persisted in his awkward attempt to seduce her.... Instead of rolling around naked on the living room rug she was sitting alone in her room, the whole day in front of her. The need to compensate for a feeling of emptiness and frustration by wanting something she couldn't have was a throwback to all the feelings she'd experienced in high school, when she stood in front of the mirror in the bedroom of her parents' house and tried to imagine why anyone would want to make love to her. A drink, a cigarette—her vices, if you could call them that, were mild compared to the things other people used in an attempt to forget themselves. She knew she was using drinking as a way to get Frank to notice her. On nights when he didn't come home she'd leave an empty whiskey bottle visible on the kitchen counter. She wanted to make him think she was drinking heavily to assuage her guilt. Possibly the thought that she was suffering horribly would be enough to make him overcome his anger and stubbornness. She was drinking so as to appear unhappy in his eyes. Craving something other than the presence of another person had its usefulness, though occasionally getting drunk made her more unhappy than she already was. She'd lie in bed, alone, a drink in her hand, and try to see herself from a distance, as if she were acting out a part in a movie or play. When Frank came home and she was still awake she tried to will him upstairs so he could see her in this pose. She'd light one cigarette from the tip of another, in the hope that he would enter the room at that precise moment and see for himself how self-destructive she was being. She wanted him to admonish her for smoking too much; at least that would be a sign of concern, that he still cared. But the only time he came upstairs was in the morning, before leaving for work, in search of clean clothes. He would rummage through the drawers of the bureau or bang the closet door and she'd wake from the middle of a bad dream and find him standing in the center of the room with a shirt in his hands and a look in his eyes that made her think, even half-asleep: If I say the wrong thing he's going to kill me.

Her first thought, when Joe arrived, was to offer him a cup of coffee. She closed the door behind him, paused for a moment, and then locked it. It was the first time in the more than two years since Frank had first introduced them that she and Joe had been alone together. The only times they'd ever talked during all that time had been at parties, both of them high, and being with him now made her wish that she had a drink in her hand, at least for the moment when neither of them could think of what to say. She wondered if he was visiting her to talk about Frank ("This whole thing that's happening between you two. . . .") and how it was affecting his work. She knew that Frank often visited his friend's house, not so much to talk to Joe but to see Irene. At parties they— Frank and Irene—would often go into a corner together, or sit for hours on the couch, and Gina would spy them from across the room with their heads close together as if they were trading secrets, lost in a world of their own. She could see Irene's lips moving, while Frank nodded and occasionally said something, and later, when they returned home and were lying in bed, she'd say, flippantly: "What were you and Irene chatting about?"—they were reviewing the party—and Frank, too dumb to catch that she was actually jealous, "Oh, you know, the usual, Joe, the kids," pretending whatever had been talked about wasn't worth repeating. These parties were attended mostly by cops and their wives. Gina resented being thought of as merely an adjunct to someone else and resisted acceptance into this fraternity. When one of the wives showed up at a social gathering with a black eye or a bruise on her cheek, no one was shocked, and even the woman with the bruise made jokes about what had happened—no attempt at saving face, no subterfuge, no lie—as if being beaten by one's husband was a natural thing, an everyday occurrence, something all women should expect to happen in the course of their lives.

At parties you could always hear Joe's laughter from across the room. If you were in one room and he was in another you could hear his voice, unmistakably his, rising above the music. And when the party was drawing to a close you could see him with his arm encircling the waist of a woman, not Irene but the wife of a colleague who had passed out on the front lawn or one of the few single women who came to such parties, drawing her off into a dark corner.

He followed her into the living room—"Would you like some coffee?"—and sat down at the end of the sofa while she hurried nervously into the kitchen. (If she'd been more clearheaded, more aware of her own feelings, she'd have taken his hand and led him right upstairs to the bedroom.) She leaned back against the refrigerator, which was humming wildly and in need of repair, watched the blue flame leap up along the underside of the coffee pot, and when the coffee was ready carried the pot and two cups and a container of milk on a silver tray into the living room, perched on the edge of the sofa like

a good hostess and poured the coffee from the pot, tilted the milk container over the cup ("tell me when") and
handed it to Joe without looking at him. Then a cup for
herself. She wondered if Joe was wearing a gun under his
jacket, as Frank did on his day off. "How's Irene?" she
wanted to ask. "How're the kids?" At parties you could
always get drunk and gossip about all the other people in
the room, that was one form of flirtation, but at ten in the
morning it was harder to translate thoughts into words
without feeling that you were saying the wrong thing.

She watched the steam rise form the cup between her
hands. Joe had placed his cup on the coffeetable without
drinking it, and Gina was tempted to reprimand him and
slip a coaster under the cup so it wouldn't stain the wood.
Frank and her father had carried the table over from her
parents' house soon after they were married. Her mother
had been worried that they wouldn't have enough money to furnish the house properly—"properly" meaning
as she herself would furnish it—never realizing that her
sense of largesse might be a source of embarrassment
to Frank, who preferred an empty house, though he
wouldn't say as much, to a house filled with someone
else's discards.

Gina didn't want Joe to think she was the type of person who really cared about whether the table was stained
or not. She didn't want to do or say anything that might
remind him of his wife.

When her teacher at college had asked, after class, if
she wanted to drop by his place for a drink, she'd consented, innocently, not knowing what to expect. Her first
thought, as they walked to the apartment a few blocks

from the campus on the Upper East Side, was that she had to call Frank to tell him she was going to be late. But she couldn't think of any reason why she might be late (telling the truth—"I'm going to have a drink with my professor" was out of the question), she was never late, she always came home on time, and once she arrived at the teacher's apartment she wasn't about to say: "Can I use your phone?" The phone, she noticed immediately, once he'd switched on the lamp at the side of the sofa, was on the floor in the center of the tiny apartment, and even if he went to the bathroom or pretended he was engrossed in making drinks in the small alcove that served as the kitchen he would overhear everything she said. She removed her coat and made herself comfortable on the sofa, sinking into the leather cushions, much in the same way she was sitting now, with Joe beside her, while Eric, that was her teacher's name ("call me Eric," he said), handed her the drink he'd made, placing his own glass— he'd taken a sip and smacked his lips in approval—onto the coffeetable.

The shallow glow of light reflected the glossy covers of the expensive art books, magazines, and ordinary paperbacks that filled the bookcase facing the sofa. Hanging from the wall alongside the bookcase were framed reproductions of various paintings, and Gina was tempted to cross the room, drink in hand, as if she were at a cocktail party or a gallery opening, and pose inquisitively, as she imagined people did, but the thought of trying to summon an opinion about anything made her decide to stay put; the last thing she wanted to do was reveal her ignorance. Beneath the windows there was a large bed on which an assortment of diamond-shaped throw pillows, of various prints, had been carefully arranged ("too carefully," Gina remembered thinking, as if someone had set the scene for a play). The apartment was truly a pied-à-terre, since the teacher was married and lived with his wife and family in a house in Westchester; it wasn't even his apartment, but the apartment of a friend who was out of town. The friend, so Eric told her, had given him the keys and he often slept over when he had classes on two consecutive days.

The class ended at eight. Most nights it took her an hour to get home by subway. Frank was always home when she arrived. If she didn't call he might telephone her mother just in case she'd stopped off at her parents' house for some reason. She imagined him sitting at the kitchen table, drinking beer from a bottle and reading the newspaper, but when Eric bent forward and kissed her, moving his lips from her mouth to her ear to the side of her neck, her thoughts of Frank vanished. She could have said "I can't, don't, I have to go home," but she didn't say anything. If she were going to worry and feel guilty about Frank she might as well have said "no" when he asked her for a drink. Thinking of your husband or wife when you're with your lover was a sure way of undermining the potential pleasure of the moment, a pleasure that involves, among other things, the risk that by loving one person you might cause pain to someone else. (If you're going to hurt someone by what you do the pleasure you receive better be worth the effort.) She knew that at some point she'd have to say "It's time for me to go" but that didn't mean every moment between now and then had to be fraught with the tension of leaving. It was only when Eric—she was still uncomfortable calling him by his first name after a month sitting in the front row of the class thinking of him as "my professor" (at least that's how she referred to him when talking with Frank)—seemed to get hung up kissing her breasts that Gina realized she had to do something to speed things along, and pushing him aside as gently as possible (his hair was thinning, something she hadn't noticed before, and there was a small bald spot on the top of his head) she undid the button on the top of her pants and slipped them off, along with her shoes and underpants, while Eric, taking his cue, stood up and began undressing.

"What time is it?"

She bit his shoulder, playfully, as a signal that he should make a move, get off her, do something. It was difficult to pretend you were in a hurry—especially after making love—without being rude. No matter how accommodating you were, it was still possible for a man (as much as for a woman) to feel he was being used. She wondered whether she should get dressed in front of him or go to the bathroom and wipe off the semen dripping down her leg but decided she could always wash up when she got home. She'd already decided that the best way to console Frank for not coming home on time and for not calling to say she'd be late was to seduce him: they could make love on the kitchen floor or the kitchen table if he wanted. She knew that Eric felt disappointed in himself for coming so quickly, and ultimately in her, for not giving him a second chance, but there was no way of denying that she did feel guilty, and foolish for not having arranged the situation so she could take her pleasure more leisurely. It was a start anyway. She'd had a crush on Eric, no denying that either, since the first day of class, and knew that if she didn't sleep with him someone else in the class would. Most of the other women in the class were unmarried and for all she knew he'd already seduced at least one of them. It was very convenient having an apartment so near the campus. Surprising he didn't ask her why she had to get away so quickly, but seemed content to sit back and sip his drink meditatively and watch her as she dressed. The next time would be different.

The next time was different. Before Frank left for work in the morning she told him she'd made plans to go to the movies with a friend from school. After class. Don't be worried if I come home late. She was wearing the night gown with the blue flowers he liked so much and as they said goodbye she pressed against him as a reward for not questioning her about whom she was going out with. When she came to class and took her seat in the front row Eric smiled at her, significantly, and in a way that made Gina think everyone else in the class now knew they were sleeping together, as a signal that she should wait for him after the class ended. Once back in the apartment (and though she'd lied to Frank and could stay out later than usual time was still a matter of concern) it was no longer necessary to proceed with the formality of offering and fixing drinks. She'd worn a skirt, as well, with a small slit at the hem, to save time dressing and undressing, and because making love with their clothing on was something she and Frank rarely did.

"Don't turn on the light," she said. She reached forward, bending slightly, and unbuckled his belt. She liked the idea of playing the role of the aggressor, of being the person who made the first move, especially since Eric had assumed it was he who had seduced her. A few minutes after they'd arrived in the apartment she was lying on her stomach on the bed in the corner with her skirt pulled up to her waist. When he entered her from behind, her head buried in the pillow, she pushed back against him: "Oh shit," it was what he said when he came too quickly.

The night after she told Frank she was sleeping with Eric, though she didn't mention Eric by name, she went to his apartment after class knowing she might be going there for the last time. She didn't want to make a choice between staying married and having an affair (though it was she who'd given herself this ultimatum, not Frank) and knew that part of the reason for confessing to Frank was that it would force her to stop seeing Eric. All the lying and the subterfuge that went along with having an affair was too exhausting and she was anxious for things to return to normal. To normalcy. At least she thought she knew herself that well. She propped the pillows against the wall and lay back on the bed, Eric's head buried between her outstretched legs, his fingers moving inside her, and looked over his shoulder at the room where she'd spent two nights a week for the last two months. "I'll never see this place again," she thought, realizing, without regret, that sentiment and sex didn't mix. She raised her legs slightly, as if she were levitating off the sheet. (If Eric were a better lover it might be more of an inducement to continue the affair, but what went on between then seemed to her as desultory as what she imagined took place between people who had been married for many years.)

Afterwards, as Gina lay alone on the bed, glowing slightly but still nervously contemplating whether she should confront him with her decision (he knew, by now, she was married, but didn't know that Frank was a cop), and Eric fixed drinks by the light of the refrigerator—it was the only light on in the apartment—the doorbell rang, three short rings, a signal, and Eric, making no attempt to get dressed and showing no surprise, turned the knob and opened the door without even asking, "who's there?" As Gina pulled a blanket around her body and sat up, petrified, assuming the person at the door was the mysterious friend who lived in the apartment, a woman in a beige raincoat and with a silk scarf protecting her head ("Hello dear," she said, kissing Eric on the cheek) stepped out of the shadows of the hall into the center of the room.

"Don't be scared," Eric turned toward the bed and squinted at Gina. "Gina," he said, "I'd like you to meet Susan, my wife. It's okay—I've told her all about you, and us."

The woman unbelted her raincoat and tossed it onto the sofa. Before they began sleeping together, Gina had seen a framed photograph of her on the desk in Eric's office. "So that's who he's married to," she'd said to herself, experiencing a trace of jealousy and feeling her old dumpy self. She was in her mid-thirties, neatly dressed in an expensive suede skirt extending a few inches below her knees, a crocheted blouse through which, in a better light, you could see the tips of her breasts through the tiny openings, and high heels, which she didn't need since she was almost six feet tall without them.

"Don't be scared," she repeated Eric's words. "You're even lovelier than I imagined."

As she sat down beside her on the bed, Gina—who couldn't help feeling like a piece of merchandise up for auction—noted the red paint on her nails (she'd probably had them done that day) and the smooth white skin (it took energy to remain young) on the side of her long neck. Sometimes, before class, Gina would see women like this, fastidiously groomed and emanating self-confidence (like goddesses descended from the clouds for a view of their domain), strolling down the aisles of Bloomingdale's, fingering the scarves and the hundred-dollar handbags, or staring at their reflections in the windows of expensive boutiques.

It was raining out. She could hear the rain falling behind the heavy curtains that covered the windows, and the hum of traffic. Before joining them on the bed, Eric—who had returned to the kitchen to finish fixing the drinks—put on a record by Dinah Washington, an "in concert" record, there was a burst of applause and then Dinah Washington began singing "Red Sails in the Sunset." He stretched out behind her on the bed and Gina extended her arm from beneath the safety of her blanket and took a glass from the tray, hoping that by drinking she might be able to see things more clearly. Neither Eric nor his wife seemed nervous or tense. They were acting casual—or pretending to act casual—in thehope that their mood would make Gina feel at ease. Pretending the three of them together was the most natural thing in the world. Eric began playing with the strands of Gina's hair, trying to convince her of the pleasures of making love to two people at the same time, while his other hand disappeared beneath his wife's skirt. Gina was too numb to move, too frightened to fight against them, and for a moment didn't know whose hand—the man's or the woman's—was touching her breast. She'd been anticipating making love with Eric one last time—it was going to last forever, she was going to make it last—and then leaving, without saying anything. She'd drop out of school and never see him again. She'd never been in bed with a woman before and it angered her that Eric assumed she might want a third person—man or woman—to join them. She wanted to shout at him: "I've risked my marriage by coming here with you," but she knew it was past the point where saying that would make any difference. Sometimes thinking of things simplistically was the best way to overcome feelings of anxiety and nervousness. She didn't want to admit that the hands touching her body were making her feel excited and that part of her wanted to stay, if only to see what would happen. It was the thought that she'd been betrayed, that intimacy, in its most narrow definition, was limited to what happens between two people (even though in her own mind she'd created a kind of triumvirate between Eric, Frank, and herself, and all the time she was seeing Eric she'd been sleeping with Frank as well), that made her, finally, push them both aside—"There's nothing to be frightened of" "I thought you said she wanted to" "Don't go!" "We just want to talk to you"—find her clothing "Where are my shoes?"—and slam the door in their astonished faces.

9

His name was Miguel. Her name Bienvenida. When they were both in high school they passed each other in the hall. "That's when I fell in love with you," she told him later. He was a senior, she was only a sophomore, but they lived in the same neighborhood and after he graduated they saw each other on the street, her sister knew his brother, his friends called him Mickey, he wore a jacket with the word Cobra written in orange script on the back, he had girlfriends—every time she saw him he had a different girl on his arm—and a part-time job, but after he lost the job she would see him hanging out in Seward Park after school, she would point him out to her friends as they walked home from school to the projects where she lived with her parents overlooking the river, she'd watch the lights on the bridge from her window and listen to the radio and think about him before she went to sleep in the room she shared with a younger sister, her older sister had moved out by then and when Bienvenida ("Benny" to her friends) was old enough she'd move out too, she'd graduate high school and get a job and when she saved enough money she'd find an apartment, Mickey had his own place for awhile but now he stayed with friends, with different friends or different women every night, sometimes he even slept in the storefront the Cobras called their clubhouse and where late at night they'd shoot pool and listen to the radio, it was there that they met again ("Don't I know you from somewhere?"), Mickey meet Benny, she'd graduated from high school and had a job in an office uptown and the first night they slept together she told him about her plan to get her own apartment, her friends warned her against him, her parents advised her to move out of the neighborhood if she had a chance, her sister lived in the suburbs with her husband and two kids, they slept together and then the next day she saw him on the street with his arm around someone else's shoulders, how could she expect to keep track of him when she worked all day and he was free to hang out in the park, he took pills that affected his mood and sometimes he didn't even feel like fucking, sometimes he'd notice her from a distance and call out to her, stop traffic just to get to the side of the street where she was walking, other days he'd pass her on the sidewalk without seeing her, she knew the names of all her rivals, she thought that if she had her own apartment she would meet him one night—this was her fantasy— and that he would come home with her and stay forever, when she got up to go to work she would say: you can stay if you want, here's an extra set of keys, and when she returned from work he'd still be there, sitting around the kitchen table drinking beer with his friends, if he wanted, even though she worked all day, she'd fix dinner for him with the food she'd bought on her way home, his friends would leave and he'd turn on the radio and dance her around the room and then, if he felt like it, they'd go to bed before dinner, she'd bring him a beer to drink in bed while she made the food and when dinner was ready they'd eat in bed together, when she was inside fixing dinner he'd taken a pill with the beer and that made him anxious to finish dinner as quickly as possible and go out somewhere and spend the money that she made working, she'd always give him money so he could pay if they were going somewhere though some days he had money of his own from selling pills in the park. You could see his ribs through his flesh, he was that thin, but being with one person was probably good for him, "you're the best thing that happened to him in a long time" his friends would say. When she told him she didn't care what he did except if he brought other women back to the apartment when she wasn't there he smiled and said "I don't want other women" and it was true in a way, he was tired, he was happy, he thought about getting a job but he knew the only way anyone ever hired you was if you knew somebody and that only jerks actually spent their time looking, his best friends, the guys he'd been friends with in high school, the Cobras (but the Cobras no longer existed in any formal way, their clubhouse was a bodega now) all hung out in the park, though some of them worked odd jobs most of them sold dope, some of them had died, Benny had lied when she said she didn't care what he did but she didn't want to tell him not to take drugs, she was frightened he would leave her if she said "don't do that," all her friends warned her against him, some of them had even slept with him years before, but she just laughed. Her parents thought she was crazy when they found out he was living with her so she hardly saw them any more but she still kept in touch with her sisters. She began taking pills because she knew it would make him happy and because the effect they had on him made her curious about taking them and when she came home from work they'd get high together and go out and see his friends since most of their friends now were his friends and on warm days she knew if he wasn't at home when she returned from work he'd be in the park. She'd go and meet him there and they'd sit on the benches or lean against the railings drinking beer until the sun went down. It wasn't his fault that he couldn't get a regular job and it wasn't as if she were supporting him since often he did have his own money, he liked to play cards and bet on the horses, he'd take a pill and stay up all night playing poker with his friends.

When she and Mickey began living together the people she worked with noticed a change, not only in the way she acted—her attitude towards her work—but in her appearance. In the past she'd been compulsive about her clothing, laying out what she was going to wear before going to bed; now she often picked up whatever was close at hand, the wrinkled blouse thrown over the back of a chair—the one with the missing button—or the skirt with the stain which she hadn't had time to take to the cleaners. Her first few months at the job, and while she was still living at home, she'd spent most of her money on new clothes. After work she'd mull over her wardrobe, matching skirts and blouses, ironing and sorting, in an attempt to see how long she could go without wearing the same outfit twice.

The other women at work, with whom she'd talk about clothing and hair styles, felt snubbed by Benny because she seemed reticent about confiding in them. They knew she had a boyfriend, no one had ever called her at work before, and Mickey called her at least twice a day, not for any particular reason but just to check in. The calls would nullify her attempts at concentrating and she'd have to type everything at least twice before getting it right. All her thoughts when she was at work involved Mickey and what he was doing. Her hands were trembling from lack of sleep and she had to watch the keys while she typed and that made her make mistakes she wouldn't normally make, and when she read over what she'd typed checking for errors her mind wandered and the boss's secretary would call her over and with a wary eye mark up the clean copy with a thick red pencil. And then she'd have to do it all again.

One morning she came in late and knew by the way the people looked at her that it was just a matter of time—days or weeks, how could it be measured?—before she lost her job. And maybe it was just as well; if they fired her she could always get unemployment and in the meantime look around for another job. Maybe if she spent more time with Mickey she wouldn't worry about him so much. She could sleep late, like he did, and go to the park. She'd call up all her old friends and surely one of them would help her find work. When she told Mickey her fears about losing her job he didn't seem concerned; though he knew how much the job meant to her he made no effort to discourage her from taking pills or encourage her to go to bed early so she could wake up reasonably sane and not have to take yet another pill just to get herself dressed and onto the subway, it was the ride uptown on the train that she hated most about the job and on mornings when there were no pills she'd call in sick and sleep all day while Mickey went to the park to see what he could score.

While at least ten percent of the country suffered the indignities of unemployment, she went to work each day hoping to get fired. It occurred to her that possibly they were waiting for her to quit so she wouldn't be able to collect, but she would never quit, she would type every word backwards and hand it to the boss's secretary who would eye her coolly above her horn-rimmed glasses and repress her racist thoughts, she would saunter into the office an hour late and spend another half-hour combing her hair while the work piled up on her desk, she would flirt with the men in the office, brushing her breasts against their bare arms as she leaned over their desks, engaging them in conversations about subjects that had no relevance to what they were doing. She was a good actress, it was her calling, she could charm anyone.

Sometimes, unable to sleep, she'd lie in bed remembering the days when she would have given anything to have a job, as if working for its own sake was the key to freedom. She had played the role of docile office worker but after two years at the same job she was still at the lowest rung of a kind of hierarchy that existed so other people could play out the roles of authority and power. She couldn't help feeling that the people she worked for thought they were doing her a favor by letting her have this job. She was seeing the world through Mickey's eyes—however glazed, his vision was clearer than that of her parents, clearer than her sisters' or that of her friends at school—and her former dreams loomed above her head like tarnished icons: there was no goal, no sense of "getting ahead." The only thing she believed in was her feeling for Mickey, and he didn't care whether she worked or not. "We're a good team, you and me," he'd say. The implication was that no harm would come to them as long as they stayed together.

It was a cold February day with flurries in the air when the end came, so to speak. "We think you might be better suited working somewhere else," the boss said, employing the ambiguous "we" to deflect the burden of making the decision from himself. Benny couldn't help think that he'd said the same thing, or a variation, a hundred times before to a hundred women (if she were a man he might have stated it differently) who were so much like herself she might as well have been a shadow or ghost poised at the edge of her chair. As he spoke he stared out the window at the downtown Manhattan skyline, wondering how he would get home that night if it continued snowing. He made a mental note to tell his secretary to reserve a room for him at a hotel, just in case. It would take a bomb to destroy the skyline, but before that happened more and more buildings would be built containing offices where men like her boss would light their pipes and tilt back in their plush leather chairs, while women or girls like herself innocently adjusted their skirts—pleated or straight, whatever the fashion—so as to appear modest in the eyes of their superiors. She wondered if the woman who replaced her would feel the temptation to offer herself to this person as a form of compensation for being hired. The only compensation for being fired was the feeling of freedom. In her mind she said goodbye, not sentimentally, to her desk, her chair. To Pete—the man who operated the elevator—she talked about the weather, the same way she did every day. "I'll never see you again," she wanted to say. He was friendly, docile, a veteran: there was no way he'd ever be fired. He was grateful to be where he was, and expressed his gratitude by being invisible.

Losing one's job, in Mickey's eyes (whether you quit or were fired, what difference did it make?) was a happy occasion, an excuse to go out and get smashed. They walked through the snow to a bar where they would be certain to meet people they knew. Coincidentally, Mickey had made some money that morning selling pills, and bought everyone drinks. He tried to be more attentive to Benny, reassuring her that losing her job wasn't the end of the world. When they first started living together he had sensed how much having a job meant to her; what he didn't realize at this moment was that her sullenness wasn't the result of feeling insecure, but a way of hardening herself against the outside world. If you could become like a stone and not need anything then maybe even money wasn't necessary. She swallowed a pill with her beer and her sullenness vanished. Mickey's friend Eddie winked at her and Benny thought that if Mickey weren't around she might go home with his friend. She still loved Mickey but her dreams were in disarray; the will power necessary to adjust one's state of mind to the changes in one's life was no longer needed if you could take a pill. It was easier to change every minute or every day than not to change, to stay the same person—at least on the surface—for years on end. Easy to dismiss the voice in one's head that translated one's instincts into verbal structures, easy to act contrary to the voice of conscience if only to see if one could take the consequences. The voice of pleasure, the voice of pride, the voice of doom: one could be obedient to any of these. Mickey answered to the voice of survival, but nothing prevented him from going to the edge and courting disaster. Survival meant knowing when you were going to lose control, and then stopping. (Losing control meant that there were no more voices.)

One morning they woke to a cold apartment. No heat, no hot water. Mickey knocked on the door of a neighbor who told him the boiler was broken and that they shouldn't expect heat for two weeks. He boiled water for instant coffee and brought Benny a cup in bed. It was ten degrees, but the windchill factor, if you believed such things, made it feel like ten below. At first they enjoyed the novelty of not having heat, and joked about the prospect of spending two weeks in bed. They eased their bodies beneath layers of quilts and coiled their arms and legs around each other for warmth. They fell asleep, woke up, and sat in the kitchen near the stove. They rubbed their hands together in front of the stove as if the stove were a fire and they were living outdoors. The window frames were old and fragile and the wind whistled a piercing tune, the high-pitched note of a bamboo flute, as it blew through the cracks. The windows themselves were covered with frost.

Days passed and it seemed no work was being done to fix the boiler or install a new one. There were conversations among the tenants about withholding rent. A man who introduced himself as a tenants' organizer canvased the building and advised each of the tenants to call the heating inspector and complain. Mickey and Benny went over to a friend's house to take a shower, but turned down his offer to sleep on the floor. With her first unemployment check they bought a small cube of hashish and sat in bed smoking and laughing, watching TV. Benny told Mickey the story of how she'd first seen him in the hall of the school and how she'd had a crush on him from a distance for two years before he even noticed her. It was a story she'd told before, but he liked to hear it. One morning they woke up sick, unable to talk. They were drinking too much wine and beer, taking too many pills, rarely eating. Even though the unemployment check Benny brought home was only half her former salary they always had enough money, or so it seemed, to get along. With her first paychecks, two years before, she'd bought her first real winter coat, with an imitation fur collar meant to resemble some poor animal, a fox or a lynx. Maybe a raccoon. Benny had never seen a fox, a lynx or a raccoon, but she knew what a skunk smelled like. In those first few months she'd bought enough clothing to last for years. "Now that I don't have to go to work every day it doesn't matter what I wear." During the two weeks without heat she often slept in her clothes.

"Do you have a cigarette?"

When they smoked all the butts in the ashtray he went downstairs to get some more. He was sick all the time, his nose running constantly, and he coughed for about an hour every night before falling asleep. Sex was performed hurriedly and with as little thought as possible to the memory of what it had once been, and if they made love often it was only because they spent most of their waking hours in bed. They assumed that either the weather would become warmer or the boiler would be fixed and they'd be able to live normally. In the back of her mind was the thought that when spring came she'd go out and look for work and part of her almost wished she still had her job so she could go some place where it was warm during the day. The balance in their relationship was shifting; she saw how passive Mickey could be, especially when he didn't have pills, and that he now needed her and depended on her as much as she had once needed him. The person she'd loved from a distance was different from the person she spent every moment of the day with, and some days it required an effort to remember how she felt when she first saw him in the hallway at school.

She missed her family and all her old friends and whenever Mickey went to bed in the evening she sat up and made phone calls in an attempt to reconnect past and present. She'd make offhand comments to everyone about looking for work. She would ask her old friends if they knew of any jobs, and if they did hear of anything to please let her know. Some of these people sounded distant, while others were pleased to hear from her. Nobody dared to say "I told you so," though Benny could sense that that's what they were thinking. We told you not to get involved with that guy. She wondered why it was so necessary to defend Mickey to people who didn't seem any better off themselves. Everyone she talked to was having a hard time, and it was almost a cliché to complain about rents or the prices of food or the way landlords were harassing tenants so they'd eventually move out: if there was a big turnover the landlords could raise the rents. When she hung up the phone after one of these conversations she invariably burst into tears, not realizing that Mickey, lying in bed but unable to sleep, had heard everything she'd said, and could hear her now. Listening to her cry made him think that she regretted their life together. To say "things will get better" was like believing in religion; no reason to worry as long as you kept the faith.

When the weather turned warmer they began hanging out in the park again. Once a week she went downtown to get her unemployment check and maybe once every two weeks she traveled uptown under the pretense of looking for a job. She would ride the elevators of the huge office buildings and fill out applications, avoiding eye contact with the prissy receptionists, who regarded her with open hostility as if she were a threat to their jobs. "Nothing's available now but if anything comes up we'll call you," became a familiar refrain. She wondered what kind of reference her previous employer would give, if any, and part of her had the peculiar idea of returning to her old office—what could she lose?—and requesting her job back. For about an hour a day she contemplated what their lives were going to be like when the unemployment checks stopped, but the rest of the time it didn't seem to be a matter of urgent concern. She couldn't understand why they couldn't both find jobs, and why Mickey didn't seem inspired to even make an effort. To amuse herself she added up in her mind how much money they would have if both earned decent salaries. She tried to imagine what he would say if one day she told him she was pregnant. Would he get a job then?

Once a week Mickey took a bus uptown. There was a doctor in the East Sixties who performed abortions and dispensed pills. For twenty dollars Mickey could buy a bottle of thirty-six spansules and sell them in the park for a dollar each, sometimes more. He would buy two bottles so he and Benny could have a stash for themselves. The pills were green and white, diet pills, he didn't know what they were called. There were red and black spansules that were more potent but more expensive. After the introductory visit Mickey never saw the doctor: a middle-aged nurse checked his name on the register and filled his order. Most of the women who came to the doctor for abortions were call girls who lived and worked in the high-rise apartment building adjacent to the building where the doctor had his office.

Benny often joined him on the trip to the doctor. They took the last long seat in the back of the bus, even if the rest of the bus was empty, and stared out the window, pointing at people, buildings, the display of plants in the front of a store, the insignia on the grill of an expensive car. Being together in what they thought of as "the outside world" made them realize how isolated they'd been all winter.

Taking pills placed them in the center of their own lives so completely they'd forgotten anyone else existed, or that it was possible anyone else could be any less self-involved. It was a fact of life, of being inside your body. Being together they became like children wandering through a strange city. Weeks went by and they didn't leave the neighborhood except to go uptown for pills, downtown for money. The park was their second home. The local bar, a party at a friend's apartment, the movies—when they had money they'd go to the movies twice a day. Some nights when they didn't have money to go anywhere, but still had a few pills, they would spend hours listening to the radio and rear ranging the furniture in their apartment. When they had a lot of excess energy they would walk the streets looking for chairs and end tables, anything light enough to carry home. Whether they needed it or not wasn't important; the prize itself had a meaning that transcended its potential use. Benny had watched other people scavenging the garbage at the edge of the curb and it shocked her slightly to see herself as one of those people her parents had always warned her about. When they arrived home they'd lie in bed, exhausted, staring at the new object as if it were a rare antique.

If it wasn't worth anything to them it might be worth something to someone and now that it was inside their apartment they were the owners, at least technically. What did they need a bookcase for? They had no books. For a brief period of time the apartment seemed too cluttered. The surfaces of tables littered with newspapers, magazines, unpaid bills. Disconnect notices. Then one day a friend would visit, offer them twenty dollars, and cart away all the unnecessary furniture. Benny remembered the volumes of the encyclopedia in her parents' living room. Hours in the library, doing her homework: head pressed so close to the page her mother thought she might need glasses, copying words for a research paper into her spiral notebook, holding the pencil between her teeth as she tried to concentrate. Mickey said his mind moved too quickly to read. When he opened a book his eyes wandered toward the margins. He preferred movies. television, he liked the sound of a television even if he wasn't watching, sometimes, absentmindedly, he kept the TV and the radio going at the same time, he liked to lie in bed and watch TV—that had been his favorite occupation during the winter of no heat—he would watch anything, *Gilligan's Island*, *The Dukes of Hazard*, the ballgames, old westerns. Benny liked to read fashion magazines: *Vogue*, *Harpers*, *Mademoiselle*, *Glamour*. She stared at the faces of the models, the way they held their bodies. She liked to read the descriptions of clothing: "Bold in black and white, but soft, with big full sleeves, dropwaist and a tempting mid-thigh hemline. Dress by Oscar de la Renta, in hand painted silk, $900." Mickey would bring her back issues, he had a knack for finding them in the street, and occasionally he'd hand her the most recent issue which she knew he'd stolen, stealing was worth the risk if it gave her pleasure, she would turn the pages and stare into the faces of the women modeling bathing suits on the decks of yachts, she loved the thickness and smell of the pages, she liked nothing more than to sit at the kitchen table smoking a cigarette and drinking a cup of coffee, wearing only a black slip, and allow herself to be hypnotized by the faces of the women in the magazine, she would read every word of every ad: "Eclipse—The tan you want...the protection you need," "A woman's body chemistry changes from day to day, not just during menstruation but every day, that's why you should think about using FDS Feminine Deodorant Spray every day," "One touch waxing. It promises you the moon. And delivers." Most of the clothing Benny wore when she had a job no longer fit. Her breasts were growing smaller, she'd lost her appetite. She ate chocolate, drank coffee, and smoked whatever cigarettes Mickey brought home. The lines of her face were changing and people told her she looked older; when she was alone she stood at the mirror and traced the wrinkles with her hand. She was flowing forward into the feeling of the person she was becoming and it seemed pointless to question what was happening: to ask too many questions would only make her sad. She was watching herself cease to be the person who observed everything that was happening inside her, and now she was gradually ceasing to be the person who was aware that any changes were taking place at all. One could be faithful only to the idea of cynicism that informed you that no one, not even the young women modeling clothes, was exempt from the harsh glare of the colored bulbs that encircled the world, and which made everyone's skin appear sallow and unhealthy. A jaundiced yellow.

She felt busy in her head all the time, one thought colliding with another, like dodgem cars. The thoughts canceled each other out and were occasionally connected by some vague feeling that was a combination of all the residues of nostalgia she felt for a part of herself she could still remember. Her thoughts were convoluted, like sentences in a novel by Henry James, or Proust, and there were no sharp lines demarcating wakefulness and sleep. She was lying in bed thinking about something someone had said or fantasizing about what it might be like to sleep with Eddie, Mickey's friend, and trying to fall asleep at the same time. And then she would be asleep but the thoughts would continue, along with the secondary thought (as she slept, and dreamed) that I'm really sleeping. Making love or thinking about it, with Mickey or anyone else, only made her more wakeful. For Mickey sex was a means to exhaust himself so he could fall asleep. There were no preliminaries and it never lasted very long and sometimes he fell asleep in her arms minutes after it was over. She would stay up late and watch him sleep, curled on his side, back facing her. His bony wrists and ankles, the knots in his spine, the bruises on his arms and ribs—for a moment, asleep, he resembled a battered child. Benny's clearest thought, but one she'd never admit to anyone, was her acknowledgment of the difference between the way she'd thought and felt about Mickey before they started living together and the way she felt about Mickey now. It was a difference that had to do as much with the value of feelings as with ways of perceiving someone over a period of time, painting a portrait of him in the present (lying on his side, breathing gently) and comparing it to a portrait a stranger had painted of him then.

The days were painted as well, in bright fauve colors. It was useless to stare at the painting and ask oneself: What does this mean? Even the blacks and grays were exhilarating and electric and seemed to leap from the canvas in a way that transcended the simply mournful or elegiac. It was possible to say to oneself "I must get up early and enjoy the daylight" and take pleasure in having the thought, without necessarily doing anything about it. In some cases thinking about doing something was easier than doing it, more rewarding. The truth of the moment, any moment, was that it had already gone by.

Later, Benny wouldn't be able to remember with any clarity what they'd done that particular night. She remembered looking at her wristwatch and thinking that for the first time in weeks she felt genuinely tired, like she could fold up and go to sleep without any trouble, that her body craved sleep and how great it was that she didn't have to get up the next day and exhaust herself further by traveling to a job she hated.

"I'm going to bed now," she announced to Mickey, who was sitting in the kitchen talking to his friend Pedro. It was 4 a.m. She removed her skirt and blouse, draping them over the back of a chair, unhooked her bra and stepped out of her underpants, stood at the window wondering if anyone from any of the nearby buildings was spying on her, then closed the curtains and lay down on the bed, on top of the blankets, wishing that Pedro would leave and that Mickey would join her. Whenever they were gone from the apartment for long periods of time, and these days "long periods" meant a few hours, she began to miss the feeling of intimacy that could only exist when they were alone together, not in bed or even in the same room but in the apartment doing separate things. There was a tangible feeling in the air at that moment which she could recognize and understand as if it were in her blood, some kind of biologic instinct that made her think, in the cosmic sense, she was where she should be. It was the closest feeling to what she imagined marriage was like, it made her feel sane and allowed her to forget her hatred and jealousy of the women in the fashion magazines and all her old women friends who snubbed her when they passed on the street. She lifted her bare arms into the air and stretched, made hand shadows on the wall in the light from the kitchen. She tried to hear what Mickey and Pedro were talking about. She unfastened her wristwatch, a gift to herself when she began working, and held it to her ear to check that it was still ticking. More than once she'd been tempted to sell it so they could have money to buy pills but Mickey doubted they'd get enough—maybe five dollars at the most—to make it worth the effort. The silver digits of the tiny clock glowed in the dark.

She was asleep when Mickey and Pedro left the apartment. When she thought about it later she couldn't remember hearing them leave. She was fairly certain they were there when she went to sleep, but she wouldn't bet on it. When she worked all day she would sleep with an alarm clock on the floor near the bed but when she quit her job Mickey, in a symbolic move, had thrown the clock away.

"You won't be needing this anymore," he had said. She was asleep, it was almost dawn, she slept on her side under a single sheet. There was something luxurious about being so tired you couldn't think. The mind went blank by itself, without effort, and began to drift. It was a pleasure to be lying in bed alone. No matter how tired she was Mickey's nervous energy (he had a habit of turning from his side to his back to his stomach before falling asleep) kept her awake.

Pedro claimed to know where they—he and Mickey—could buy some pills, but when they arrived at the person's house, a tenement building on 2nd Street, just off 3rd Avenue, no one was home or no one was answering the downstairs bell. Pedro was apologetic. "I'd call them," he said, "but they don't have a phone." They leaned back against a parked car on the deserted sidewalk and stared upwards at a window on the fourth floor, the only window in the building where there was a light, debating whether they should shout out the name of Pedro's friend. "They told me they'd be up, that I could come by any time." Pedro seemed genuinely disconsolate about steering his friend down a blind track and Mickey tried his best to convince him that he didn't really need any pills, that he could wait till tomorrow, even though he'd taken his last pill twelve hours earlier and had ceased to be able to think clearly, part of him craving sleep or a pill to put him to sleep, part of him wanting the security of knowing that when he woke the next day he'd have a pill to wash down with morning coffee, and get him going, just one pill would do it. He felt like all the blood had flowed out of his legs and that he should stand on his head, right on the sidewalk, to get the circulation going.

If Pedro decided to shout out the name of the person with the pills, risking the chance that the sound of his voice would wake someone in the same building, someone who'd stick his or her head out the window and threaten to call the cops if they didn't pipe down, though the terms of the threat couldn't be described as being civilized or polite, Mickey didn't want to be around to deal with the consequences. Pedro didn't have a pill habit, though he enjoyed taking them when offered, and the only reason he'd offered to help at four in the morning was as a favor to his friend. They decided to walk up Second Avenue and stop in an all-night restaurant for coffee on the chance that they might run into someone who could help them out. It was warm enough for the men on the Bowery to be out on the street, sleeping on benches where in winter they'd gathered around bonfires, or in doorways, with their heads cradled in the folds of a black garbage bag. The two men didn't say much as they walked. They'd known one another for a long time and if someone were to ask Mickey if he had any brothers he would say that no, he didn't have any brothers, but Pedro might as well be his brother, they were that close. He would hold out two fingers and press them together. "We're like that."

What made their friendship special was their common attitude to money. It could be said that they had an understanding, that they were partners as well as friends. When one of them had a few extra dollars and the other was broke the person who was broke didn't even have to ask to borrow money. Any money one of them had was for both to share. There was a way of being generous that didn't involve trying to manipulate the other person in order to see how much they would give in return. When Pedro gave Mickey money there was no sense that it was payment for an old debt. It wasn't necessary to say "I'll pay you back on Friday" when it was obvious that Mickey would have no more money on Friday than he'd have today. The give and take didn't exist in the moment but took place over a long period of time. Neither of them kept even a mental record of who owed who money. They assumed that eventually everything would balance out and if it didn't what did it matter as long as their friend-ship remained intact.

Initially, Benny had been jealous of the time the two men spent together. Mickey had warned her that Pedro was like "family," but Benny hadn't realized how close that meant. When she was working, and Pedro was visiting when she arrived home, she would go to the bedroom, close the door and wait for him to leave. She realized she was acting irrationally but working all day at a job she hated entitled her to be selfish, or so she felt. When she came home from work she wanted to be with Mickey. She would sit on the edge of her bed and brood. It was more than a matter of pride that made Mickey encourage Pedro to stay when he knew that Benny wanted to be alone with him in the apartment. Living with a woman didn't mean you had to sacrifice all your male friendships. He didn't want to be in a position where he had to choose between Benny and all the rest of the people in his life. It would take him a while to learn that acknowledging another person's feelings was as important as not compromising one's own.

Sometimes when she climbed the steps to her apart-ment after a day's work she would make a pact with her-self not to get angry if Pedro was there. She hated feel-ing petulant and the sense of distance it created and all the time and energy spent trying to avoid feeling angry all because another person—the person you lived with, your love—was acting in a way that you thought of as in-considerate or thoughtless. She climbed the stairs—there they were, at the kitchen table—hung her pocketbook from a hook on the door and went to the refrigerator for a beer. She didn't want them to feel they had to stop talking just because she was there, but it was her apartment and she could do as she pleased when she came home from work. Pedro, at these moments, usually hung his head guiltily, downed his beer with a flourish: after I finish this one I'll leave. He was always surprised when Mickey encouraged him to come over just at the time when he knew Benny was due home. He'd lived with a woman before and knew how possessive they could be. The last thing he wanted was to start any trouble; on the contrary, he liked Benny and wished they could be friends. Whenever they found themselves sitting opposite one another at the local bar he would try to initiate a conversation with her in an attempt to prove his friendship with Mickey was genuine, and that he had no intention of coming between them. He'd tell her stories from "the old days," what Mickey was like as a kid, how they used to hop rides on the back of the crosstown buses, heading west, and sit on the pier looking out over the Hudson when they should have been at school: harmless memories, blurred snapshots. She, in turn, would ask him questions about his life: What was the woman he'd lived with like? Why had they split up? The first time Mickey gave Pedro money in her presence she was appalled; she was the one who was working, after all, and in a way the money he was handing out was hers. Then she saw how, a week later, Pedro would come over at dinner time with a bag of fruit and a bottle of wine, and she would realize with a trace of envy—she had few enough friends of her own— that their relationship wasn't one-sided or manipulative, but that the two men were truly devoted to one another in an unusual way.

They said goodbye outside the building on Broome Street where Pedro was staying—it wasn't his own apartment, but the apartment of a friend of a friend who'd gone out of town for a few weeks (he hadn't had his own place since he and his girlfriend had separated)—and with the sun rising in his face, it was too hot for late May, Mickey headed back across town. He didn't want to go home till he had some pills or money, preferably pills, but the list of people who would loan him anything ("I'll pay you back tomorrow") was narrow. Not having money, in a chronic way, made it hard to cultivate casual acquaintances, since it was difficult to know when someone you didn't think of as a true friend was feeling generous or how often you could ask that person for a favor before they began crossing the street when they saw you coming. You could borrow money from a person you didn't know well and not pay it back at the exact time, but you couldn't do that more than once. Even if you did pay the person back, eventually, you would be pushing your luck to attempt to ask the person for money again. Sometimes he thought that living with a woman had made him weak: he couldn't remember who he was as a separate person trying to survive in the world, and surviving— up until the time he began living with Benny—was the thing he'd done best. If it weren't for Pedro—who was the only person to whom he confided his feelings for Benny—he would have gone insane long ago. "You should be lucky," Pedro would say when Mickey complained about Benny (he didn't mean to complain but it was possible to interpret anxiety—if that's what he was feeling—as a sign of ambivalence). "After you've lived with someone for awhile it's hard to live alone."

Mickey knew that Pedro was talking from his own experience. After Pedro and his girlfriend Mary split up Mickey had spent endless nights getting drunk with his friend, listening to him rant about all the hideous things each had done to the other; and it wasn't as if either of them were playing around with other people, it was just living together and trying to relate to what the other person expected at any given moment: "I can't even remember what we fought about but you better believe that's what we did from the moment we woke up till we got into bed. It was as if that's what we wanted to do as an excuse to get stoned maybe and then make up briefly but after awhile you just begin to hate and resent that person, you want to bang her head against the wall, shit, it's like a drug, being that person and feeling these things. I can't believe all women are like that," a drunken pause, "I still love her, that's the worst part, I'd move back tomorrow if that's what she wanted."

There'd been a time when they could brag about all the women they'd slept with, compare notes, all the dates they'd go on together when one of them had a girlfriend and she would bring a friend with her and they'd all ride off together in someone's borrowed car. Possibly being free involved a kind of immunity from feeling anything; feelings led to suffering and that's what made you old. That's where those lines in your face come from. That's what all the sadness is about. If that person lying in the doorway were to tell you his or her story, it wouldn't be much different from your own.

It was 8 a.m. by the clock in the coffeeshop on Essex Street. At last he had a destination, a place to go. He felt like raising his middle finger in the air as a salute to all the people passing by in their cars on the way to work. Pedro had given him five dollars and if he wanted he could join the crowd at the counter for the breakfast special: two eggs, toast, hash browns, coffee and juice— fresh juice but unlike everyone else he didn't need a hearty breakfast to get through the day. He might just as well stuff the five dollar bill into the shirt pocket of the man sleeping on the bench in Seward Park, a threadbare winter coat pillowing his head.

Knots of students with notebooks and briefcases mingled on the sidewalk outside the high school where Mickey and Pedro and Benny had spent four years of their lives, "the best years," Mickey would say. He wasn't one to offer advice but if someone were to ask he'd set them straight about what it was like when you got out of school and how nothing that happened in school prepared you for going hungry or being perpetually broke. It was rare to find a teacher who was genuinely interested in sitting down and listening to your problems. Even rarer to find a student, who, by the time graduation day rolled around, was still so innocent he or she would actually see the occasion as a stepping-stone to a way of life they didn't yet know was an illusion.

The teachers weren't models, nor did they attempt to be. The Platonic equation of knowledge with health wasn't a very realistic ideal. One became a teacher not because one had any particular attribute that made one a good teacher (or a better teacher than the next person) but because one thought, in a rational way, that it was something one could do. It was a position that commanded—at least in the past—a modicum of respect within the so-called community. "What do you do for a living?" "I'm a teacher." (I'm just doing it for the money.) The teachers drove up each morning to the school in their small foreign cars. Most of them lived in other neighborhoods. They came from Brooklyn or the Upper West Side and parked their cars outside the school. On the windshields of the cars were the stickers that identified the owner of the car as a teacher or administrator connected with the school. One way of getting revenge against a teacher one disliked might be by slashing the tires of his or her car. They parked their cars and walked up the steps to the school. (When Mickey was a senior one of the Cobras had been arrested for assaulting one of the women teachers in an empty stairwell.) They went to their rooms. They sat behind their desks. They read the newspapers while waiting for the students to arrive. Some of them congregated in the teachers' lounge drinking coffee. Being distant, as in any relationship, was a form of protection, and everything the teachers did was with the purpose of creating as much distance as possible between themselves and the students.

As he climbed the front steps of the tenement on Henry Street he had the thought that maybe he was better off just going home and getting some sleep. He had met his cousin Esteban ("Essie") on the street a few weeks before and Essie, who was a few years older, had mentioned that he might be able to help him out if he ever needed any pills. There had been no mention of money or whether if Mickey needed pills and didn't have any money Essie would give him the pills outright or let him have a few on credit. He could always give him the five dollars as a kind of token payment until he did have the money. Mickey hoped to catch his cousin before he left for work. He stood in the downstairs cubicle, rang the buzzer next to his cousin's name, and was surprised at his own feeling of elation when someone buzzed back, almost immediately. At the same time he felt like he could just as well lean against the wall of the cubicle and fall asleep. The quest to fulfill one's momentary needs wasn't worth the effort. The lines in his face were a sign that he could no longer trust his own thoughts. "I've been here before," he said to himself, as he paused on the landing between floors, "here" meaning a state of mind, not the actual building. ("But I've been here before, too, I've walked up these steps...." He was singing a song in his head to stay awake.)

At the sound of his steps on the landing a dog barked behind a door. The building was waking up. People, late for work, were hurrying through their morning rituals. A man and a woman—one hesitates to say "husband and wife"—were bickering over a minor household detail, something that had happened the night before and which had been left unresolved. It's not a good practice to go to bed angry, always best to wake in a good mood. It's no fun walking around fuming all day, inventing small dialogues between yourself and someone else in your head. "Don't shout," the woman was saying, "the neighbors will hear." They kept that dog locked up in the apartment all day. When it barked everyone on the floor could hear; it was a way of alerting the tenants that someone was in the hallway, a potential thief, perhaps; every building should have its own watchdog. "They're fighting again in 3-B." Radio music—someone was turning the dial from station to station, someone else was singing along. You place one foot in front of you; you move forward at all times. A child might feel inclined to count the steps; the result of anything, even climbing a staircase, is a form of achievement. Each landing was lit by a bright bulb screwed into the ceiling. The walls were encrusted with thick layers of yellow paint. One building like this might remain, say, a hundred years from now, as an example of a typical dwelling in what was then known as a "slum."

So a person Mickey's age, at some future time, would marvel over the way people used to live. Such ingenuity! Such forbearance! There was always the possibility that people a hundred years from now would be worse off than people today. A room in a building like the one you used to live in would be equal in size to a whole apartment! There were too many people, too few places to live. Robberies were commonplace. One entered an apartment by force and took what one wanted and if by chance the occupant of the apartment returned and caught you in the act you could always brandish a menacing weapon and force the victim into a closet. The wealthy lived in structures resembling castles or churches, surrounded by moats, while the poor victimized the poor as a part of an unending cycle that could only culminate in a revolt by the lower against the upper classes or by the arrival of a kind of Messiah whose very presence on the planet was a signal in itself that the structure was all wrong.

He knocked and announced himself, "Essie, it's me, Mickey," before the person on the other side had a chance to say "Who's there?" The door, caught on a sliver chain, opened a few inches. Mickey could see the top of a woman's head but couldn't remember whether his cousin was married or whether this woman was someone he was supposed to know. Would she recognize his name if he told her? Her bleached blonde hair looked like a thicket streaked by sunlight. She wore a bright orange bathrobe, belted at the waist. In the dim light of the hallway bulb he could see the dark furrows under her eyes, as if she, like himself, had been awake all night.

What registered most emphatically in Mickey's mind was that she was a white woman, not that that made any difference, but a fact he would note and file away for some later date when he might be called upon to make an assessment of his cousin. If he'd been more alert he might have made an attempt to charm this woman, who was in her early thirties but looked older, into letting him into the apartment, flash the famous smile Benny often reminded him had been the reason she had fallen in love with him in the first place, though it had been awhile since she'd recounted the story of what she felt like when she saw him in the hallway at school, and the subsequent years of trailing him around like a small dog. He had lost his confidence with women—that much he understood about himself—and his desire as well. He was like an athlete who'd lost his skills, who could feel, as he grew older and played more, his motivation to be successful, to win, to conquer, fading away. Instead, when it was obvious that Essie wasn't at home ("he left for work an hour ago") Mickey just backed away, not wanting the woman to get the impression that he was going to make an attempt to

get into the apartment by force, or that there was anything desperate about the way he was feeling. She stared
out at him through the crack, her dark eyes flashing. He
was tempted not to leave his name, but figured that after
the woman described him Essie would guess his identity.
Essie would know what he wanted, and that he probably
was desperate; no other reason Mickey would bother to
visit him at nine in the morning. "Tell him Cousin Miguel came by. And that I'll stop by later."

He turned and started down the staircase. At each floor
there was a window open a few inches from the bottom
to let a small amount of sunlight and air into the hallway.
He thought of Benny—before leaving the apartment,
with Pedro, he had checked to see that she was asleep—
and knew that she was past the point of being jealous or
worried because he'd stayed out the entire night. If she
were angry about anything when he came home it would
be because he arrived empty-handed: no money—or not
enough to make much difference—and no pills. It would
be her turn to go foraging and she wouldn't know where
to begin. There wasn't even any coffee left and on good
days she needed at least two cups to feel, as she put it,
half-human, though she needed a lot more than coffee to
feel like she could face the world at all.

"Remember to buy coffee," he said, not to himself, but
aloud, as if the part of himself that was responsible for
such chores had floated off into space. He had reached
the second floor of the building when he heard the front
door open. He peered over the landing and saw an elderly woman carrying a shopping bag standing in front of
what was probably the door to her apartment. She was

searching her pocketbook for her keys. The pocketbook, which possibly contained a wallet filled with money, or maybe only some money, was on her arm. The shopping bag was on the floor. It was a plastic shopping bag with the words Met Foods printed on the side in big red letters. Obviously this woman believed in getting a jump on the rest of the world by doing her chores early. No interminable waits at the counter in the supermarket or at the bank. When he was in high school, and the Cobras were flourishing, he'd stolen a pocketbook from a woman on the street—an older woman, much like this one, too helpless to resist—and though the police attributed most of the petty crimes in the neighborhood to the Cobras he had never been caught. There'd been the rush of adrenaline when he stripped the pocketbook from the woman's arm in broad daylight and made his escape, not running but walking as fast as he'd ever walked, disappearing down a subway entrance where another member of the gang was waiting. He gave the stolen object to his comrade and they both took off on different trains, going in opposite directions. At an appointed time they met and shared their plunder, which was never enough to compensate for the risk of being caught or imprisoned, but in those days it wasn't the money that was as important as the feeling involved in taking any risk at all.

He waited till the woman was halfway in the door of the apartment before making his move. There was no possibility of even attempting to think clearly about what he was doing. He didn't have a plan. For all he knew there were two or three other people in the apartment, or at least one person, the woman's husband. If he'd been capable of thinking clearly he would have questioned his own ability to be prepared to perform two or three quick actions at the same time. Clamping his hand firmly over the woman's mouth and closing the door behind him, not slamming it, then locking it from the inside—all this required a certain amount of precision. "Don't scream, don't make a sound," he hissed in the woman's ear, pointing his thumb into the base of her spine as if he were holding a knife or a gun. An orange squirted out of the top of the shopping bag and rolled, like an 8-ball, across the linoleum squares, coming to rest against the leg of the kitchen table. She raised her arms into the air as if she were going to protest or fight back—he had one hand around her mouth, the other on her neck—then fell against him, limp, her hair in his face. Slowly, he lowered her to the floor—this was easier than he'd thought—and, assuming she'd fainted, slipped the strap of her pocketbook from around her arm. There was no thought of being meticulous or neat: he dumped the contents of the pocketbook onto the floor, ignoring the nickels and dimes that spilled from the change purse of her wallet and rolled off along the linoleum. There was no thought about whether he might be leaving fingerprints. Without thinking twice he emptied the wallet onto the floor, taking only the roll of bills, ignoring the photographs and whatever identification papers the woman carried. He wasn't curious about who she was. He wasn't about to kneel on the floor and count the money of this woman who wouldn't even be able to recognize him—had never even seen his face—when she woke up. If it felt like a lot of money, well, it was about time something lucky happened to him.

The woman was lying on her back on the floor. She was wearing a woolen coat, unbuttoned, over an old-fashioned striped housedress. As he stood over her his shadow fell across her bare legs. She wore no jewelry, only a silver band on her finger, but he didn't have the strength to pry it off. There was a part of him that had performed the act and another part that had watched it all happen, and as the two parts merged he felt the weight of centuries descend upon his shoulders. (When something lucky happens it's often just a sign that the gods are trying to trick you into thinking they're on your side.)

The roll of bills was secure in the front pocket of his pants. He turned from the body of the woman and opened the apartment door an inch at a time, measuring the distance between the knob in his hand and the identical knob of the outside door leading to the street. He fixed his attention on that door, breathed deeply and listened. No one was coming down the staircase inside the building but it was possible that someone was coming up the steps outside. This moment was as good as any other. He refused to turn his head and stare at the woman on the floor for fear she might rouse herself; in the moment their eyes met he would be forced to extend beyond himself to a point neither he nor Benny nor Pedro nor anyone he knew would understand. He would be forced to commit an act that would alter his life so irrevocably that he himself might as well be dead.

"Where have you been?" Benny wanted to know when he staggered into the apartment. She was standing in the kitchen looking through all the tins and containers with colorful labels which lined the cupboard shelves. When she saw the brown paper bag in Mickey's hand she eyed it greedily. (She had assumed that Mickey, in the course of his peregrinations through the city streets, would forget they needed coffee, that she needed coffee, and that whatever money he had allotted to buy the coffee he had spent on something else.)

"Don't worry," he said. Later, when the cops questioned her, she would remember that those were his exact words. If she were asked to describe further what had happened when he arrived home she would respond by saying he looked tired, but no more tired than she'd seen him on other occasions when he'd stayed up all night. And that there was nothing unusual or paranoid about the way he was acting. Nothing to make her think anything out of the ordinary had happened. She also had to admit that when he walked through the door she was more preoccupied with her own state of being than with his, and that her main concern was whether he'd found any money or pills and whether she'd be forced to begin her day without a cup of coffee.

He emptied the bag on the kitchen table. A can of Bustelo coffee—her favorite brand—and a pack of smokes. From the pocket of his pants he took a small container of pills and placed it next to the coffee. He didn't say anything about the roll of bills or where he had gotten the money to buy the drugs. What was the point? It was only the next day when she read about the death of the old woman in the paper that she began making the connections. "I don't think I want to go to the park today," Mickey said, as the day drifted along. She remembered that when she confronted him with the question of what he'd done that night—or early that morning—he had denied knowing anything about what had happened in the apartment on Henry Street. She knew him well enough to know that he was lying but didn't want to act—not without further evidence, anyway—as if she were accusing him of something he might not have done. If he didn't want to go to the park that was fine with her.

That morning, when he came home, all she wanted was a cup of coffee. She would have liked to make love to him as well but by the time she'd finished her first cup—a cup of coffee and a smoke were pleasures that couldn't be postponed—he was already asleep. Still dressed. Lying on his stomach, face buried in the pillow.

Dead to the world.

10

As soon as Irene eased the car out from under the trees in front of the house she realized she'd neglected to tell Janice, the babysitter, what she should say if Joe called. He'd already called once that day to inform her he'd be coming home late and not to wait up, but the call had taken her by surprise; she didn't have the chance to tell him she might be going out as well and if he did come home and she wasn't there and he was hungry to heat up the left-over chicken in the icebox. She would have liked to say "don't wait up" in the same cavalier tone he used when he said it to her, but she didn't have the nerve. She never questioned him, not even in her own mind, when he said he was going to be late (when she had in the past, he had always countered with a ready-made speech referring to whatever case he was working on at the moment), and whether he was seeing another woman, which she doubted, was no longer an issue. It was only during the last year that she'd begun going out alone or with her friends on nights when she knew that Joe was working late, and though she never abused the privilege (if it could be thought of as that) Joe wasn't overjoyed at the idea, acted sullen for days afterwards. "You're crazy just to sit home alone all the time," her friends admonished. If they could live autonomous lives, independent of their husbands, at least on the surface, why couldn't she?

Joe tried to appeal to her sense of guilt: how would she feel if she went out one night and something happened to the kids, as if the house couldn't burn down with her

212

there as well. Her sudden need for independence made him suspicious. What did she do all day, anyway, and who were these so-called friends? "Debbie's going to have another baby" or "Ilona's going back to school" or "Virginia just got a job in a dress shop on Madison Avenue"—for Joe, who spent only a fraction of his waking hours in the neighborhood, these women, who lived in houses around the corner or a few streets over, were like characters in a story out of classical mythology (Diana, Helena, Athena), and talking about them in this intimate way only fed his feeling of resentment that she should crave a life of her own while he was out working. He didn't understand why she couldn't make friends with the wives of his friends, and why, when some of the guys and their wives got together for a party, or went out to dinner at a restaurant, she invariably ended up talking with one of the men. He knew that she wasn't particularly fond of Gina, and that the feeling was mutual, but that didn't mean she couldn't find something to talk about with one of the other women. "Really," she would say, when they returned from the party or restaurant and he would berate her for her antisocial behavior towards the members of her own sex, "I didn't know I was acting that way." It was his instinct, based on all his dealings with all types of people during all the years he'd spent being a cop, that Irene might entertain the idea of going out and finding a lover, if only for one night, that made the issue of her going out seem like such a threat. He couldn't believe that after all these years she was no longer frightened of him, and that if he were to say "You can't go out tonight—I want you to stay at home" she might hang up on him or laugh in his face. In recent years his own infidelities had become more and more transient, which was too bad because he'd finally learned the art of discretion and could actually go to bed with someone from time to time, without broadcasting it to half the world. Most of the time when he called to say he'd be coming home late because he had to work overtime on a case, he was telling the truth.

The bar was located about a mile from where she and Joe lived, on the corner of a street in a neighborhood where she didn't know anyone. She'd passed it driving home late one night with Joe—she couldn't remember where they were coming from, only that they were bickering, as usual, about whether Joe was too drunk to drive, and how she was a better driver than he was, drunk or sober. The bar was called Butterfield 8—the name spelled out in an orange neon gash across the front—after the John O'Hara novel, which she had never read, and the movie starring the young Elizabeth Taylor as Gloria Wondrous. As they stopped for the light on the corner opposite the bar she saw three men and a woman standing in a circle out front. The men were all dressed casually, in corduroy pants or dungarees and shirts with wide open collars. The woman, wearing a long loose wrap-around skirt and a Mexican peasant blouse, was clinging to the arm of one of the men and laughing at something that one of them had said. As they paused at the light, Irene could hear the woman's laughter, so breathy and human-sounding it made her realize she'd forgotten what it felt like to respond to something genuinely, and with one's whole self. It also inspired her to think that if she wanted, she could enter that bar alone some night and not be harassed or attacked, not by people like this. (It was one thing to want to go out alone at night, but what to do once one had one's freedom was always a problem.) The people she'd seen on the corner looked like they'd stepped out of an advertisement for life itself, or the elixir of life. Perhaps the men had all known one another for many years, and then one of them had married this woman who had become friends—"they're not just my husband's friends," she would say, "they're my friends as well"—with each of the men. Unlike many women, she hadn't tried to possess her new husband to the extent that he would be forced to break off his two oldest friendships. She was happy because being with his friends made her husband happy and she herself was happy to have made two new friends herself.

Most of Irene's friends—Debbie, Ilona, and Virginia, to name three—were women she'd met in the five years since she and Joe moved to their present house (in Staten Island, where they lived before, she'd had a hard time meeting anyone), and the only man whom she'd consider her friend, though they rarely saw each other, was Frank, Joe's partner. When they were first married, in the days when she was too young to know better, Joe discouraged her from keeping up close ties with anyone but her immediate family, most of whom—sisters, brothers, and cousins lived in places like Fargo, North Dakota and Tacoma, Washington, too far away to make any difference. She'd return to that bar some night when Joe was working late, confident that no one would bother her unless she wanted them to. (She'd recently read an article in the newspaper about a woman who'd been raped on a pool table in a bar in Boston while the patrons of the bar looked on, cheering the participants and making no attempt to call the police, but when she pointed out the article to Joe he just shrugged, "Things like that happen every day," indicating, as well, that it had been at least partially, if not entirely, the woman's fault for venturing into a strange bar unescorted.)

She had to admit that the thought of meeting someone at the bar was more than a remote possibility—at least the space in her mind she allotted to such thoughts grew larger as the time for leaving grew near—and she ended up spending as much time in front of the mirror (changing from a simple skirt and blouse to a pair of tight jeans and a sweater to the black-and-white polka-dot shirt-waist that she finally chose to wear) as she would if she were going out for the evening with Joe and wanted to impress his friends. Even the babysitter, Janice, had complimented her on her appearance. (Janice, a tall thin girl wearing shorts and a T-shirt with the words "Kool & The Gang" stenciled along the front, was secretly anxious for Irene to leave so she could call her boyfriend Tom. A few days ago Virginia, Janice's mother, had complained to Irene that Janice was in the habit of staying out till three or four in the morning on weekend nights, and was concerned that her daughter was possibly sleeping with this person Tom, who didn't even go to the same high school as Janice and whom Virginia herself had never formally met: "He just drives up to the front of the house and honks his horn." If they were sleeping together she wondered whether she, Virginia, should try to have a heart-to-heart talk with her daughter about birth control: "Even if she knows more about it than I do I still think I should make the effort, right?")

Now, as Irene neared the street where the bar was located, she was conscious of the outline of her body beneath her dress and tried to imagine what she looked like to someone else. She rejected the idea that wearing makeup and tight clothing was a way of inviting trouble. There was no way to hide her age, after all; even makeup couldn't obscure the circles beneath her eyes, not even in a bar where the lighting was dim (though it was possible the combination of poor lighting and being half-drunk might make someone think she was younger than she was, in this sense, meaning more desirable). Joe often complained that she didn't wear enough makeup, that she should devote more energy to her appearance, as if he were some kind of connoisseur of her looks, though of all people he was the most conscious of the fact that she was getting older, and he preferred, selfishly, the image of himself walking down the street with a younger, more attractive woman on his arm. Irene had no image of a possible alternative to Joe—though in his present state he was hardly an image of anything; she would have to be presented with a few possibilities (a lineup of potential suspects) before making her choice.

The neighborhood around the bar was similar to the one where she and Joe lived, attached red-brick homes with driveways and garages surrounded by neatly clipped hedges and manicured front lawns. Neighborhoods—it was a familiar story—where generations of families somehow coexisted, where the men went to work every morning and returned home at dusk, where the children bicycled innocently along the treelined streets after school, where the wives spent their afternoons posing indolently in front of their full length mirrors or sat by the phone waiting for their lovers to call. Now the street was empty. Anyone walking by could pause on the sidewalk and stare through the windows of any of the identical houses and watch the occupants going about their lives. (It was after dinner and the woman of the house stood at the kitchen sink in a soiled apron, scrubbing the grease from a skillet, while her husband fixed himself a drink at the basement bar before climbing the steps to the livingroom where his daughter—"isn't it past your bedtime?"—sat on the living room floor cutting pictures of toads and turtles—"she's doing her homework"—from an old National Geographic.) There was a parking space beneath a tree right across from the bar but instead of stopping the car, putting it into reverse and backing into the space, she cruised by, turned the corner and drove around the block: she was losing her nerve. It was one matter to sit at home and daydream about going out alone; actually doing it was a different story. The day after the woman had been raped on the pool table in the bar in Boston the residents of the neighborhood—no doubt a neighborhood much like this one—had bulldozed the building ("how could something like this happen here?"), and a coalition of women's groups had staged a candlelight protest outside the courthouse where the suspects were being held. If her main purpose was to meet someone she was better off going to one of the bars along upper First Avenue in Manhattan which single people frequented with the sole purpose of finding a partner for the night. ("But I'm not single," she reminded herself, "I'm a married woman with kids.")

She came around the block a second time, stopped, eased into the space—Joe always ridiculed her parking technique—rolled up the windows and slipped a sweater over her bare arms. The dress she'd chosen accentuated her breasts (in a way that would have met with Joe's approval) and extended modestly a few inches below her knees, so when she crossed her legs only the lower part of her calves were visible. (She had skirts and dresses in her closet which were shorter but she didn't want to be too obvious.) Her brown hair was combed straight back, reaching mid-way between her shoulders an'd waist, and she'd parted it in the center (rather than off to one side) to give her face symmetry. She didn't want to think that someone's interest in her could be so determined by her appearance but thinking like that was a way of encouraging a defeatist attitude (if she were truly looking for someone to sleep with, and nothing more, there was no reason why she shouldn't make herself as attractive as possible). She wondered what Frank—Frank, of all people—would think if he knew what she was doing. He'd called her a few times over the last few weeks but they hadn't seen each other since the morning he arrived at her house with the news, no surprise to anyone, really, that Gina was having an affair. She'd always been amazed that Frank had chosen to marry someone who was so obviously attractive to other men and who made no attempt to mute her attractiveness (even though she was now "a married woman"), since he was obviously not the type who could handle a situation where his wife might be unfaithful to him. To her mind, he was as unsuited to playing the role of Gina's husband as he was to being a detective. ("I hate the sight of blood, it makes me sick," he once confided to her.) Frank needed a woman who would mother him, someone who would be content in taking care of him, and who didn't make many demands. When she expressed her thoughts about Frank and Gina to Joe ("you think you'd be perfect for him, don't you?") he looked askance.

No one stopped what they were doing or stared at her when she entered the bar—not a good omen, but Irene, nonetheless, felt relieved. The men around the pool table and pinball machine in the back were engrossed in their games and at first glance didn't seem the type who would drag her to the pool table and rape her. There was an empty stool at the curve of the bar nearest the door—in fact, the entire section was deserted—and that's where Irene chose to sit. A few couples and an occasional single person occupied the booths along the wall and at the far end of the bar the bartender, a curly-haired man in his mid-twenties, possibly the owner's son, was involved in a conversation with a woman much like herself ("you see, I told you it was safe to come here"). Now that she was here it almost didn't matter whether she met someone or not. She'd dressed up ("you look beautiful," Janice had told her), and driven her car into the night. That was the first step and she congratulated herself for having come this far. Now all she had to do was light a cigarette and ask the bartender for a beer. She fingered the string of blue pearls around her throat, crossed her legs, and caught his eye.

Max waited till the day after his mother's funeral before calling Caroline. He hadn't forgotten her—it had only been twenty-four hours since he'd last seen her—but he hadn't thought about her much during that time and it worried him how easily she'd slipped from the center of his thoughts, as if she were already part of the past, "my year in California." It was easy, as well, to feel he'd never left New York at all, the streets and the feeling in the air were so familiar, he could leave for twenty years and probably still feel this way. Being back in the city was like slipping on a familiar jacket or sweater. He'd spent a year in California feeling self-conscious about his instincts and it was a relief to know there was a place where he could relax, this was his home.

He sat at the kitchen table of the apartment on Henry Street, only a few feet—according to the police—from where his mother had been murdered. It was 1 p.m., 10 California time. By now, Caroline would be finished with her yoga exercises. He imagined her in the kitchen of the house across the continent—her black leotard, the island of freckles on her bare shoulder—lighting a flame under a pot on the stove, brewing morning tea. After she lit the stove she placed the used match in a box on the counter (Caroline had a hard time disposing of anything; even a wooden match might come in handy someday) and opened the door of the cupboard.

If anyone was spying on Max, through the keyhole or window, they'd think he was doing nothing but staring into space, and it was true, being back in his old apartment put him in a state of mind similar to what people call a "brown study"—a waking state of abstraction in which one doesn't know what one's thinking. Occasionally an object in the apartment would catch his attention, the calendar on the inside door of the cupboard above the stove, for instance, held in place by a blue thumbtack, the top part of the calendar a child's drawing in bright colors of buildings, sky, people and clouds, with a flying saucer in one corner. The saucer, looming over the city, looked like the body of a weird spider, an oval with a lot of prickly thorns. The table was the same table where he'd sat with his parents, and then, after his father died, alone with his mother. If he and his mother didn't exactly make animated conversation, at least they took pleasure in what they were eating. A person, someone he didn't know, or so he assumed, had walked through the door and strangled her.

Before getting into bed the night before he'd positioned a pint of Jack Daniels on the bedside table, just in case he had trouble sleeping. He'd surprised himself by falling asleep almost immediately, and woke, ten hours later, feeling slothful, as if he could sleep ten hours more, that he deserved sleep, his heart and mind needed a rest. He didn't want to waste any of his pills when he knew he might need them during the day and at this point he wasn't sure where he could get more if he ran out. He wasn't even sure how long he was going to stay in the city and part of the reason he was anxious to talk to Caroline was to find out what she was thinking—was there any reason he shouldn't return? He would know, from hearing her voice, whether she truly wanted him to come back.

He could instruct his uncle to sell the building, clean out his mother's apartment, pack up all his old books and papers and ship them out to California, then fly back himself, assuming the cops didn't need him. That was one possibility. And he hadn't even needed the bottle of whiskey: there it was, unopened, on the table near the bed. His old mahogany table with the bad leg that he would prop up by wedging a thin paperback beneath it (the same book, a copy of Shakespeare's *Sonnets*, was still there), the bed the same narrow monk's bed he'd slept in all through childhood and adolescence. He didn't need to get drunk to close his eyes and hear, in his mind, the sound of his parents bickering, but rather to drown them out, that chorus of gloomy voices. The cupboard and all the drawers were cluttered with the same objects and utensils he'd lived with as a child. His mother, like Caroline, was compulsive about saving things; just because something was old didn't mean it wasn't useful).

There'd been a calendar on the inside door of the cupboard for as long as Max could remember. Every year banks, meat markets, and insurance agencies gave them out free to steady customers. One year Max had given his mother a calendar for her birthday, one with photographs of the Lower East Side at the turn of the century, but for some reason she never tacked it in the place of prominence on the cupboard door. Once he started sifting through her things he'd probably find it in a carton at the bottom of the bedroom closet.

It was time to go to the bathroom and wash up for dinner. Time to set the table. Time to go into his room, sit at his desk, pretend to study. It might be said that if your parents give you a great deal of attention when you're very young, it doesn't matter what their attitude is towards you when you're older. Now that his mother was dead, Max wished he could feel more forgiving toward his father, but it was hard not to blame him for everything that had gone wrong. Max used his father as a scapegoat for his own inability to finish things he'd begun, as if procrastination and self-doubt were inherited traits. "At least," it might be said for him, "he didn't desert us," as other fathers had done to other families, but that was kind of a negative defense, and who knows, it might have been better for all of them if he had left, dropped out of their lives forever. One accepts the possibility that a phone call might bring bad news, disrupting the otherwise peaceful rhythm of one day passing complacently into the next, no one worrying whether they were drunk or sober as long as they knew there was a bed to sleep in and a person, the same person every night, to share their miseries. After awhile, though, it's sickening to contemplate possibilities. If you don't have a solid base on which to stand the first strong wind of autumn will blow you away like a discolored leaf, leave you abandoned to the venom of the even stronger winds of winter, stormclouds filling the sky like a migraine for which there's no cure but the deft fingers of a professional masseuse who is also your lover.

* * *

At any moment he could remove the gun from his shoulder holster, press the cold barrel to the side of his head, wink at himself one last time in the bathroom mirror, and pull the trigger. What stopped him from even contemplating suicide was the thought that no one would truly care. Maybe Joe Hopper and some of the other guys would express feelings of guilt. They'd noticed something was wrong and had assumed it wasn't their business. "He was always acting a little strange" "Not exactly one of the boys" "Why he ever became a cop is beyond me" "A loner, except for Joe I don't think he had any friends" "I never liked the guy much but I'm sorry he died." It wouldn't be the first instance of a cop taking his own life with a weapon he'd been trained to use in defense of other people. It was a point of honor—at least this is what he'd been taught—not to let other people know you needed help (especially the people you worked with, who would take it as a sign of weakness). If you couldn't take care of your personal life without involving other people, then you might as well kill yourself. It was also important never to confuse your personal problems with your work as a cop. "But I never wanted to be a cop to begin with," you might say. Sometimes, when he walked down the street, he stared intently into the faces of the people he passed, in the hope of finding some indication that beneath their facades they were suffering—even if not for the same reasons—as much as he. Frank was only thirty; one looked to chronology for support. If he didn't like being a detective there was still time to do something else. (If when he was younger and people had asked him what he wanted to be when he grew up he had said "I want to be a cop—just like daddy" it was only to please his parents, but realizing that now only added to his confusion.)

Just because he'd never sat down and thought about "an alternative vocation," as guidance counselors might call it, that was no reason for him to assume he had nothing to do, or that the end of the sentence that began "I want ... " just trailed off, a blank space, a blinking star, the ripple at the bottom of a well. "Where's Gina? I thought you said she was coming."

He entered the apartment to the shouts of his nieces and nephews, who greeted him in the hope that he'd brought them a new toy. When they realized he'd arrived empty-handed they lost interest in him and returned to the broken toys spread out over the living room floor. Frank's parents had somehow accumulated the toys over the years and they brought out those dolls and racing cars and miniature dump trucks to amuse their grandchildren once a month. As always, the women of the family—Frank's mother, his sister and sister-in-law— were in the kitchen ("I think I used too much garlic" "Did someone come in?"), while the men sat like zombies in front of the TV (there was more than one television in the apartment but the. one with the best reception was in Frank's old bedroom), engrossed in a sporting event on which they'd bet modest sums of money. There was no chance that Frank could sit down with any of these people and tell him or her what was on his mind, nor would any of them—if they were attentive enough to observe that something was bothering him—initiate such a conversation.

Gina's no-show wasn't a cause for alarm, though Frank knew his mother would be secretly insulted, and consider her daughter-in-law's absence ("she didn't even call!")

a breach of etiquette, Frank had been the last of the children to get married and it was too bad he hadn't chosen someone who was willing to make even the minimum effort to get along with his family. If she thought she was too good for them—well, she should check out her own family, they were certainly nothing to write home about. Frank and Gina's parents had made it clear, early on, that just because their children had found enough in common to want to spend their lives together, it didn't mean they had to go out of their way to socialize. "I didn't marry your mother and father, I married you." Frank could argue, though he didn't really try, that one afternoon a month spent with his family wasn't too much to ask, and that he himself had gone out of his way to be civil to Gina's family. He could honestly say, in fact, that he liked being with them, especially her brother Ted. He'd been tempted to call his parents and tell them he wasn't going to come; he could lie to them, invent an illness that might actually be half-true, since he was sick, sick at heart, and was barely capable of making the type of conversation necessary to get through an afternoon with the family: these people were his relatives, his blood relations, but he had ceased feeling any real kinship, they might as well be strangers he was passing on the street, even his brother-in-law (also a policeman) seemed more a part of the family than he himself did and the only way Gina would ever really be accepted was if she had a baby—why did they bother getting married if they weren't going to have kids?

"Hey Frank, how's it going?" was as much as any one of them could say. "Pull up a chair."

It was another languid afternoon at the end of the heat wave that had begun in mid-May. At least everyone hoped it was drawing to an end. The crime rate tended to soar once the warm weather set it. Tempers flared under the pressures of being unemployed; simple domestic quarrels escalated into mass murders. There was nothing to do to relieve the tedium except take the subway out to Coney Island or Manhattan Beach and catch the breeze blowing in off the ocean (but some people didn't even have enough money to do that).

Frank's father, in a white T-shirt and baggy trousers, hadn't even bothered to shave for the occasion—though it was hardly that, in the formal sense, just a family get together. "It's my house," he'd insist, "and I can wear what I fucking want." Since his retirement from the police force two years before, and despite his wife's admonishments, he refused to take any interest in his physical appearance. He was literally caving in: head sinking into neck, neck into shoulders, shoulders into chest. Staying home all day ("you should get some exercise") was making him crazy. It was even crazier that all four men in the room were cops, or had been cops, and that this was supposed to create a feeling of camaraderie that enabled them to occupy the same space once a month without questioning what one or the other of them was doing with his life. As Frank's father leaned forward to tip the ash from his Chesterfield into an empty beer can, Frank noticed that the older man's beard and hair (once black with a streak of white) were almost totally gray. Frank didn't understand why his brother and brother-in-law didn't see that his father was a mirror image of what they'd become if they weren't careful, and that it was hardly an image anyone in his right mind would aspire to. "If I just went along with everything without questioning what I was doing then I probably wouldn't care either." It was the questioning that created the conflict. It was Gina, his adulterous wife, who had put these thoughts into his head, or brought them to the surface. When he saw his family through her eyes, as he'd been forced to do, he knew she was right for not wanting to come here. "All they ever talk about is babies and food," she'd complain as they drove home through late Sunday traffic after visiting his family. He wasn't responsible for his family but he didn't want to be put in a position where he had to defend them either.

For the first time in a month he realized how much he missed her— "if the Celtics don't win by 11 I'm out $50," his brother-in-law said to no one in particular—and how much her presence here made these afternoons bearable. What difference did it make if she slept with someone else? It was over, she'd told him as much, it wouldn't happen again. There was still time for him to say "let's forget it" and start anew. She was leaving it up to him, giving him the chance to show his generosity—the part of him that wasn't a cop with a rigid sense of honor about the way things should be. He imagined her sitting in her blue and white nightgown, the one with the flowers embroidered around the collar, at the kitchen table—it was mid-afternoon and she hadn't even bothered to get dressed—staring dumbly through a space between the curtains at the empty street.

"I've met your parents and you're not like them at all. Thank God!"

* * *

Sally didn't say much until after they made love but the silence had an inverted glow, like the reflection of the moon in an abandoned well. They'd cling to one another as if they were clawing the damp walls, slipping a little farther into the darkness each time they moved. (Maybe the first time people sleep together is the only time it's possible for them to disappear completely into one another's skin, and maybe this conveys a knowledge that goes beyond words.) For a moment Rosemary had the precarious feeling Sally was going to leap from the bed, pull her dress over her head ("would you zip me up?") and leave without saying anything. (The flicker of a memory of being in bed with someone else, a man, and having nothing to say to him after they'd made love— looking across the pillow into the face of a complete stranger—flashed through Rosemary's mind.) Instead, and to her relief, Sally leaned back against the pillows, stacking them carefully so her head didn't touch the wall, and closed her eyes.

She had been anticipating a quiet night at home, and had been caught unawares when Sally called and said she wanted to visit, not meet for a drink or for dinner but come right to her apartment. "I'll be there in ten minutes."

"Does Maureen know?" she felt like saying, but it was only after making love that Maureen's name was mentioned.

As soon as she asked the question Rosemary knew she'd made a mistake.

"Hand me my pocketbook, will you," annoyed, "I want a cigarette." It was a way of changing the subject or postponing it—who wants to talk about *her*?—till some other time.

Rosemary leaned backwards, rolling over onto her stomach, and fumbled along the floor near the side of the bed.

"Do you remember where you put it?"

"Maybe on the chair over there. Oh forget it, I don't want to smoke anyway."

"Do you want anything? A drink?" Rosemary didn't trust her own voice.

"Some water maybe, but later, don't move. My husband always liked to jump up right after we fucked. It was either a smoke or a beer, anything to get out of bed. Sometimes, right away, he'd go to the bathroom. It didn't matter whether I'd come or not. As soon as he had his fun, sex—if you could call it that—was over."

"How long were you married?"

"If I'm going to tell you the story of my marriage I will need a cigarette. A whole pack—and a beer."

"No beer, I'm afraid. Let me get dressed and go down."

"It's not worth it."

"Well, I want one and you said you wanted one and there's a bodega on the corner that stays open late. I'll be back in five minutes."

"I guess you do want to get out of bed."

"You keep saying you want things but when I offer to get them for you you act insulted."

Rosemary was tempted to bury her head between Sally's legs and make love to her again. If she resisted, or wasn't in the mood, so much the better. She didn't understand why she seemed so anxious to bicker, and ruin what had been a pleasant evening, though "pleasant" was hardly the word. It was too hot to fight. In the interval between the time Sally called and the time she arrived Rosemary had managed to straighten things up a bit, she'd even carried all the empty beer cans and black plastic bags of garbage into the street and dumped them into the trashcan out front, she'd sat on the side of the bed brushing her hair, wondering what the apartment looked like through the eyes of a person seeing it for the first time. But when Sally arrived it was as if the apartment was nothing more than a faded backdrop to some play that had folded after one performance, they could have been anywhere ("I've been thinking of you ever since the other night," was all Sally said as they helped one another undress).

Rosemary couldn't help remembering the time, only a few days before, when she'd thought of Sally as her adversary, and how miraculous it was that everything could change so rapidly.

"I have to go to the bathroom." Finally, it was Sally who would get out of bed first.

Rosemary lay on her back, knees raised, her arm beneath her head, and when Sally returned, the shadow of her body cutting across her own, she pulled her down, playfully, so that they were lying directly on top of one another, face to face, legs intertwined. She was anxious to tell Sally that she was only the second woman she'd ever made love to, that Maureen had been her only previous female lover (either way it meant the same thing), but she was frightened to bring up the subject. The past—at least the immediate past—could wait. Part of her thought they should be grateful to Maureen for introducing them and that there was no reason why they couldn't talk about anything—not only Maureen, but Sally's husband, all the lovers they'd ever had, any subject at all—with the same lack of inhibition with which they'd just made love.

"When will I see you again?"

"Why don't you stay over? You can if you want."

"Maybe tomorrow night—if I can see you tomorrow. Why don't you buy some food and we'll make dinner together here."

Rosemary propped herself on one elbow and watched Sally put on her clothes. It was after 1 o'clock and she couldn't understand why she didn't want to sleep over but the last thing she wanted to do was argue about anything. If getting along with another person meant acquiescing to their needs, even if their needs seemed irrational at times, that was okay with her. If I were in her position I might not want to sleep over either. I'd have to get up and go to work the next day and I'd want to wake up in my own place, shower, change my clothes, feed the cat, whatever. She remembered all the nights when she'd put her own feelings aside and stayed over at Maureen's apartment rather than arguing with her about where they should go. "But you don't even have a shower," Maureen—who had a bad back as well, and complained bitterly about the state of Rosemary's mattress—would say, and it was true, Maureen's apartment was almost luxurious compared to her own. Sex often gives one of the partners the feeling he or she has access to some secret or power over the other person, and that this gives them license to dictate to the other about what they should do. One could be aggressive sexually while being a passive person about everything else. ("I hate wearing dresses," Sally said, "but this is the coolest thing I own.") The ideal situation would be to tell your lover, either by words or signals, exactly what he or she should do to give you pleasure.

The next night when Sally arrived at the apartment the two women embraced on the threshold and with their arms around each other walked to the bed and undressed. Dinner could wait.

"I've been thinking about doing this all day," Sally said.

* * *

When Mickey returned home Benny was leaning over the stove, staring into a saucepan of boiling water.

"The cops were here," she said, not looking up at him.

She turned off the gas, emptied the contents of the pan into the mug on the counter, and carried it between her palms to the kitchen table. It was almost 90 degrees outside, hotter indoors, and the last thing she wanted was something hot to drink; the only reason to drink coffee was the hope that it would wake her up. The effect of the pill she'd taken a few hours earlier was wearing off and she knew if she drank a beer—there was a sixpack of Millers on the bottom shelf of the icebox—she'd either get sick or fall asleep. The visit from the police had unnerved her, to say the least.

"They asked if we knew anything about the old woman who was murdered a few days ago. Remember Pedro telling us the cops were asking people questions in the park? Well, someone must have given them our address."

"What did you say?"

"They asked where you were and I didn't lie or anything, I said you'd gone out and I didn't know when you'd be back. That's the truth, isn't it? They said I should tell you they were here and that they would try to get in touch with you later. Or if you knew anything about it you should get in touch with them. They left their phone number. I told them that as far as I could remember you were home with me the night it happened"—for a moment Benny wasn't sure whether this was true— "that's right, isn't it?"

She stirred the coffee with a spoon, wishing her electric coffee pot was working so she could make herself some iced coffee, that was her favorite hot-weather drink. She could hear Mickey in the bathroom, washing down his pills with tapwater. At least that's what she assumed he was doing. Since quitting her job she noticed that Mickey was more private and less generous about his pills. Now that they had less money the number of pills that entered the house were fewer, and Mickey didn't like to think Benny needed them as much as he did. He put her in the awkward position of having to ask if he scored any pills, and occasionally he lied to her and told her he had none when in fact he had managed to score maybe half a dozen, enough to get one person through a day, nothing more.

He emerged from the bathroom shirtless, sweat dripping from his shoulders and arms. The hair on his chest was shiny with moisture, as if he'd just taken a long swim. Benny wished they could go to the beach someday, take the train to Coney Island or the Rockaways or even Jones, just to cool off and get away from everything for awhile, break their normal routine which seemed to be centered so obsessively on money and drugs. As she sipped her coffee Mickey went and stood by the window and stared across the air shaft at the windows of the neighboring apartments. There was a high school girl who sometimes dressed and undressed in front of her window and Mickey would kneel at the ledge and watch her, but today her apartment was dark. As he looked out the window he drummed on the sill with his fist. He hadn't spoken more than a few words to her since the night he'd gone out with Pedro, presumably looking for pills, the same night—according to the cops who just visited—the old woman on Henry Street was murdered. There'd been other periods of time in their life together when he didn't say much, when it seemed like there was no need for either of them to say anything, but usually those were times when there were no pills around at all, and no money to get them even if they were available. But this was different. For a change, there didn't seem to be a lack of either money or pills. He went to the icebox, helped himself to a can of beer, flipped back the lid with the edge of his fingernail, swallowed, sat down in the chair opposite her, then stood up again, leaving the beer on the table, and stomped to the bedroom, muttering under his breath in Spanish.

"You don't think I know anything about the murder, do you?"

All she had to do was sit there, stir her coffee till it was cool enough to drink, and he'd tell het everything presuming there was something to tell. It was true that the cops hadn't acted as if the visit was anything but simple routine. Mickey's name was probably on a list of everyone who hung around the park—was that how the cops worked? did such a list exist?—and it was part of their job to question everyone on the list. It was just a job. The two men who entered her apartment—the tall thin one with the hollow rings beneath his eyes who didn't say a single word all the time they were there and the stocky, middle-aged stereotype of what she imagined every cop was like, who never shut up and who seemed as nervous, and jittery, in his way, as Mickey—didn't seem to have any personal interest in either Mickey or herself. She'd noticed that the tall silent one had been staring at her in an odd way and she'd instinctively pulled her skirt over her knees and fingered the buttons on her blouse as if perhaps one were missing, his attention indicative of some weird undercurrent of perversity (as if she didn't have enough of that already in her life), and as if the questions they were asking really implied something else. It was odd, as well, to be in the apartment with two strange men who were perhaps only posing as cops and there was no denying that she'd seen the thin one's expression on the faces of other men in other situations. Mostly they both appeared to be biding their time, repeating the same questions in different variations, in the hope that Mickey, the person they really wanted to talk to, would suddenly return.

Finally the stocky one consulted his wristwatch. "Tell Miguel to call us, OK?"

The night after the morning when the old woman was supposedly murdered Benny woke up to go the the bathroom for a drink of water and when she returned to the bed Mickey was lying on his stomach, bathed in sweat, moaning into his pillow. She tried to comfort him by waking him from what was obviously a bad dream but he just pushed her hand aside as if comfort was the last thing he wanted. Someone in the apartment above them was playing the radio and she lay in bed listening to the music, unable to fall back to sleep. Occasionally Mickey would pound the pillow with his fist, and curse—she couldn't tell whether he was asleep or awake—but his head was turned away from her and if he said something else she couldn't hear.

He was in the shower for about fifteen minutes and this time he emerged from the bathroom with a yellow towel wrapped around his waist. He took another sip from the can of beer, looking at Benny—still sitting at the table, immobile, staring at the now empty cup of coffee—as if she were a stick of furniture, or a stone. He'd slicked his wet hair back from his forehead and for a moment resembled a younger version of himself, the person Benny had fallen in love with in the hallway of their high school years before.

"Do you want to go to the movies?"

"With what money?"

"I have some money. I told you a few days ago I had some money, remember?"

"Where did you get it?"

"Where do I ever get it? How come all the questions?"

So it was true, he did know something about the murder. You can't live with a person for more than a year without knowing when they're lying or telling the truth. The visit from the cops hadn't been routine at all. They wouldn't be wasting their time if they didn't suspect that he knew something. ("Suspect" was the key word. You could suspect someone of something but that didn't mean the person was guilty. But if you were a suspect it meant something more than just knowing about the crime.)

Benny couldn't deny that the night or morning of the murder Mickey had been out of the apartment. If she were to tell the cops he was with her, as she had in fact told them, she was lying. He had left with Pedro at 4 a.m.—she remembered hearing their voices, and the line of light beneath the kitchen door—and had returned to the apartment after ten the next morning. She could see the gold dials of the clock glowing in the dark.

"So if you don't want to go to the movies what do you want to do? I'm sick of sitting around this place doing nothing."

It was hard to get used to the idea that the man she lived with was a murderer, someone "wanted" by the police. If in fact he was the murderer. She imagined herself sitting in a bare room in the police station, a naked lightbulb dangling from a thread of wire, surrounded by the two cops who'd visited her that afternoon, the thin one who never said anything (but who in his own way fit the profile of someone capable of committing a murder) and the stocky, red-faced man who never stopped talking. "But you said he left the house at 4 a.m. and didn't return till some time the next morning. That means he wasn't with you when the murder was committed. Is that correct?"

They would wear her down till she told them everything, that yes, it was true, he went out, he wasn't there. Cops had methods of extracting confessions too devious to even contemplate. Perhaps the information she was giving them wasn't even necessary except to corroborate what Mickey had already told them. They were trying to test her, they were playing games. In another room in the same police station Mickey had confessed everything. How the life of the poor old woman had melted away beneath his hands.

She rinsed out the cup in the kitchen sink and set it on the drainboard. She had the feeling some new phase of their life was beginning—or perhaps it was only her own life, separate from Mickey, that she was thinking about now. The person thinking these thoughts was someone new; the image she'd always held sacred in her mind—two people, herself and Mickey, walking across a field in the country, arms around each other, inseparable—had faded away. Possibly a few hours in an air-conditioned movie theater would be a good distraction for both of them—even though the visit from the cops made life feel more like a movie than any movie could possibly be. When they first started living together they'd spent at least half their time going to movies, and doing that now would be one way of reconstructing some past feeling of camaraderie and love. Mickey was at the door, ready to go, waiting for her, tapping his feet. She felt like they were in a boat that had capsized out at sea—a picture of bodies flailing as the waves washed over them passed through her mind—and if she didn't do something quick they'd both go under.

It was a ten minute walk from her house to the house of her parents, where she had lived until she moved in with Frank, and Gina stretched it out—it was too hot to rush and no one was expecting her—by stopping at the corner grocery for a Coke. The white-haired man behind the counter, whom she'd known since childhood ("well, look who's here") asked her, as he always did, how her husband was doing.

"He's working on the Henry Street murder—did you hear about it?"

The murder of the woman on Henry Street wasn't exactly front-page news and the old man shook his tousled head, astonished that this young woman, whom he still remembered as a little girl in pigtails clinging to her mother's arm, and whom he'd offered hard candy whenever she came into the store, would bother telling him anything so specific about what her husband was up to. Even Gina was. surprised that she'd blurted out this fragment of information; normally, all she would have answered was "he's fine" or "very busy." If she'd been asked, however, to elaborate on the particular case he was working on she would have been unable to, since all she knew was what she'd overheard Frank talking about, one night on the phone—he must have been discussing it with Joe, but Gina didn't even know that for certain.

As she left the store she noticed the young Spanish stock clerk, unloading cartons of pet food in the back, pause in his work and stare at her legs. Gina had once come to the store when the old man wasn't there and the stock clerk had rung up her order. "Do you live in the neighborhood?" he'd asked, trying to make conversation. His English was perfect, but the question seemed one she should be asking him since there were so few Spanish families in the neighborhood, where does he think I live, Brooklyn? There was something wild about his appearance and Gina felt she was in the presence of a caged bird, some exotic strain. She focused on the veins in his arms and the point where they disappeared under the sleeves of his white T-shirt and the way the shirt gripped his chest as he placed each object in the brown paper bag. Then he handed her the groceries with a big smile, as if fitting the objects into the bag was some major accomplishment for which he'd be rewarded by nothing less than a kiss on the cheek.

Since the night Eric brought his wife into bed with them (or tried to) Gina hadn't slept with anyone. Her visit from Joe had seemed an indication of what life might be like as a single person, free to go to bed with whoever she wanted. But of course she wasn't single, just biding her time till Frank decided what he was going to do, ask for a divorce or forgive her and start anew. The longer it took him to make up his mind the less Gina cared. It was obvious that he was content to prolong this state of tension between them indefinitely. Though she missed making love to someone—not to mention falling asleep in the same bed with another body close by—Frank hadn't exactly been the ideal, or most adventuresome lover. (The second time they made love she asked him, in a way she hoped wouldn't sound insulting or imply that his ability as a lover was inadequate, how many women he'd gone to bed with before her, and without hesitating he'd answered "you're the third.") Part of her wished she'd stayed around to see what sleeping with Eric and his wife was like, if only to have the experience to hold up in comparison to other experiences, past and present. She wasn't sure that she had the strength to tell her parents she and Frank were breaking up—getting divorced wasn't part of the repertoire of possible things that could happen to someone they knew, much less their daughter—if that was what they were doing. She still loved Frank, in a way, loved the idea (growing more nebulous as time went by) of things continuing the way they were before, but no longer trusted herself, and couldn't be sure, if they did get back together again, another Eric wouldn't appear. (In this sense, she was beginning to remind herself of the nymphomaniac played by Lee Remick in the movie *The Detective*, which she and Frank had watched one night on TV.) She'd had it with all the lies and subterfuge. She couldn't imagine living in the house in the Bronx without Frank and carrying on affairs with all the local stock clerks and gas station attendants, though she couldn't deny a stir of feeling at the thought of being in bed with the young man in the grocery. (In response to his question about whether she lived in the neighborhood she might have written her address on a piece of paper and told him to "come by" when he was through with work, if only to see the expression on his face.)

She was wearing a pair of yellow running shorts with a green stripe down the side, a blue short-sleeved blouse, no bra or underpants, and a pair of yellow high-heeled shoes. When she crossed the street the man in the cab of the truck waiting for the light to change honked his horn, but she didn't look back. At one time in her life she might have turned to him and given him the finger, but now it flattered her and gave her reassurance to know there still were people who were attracted to her. Every time she passed a man on the street she was tempted to turn around to see if he was watching her. She'd never worn the shoes before—she'd always had a problem with high heels—and was conscious that she was walking in a different way, rolling her hips slowly and languidly to keep her balance, as if she were just cruising the street, sipping her Coke from a straw, with nowhere to go.

She wondered what Joe was doing, and about her first boyfriend, Dick Miller, who had died in an auto accident about a year ago. She stopped at the window of a pet store that had been in the neighborhood since she was a kid and stared at her reflection, brushing the hair from her eyes. There was a parrot in a cage in the window, a big empty tropical fish tank, and a few rabbits eating tiny scraps of lettuce in a corner. As a kid she'd had, at various times, a parakeet, goldfish, and a gerbil, but no matter how conscientious she was about feeding them they always died. She remembered a summer when she was eleven; her parents had rented a small cabin on a lake in upstate New York, and her father had tried to teach her how to fish from the end of the dock. They didn't use a fishing pole; just a stick with a string, a hook with a piece of meat at the end. There was a school of small fish that lived beneath the dock. Every time she caught one her father would remove the hook but instead of watching him do it she closed her eyes. Then he would throw the wounded fish back in the water. There'd always be a lot of dead fish floating on the surface and Gina, who loved to swim, began to hate going into the water, for fear one of the dead fish might brush against her skin. After a storm, the shore would be littered with the swollen bodies of the dead fish. They would stay there for days, rotting in the sun, till the caretaker of the docks, a man named Tobey, who had no teeth and who was often drunk, swept them into an old oil barrel and carted them away.

She remembered how the two men used to stand at the edge of the dock talking while she lay stretched out on a towel nearby. Sometimes she sat at the edge of the dock writing a letter to her best friend in the city, the margins of the note paper embroidered with wreaths of tiny flowers. As she dangled her feet in the water the fish beneath the dock would nibble at her toes. Every time Tobey came down to the lake he touched her shoulder with his huge furry hand. "How's it going today, Gina?" When they went for a drive there were always a lot of dead animals down the center and along the side of the road: raccoons, skunks, chipmunks, squirrels. Her father would drive right over the bodies. At night before going to sleep she listened to the katydids and the frogs, and in the morning to the birds who lived in the branches of the huge pine trees surrounding the cabin. She remembered Tobey coming to the cabin when her parents weren't home, the touch of his hand on her shoulder like a dead fish. After he left she went to the bathroom and washed the place on her shoulder where he had touched her. In the evening, after dinner, she would go down to the dock, alone, and feed breadcrumbs to the fish, lying flat on her stomach along the wooden boards. She could still see the wounded fish squirming in her father's hands. "If you don't watch closely," he would say, "you'll never learn."

* * *

Sept. 8. Went to Jones Beach. Tried to make love under a blanket—or wanted to—but there were too many people around. Sonia, in her competitive way, swam out farther than I did, and kept waving to me to follow her. I like standing in the shallows and diving into the waves, like I used to do when I was a kid. Then back home on the bus and subway—it took over two hours—covered with sand. Told Sonia I was going to drop out of school for a term so I could get a job and some money to find my own apartment, but she didn't seem very encouraging. Whenever I begin talking about the future she presses her finger to my lips as if she doesn't want to hear anything about it. Thought of going to the movies but we were both too tired so decided to take a bath and stay home. Beer at the beach, wine in bed. Sonia told me about her childhood—sometimes she repeats the same stories but I don't mind hearing—and a little about her marriage. She interrupts herself and asks me if I'm really interested. Somehow she assumes that she won't be able to have any kids, though she doesn't know for sure. She confessed that what attracted her to me initially was my inexperience (in bed), which hurt my feelings a bit, as if we were just playing roles (student and teacher). We talked about ambition and whether it was important to want to be anything or whether it was enough just to live from day to day. I said that not wanting to be anything was easier, but possibly more frustrating. Doesn't everyone want to be something? Maybe most people, like my father, just succumb to the randomness of everything, never questioning whether they like what they're doing or not. The responsibility of earning money to support your family makes people end up doing things they don't really care about—but that explanation seems too simple in a way. Sonia says that only people from the middle classes have the luxury of being able to dream about doing something. We talked about how both the man and the woman had to shoulder the responsibility of supporting the household, and that merely working for a living—this is one of the few things we agree upon—without any goals (or pleasure) was like being in prison. Somehow her apartment seems conducive to such conversations.

When I told Sonia I was keeping this journal she was shocked, not because I was writing about her, but because she was certain that my mother was reading it. She started beating on my chest—we were lying in bed—and shouting "You fool, you fool!"—half-playfully, but I knew she was serious. I think the fact that I'm her landlady's son makes Sonia feel more committed to our relationship than she would be otherwise (if she were to break up with me I might turn my mother against her), though maybe I'm underestimating everything as a way of protecting myself. Made plans to meet and see *Tokyo Story* tomorrow night when she gets back from work, so I imagine we'll talk more about all this. (Oddly, when I just came home—2 a.m.—my mother was sitting in the living room waiting up for me. At first I didn't see her because the lights were off but just as I was about to go to my room a car went by and I saw her in the headlights as it passed our window. I asked her what she was doing but she didn't answer which makes me think maybe Sonia is right and she has been reading this journal.)

Sept. 9. When we came back from the movies I expected to go upstairs with Sonia but she said "no, not tonight," and when I asked her why she said "I'm tired." We stopped at the coffeeshop on the corner of Canal and East Broadway and talked for awhile at the counter. (The man who works there knows us by now and just brings us our two coffees without saying anything.) Sonia went upstairs first—just in case my mother was watching at the window—and I drank another cup, though I realize drinking coffee just makes it harder than usual to fall asleep, and brooded. I shouldn't feel sexually frustrated, but I do, and in my thoughts—whcn Sonia left me—1 was unfaithful to her almost immediately, staring at the two young women across the counter and then, when they left the restaurant, turning to watch them as they walked out. (The man behind the counter, old enough to be my father, was watching them too, and when they were gone he winked at me, conspiratorially, and smiled.) I always feel a sense of superiority when I see men leer at women sexually, even though I'm guilty of it too. Sometimes Sonia teases me and makes me wonder if perhaps the difference in our ages is too much for her. In the movies I wanted to hold hands but it was obvious that she didn't, and when I put my arm around her shoulder she didn't respond, or lean back against me. "Will I see you tomorrow?" I asked as we were walking home. There are times, when we're together, when I know that she's not really with me, that she's thinking about something else which for some reason (and no matter how often I ask her "what are you thinking?") she won't tell me, and tonight was one of those times. All the subterfuge surrounding our relationship makes me feel (from her point of view) that I am too young for her, and that all this secrecy is the last thing she needs, another dead end. The movie—which Sonia had already seen—was very slow moving, but beautiful. I think it made Sonia a little homesick for Tokyo, where she still has relatives.

When I came home, finally, the door of my parents' bedroom was closed. Earlier, my mother acted as if nothing had happened the night before—while in fact nothing did. It's sad that no one in this household can speak openly, including myself. My father seems oblivious to everything, and is barely able to say "pass the salt" while we're having dinner. (Before and after dinner he sits in his chair in the living room, hidden behind one of the several newspapers he brings home each day.) After dinner I help my mother clear the table—she won't let me wash the dishes—and then go to my room, where I'm sitting now, and contemplate all the things I have to do, while (secretly) all I want to do is go upstairs and be with Sonia.

Sept. 10. Took the subway up to school (first day of classes). Met Sara, who was in my psychology class last year, and we walked up the hill together. We compared schedules and discovered we had another class together this term, introduction to philosophy. Whenever I'm walking alongside a woman I feel tempted to take her hand. It seems unnatural to be in such close proximity without making physical contact. I told her (Sara) that she reminded me of Vivie Warren, the heroine of *Mrs. Warren's Profession* by Shaw, which I just finished reading. She told me about her analyst (a Freudian) whom she goes to twice a week, $50 a session. ("My parents"—she still lives with her parents, apparently, in a big apartment overlooking Central Park West—"are paying for it.") She was wearing a tight black turtleneck sweater, though it wasn't particularly cold, and a red and blue pleated skirt, and as we said goodbye I couldn't help turning and watching her as she walked away. (I wish there was someone at school I could talk to about Sonia—maybe I'm the one who needs an analyst!—but there isn't.)

Sept, 12. I've been calling Sonia every few hours for the last few days but she's either not at home or not answering. I'm sick of all this secrecy. Every time I want to call I have to go outside to the phone on the comer, and each time I leave the house I have to think up a different excuse. Whenever I go I'm tempted to sneak around back and enter the building through the basement, but that still means passing by my parents' apartment. I'm torn between not wanting to hurt my mother and my desire to see Sonia, but I'm beginning to wonder—and I know Sonia feels similarly—whether all this sneaking around is worth it. (Even getting my own apartment would be no real solution, since it would still mean encountering my parents—or at least the possibility of that happening—whenever I visited Sonia.) And as long as I'm still in school there's no chance of getting my own place.

Met Johnny Jerabek in the cafeteria at school and he

invited me to a party at his apartment (Friday night).

Then Sara, who I keep running into, asked me if I was coming to the same party (I didn't know they knew each other). The way she asked made me think it was important to her that I was there. I told her "I don't know" but (as I told JJ) "I would try to make it." At dinner my father actually asked me "how school was going?" Roast beef, mashed potatoes (no gravy), string beans (frozen). My mother asked if I was going to be involved with the drama club, as I was last year, and seemed disappointed when I said "no." (It occurred to me that if I had a girlfriend at school I could use that person as a decoy to continue seeing Sonia. Is it possible to be that manipulative?)

Sept. 13. Until I started seeing Sonia I was always open with my mother about all my girlfriends. But now everything's different; my mother acts like she's my girlfriend, and that I'm being unfaithful to her by seeing Sonia. She certainly seems to go out of her way to make me feel guilty. Every time I leave the house, even if I'm going to school, I know that she thinks I'm going upstairs to see Sonia. This feeling that everything I do is being scrutinized makes me want to defy her even more; at the same time I miss the intimacy between us that now seems like a memory. Perhaps—and maybe this is what getting older means—that part of our life is gone forever.

Called Sonia between classes and we met uptown, at the entrance to Central Park at 59th & 5th. It's always a relief to get out of the neighborhood. Walked west, around the pond, and sat down on a hillside under a tree. She wanted me to tell her, in detail, everything that my mother said, whether she ever mentions her (Sonia) by name, and what the feeling in the household was like. After I finished telling her we sat in silence for a long time, watching the wind blow the ripples across the surface of the pond. She asked me if I'd read the book she loaned me, *Beauty and Sadness*, by Kawabata, and I confessed I hadn't, that I was too busy with schoolwork (which isn't exactly true, I'm just too distracted to read anything). We took the subway downtown together and made tentative plans to meet at the coffeeshop, "just in case." I didn't tell her that I was going to Jerabek's party; at least I think I am.

Sept. 14. I don't think my mother believed me when I told her I was going to the party, but what can I do? I have to go out sometimes. Jerabek lives in the West Nineties, another endless subway ride, and I don't even know why I'm going. The apartment was filled (about 20 people) when I arrived, but I didn't know anyone except Sara and Johnny, though a few faces were familiar to me from the cafeteria at school. Sara didn't know anyone there either and seemed happy to see me. We sat on the couch together, talking (the music was very loud and we had to practically shout at one another), and shared a joint. She was wearing a white silk blouse and a tight black skirt with a small slit up the side. Each time I handed her the joint she gave me a quick smile and once, in the midst of a long, convoluted story about a camping trip she'd taken to Fort Ticonderoga, she placed her hand on my knee as a way of holding my attention. I kept thinking of Sonia and what she was doing and just the thought of her alone in her apartment made me want to go into the next room

and call her or leave the party and return downtown—
who cares what my parents think? It seemed possible to
take any thought and sink into it until it became nothing
but an endless circle, spreading out and contracting at the
same time. Sara asked me if I wanted to dance and as we
stood together in the center of the room she locked her
hands behind my neck and swayed in front of me with
her eyes closed. Then she tilted towards me and buried
her head in my shoulder and we just stood there while
the other dancers circled around us, as oblivious to us as
we were to them. As we danced I slipped my hand under
her blouse and touched her back with my fingers; her response was to press herself even closer to me, I could feel
the pressure of her knee between my legs, a small very
bright light bulb burst into flames in my head....

Later, what seemed like much later, we took a cab
back to her parents' apartment. I'd been to a party there
last year but I'd forgotten how vast it was and I couldn't
help feeling envious as I imagined myself in her place
and what it would be like to live there. "I wanted to make
love to you all of last year but you never seemed interested." She let me put my hand under her skirt but when I
slipped my fingers beneath the seam of her underpants
she pushed me away. "I still want to make love to you,"
she said, "but I can't." She took my hand and led me out
onto the balcony, with its view of the park. "I got into
trouble last year and had to have an abortion during the
summer. That's one of the reasons my parents are sending me to a psychiatrist. I want to make love to you, I
still do, but I can't, I'm frightened—at least not yet." And
then, when I didn't say anything (I was thinking of So-

nia, and the story of her abortion, her marriage, and how she probably won't be able to have children), she turned me around so I was facing her and stared at me intently, holding my face between her cold hands. "You understand, don't you? You're not angry?"

When I came home it was after three in the morning. I found the book by Kawabata that Sonia loaned me and read myself to sleep.

Sept. 15. On the roof with Sonia. She seemed happier than I'd seen her since we went to the beach last week. I was tempted to tell her about the party, but I decided not to, even though (in the past) she'd encouraged me to "go out" (as she puts it) with other women. But I can't imagine confiding to her about Sara, and I know that I'd feel jealous if she were sleeping with anyone else. Later, sitting on the floor of her apartment, drinking brandy, I asked her what she felt when we were making love. Part of me wants to pry into her past: I want to know everything about her old lovers and what they were like. For a change we didn't talk about my mother, though I reassured her by saying I'd found a hiding place for this journal. ("Hi Mom!")

Sept. 17. Sara called when I was out and left a message with my mother. When I returned the call I made sure my mother was in the room, so she could overhear everything I said. Planting the idea that I'm going out with someone from school in my mother's head has had a good effect on her mood, and at dinner she seemed more like her old self, even tried to engage my father in some vague conversation about politics, which is all he ever wants to talk about, though even then it's like pulling teeth.

My mother took the liberty of asking me about Sara and I told her everything: how I'd known her at school last year, how she was in one of my classes now, where she lives, etc. (I hate the idea of using Sara in this way, especially since she's obviously gone through a lot this past year, and I know she's more involved with me than I am with her, but regardless.... The only person I really want to be with is Sonia, in her bed or on the roof or sipping sake on the floor of her apartment.)

Sept. 19. I can't tell my mother that I'm seeing Sonia and now I can't tell Sonia that I'm seeing Sara. And of course, I can never tell Sara about Sonia. Last night met Sara uptown and we went to see *Hiroshima, Mon Amour*, which I'd seen before, and afterwards we went back to her parents' apartment. I think part of my interest in Sara is this apartment: the paintings under glass, the walls lined with bookcases, the balcony, the baby grand piano in the living room, all the objects which—according to Sara—her parents bought on their travels (I've never met her parents but can't imagine them meeting mine, or how Sara would react if she ever visited me on Henry Street). I realize that Sonia's power over men (or over me) is her ability to make me relax, and feel myself, whatever that means, while with Sara I'm always thinking about what to do or say, my next move. "We have to be quiet," placing a finger to her own lips (apparently her parents are sleeping somewhere in the apartment) as she takes my hand and leads me down the hallway to her bedroom. It's possible, for a few moments anyway, to forget about Sonia, forget about the problems with my parents, at least until after we've made love and I suddenly look into the closed eyes of this stranger lying beneath me and can't believe I'm really there: all I want to do is get dressed and leave. I wonder what happened since the last time I was here that made sex possible—maybe she thought if we didn't fuck I'd lose interest, while on the contrary I couldn't care less.

Sept. 20. My mother has been in unusually good spirits recently, but it wasn't till I spoke with Sonia that I realized why. Apparently, my mother offered Sonia a new lease at double what she's paying now. "It means," according to Sonia, "I have to take her to court or move out." We met in the coffeeshop on Canal and she looked terrible, as if she'd been awake all night—and the night before—weeping. "If you move I'm going too." As soon as I said it she started crying, shaking her head, her hair practically falling into her coffeecup as she bent over the counter. I went back to the apartment and confronted my mother, who was washing the dishes and humming contentedly to herself, and asked her if it was true, and how she could do such a thing. My father was sitting in the living room watching television and when I started shouting turned around in his chair and said: "Don't talk to your mother that way," as if I were a child ("go to your room.") Instead I felt like telling him to go fuck himself, but didn't (it all seemed so pointless)—I left the apartment. I wandered around, heading uptown toward Second Avenue, trying to decide what to do: how I would drop out of school and save my money till I could find my own apartment so if Sonia did move out we could continue seeing one another. How I resented my mother for interfering with my life—and how, for whatever reason, she felt she knew what was best for me. When I returned home it was after midnight and my parents were asleep. There was a note on the kitchen table in my mother's handwriting informing me that Sara had called and that I should call her back when I came in, but. of course I didn't.

Sept. 25. Saw Johnny Jerabek at school and he asked if there was something "wrong" with me, and why wasn't I returning Sara's calls. I told him I assumed I'd see her in class and he informed me that she was sick and that she would appreciate it if I called. Why can't people mind their own business? At this point I'm barely capable of getting through the day at school, much less returning home and trying to get any work done. Already I'm falling behind in all my courses. I speak to Sonia every day on the phone: she'd made contact with a lawyer but doesn't have the money to hire him and go to court. According to the lawyer what my mother is doing is illegal and he has no doubt that Sonia will win and is encouraging her to go through with it. Sonia seems to think she'd be better off moving; even if she sticks around things can only get worse. She's talked to a few other tenants in the building and none of them are willing to go to court with her and take her side against my mother. Needless to say, things are tense at home. I try to avoid being around during the dinner hour and when I do come home I go straight to my room. Sara calls once, sometimes twice a night, and seems to imply that she wants me to have dinner with her and her parents—she's still sick, but nothing serious. I begged off with the excuse that I had too much schoolwork to do, and I could sense the disappointment in her voice when we hung up—as if my response indicated some version of her worst fears. Regardless, she keeps calling and invariably ends up chatting with my mother, who once told me she thought Sara sounded like "a nice girl."

Sept. 28. Saw Sara at school—there's no way to avoid seeing her since we're in the same class—and she tried to encourage me to come home with her in the afternoon, cut my other classes, etc. I said it was impossible but promised to see her over the weekend. Jerabek continues to act very self-righteous about it all, though I don't know what his interest is—maybe he wants to sleep with her too?

Sept. 29. A big scene at home. As I was leaving the house my mother asked me where I was going. "Upstairs," I said, not looking at her, and she followed me out the door screaming at me, but I never turned back. There's no reason, now, to hide the fact that I'm seeing Sonia, and it's almost a relief to have everything out in the open. When I came in Sonia was on the phone with a friend who said she could move in with her any time. We sat across the kitchen table from one another—Sonia wearing her white kimono, the one I like best—and stared sadly into space, neither of us saying anything. "I can't take your mother to court," she said, finally, "and she knows it." "But if she takes you to court, and you win...." "It won't happen that way. If I ignore the eviction some federal marshals will come and throw me out into the street. I have to take her to court if I want to stay and I'm not going to." And after another long silence: "Maybe it's better this way. Better for you too." When it was time for me to go she held the door open, standing back in the shadows, and I wondered if this was the last time we'd meet together in this way. I wanted to say: "Let's go up to the roof"—not to make love, but just to be there together again. And then I realized, when she closed the door, that I couldn't simply return to my parents' apartment, not after what had happened. I couldn't face my mother and the claustrophobic feeling of being alone in my room. So I went up to the roof alone and stared out over the city, at the bridges and the cars passing, and the airplanes flying low beneath the clouds, hoping that if I stayed away long enough my mother would be asleep when I returned. But of course she wasn't, she was sitting in the living room again with the lights off, and as I walked past her on my way to my room she said, "How could you do this to me?" more bitter than angry, and in a way I know was intended to make me feel guilty, but "guilt" is the last thing I'm feeling.

Oct. 1. Jerabek called to tell me that Sara is in the hospital. Apparently she overdosed on seconals and left a note implying that her "affair" with me was part of the reason. "I just thought you might want to know, you prick," he said, and hung up.

Oct. 3. Sonia moves out. ...

* * *

Frank unclipped his pen from the pocket of his white cotton shirt and leaned forward over the kitchen table like a schoolboy doing his homework, the point of the pen poised in midair. He'd already written something on the page, maybe a half-hour before, someone's name and address, an apartment number. He'd been in his office at the precinct, the office he shared with Joe, when the call came with the news that another old woman had been found dead in her apartment, right around the corner from the building on Henry Street where only last week… one hesitates to complete the sentence.

When the call came he'd been sitting at his desk, staring into space, sipping from a container of iced coffee. The air conditioning system in the precinct had broken down, no surprise to anyone, and the room, even with the window wide open, was stifling; the cubes in his container of coffee had melted long ago. Frank was daydreaming about Gina—the way she used to wave at him from the driveway every morning when he left the house. Even in the middle of winter, when it was zero degrees or colder, she'd come outside or stand in the doorway while he warmed up the car. She'd put a down jacket on over her nightgown, pull on a pair of suede boots, and walk with him through the banks of snow. If the snow was particularly heavy and he had to shovel it from around the tires or scrape the windshield she'd stand alongside him, hopping from one foot to another. Through the rearview mirror he could see her standing in the driveway as he pulled away, waiting till he was out of sight so she could call up her lover. "He just left, you can come over now." Was that the way it happened?

He'd left the office and now he was in the car, with nothing in the rearview mirror but the junkies and winos perched on the railings around Seward Park, all the old men and shopping-bag ladies displaying their goods on the benches—none of them had licenses but it was department policy not to hassle them—all the prostitutes in their spiked heels and short, tight dresses at the intersection of East Broadway and Canal, girls from another planet with names like Yvette, Ruta, or Sue Ann.

He didn't have to inspect his notebook to know which building he was going to. There was a uniformed policeman talking with a person who was probably the super of the building—middle-aged, Spanish, with a mustache and gray sideburns—standing out front. It was the super who had found the body and who now led Frank up the tenement steps, the uniformed policeman trailing behind.

Frank didn't know enough Spanish to translate what the super was saying. The man kept pointing to the door "puerta, puerta"—trying to convey the fact that it had been open when he found the body. He extended his hands to measure how many inches or feet the door was open, but questioning him further was useless, he just didn't understand, or didn't want to. The cop was no help either—knowing the language of the people in the neighborhood where you worked wasn't a prerequisite for becoming a policeman—and seemed more intent on lighting his cigarette (something was wrong with his lighter and he kept flicking it on and off) than on understanding what the super was trying to say. Frank sighed—he should have known better than to think he'd get help from anyone and wrote down the super's name ("Will you spell that?") in his notebook. He checked his wristwatch, as if the time of day were important, and circled around the woman's body till he reached the window that faced the street, from which he could see his car, parked next to a hydrant out front. Both the super and the policeman hovered around the door—the famous "puerta"—waiting for a signal from Frank (he was the boss, after all) telling them what to do next.

The woman under the sheet—Frank had drawn it away from her body, momentarily—was the same age as Bette Eckstein. Her murder—Frank didn't want to think about it—was still unsolved; in fact, there weren't even any clues worth mentioning. He and Joe had gone around questioning all the woman's friends; what else could they do? Even the informers they usually counted on didn't know anything. From the autopsy they learned that she'd died, not of strangulation or a knife wound, but from a heart attack. Someone had followed her into the apartment as she was returning home from an early morning shopping trip to the local supermarket. The person had approached her from behind, scaring her, and placed his or her hands around her throat. (One advantage of assaulting the elderly is that in most cases a weapon isn't necessary.) According to her doctor, Bette Eckstein was taking medication for a heart condition. Her medicine chest was well-stocked with both prescription and over-the-counter drugs and there was a cigar box on the shelf in her closet with a lot of empty pill containers. Purposefully creating a situation where a person with a heart ailment might become overly excited was a form of homicide, and the fact that there was no weapon involved (no overt intent to harm or disable) didn't make a person less culpable.

The dead woman under the sheet was named Rosa

Rodriguez. She lived alone, and if anything her apartment was neater and sparser than Bette Eckstein's. There was a neatly arranged stack of religious magazines on the coffee table and a laminated portrait of Jesus, in bright colors, on the kitchen wall. Clean dishes in the drainboard and a yellow container of Joy (the same brand of dish detergent Gina used) on the edge of the sink. These facts, however, added up to almost nothing. A religious person (surely she had a family somewhere who would light incense and perform the proper rituals when they learned she was dead) who washed her dishes.

"Did you check out the bedroom?"

He turned to the policeman, who jumped slightly as if Frank's question had broken a train of thought that had nothing to do with where he was. Something about the way he was standing, leaning against the front door, smoking, reminded Frank of an actor in a movie he'd once seen. With his short blonde hair peeking out from beneath his hat and his light blue eyes, he was too good-looking to be a cop. Frank had seen him around the precinct but they'd never spoken. He remembered sitting in a theater not far from where they lived; as the movie began Gina leaned forward and placed her hand on his knee. Then the face of the actor who resembled the cop (or vice versa) appeared on the screen. If Gina were here she would remember his name.

Frank wondered what Rosemary was doing and whether Rosa Rodriguez had any neighbors who might like to invite him in for a cup of coffee. He was tempted to walk across the room and inspect the icebox to see if there was anything cold to drink—a beer (though it was hardly likely that Mrs. Rodriguez was a beer drinker) or a glass of club soda would taste good about now—but he couldn't imagine sitting around drinking while the policeman and the super were still there. There was no question that this life of stumbling around strange apartments searching for clues to why people he didn't know had died or were murdered was a kind of hell, and that most days he felt like he wanted to reach out and strangle someone: his own mother, Gina, a stranger on the street. The thoughts in his head resembled a huge wall fringed with barbed wire. Even if he managed to leap over or circumvent it there was no assurance that there weren't a pack of wild dogs waiting to pounce on him on the other side. But to think so much about oneself and one's problems—here, in this world, where people were dropping like flies—seemed self-indulgent, the same way thinking about sex (or so some people believed) dulled one's aspirations to something higher. The woman under the sheet—ankles and feet protruding from one end, a wisp of gray from the other—was more real than the two men who stood around like statues, waiting for someone to tell them what to do. The weight of one's thoughts—as heavy as the air in a smoke-filled boardroom where politicians and businessmen planned the future of the world—made it hard to center one's interest on a shaft of sunlight or a burning ash, much less the body of a dead or murdered woman. It seemed possible, if this moment could be seen as a kind of epiphany, a fork in the road rather than the prelude to cracking up, that Frank could continue sitting at the kitchen table in the dead woman's apartment till he heard the whine of the approaching ambulance, and that after the orderlies in white had climbed the steps bearing a stretcher on which they would then lift the body of the dead woman, he would stand up, replace the notebook and pen in his jacket pocket, dismiss his subordinates, and return to the Bronx, to his house in the Bronx where Gina would be waiting, sitting on the living room sofa with an open can of beer in her hand, as pristine and demure and cool as the day they first met.

* * *

Marriage is like a fantasy or a dream of being rich or famous, something to contemplate when you're too young to know better. A woman in a low-cut gown, with bare shoulders and crimson hair, as depicted on the cover of one of the "adult novels" your parents borrow from the library or buy in the drugstore and leave around the house, the man behind her with his shirt open to the waist, his lips pressed to the nape of the woman's neck, might give you the impression that this was what "marriage" or "love" was all about. You assume you're going to get married (and that the only way to experience the feeling simulated on the cover—the woman with eyes half-closed, her arms reaching behind her to draw the man closer—is to be married) because your parents and everyone else you know expect it to happen; all your older brothers and sisters are married as well. Of course there are always an iconoclastic few who go around saying they don't believe in marriage, They're the people who end up living together, "living in sin," as your mother, flexing her silver knitting needles and pointing them toward you accusingly, might say. They're the bad examples. You can hear your parents discussing them late at night under the drone of the radio or television when they think you're asleep; hopefully our own kids won't grow up to be like them. When Sally told Rosemary about her life as a married person it was as if she were discussing a person who had once been her friend and with whom she no longer had anything in common. And it hadn't been that long either, less than two years since she'd left her husband, the small town in New Hampshire where she was born, and the diner where she worked, and had traveled to New York, by bus, with a single suitcase.

They were born in the same year, only a few months apart, Rosemary on the cusp of Aquarius and Pisces, Sally in Scorpio with a moon in Taurus. Their closeness in age made it hard for Rosemary to believe that Sally had actually been married for five years. It made her seem like she was in another league, if one could be so crass as to categorize people this way, to have gone through all that, and now be this person lying in bed with her. Nothing in her own experience could compare to what she imagined living with someone for five years was like. Some days Rosemary couldn't imagine ever living with another person (not that there are people lining up around the block to live with me), while other moments—when she'd see a couple who were obviously in love walking arm in arm down the street—it was the thing she craved most.

They were lying on the bed, on top of the sheet, naked, Rosemary propped on one elbow, while Sally lay on her back, head on pillow, reciting the litany of the aftermath of her marriage in a low monotone, as if she were talking, not to Rosemary, but to the glass of vodka and tonic in her hand, to the ice cube in the glass, or to the tip of her cigarette that she'd occasionally point to the ceiling before letting the ash drop into the ashtray both women shared. It was scary to feel so immersed, as if they were slipping into each other's person, falling freely through an inner space where past, present, and future intertwined, and smoking and drinking were ways of keeping in touch with the outside.

"When I arrived in the city I stayed with a friend of mine for a few days—someone from the same small town where I was born who lived with her husband on the Up-per West Side, near the park—but her marriage was on the rocks as well and my being in the apartment didn't help things. I had a little money so I found a room in a residence hotel—a hotel for "women only," but most of the other women were twice my age—and a job, I worked in a diner back home for five years so even though I hated the idea, I found a job in a restaurant just to get through the first few months; it was a restaurant on Spring Street that was also a bar and I worked nights, which I hated, until finally I found a job in an office uptown, I was always a good typist, that paid less than I made as a waitress but wasn't as tiring, and eventually I saved enough money to get my own apartment, one room, really, with a bath and a small kitchen. It wasn't easy, in the beginning, coming to the city and knowing so few people, but after awhile I made friends with the people who lived down the hall, and gradually—when I realized that people in New York aren't all ogres—with people at work, you wouldn't know it by the way I am now but I was too shy to say more than two words to anyone, and now—look at me—I can't shut up. Since the last thing I wanted to do was get involved with another man most of the people I made friends with were women. People live alone for a lot of different reasons and most of the women I met—and I don't want to sound like I'm making a speech about anything since you live alone and maybe people who live alone do it out of choice, though I can't imagine why—weren't necessarily interested in sleeping with other women, though some of them were, but they were alone because they couldn't find any interesting men. A lot of them are older than I am—than we are—and would give anything to fall in love with a man and have kids—most of all there was this desire to have children—but the men they met had no interest in taking on the responsibility of having a family, or didn't want to do it (though I can't imagine why) with these particular women. I tried to stay clear of couples—when you' re single they always want to match you up with one of their single male friends, either that or the husband makes a play for you or the woman thinks you're after her man. And no matter how hard you work making it clear to these people—and it's a waste of time, since what they all really want is to add a little drama to their lives—that you have no intention of breaking up their marriage, once you start playing games there's no turning back. How can you be friends with people you don't trust?"

Most mornings, Sally would wake up first. "I don't need an alarm," she said, "something just goes 'pop' in my head." She was working as a temporary typist in an office in midtown and it was important that she be punctual, though important to whom was open to question. If she were late and she was fired she could always get another temporary job through a different agency, or go back to being a waitress. No matter how late they stayed up the night before, or how much they had to drink, she always woke with enough time to smoke a cigarette over a cup of coffee, and in general compose herself before she went out to face the world. Rosemary didn't have to be at work at the library till noon but she got up anyway, fixed the coffee while Sally dressed. Neither of them woke hungover or in a bad mood, but there was a long moment when it was necessary that neither of them say anything. By the time Sally emerged from the bathroom the cup of coffee would be on the table. ("No one ever made coffee for me in the morning," Sally once confessed.) It wasn't necessary to speak, but it was a pleasure to sit at the kitchen table and stare at one another, greedily, thinking about the night before. They'd kiss goodbye at the door—one of them would say "I'll call you later"—and Rosemary would stand on the threshold, with the door ajar, and listen to her lover's footsteps on the staircase. Though they'd been together less than a week Rosemary felt like they'd known one another for years, and it seemed odd that their relationship had begun the same day she'd discovered the body of the woman in the apartment below: if that hadn't happened she might never have gone to the bar. (The first night they spent together Rosemary told Sally about finding the body of the dead woman and the visit from the detective and a few nights later when they came home late from the bar—the same bar where they first met—they saw someone whom

Rosemary later said she thought was the dead woman's son—"I only met him once, a long time ago, so I'm not really sure"—sitting on the front steps of the building drinking a beer. He'd moved to one side so they could get by and Rosemary had been tempted to introduce herself and offer her condolences—he seemed so lonely sitting there by himself, a bottle of beer on the steps between his feet. But she was a little drunk herself and anxious to get upstairs before it got too late, so she didn't say anything. Sally had to be up early the next morning and both of them were anxious to get into bed.)

She hadn't seen Maureen since the night the three of them slept together and part of her dreaded the eventual confrontation; the other part of her, with Sally's encouragement, was anxious to get it over with, if only so she could proceed with her life in an honest way. What would bother Maureen wasn't that Rosemary wanted to break up with her but that she was leaving her for someone else, and that it had been Maureen herself who had brought them together. Rosemary could imagine a moment when she and Maureen and Sally could all be friends, but at this point she regarded everyone she knew, Maureen especially, as a potential trespasser on her life with Sally. She knew that Maureen was capable of some minor dramatic episode, storming into the library, for instance, and demanding to talk with her, oblivious of anything but her own selfish needs. She, Maureen, was capable of denying that they were drifting apart and that they'd probably have broken up anyway whether Sally had come along or not. After Sally left for work Rosemary would return to bed with a book and a cup of coffee and pretend to read, but mostly she just sat back against the pillows staring at the space on the bed where Sally had been asleep a few minutes before (and where her cat was now curled up on her side, anxious for a little attention of her own), listening to the birds on the windowsill, and contemplating the life ahead.

* * *

Irene stood near the pinball machine watching Harry's friend Mel work the flippers. After much hesitation Harry had placed his arm around her shoulders and she'd responded by slipping her own arm under his jacket and around his waist. Anyone entering the bar at that moment and seeing them together would think, if they didn't know better, that they'd been lovers for a long time. Whenever it seemed like one of the silver balls was going to slip through the zone between the flippers or down one of the chutes that ran parallel along the sides of the machine, Mel pressed forward with all his weight and uttered a high-pitched shriek that made the other bar patrons tum and look.

The motif of the machine centered around a super-woman figure, a true giantess, with a sword in her hand and an entourage of male cohorts or consorts wearing helmets and brandishing similar, but smaller, swords. Some of them were posed on their knees with the swords raised triumphantly while others were shown in profile with the swords pointed directly in front of them as if they were dueling with an invisible opponent. The woman had long red hair and stood upright across the face of the machine, her legs spread apart, her eyes fixed on a point in space that was meant to correspond to the eyes of the person at the flippers, as if she were defying you to look up at her. When the silver ball bounced off the various targets in the center of the machine the point of her sword burst into flames.

Two other men, friends of Harry and Mel—Harry had introduced them to her but she couldn't keep track of their names—sat at a booth on the other side of the pinball machine, drinking beer and smoking. Irene held a beer bottle in her free hand: every minute or two she lifted it to her lips. The bottle was empty—she knew it was empty but she didn't want to spoil the moment by asking Harry to buy her another drink. She'd been in the bar no more than ten minutes before Harry (chatting with the bartender and ordering another round for his friends, he'd noticed her sitting alone) had struck up a conversation. Irene, already on her second beer, had found it easy to respond to his questions, and realized she could help the conversation along by asking a few questions of her own. Asking questions was a way of showing interest, wasn't it? She learned that he lived right around the corner and had lived in the neighborhood his entire life and that he, Mel, and the two other men were partners in a company that specialized in installing aluminum siding, "and other home improvements," and that earlier in the day they'd closed an important contract with a real estate firm that was building a series of condominiums in Queens. When Harry asked whether she wanted to join him and his friends she slipped off the barstool and took his arm, as she often did when she was out with Joe, and allowed him to escort her, his face beaming, from the bar to the booth where his friends were sitting.

All the men stood up when she approached the table and Harry introduced her to them: "Don, Roy—this is Irene." She squeezed in between Mel and the person named Roy, nodding attentively when someone addressed her. Her presence, rather than inhibiting the men, only made them talk louder and more assertively, each one attempting to out-shout the other. Every time she moved, either to reach for her beer or to slip a cigarette from one of the packs on the table, she was conscious of brushing against either Harry or Mel, and part of her wished that Mel had been the person who'd spoken to her first. He was better looking than Harry, with wavy brown hair combed back from his high, wrinkled forehead, and an innocent wide open face, as if he'd just come down from a fire station in the mountains for a night in the city. She'd pegged Harry as a relatively shy sort of person and doubted whether he'd have the nerve to attempt to seduce or proposition her, even dream that's what she wanted, though with a little encouragement on her part he might get the point. All the men had obviously dressed up for their business meeting—their suit jackets hung from a coat rack in the corner—and only Harry was still wearing a tie, a dull stripe of metallic gray, though as a concession to the potential frivolity of an evening out he'd opened the top button of his white shirt and rolled up his sleeves. He'd never anticipated picking anyone up, but Irene's appearance in the bar, given the events of the afternoon (and the fact that his wife was visiting with her parents for the week), seemed like a good omen.

She didn't know what time it was or how long she'd been in the bar but assumed that Joe would be home soon, and standing around watching pinball wasn't worth the argument that would undoubtedly ensue if she came home too late. She was tempted to press her nails into the skin beneath Harry's shirt and whisper something shocking ("Do you want to fuck me?") in his ear, just to see what he would do, but she didn't want to risk spoiling his moment either. Another beer, though, and she might say anything. She found herself wondering what it would be like to meet Joe under these same circumstances, and couldn't imagine him letting so much time pass without making a move.

"Give me a quarter," she said, pinching Harry in the ribs and stepping out from under his arm (he was more like an older brother than a potential lover), "I want to play the jukebox."

Harry fumbled in the pocket of his trousers, found the coin, and delivered it to Irene's open palm. She walked across the room, bypassing the men playing pool but noting the size of the pool table and remembering the woman who was raped in the bar in Boston. Her instinct about this place had been correct. If she hadn't respond-ed to Harry in a way that made him think she was inter-ested in talking to him, he wouldn't have pursued her (if he had, the bartender would probably have thrown him out). She leaned up against the machine with her back to the bar and wondered if anyone was staring at her, whether Harry was consulting his friends ("Maybe we should all go back to my place: Linda's at her mother's") about what to do next. She slipped the quarter into the slot and began reading the names of the songs, but the only title even vaguely familiar was "Georgia" by Willie Nelson: it was Joe's favorite song. She pressed the corresponding buttons and by the time the record had slipped into the proper groove Harry had joined her, his welcome arm around her shoulders once again. She returned her own arm to his waist—it seemed like the natural thing to do—and he turned her around so their bodies were facing each other("May I have this dance?") and tilted her chin upward as a way of preparing her to be kissed. From the corner of her eye she caught a glimpse of the men playing pool, Harry's friends arranged in a circle around the pinball machine, all the people she didn't know sitting at the bar, but as she darted her tongue between his lips and placed her hand on the back of his neck, all the pictures and faces, like images in a dream, began to blur. The voice on the jukebox reminded her of Joe; she could hear him singing "Georgia" to himself in the shower, and she wished she had played something else instead. She closed her eyes and rested her head on Harry's shoulder—"I'm drunk," she thought, "and happy"—until the song was over.

* * *

Just as Rosemary expected, Maureen came to see her at the library.

"I figured that's why you were late," Sally said when they were back in the apartment together. "What did she have to say?"

"Nothing good about you, I'm afraid."

Rosemary stood in the center of the kitchen and lifted her dress over her head, extending her arms quickly through the sleeves before dropping it carelessly over the back of a chair. The first time she'd made love to Maureen she'd been wearing the same dress, a fact Maureen pointed out to her—"I still love that dress"—as they sat at the restaurant on the corner of East Broadway, the same restaurant where the detective had taken her for lunch a few days before, the morning after the first night she'd slept with Sally. Maureen had always been critical of the way she dressed and most of her wardrobe consisted of clothing Maureen had bought for her or had given her ("it's probably too big for you, but try it on anyway") out of her own wardrobe. The white cotton high-necked dress—she'd bought it one morning before work at a discount clothing store on 14th Street—was one of the few articles of clothing that dated from the time before they met.

"I have my period," she said to Sally, joining her on the bed.

Making love before dinner had become a ritual. It erased everything that had happened—the boring job, the conversation with an ex-lover, the long ride on the subway (Sally always complained that men tried to molest her on her trips to and from work, and Rosemary, to whom this had never happened, but who rarely took the subway anywhere, wondered whether Sally was being overly sensitive: she could understand it happening once—"you don't know what it's like"—(but not every day) since they'd seen one another that morning.

They were sitting on the edge of the bed, engrossed in

a long kiss that would end with both of them falling back onto the crumpled sheets, locked in one another's arms. They'd make love to each other simultaneously, or take turns, one of them lying back with her head on the pillows, while the other stretched out between her legs. "Is she as good as I am?" Maureen asked, meaning is she as good as I am in bed. Love makes people say things they don't mean, and Rosemary, sipping a cup of coffee, chose not to respond. Before making love she reached between her legs and removed the tampon she'd inserted in the bathroom at the library before leaving work. The first day of her period was usually the heaviest. If she ever needed any painkillers she could always get something from the drug dealers in the park, who sat along the railings openly hawking their various products. Grass? Valium? Hashish? "I want to talk with you," Maureen had said, rushing up to the main desk of the library where Rosemary was checking out a novel by Barbara Cartland (the world's best-selling novelist, according to The Guiness Book of World Records) for one of the old women who lived in the middle-income housing projects bordering the park. Out of the corner of her eye Rosemary could see her co-workers smiling to themselves, as if Maureen's mannish appearance corroborated what they'd suspected about Rosemary all along.

If there was a listing in The Book of Records for "fastest orgasm" Rosemary would probably win. Sally, on the other hand, took longer, and usually ended up apologizing midway for all the work ("but I love you, I love doing this") that having an orgasm seemed to entail, as if possibly it wasn't worth it, or it didn't matter whether she had one or not. "This guy kept rubbing his elbow against my breasts, all the time pretending he was reading the newspaper as if he didn't know exactly what he was doing." Rosemary wished she could do something ("I'll do anything, just tell me what you want") that would make sex easier for Sally. She wished she could say something to Maureen that would make her less angry or not feel she'd been tricked or deceived. ("You guys fucked me over" was the way she put it in the restaurant, standing up dramatically—was anyone watching?—as if she were auditioning for a part in a play, and then sitting down, spilling her coffee, remorseful, bursting into tears.) She guessed Sally's problems had something to do with having been married to a man who abused her, and just the thought made Rosemary hate all men, the men in the subway, the men in the park, even men she herself had once loved ("how could I have ever let them touch me!"). But whenever she tried to be solicitous or gentle when they were making love (men often feel squeamish about making love to women when they're having their periods), Sally lay back with her eyes wide open, immobile, as if she were bored.

Sally's period ("a doctor once told me I had amenorrhea") was always late. Occasionally, when they were making love, she would mutter the word "harder" in response to something Rosemary was doing. It made Rosemary wonder whether she liked being roughed up, whether all her complaints about men were a way of disguising what she really wanted.

"He'd come home drunk and if I didn't wake up and want to fuck. . . ."

They were lying back, exhausted, and covered with sweat, and Sally was telling Rosemary about her life in the small New England town where she'd been born and where she lived all the time she was married, often forgetting that she'd already told Rosemary most of this before, a cigarette, a beer, should I make some food, are you hungry? They would get up and walk naked around the apartment, oblivious to the possibility—and in New York one never knows—that someone in an apartment across the courtyard might be spying on them through high-powered binoculars. It was just a matter of time—days, weeks, months—before they'd borrow a van from someone one of them knew and cart all of Sally's possessions downtown from the apartment she lived in now, just a room in a larger apartment that she shared with two other women. There were things about themselves that neither of them knew and they would only learn by living together; they hoped there was nothing either was keeping secret from the other that would prevent one of them from loving the other more. At the moment, however, there was no "more" or "less." As soon as she had some extra money, though when that would happen was anyone's guess, Rosemary planned to buy new clothes so she wouldn't have to wear the dresses, sweaters, and blouses Maureen had given her. If Sally did move in they could probably share each other's clothing, since they were closer in size than she and Maureen, and maybe—since there wasn't enough room in the apartment for both of their sets of clothing—she would get rid of everything that reminded her of her ex-lover, call up the Salvation Army and have them come and cart it away.

In a tenement apartment on Bathgate Avenue in the Bronx, little Arabella Jones spilled a cup of vanilla yogurt down the front of her bib. Leon Phelps, a stoker on a barge carrying trash down the East River, looked over the edge of his boat and saw the body of a naked young woman floating on her back, her long yellow hair streaming behind her like a torch. A Greek restaurant owner, Nanos Popodorus, who was hit over the head with a baseball bat as he closed his restaurant the night before, died on the operating table at St. Vincent's Hospital. At the Astor Place subway station a man wearing lederhosen was trying to bum money to buy a token so he could go home to Brooklyn. A cocktail party in a penthouse apartment in a new condominium highrise on 68th Street and York Avenue was canceled because the husband of the woman giving the party had died in his sleep the night before. Dennis Belfor and Randy Bowen sat in the last row of a movie theater on Times Square, holding hands. In the Key Food Supermarket on 4th Street and Avenue A, Susan Cooper, a Welfare recipient and the mother of three, slipped a 1 1/2 pound package of hamburger meat into her pocketbook. A fifteen-year-old girl, recently arrived from Omaha, was seen accosting strange men on the main floor of the Port Authority Bus Terminal. Ed Marshall, a poet, stood in a bookstore on St. Marks Place, watching a girl in black leather pants and a black blouse, with a gold chain around her neck and almost no hair, thumb through his first book of poems and return it to the shelf. Martin Rosco went into the bathroom of the Beekman Theater on E. 64th Street but there were no more paper towels in the dispenser so he had to wipe his hands on his pants. There was a fire raging in a nursing home in Hoboken; three sisters, ages 85, 81, and 79, would die of smoke inhalation. Debra Palozzi, a cleaning woman, set up her vacuum cleaner in the center of the office of the president of the Sirovitz, Rosenfeld, and Larsen ad agency on lower Fifth Avenue, inserted the plug into the socket, received a mild electric shock and fainted. Mark Hathaway got up his nerve to ask the pharmacist in the all-night drugstore on the corner of 6th Avenue and 8th Street for a remedy for crabs. The stewardess from the Trans World Airlines flight 706, Athens to New York, checked into the Howard Johnson motor lodge adjacent to the John F. Kennedy airport, removed her uniform and hung it carefully on a hook on the closet door, covered her face with Nivea cream, swallowed a birth-control pill, and turned on the bath.

On a warm night, a Friday, during the spring of his senior year in high school, when he was still only seventeen, Frank descended the steps to the subway and boarded the F train to Manhattan. He'd been to the Village a few times before, mostly in the company of friends, and especially one friend, Nicky d'Angelo, whose father occasionally let him borrow his car. The two friends would cruise over the bridge into lower Manhattan and drive around the Village, from East to West and then back again, drinking beer, listening to the radio, and staring at all the people. The last time he and Nicky went to the Village together Frank made a silent pact with himself to return, alone, and really explore the place; the problem with Nicky was that he never wanted to get out of his car. "If anything happens to this car, man, I'd be in deep trouble." It was as if the car were some kind of protective armor, shielding them from a world of which they weren't a part, where anything could happen. It was one thing to drive by, say, O'Henry's steakhouse, on Sixth Avenue, with all the people at the outdoor tables eating dinner, and another thing to be one of those people—"would you like some more wine?"

He emerged from the subway at the corner of Second Avenue and Houston. Heading uptown, the only people he encountered at first were the winos overflowing the steps of the Men's Shelter on East Third Street: leaning drowsily out of the shadows of the storefronts, some of them shirtless, others on crutches, they'd stare furtively, like wayward angels, at every stranger who passed, lacking even the energy to step forward and ask for money. As he approached St. Marks Place the scene on the street grew more lively; every half-block someone asked him for a dime, but the people asking were different from the winos, more demanding and assertive, as if it truly mattered whether you responded to them or not. (If you didn't respond they might shout something insulting at you behind your back, daring you to turn around and get involved.) Frank walked quickly, ignoring the pan handlers, focusing on the back of a person a few yards ahead, and then gliding by, casting a sideways glance but averting his eyes at the last moment so the person, male or female, wouldn't think he was staring at them. The trepidation he'd felt before getting on the subway in Brooklyn had been replaced by a feeling of exultation; he was actually here, striding purposefully across the pavement, absorbing everything, the air, the lights, the drone of conversation. In the back of his mind was the thought that before returning to Brooklyn he'd stop somewhere for a drink—though he was underage he'd never had much trouble going into bars and it had been awhile since anyone had asked to see his I.D.—but where to stop? This place with the striped awning or that one with the cactus plants huddled in the window? Maybe it was best to keep on walking till he was so out of breath it wouldn't matter where.

He crossed Astor Place and continued west along 8th Street, not certain where he was going but only aware that this was the most well-lit, well-traveled street, and though the crowd made him impatient since it meant he couldn't walk as rapidly as he wanted, it was all the people milling together that gave the place an air of excitement. Standing on a street corner waiting for the light to change someone behind him accidentally pushed him against the woman in front, so close he could smell her hair, and for a moment he felt like turning around and taking a swing at the person who'd jostled him; back in Brooklyn he'd never let some thing like that happen without a fight, but here it was impossible to walk without making some kind of physical contact with other people, and the woman in front only turned to him and smiled. Small infractions like bumping someone accidentally obviously didn't matter here; people had more interesting things to think about. The woman in front of him took the arm of the man she was with and when the light changed Frank watched as they crossed the street, the woman's hair loose along the back of her denim jacket. Thinking about anything—the awareness that other people might think differently than you—was all new to Frank, and he wished he could somehow get into the minds of these two people ("How come they're walking down this street right now, and me too, maybe I should follow them to see where they're heading?"), sift through their memories and dreams till he discovered what made them tick.

He continued west till he could see the black hulk of a liner parked at a distant pier. In the sky above the river an airplane was circling in the spaces between the clouds, which seemed to be lit from behind by the stars or the moon, like clouds in a stage setting. What was happening up there had little relation to what was going on in the street below, where no one was willing to risk admitting that there was more to life than they already knew: the shop windows, the bars, the pavement under their feet—only the most tangible things were real. He'd felt what it was like to wander around here alone, to be caught up in the throng of strange faces and bodies, to be singular, himself, an individual person, and yet at the same time to be one of many, an innocent spectator. It was amazing to be surrounded, hemmed in, jostled, trampled upon, stared at vacantly or ignored, and yet still feel free—free to descend the subway steps, if he wanted, and vanish forever. He was there, on the earth, no different from anyone else, and beyond him there were the stars, and the great pale dome of the sky. In the old days you could follow the stars, or the flights of the birds, and find your way home, but now, instead of using your senses, all you had to do was spread a map over your knees and draw a line from one point to another. It was too easy; he could return to the neighborhood the next night, and the night after. Soon these streets would be as familiar to him as the streets of the neighborhood where he was born. He would wander the avenues and the alleyways canvasing the faces of everyone he passed in search of someone whose profile matched that of a potential thief or murderer. Late at night, when the streets were empty, he would test the knobs on the doors of all the shops. He would arouse a drunk who had fallen asleep in a doorway and send him reeling homeward across the gutter. Some people would look at him with respect (or hatred) and turn to him if they needed assistance. They would pick him out of a crowd because he wore a uniform. It was his job.

In a few months he'd be graduating high school, his uncle had promised him work in his clothing store for the summer ("you could use some new clothing for yourself, Frankie"), and in the fall he'd be entering the police academy. All the questions about what to do after leaving school had already been answered. He even had a plan to ask Nicky's twin sister Debbie to go with him to the senior prom: afterwards, Nicky and his date and Frank and Debbie could take Nicky's father's car to the Village and Frank could surprise everyone with his knowledge about where to go. "Do you come here often?" Debbie would ask; knowing his way around Manhattan would make him a hero in her eyes. He patted the wallet in the back pocket of his trousers and stared through the window of a bar on the corner of the street facing the river—it was as far west as he could go, nothing to do now but turn around and head back—debating with himself whether or not to go in. The thought of Debbie ("maybe she already has a date") gave him something to aspire to, and he wished she was with him now. ("Oh, let's go in here, Frank," she would say, taking his arm and steering him toward the door—it was that simple.)

Debbie wasn't there, but the place looked harmless enough. The worst thing that could happen was that the bartender would try to kick him out. He rehearsed in his mind what he would say if anyone did question his age: create a scene, act belligerent, ask to see the manager. He imagined everyone in the bar looking in his direction, taking sides. "I'm sorry, it's the law," the manager would say. Frank would wait till the last moment, then take out his wallet and present the fake driver's license his brother had given him for just such occasions.

He threaded his way around the tables in the center of the large room till he reached the long mahogany bar extending the length of one wall. The people at the tables were eating by candlelight and in the dim glow it was hard to see their faces, only the outlines as they leaned forward to inspect the food on their plates or pour out another glass of wine from a carafe. There were only two or three people standing at the bar and no one paid much attention to him. It was only after he ordered a beer and turned back toward the tables that he realized all the people around him were men. He sipped the beer slowly—no one had asked him about his age—and stared at his reflection in the glass panel that covered the wall directly opposite him, behind the imitation tiffany lamps and the pyramids of bottles (not narcissistically, but just to check that he was still himself). "I'll just finish my beer and leave," he thought, when the person standing a few feet away turned in his direction and stared at him over the tops of his glasses.

"A little young to be hanging out in bars, aren't you?" As soon as he spoke the man burst into laughter, loud enough so the people at the nearby tables looked up. Frank eyed the bartender nervously but couldn't tell whether he'd been listening. The man edged his drink along the surface of the bar and moved closer to Frank. "Only kidding," he said. "Do you mind?"

"I'm old enough," Frank lied, "and no, I don't mind. Why should I mind?"

"I always have a hard time meeting people, and one way of doing it is to try to be funny. Cute. But usually I'm the only one who thinks my jokes are cute."

Frank bit his lip, as he often did when he was nervous, and didn't know exactly what to say. His fantasy of wandering into a bar in Manhattan had centered around meeting a woman who would invite him up to her apartment. In the fantasy she conveniently lived right around the corner from the bar; it was a given that such things happened all the time. If he were in Brooklyn, and some queer made a pass at him, he'd know what to do.

The man had thin blonde hair, cut very short, fair skin, and was dressed in a dark blue sport jacket, an ascot twisted into a clever knot, tight dungarees and black loafers. He was only a few years younger than Frank's father but had worked hard keeping his body in good shape so that at first Frank didn't associate him with men his father's age. He was smaller than Frank, who was thinking that if he tried something he'd just punch him—"my name is Ed, what's yours?"—and leave. The man offered his hand, extending it across the few inches that separated them, and Frank, seeing no reason not to reciprocate, held out his own, the two hands lingering momentarily in midair.

"It's okay," Frank said; for some reason he wanted this person to like him. He'd been locked inside his own head for so long, walking around looking at things and thinking about what he was seeing in a new way, it was a relief to be able to focus directly on one other person. Even when he was with Debbie he never felt like saying much until they were alone.

When he finished his beer Ed asked him if he could buy him another. Frank nodded, "why not?", then noticed that Ed didn't order a fresh drink for himself. "At least he's not a lush," Frank thought, though it worried him; maybe the guy wasn't drinking for a reason that had something to do with trying to seduce him (more than anything Frank wanted to ask him if he were queer). All the time Ed talked he moved his hands, from jacket pocket to pants pocket, back to the surface of the bar. He lit a cigarette—"I never know what to do with my hands, that's why I smoke"—and offered one to Frank, who had a pack of his own in his shirt pocket, but took one anyway. After a half-hour—or the time it took to drink a second beer, and then a third—Frank realized he didn't have to think about what to say, he could relax, let Ed do the talking, shake his head or nod if that was what was required of him. (When he was out with Debbie he always felt tense whenever there was a silence between them, and his mind would suddenly fill up with things to say, often making it impossible to say anything.) The conversation, and the beer, and the general ambience of the bar, lulled him into some vague sense of receptivity—rather than fight against everything he would drift along, let things happen—and he wasn't surprised when Ed asked him if he wanted to have one more drink in his apartment, a night cap, before going back to—"where did you say you're from?"

Frank had never been inside an apartment in Manhattan, and part of another long-term fantasy involved eventually getting a place of his own. (If I work all summer and live at home maybe I can save enough money. Maybe Nicky and I can share a place?) Though his brother and sister had moved away from home they were still living in Brooklyn, no more than ten minutes away, and Frank had the idea that when his turn came he would do it differently; what was the point of leaving home if you were going to move down the block? "Why don't we go back to my place and have a drink?" Ed said again. Frank took a last swallow of beer and allowed himself to be escorted past the tables (no doubt all the people who were eating when he arrived had gone, and had been replaced by others, but who could tell?) and into the street.

By the time the ambulance came and took away the body of Rosa Rodriguez, the old woman who'd been murdered in her apartment on Rutgers Street, it was seven in the evening, and Frank walked around the corner and stood across from the building where Rosemary lived, staring up at her windows. It was a little cooler than it had been the past few nights, a good omen, since people were less likely to commit crimes in cool weather and even Frank felt a little less crazy than he'd been feeling, though he wasn't sure how long he could continue going through the motions of being a cop. Occasionally he could see the top of a woman's body at the window, just the head and shoulders, but from where he was standing it was impossible to tell whether the woman was Rosemary or someone else. He'd thought of visiting her before going home—possibly she'd join him for a drink if she wasn't busy—but as soon as he reached the building he knew he'd never have the nerve to go in. As a cop he'd been known for plunging recklessly into dangerous situations, but when it came to his personal life he'd always been content to stay on the periphery; easier to do that than risk going somewhere where he wasn't welcome. He'd replayed all his conversations with Rosemary and couldn't recall anything she'd said that would indicate she was at all interested in ever seeing him again. Meeting her, though, had been the one bright moment in an otherwise dismal week, and he couldn't help feeling drawn in her direction: even standing on the sidewalk outside her building was soothing (there was always the chance she'd look out her window, see him waiting there, and invite him in).

He walked around the corner to the building on Rutgers Street where his car was parked, turned on the ignition and began the long drive uptown. He'd never told Gina, or anyone else, about Ed, and it had been awhile since he thought of him, but something about the voice of the disc jockey on the radio—nasal and high-pitched, with a mixture of resonance and warmth (Ed was from Tulsa and had never completely divested himself of his Midwestern accent)—brought it all back. It was certainly more comforting to remember something that had happened in the past than think obsessively of all the dilemmas of his present life. They'd seen each other at least one night a week all that spring and into the summer. Ed would take him out to dinner or they'd go drinking or just sit around his apartment listening to records. Ed was writing the music for an Off-Broadway show and sometimes Frank would sit on the sofa and listen to him play the piano, a small upright that took. up most of the living room of his cluttered apartment. Sometimes Frank would lie to his parents and tell them he was sleeping over at a friend's house and spend the night with Ed. They would sleep in the same bed but never made love. Frank loved waking up in Manhattan; they would go out for breakfast, coffee and croissants—"you mean you've never had a croissant before?" Ed would say, "that's remarkable." Everything was "remarkable" or "amazing." When they walked down the street Ed would take Frank's arm and sometimes, when they were sitting opposite one another in a restaurant, he would reach out and ruffle Frank's hair. Frank would tell him about his parents and what he was studying in school and his feelings about attending the police academy. He would talk about his girlfriends, though he really only had one. It was becoming increasingly hard to concentrate on Debbie, or give her the attention she required—he had never got around to asking her to the prom and that had affected his friendship with Nicky as well. He had never felt so relaxed, completely open, with anyone before. Ed had a pass to a gym a few blocks from his apartment and on Saturday afternoons they would take a swim, play basketball, and lounge around in the sauna, towels draped modestly around their waists, before going to dinner or to the movies or wherever Frank wanted to go. Ed's only fear, or the only one that he expressed to Frank, was that Frank's parents would find out what was happening—even if nothing was happening, they would think something was—and was circumspect about ever calling Frank at home.

Frank remembered one night when he called Ed. It was towards the end of summer. He remembered the long silence when he told Ed that he was about to enter the police academy and that it would no longer be possible for them to meet. He didn't think (so he told Ed) that he could give his life so completely to doing this one thing and still have a secret life that was separate from everything else. (It's always easier to eliminate the source of conflict than to work it out.) It was the one moment when the older man didn't seem completely understanding of what Frank was doing, and Frank himself wasn't old enough to realize the depth of feeling involved. He didn't even feel guilty, just a twinge of regret. Ed didn't try to convince Frank that they should continue seeing one another. He didn't even get angry. "If that's how you feel, Frank, I wish you luck." And then, with a trace of bitterness in his voice: "If you' re ever in the neighborhood give me a buzz."

Gina sat in her parents' living room, staring at the TV. It was the same black-and-white portable her father had brought home when she was in high school, replacing the heavy console that had been the room's centerpiece for ten years. Whenever the TV broke down, for whatever reason, her father took it to the local TV repairman (a retired GE electrician and also the neighborhood bookie) to get it fixed. Gina had the theory that her father liked it to break down since the repairman was a friend, and Gina's father enjoyed dickering about money with people he knew well. The man would offer to fix it for free, especially if only a minor adjustment was necessary, and Gina's father would insist on giving him "something," which often turned out to be more than what he'd be charged by someone he didn't know at all. The repairman worked out of the basement of his own home and made a modest living selling used TVs as well. If someone he knew brought in a set to be repaired, he gave the person another set to use in the interim.

For all the time her parents spent watching TV, and it was almost never not on, it was odd that they didn't buy a newer model; if not a color TV, then at least one with a larger screen. They preferred to talk about buying one— at least it gave them something to talk about—the same way they discussed going to Atlantic City for a weekend, or moving to Tucson. Talking about something made actually doing it unnecessary. Gina's father suffered from asthma and the climate in the Southwest was perfect for people with breathing difficulties (at least that's what everyone said; neither Gina nor her parents knew anyone who lived there). Communities for the elderly—"no young children, no pets permitted"—were springing up everywhere. Whenever Gina's father saw an ad for one of these communities he would write away for a brochure, and when Gina and Frank came to the house he'd bring out the slick folders with the photographs and drawings of tennis courts and golf courses and landscaped gardens sloping down to the ocean, the tip of a white cloud floating serenely overhead. At first he'd act enthusiastic, as if he wanted to be encouraged, but as soon as someone said something that indicated buying one of these places might be a good idea he'd draw back, take the brochure from the hand of whoever was looking at it, fold it into his back pocket and leave the room without saying a word.

When Gina arrived at the house she discovered the front door unlocked. Her mother, wearing a wrinkled blue nightgown, her hair manacled in plastic rollers, was sprawled on the sofa, asleep. A cup of tea, the string of the bag dangling over the side, perched on the edge of the low coffee table. It shocked Gina that the front door was open and that she could walk around the house without disturbing her mother. If I can do it, she thought, anyone could. (If someone did enter the house to commit a robbery they'd be hard put to find something to steal.) Frank often said he thought her parents were too complacent; they'd lived so long in the neighborhood without ever being robbed or mugged that by now they assumed such things happened only to other people. The Bronx wasn't exactly a small town, and even small towns had high crime rates these days. One disadvantage of living with a cop was that it was easy to become overly cautious and self-protective, to the point where it was practically impossible to enjoy doing anything.

On the TV screen a young man and woman were standing at the window of a cabin in the country. The couple were ex-lovers and the woman was visiting the man to tell him she never wanted to see him again. Apparently the man was running for the state senate and wanted to marry the woman, if only to appear respectable to the people who might vote for him, his potential constituency. The cabin was high in the mountains: the only way to get to it was by a dirt road. It was raining—you could hear thunder and occasionally the lights in the cabin would flicker—and driving down the mountain road was dangerous during a storm. The man was trying to convince the woman to stay for dinner so they could talk things over. The woman said no, she was going to drive back, whether it was raining or not. The couple went to the door of the cabin and the woman, wearing a down jacket, started off toward her car, but the rain and the wind threw her back into the arms of the man. If she couldn't even traverse the short distance from the house to the car how could she expect to drive down the mountain? As the man took her in his arms you could see her resistance crumbling. Not only would she stay for dinner, but she would make love to the man—"for old times' sake"—as well.

When she first met Frank, Gina was still living at home. She was working in the clothing store on Fordham Road and thinking about returning to school. Neither of her parents had been happy with the idea of her leaving home to go live with Frank—they hadn't even met him, formally, when she broke the news—but happily the interval during which they'd lived together "in sin" hadn't lasted very long. Gina's father was pleased that his daughter was marrying a cop, but the idea made her mother nervous. She devoured every word of every story in the *Daily News* pertaining to cops, murder and arson, the more gruesome the better. Every time a policeman died there was a picture of the funeral: the wife with her hands on the shoulders of her young children, flanked by members of the immediate family. Whenever the phone rang she assumed it was Gina calling to tell her that her husband had been murdered or wounded in the line of duty.

Her mother had fallen asleep sitting up. She was breathing heavily, her head tipped forward, not quite snoring; maybe she was suffering from asthma as well? It was only slightly cooler inside the house than out— buying an air conditioner or a fan was another matter of debate between her parents. Gina fanned herself with an issue of *Family Circle* that was lying on the coffee table; she'd finished her Coke but was still thirsty. (If nothing else, thirst and hunger were incentives to make you do something.) On the TV the fiancé of the woman who had stayed in the cabin with her ex-lover was making desperate phone calls to find out what had become of her. Gina wandered around the side of the sofa where her mother was sleeping, no longer worrying that she might make a sudden noise or trip on the TV cord and overturn the coffee table, teacup and all—that would wake her. It was

2 p.m. by the clock on the wall in the kitchen, that peculiar empty time in the middle of the day when everything you planned to do when you went to bed the night before no longer seems important—I can always do it tomorrow—and the only alternative is to lie down in the shade and rest your head, let inertia take hold. Gina turned on the cold water and went to the icebox, shook loose some cubes, and dropped them into a tumbler. She sat down at the kitchen table and dialed Eric's number. She knew it by heart, though it was almost a month since she'd last spoken to him. (He'd called her at home the morning after she'd left his apartment but she'd hung up as soon as she recognized his voice.) When a woman answered she paused for a moment, then asked if Eric was there.

"No," the woman said very efficiently, as if she were dictating the message from a card, "can I say who called?" Gina was reasonably certain that the woman wasn't Eric's wife.

"I'll try later," she said, politely, though she felt like screaming.

She climbed the staircase, wheezing slightly, feeling old and young at the same time. There's no way returning to the house where you spent most of your childhood isn't going to drive you temporarily insane. Whenever she visited her parents' house she felt as if she were imprisoned inside a memory ("dumpy Gina") of what her life had been. Each object in the house signified some moment in her past and it was almost impossible to make a move without feeling she was tramping on the shadow of some person who had once been herself. Sometimes, after visit ing her parents, she tried to explain this feeling to Frank, ask if he felt the same way when he visited his parents, but Frank would either be asleep or pretending to be asleep; at any rate, she never had any sense he was even listening to what she was saying.

"Oh sure, I feel that way all the time."

"What way, Frank?"

"The way you just said."

He'd reach over and place his hand on her breasts or between her legs, as if that were any comfort, the answer to everything.

She unbuttoned her blouse, stepped out of her shorts, and turned on the shower. It was too cold at first and then the hot water came on full blast and then she realized she didn't want it too hot, a cold shower would do her good, and not only because of the heat. She rubbed the bar of soap over her neck and shoulders and arms and the parts of her back she could reach. She and Frank had never taken a shower together but they had made love, once, in the bath. She uncapped a tube of rosemary-scented herbal shampoo and squeezed the gel into her palm. The tube was almost empty but she managed to rub enough shampoo into her hair to wash it properly. It occurred to her that it might be a good idea to just cut it all off (sometimes changing one's physical appearance is the best way to improve one's mood). If nothing else, it would get Frank's attention, though it might also make him hate her more than he already did since he loved her hair long, or so he claimed, and had once, playfully, told her he'd divorce her if she ever cut it. She was beginning to realize she was no longer thinking about her life with Frank as if it were still taking place, but that it had become part of her repertoire of memories. The voice of the person who had said "I'll divorce you," jokingly, was the voice of someone she'd known a long time ago. If you could draw a line between past and present you'd have to say the present had begun the night she told Frank about Eric. Everything that had happened before that was now a memory, and that included all the good times she and Frank had had together, making love in the tiny bathtub of the apartment where they lived before they were married, soapy water spilling out over the edge onto the tiled floor.

Sometimes she wished her parents would move to Arizona. If they lived there now she could go visit them, get some distance from her life. Maybe what she and Frank needed most was time apart from one another: as long as they lived under the same roof it was impossible to resolve their problems. She didn't know what more she could do to make it clear to him that she wanted him back, not only as a physical presence, but as husband, lover, friend. At least she thought she did: what she really wanted was some version of equilibrium, an intermission in the middle of the big drama during which she could step outside, get some fresh air, smoke a cigarette, go to the ladies' room. When she returned to the theater the play (Act 2) would have already begun, and the usher or usherette (she couldn't tell, in the darkness, whether her guide was a young man or a woman) would inspect the stub of her ticket and lead her down the aisle to her seat, the warm beam of the flashlight ("did I miss anything?") pointing the way.

* * *

The ad in the Help Wanted section of the Monday *New York Times* read SECRETARY, LAW FIRM, Good Typ ing & Steno Req., and in small caps, after the phone number, "EOE." Benny, whose only previous job had been working with lawyers, had called the number "why shouldn't I?"—and the woman in personnel, at least that's whom she assumed she was talking to, scheduled her for a 2:30 appointment for the next day. When she emerged from the subway on West 47th Street she paused on the top steps, squinting into the glare, and unfastened the imitation silver clasp of the brown leather pocketbook that Mickey had stolen for her from a store on Orchard Street. She found the slip of lined notepaper on which she'd scrawled the address but couldn't read her own hand writing. Was that 8 a 3? It had taken all her physical energy to get out of her apartment and into the subway, and an equal amount of psychic energy to override her general feeling of uselessness, but all that energy would be wasted if she showed up at the wrong address.

She walked past luminous shops with intricate burglar alarm systems displaying expensive jewels behind layers of thick glass, a clothing store with a single mannequin draped in ankle-length mink in the window. Two men in beards and long black Hasidic robes and black hats wandered by, oblivious to the heat, reminding Benny of the nuns in the parochial school she'd gone to for all the years before she finally transferred to the public high school where she met Miguel. Concealing the identity of a murderer was a sin, almost as bad as committing

300

the act itself, but it had been years since she'd gone to confession or even thought that "if I act in a certain way my soul will be damned (or saved)." Her heart was like an expensive jewel that had been tossed in the gutter and crushed by a whole fleet of limousines and Checker cabs. Whenever they had any extra money Mickey always insisted they take taxis and would wait (even late at night when there were only a few cars on the street) till a Checker came into view. It was the only cab, he said, where you could stretch your legs, and it was true: the back seats of most of the smaller cabs were too narrow and made you feel that if the cab stopped short you'd be thrown against the protective panel that separated front from back. If you were going to spend all your money taking a cab somewhere—"but it's my money," Benny thought, as Miguel paid the driver—you might as well have fun. (She once suggested to him that if he liked being in taxis so much he get a job driving one—they were broke at the time and running low on pills—but he'd sneered at her—"stop nagging"—and left the room.)

"That's a good idea," Mickey said when she told him she was going to look for a job, not cynically, as she'd expected, and with no trace of derisiveness in his voice, but as if he didn't care what she did. He was still in bed, asleep, when she left, and she didn't bother to wake him up and kiss him goodbye. (A kiss is a kind of good luck charm, and as she walked to the subway she brooded over the fact that not kissing him possibly meant she wouldn't get the job.) It also occurred to her, as she turned to leave, that the next time she saw him he might be behind bars, sitting humbly on the edge of an old mattress with his head in his hands, and she wondered whether she was better off hanging around the apartment to protect him (it was her last possible excuse for not going uptown) just in case the cops showed up again. She'd been brought up to believe cops were like angels sent form heaven: no matter how carefully you hide they'll always find you. "But if they did come, and Mickey was there—what could I do?"

It was a relief to be inside the womblike lobby of the huge office building, with its high ceiling and marble walls. Out of the heat and into another world. Composed and radiating self-confidence, the people brushed by her as if she wasn't there. Odd how the security of having a job altered one's personality so radically, even if it was a job you hated. She remembered that she'd felt the same way when she was working and how, when she passed a clothing store and something in the window caught her eye, she wouldn't hesitate to enter even if she wasn't planning to buy anything. Now even browsing seemed off limits, and a form of torture. Why bother craving something you couldn't have?

When she stepped off the elevator into the lobby of the air-conditioned office she was confronted almost immediately by the receptionist—a young woman wearing a waist length red blazer over a white blouse with a wide ruffled collar and a long wrap-around plaid skirt—who handed her a questionnaire and pointed to a bank of couches in the corner. "Take a seat, Miss Gomez, and fill it out." The woman wasn't much older than Benny, and sat behind her desk like an ornament, a wind-up Kewpie doll, propelling herself sideways and back and forth as if she were in a wheelchair. Her makeup was perfect, nothing could ruffle her demeanor; every half-hour or so she left her post and went to the ladies' room to freshen up. Lip gloss, lipstick, lip liner, rouge, powder, highlighter, mascara, eye shadow and eye liner might be some of the makeup she used. Benny, who was wearing no makeup at all, felt pale in comparison, a drowsy flower on the roadside, blanched by the heat and the dust of the passing cars. It would seem that the most important attribute of being a receptionist was one's physical appearance and "a good telephone voice," the ability to sound sincere even if you didn't mean it. The less attractive women—"less attractive" as defined by the partners in. the law firm— were consigned to the tiny cubicles in back, Siberian exiles whom no one but their co-workers ever saw.

She filled out the questionnaire, listing her former employer as a reference. The receptionist was talking on the phone, occasionally bursting into high-pitched peals of manic laughter that made her sound drunk or mentally off-balance. Benny wondered how many people had applied for this particular job; it would seem, since so many were out of work, that if the job were truly desirable there'd be a line of people extending from the elevator to the receptionist's desk, not only women but men as well, each one eyeing the other nervously, while the receptionist, like the all-powerful dictator of a minor African or Central American state, chatted obliviously to her boyfriend on the phone—"I can't make it Tuesday, hon, how about Friday?" But there was no one else there, just Benny and this woman.

No traffic noise rising up from the streets below, no

indication there was another living soul behind the walls of the reception area and the single white door directly behind the receptionist's desk. The small waiting room was immaculate: lavender walls with a solitary framed painting of a bowl of fruit—overripe bananas with black splotches and half a cantaloupe on a large oval plate—which some relative of the head of the firm, or the president's mistress, had obviously painted. As she finished the questionnaire Benny found herself thinking about the mink coat she'd seen in the window on the way over, and what it would feel like close to her skin.

The receptionist tapped her pen against the desktop as she studied the questionnaire briefly, platinum tresses framing the sides of her face. When she rose behind her desk Benny was surprised to see she was as tall as a small tree—a fraction under six feet—or a shrub planted around the perimeter of someone's front lawn. Benny noted a small brown circle on the front of the woman's white blouse—a coffee stain, perhaps—and couldn't help feeling judgmental about this woman who was supposed to be judging her: just because you have a job doesn't mean you're perfect.

"We're going to give you a typing test, is that okay?"

She asked the question as if Benny had a choice: if she refused to take the test, what was she doing there? She followed the woman through the door in the wall, down a long corridor, and into a tiny room containing a large gray office desk and an electric typewriter.

"Just type it exactly the way it is," she said, pointing to three stapled pages of printed material that lay on one side of the machine. "I'll be back in five minutes." She extended her bony wrist from under the sleeve of her blouse and consulted her watch. "If you make a mistake don't worry about it, just keep going."

Benny inserted a clean sheet into the typewriter and flicked the "on" button. The machine made a low humming noise but when she began typing the keys striking the page made no noise at all. She hadn't used a typewriter since her last job, over half a year ago, and though her hands were trembling she felt a rush of adrenaline, as if all the blood in her body had congealed in the tips of her fingers.

The material she was being asked to type was a letter from a lawyer who worked for the firm to the tenants of a building whose owners wanted to turn it into a co-op. "This letter shall constitute official notification to all tenants who executed a 'No Buy Pledge Agreement' in connection with the proposed cooperative offering plan...." She forced herself to focus her attention on the words of the letter and to forget what her hands were doing. Every time she looked at the keyboard or lifted her eyes to catch a glimpse of what she'd typed, fearing that she was making errors she didn't know about or that her fingers were in the wrong position, she made a mistake. Her fingers skimmed across the keys, barely touching them, and in what seemed like no time at all she'd finished the first page of the letter.

"Time's up." The statuesque woman was standing in the doorway. Benny felt exhausted. The job didn't seem worth the effort of doing any of these things and she was beginning to think that maybe Mickey was right about never venturing outside your immediate environment.

"The only way you'll ever get a job is through somebody you know," he would say. "No one's just going to hire you." Each time he repeated this dictum his emphasis was different. Sometimes it was on the word "hire," sometimes the word "you." But by "you" he didn't mean Benny specifically, but anyone who dared to cross from their own world into another.

The woman leaned her weight on the corner of the desk and began making corrections on the pages Benny had typed. Because she was so tall she had to bend almost in half, so that her body cast a shadow across the surface of the desk and the top of the typewriter. She made the corrections with a red pencil—a quick line through the mistyped word—and for a moment Benny felt like she was back in school: at least the rush of energy mixed with anxiety was similar to what she felt when a teacher would return a test, the elation she experienced when she did well—it was like lying on a beach near the ocean with the glow of the sun in her face—and then the disappointment when she compared her marks with the people around her and learned how well or poorly her friends had done. (Once, when she didn't do as well as she'd expected, she burst into tears and rushed from the classroom, hiding in the girl's bathroom till her best friend came to console her.) "You take everything too seriously," a guidance counselor at school once told her. But the opposite of seriousness was not caring about anything, and what did that mean? Weren't you supposed to take things seriously?

"You've done very well," the receptionist smiled hopefully. "Mr. Gorman, the person who's going to interview you, is in court today. Can you come back tomorrow?"

"What time?"

"Oh—any time. Let me check his schedule."

She disappeared briefly.

"The morning would be better. How about 10 o'clock? Would that be good?"

Benny tried to imagine what this woman would look like with no makeup. The person she was at home, in bed with her boyfriend, wasn't the same person who sat behind a receptionist's desk eight hours a day. The only time she showed her real personality, and then only a glimpse, was when the young lawyers who worked in the office tried to flirt with her. Benny felt tempted to say something that might elicit a more human response from this woman but felt diffident about coming on too strong. If she were hired they would see each other every day, maybe even have lunch together, but if she weren't hired it was likely that they'd never lay eyes on each other again. In her past job she'd made friends with a few of her co-workers, but the friendships had never lasted beyond the time they actually worked together. When she first began working, her "on the job" personality, so to speak, had predominated—at least for awhile it had been a novelty to be this new person—but as soon as she began living with Mickey the balance shifted. Now that her life was changing once again what she wanted most was companionship, women in whose presence she felt comfortable and in whom she could confide.

Some people were more direct than others and were happy to tell you whatever was on their minds, even if they didn't know you well, but most people were enveloped in impenetrable layers of armor, and were reluctant to let you in on their innermost thoughts and feelings. Years might pass, and the only words ever spoken between you and the other person would be passing words of politeness (and an occasional endearment) like "Hello" or "Have a good day" or "What a nice outfit you're wearing—is it new?" or "It's hot out, isn't it?" or, ultimately, "Goodbye." Benny envied Mickey his male companions; as they sat around the kitchen table, talking and drinking, slapping their thighs to punctuate the punchline of a story about someone she didn't know, they seemed like creatures of a vanished tribe. Mickey was one person when he was with his friends and another person entirely when he was alone with her. Her place in a crowd was on the periphery—at least that was the place he consigned her to. When they got together with his friends, and his friends' girlfriends, the women always sat on one side of the room, the men on the other. Occasionally, one of these women would attempt to confide in her about the problems she was having with her boyfriend, but Benny felt that talking to someone about her life with Mickey would be an act of betrayal, and that if she said anything too personal it would eventually get back to him. It's hard to have secrets among groups of friends. "Promise me you won't tell anyone" was a meaningless thing to say if the person you said it to was the girlfriend of your husband's best friend. The person to whom you confided your intimate secrets could in turn confide them to someone else—"If she ever finds out I told you she'll kill me." There was also the possibility of manipulating some one so that you appeared (in her eyes) to be a trustworthy person, and by so doing get that person to tell you what was on her mind. "Don't worry, I won't tell anyone." Seducing people into speaking intimately was a way of feeling powerful, the repository or ark of codified data, lost secrets. If you were friends with someone over a long period of time and then you ceased being friends it was also possible that your former friend ("That bitch!") would use what you told her against you.

"I'll see you tomorrow," Benny said, turning her back to the receptionist, and poking the "down" button of the elevator with her index finger. Back on the street she paused to light a cigarette and noticed her hands were trembling, all the tension she'd managed to repress when she was taking the typing test suddenly rising to the surface. The last trace of blue in the sky had vanished and the clouds, like buoyant comforters, were massing together on the edge of the horizon. She wished she had some real news to report when she arrived home, but being able to say "I have to go back tomorrow" was better than saying "I didn't get it." Mickey's responses had become unpredictable lately, and there was no sense pondering too long over what he might say. As she approached the subway entrance she realized that all the time she'd been in the office she hadn't thought once about the murder, and the possibility that Mickey might not even be there when she came back. If she did get the job she might end up spending all her salary on lawyer's fees. It was ironic that the job would be in a lawyer's office; maybe, if she told them her story, they could suggest someone to take the case. A bearded man leaning on a crutch stood at the entrance to the subway and though she hardly had enough money of her own to buy a token she dropped a dime in his cup for good luck.

A train was pulling in to the station as she descended the steps to the platform; she ran for it, and a man standing near the door held it open so she could squeeze in. Another man sitting near the door offered her his seat— it's possible to think of someone other than yourself— and she accepted gratefully. The rush she'd experienced when taking the typing test was confused with the headlong motion of the train, which seemed to reach its maximum speed for a moment before it eased into the next station. She stared at the faces of all the people across the aisle but no one stared back. One could begin by identifying them by their genders: man, man, woman, man, woman, man, etc. Then by their ages and nationalities. One could describe all the clothes they were wearing and the color and length of their hair. One could delve into their family histories, their jobs, their sexual preferences. Regardless of all the potential differences among people, it seemed possible that at any given moment one could initiate a relationship with practically anyone at any time. (For a while, when she was in junior high, Benny had had a penpal in Norway, a girl her own age who was just learning English, and whose letters were written in blue ink on onionskin stationery that crackled like papyrus when Benny touched it. Her handwriting had been so diminutive it was necessary to use a magnifying glass to decipher her words, but what she had to say read like a variation on the content of Benny's own letters: boyfriends, music, clothing, family life, school, "falling in love": these were the vital subjects, no matter where or how you lived.)

At the entrance to the subway another old man with

a cup was waiting, but even if she had wanted to give him something she had no money to spare, not even enough for a container of coffee to drink when she came home. Men in Hasidic robes were in evidence downtown too, in even greater numbers than they were in the diamond district, but there were few stores selling jewelry and none selling mink stoles around here. For the most part, the people in this neighborhood weren't conscious of the way they looked or dressed. In warm weather, men with tattoos on their chests and shoulders walked around shirtless, mumbling popular song lyrics under their breath. The smell of restaurant food intermingled with the odor of garbage overflowing the black plastic bags heaped on the curb in front of the tenements. Small children tottered precariously at the edge of fire escapes while their older brothers and sisters played in the spray jetting from an open hydrant. A thick greasy foam oozed along the edge of the curb. The signs plastered to the store windows—GOING OUT OF BUSINESS, ALL OBJECTS IN THE WINDOWS HALF-PRICE—beckoned you inside, but once inside you discovered that all the less expensive items had been sold, and only the most expensive brands were still available.

When she reached her building the super, who lived in a basement apartment with his wife and four children, in poverty as dire as that of Karl Marx and his family, was sitting on the front stoop drinking a beer. Benny, who liked his kids and often invited them upstairs for cookies, gave him a quick "Hello" and ran past him into the building. Shortly after she'd moved in she had asked him to fix a clogged drain—this was before Mickey had come to live with her—and he'd arrived at her apartment drunk, encircled her arm with his fingers, and placed his face so close to hers ("If you don't get out of here, I'll scream") she thought she would faint. Since he was never in the building on weekends there were rumors that he had another family in Brooklyn or Queens, that he had a girlfriend down the street. Now whenever he came to the apartment to fix something Benny made sure Mickey was around.

The first thing Benny noticed as she stood at the door of their bedroom was the curve of the cheap polyester curtain as it billowed upwards from the dusty window ledge. Then, on the wide bed in the center of the room, she saw Mickey's back, with the scar on the rigid muscle beneath his left shoulder (a remnant of his days as a member of the Cobras), his spindly legs, his ass, and the soles of his feet as he arched his body into the air like a bridge, the springs of the dilapidated bed creaking furiously as he lowered himself onto the body beneath him. He moved leisurely, and with no apparent rhythm. Once, before thrusting downwards he paused for a moment, as if debating in his mind whether to continue, while in fact he was only teasing the woman as a way of increasing her excitement. Each time it seemed he was about to slip out the woman would lift herself off the sheet and jab the pointed tips of her long red nails into the scarred flesh, drawing blood and murmuring contentedly as Mickey diverted her pleasure by placing his own hands under her buttocks, propelling her upwards so their bodies coincided like trapeze artists in midair. Once he was inside her she would lock her legs around his back a if to say:

now you're my prisoner, there's no escape. For the minute or two Benny stood in the doorway, entranced and horrified at the same time, she saw the flash of a gold bracelet encircling the woman's ankle and another kind of flash went off in her head as she realized the identity of her rival, saw the whites of the woman's bloodshot eyes with their broken veins, close up, larger than life, and remembered the day only a few weeks before when this person had moved into the empty apartment down the hall and how Mickey and Pedro, who was visiting at the time, had offered to help carry her belongings up the steps—"My name's Rita," she had said, "what's yours?", extending her hand to each of them—and how after the moving was over she'd stopped by the apartment for a neighborly cup of tea, had sat at the kitchen table while the water boiled on the stove, legs crossed, displaying the bracelet below the cuff of her jeans.

Benny slammed the door of the apartment—she'd seen enough—and ran down the stairs. The super was still sitting on the front stoop and as Benny ducked past him he grabbed her arm, and spat a few words at her through his broken front teeth. "What's the big rush?" he tried to say, but he slurred his words and it came out something like "What's the brush?" She swung out at him, hitting him on the side of his face with her open palm, and he let go, covering his head with his hands as she swung again, kicking him in the ribs with the pointed toe of her shoe, until someone passing on the street pinned her arms behind her back and pulled her away.

"I'll kill you if you ever touch me again," flailing out at the man who was trying to restrain her.

As she ran from the building she could hear Mickey shouting her name—he was leaning out the window, waving his arms, shirtless—but she didn't look back.

* * *

Harry passed out in the bar, curled up in the corner of a booth, snoring, his legs dangling over the edge of the seat, trouser cuffs pulled up to reveal his mismatched socks—one green, one blue—and Irene ended up in the parking lot with Mel. He had spread his jacket on a small patch of grass, probably the yard of someone's house, and after they made love they lay on their backs, smoking, staring up at the sky. She knew it was late, and that Joe would be furious, but she didn't want to ruin the moment by saying "I have to go." The breeze felt nice on her bare legs and thighs; it had been years, she realized, since she'd made love out of doors. "You're the first person," she wanted to say, "the first person I've made love to since I was married," but she stopped herself, that kind of knowledge was too heavy to drop onto anyone's shoulders, and Mel, with a wife and children, had enough problems of his own. And Harry. Harry would be angry as well, but it had been his own fault for drinking too much and passing out. Poor Harry. Hopefully, by morning, he'd be too hungover to remember.

She was amazed how clearheaded she felt, not drunk at all. It was one of those rare moments when talking about what you were feeling wasn't necessary. It would occur to her to say something and then she would think: why bother? If I say what I'm feeling he'll only misunder-

314

stand me, confuse my voice with the voice of some person from his past. She wished she could open her mouth and say the first thing that came into her head, feel that free, without the constraint of wondering what the person lying beside her might think. "He'll think I'm crazy if I tell him what I'm feeling."

From inside the bar they could hear people laughing but the sound seemed far away, as if it were echoing down a canyon or drifting across the water from the deck of a private yacht crowded with men in black top hats and white tuxedos and women in long off-white dresses with corsages pinned to their breasts. Then a person staggered out the back door of the bar and they lay very still; it was Harry, mumbling to himself as he searched his jacket pocket for the keys to his car. It worried Irene that Harry might be too drunk to drive home, though "home," in this case, was "just around the corner," but Mel, who obviously knew him better, didn't show any sign of concern. The car wouldn't start, or he had the wrong key, and they listened as he cursed till the engine turned over and he shifted gears, in reverse by mistake so that the car skidded backwards before he hit the brakes, then forward, out the gravel path that ran alongside the bar, and into the street. Mel sighed, sat up, lifted himself slowly off the grass, turned his back to her and buttoned and zipped up his pants, smoothing the creases, and then turned toward her, offering his hands. As they kissed again, standing up, and his hands began moving along her back, and then under her dress, it occurred to her that unless she exerted some control and pushed him away—and it was the last thing she wanted to do—

they might collapse on the grass again and stay there till morning. She wondered what his wife was like, whether she was asleep or waiting up for him, putting her hair up into pincurls and rubbing cold cream into the crags in her face ("whenever I want to make love she has this stuff on her face, it feels like glue"), though maybe she'd gone out for the night as well, and when she and Mel returned home they compared notes about their various lovers. If Joe, no doubt home by now, pacing the living room floor like an expectant father, a drink in one hand, a cigarette steaming in the other, struck out at her as he once did under similar circumstances (only that time she hadn't slept with anyone, though she'd come close) she'd leave him forever, take the kids and go.

She'd gone to the bar. She'd met one person, Harry, and for a few moments it seemed they would leave the bar together ("my wife's away for the week," etc.) but she'd ended up with someone else, his friend, the person she really desired. "Not so fast"—that's what she said as they began making love, but he couldn't stop himself. As he rolled over and lit her cigarette she could feel the semen running in a cold stream down her legs and thighs and wondered if she'd have time to clean up before going home. She wished Harry hadn't gotten drunk so he could be here to take his turn. At any rate, she was glad she'd chosen to wear a dress, it made fucking less awkward. Maybe the only way to experience real pleasure was to debase oneself completely, though living with Joe, and acquiescing to his demands, was another form of debasement, and hardly pleasurable—if she could do that, exist on those terms for so long, anything was possible. At the same time that part of her could envision making love to two or three people simultaneously, another part of her felt shy, like a young schoolgirl, and wished, wistfully and with regret, that she could remember a single romantic episode out of the past that didn't involve Joe. It had been Joe ("do you want to go steady?") who had taken her to all the high school dances, and on graduation night a ride on the Staten Island Ferry. She remembered standing on the deck, the wind in her hair, as the boat crested the waves, first dawn light above the tops of the buildings, the windows shimmering like leaves on a clear day, and how afterwards—when he brought her back home and they were saying good night on the front steps—he'd torn the straps of her prom dress trying to put his hands down the front. She'd gone to her room, in tears, holding the top of the dress in place, and had spent the early morning hours trying to repair the damage. But the next day her mother had noticed, it was pointless to try to hide anything from her, the same way Joe would know that she'd been unfaithful to him when she came home, it was his nature, as a cop, a detective, to intuit the truth about what people had done.

Joe went through periods when he wanted to make love almost every night; whether Irene wanted to or not wasn't important. Other times, weeks would go by and they wouldn't touch one another. It was during those times that Irene assumed he had another lover, though she was never sure. "Not so fast"—she'd said those words to Joe as well, but his response would be to move even more quickly, as if anxious to get it over with. They would do it; he would turn over on his side and fall asleep.

Mel worked out twice a week in a gym lifting weights. He'd once spent a summer working as a logger in Oregon. Sitting behind a desk forty hours a week didn't mean you couldn't stay in shape. He was vain about his body, but not in a pejorative sense, and often tried to encourage his wife to go running with him, but she never did. The skin on his cheeks was hairless and smooth, like an overripe peach, and his boyishness—compared to men like Harry, who was already going gray—was a source of pride. It was a relief to kiss someone and not feel one was inflicting permanent damage to one's own skin. No matter now often she complained to Joe that his beard was scratching her—their first argument, after they were married a few weeks, concerned his shaving habits—he never did anything about it before getting into bed. Now it was no longer something she'd even mention, not even as a joke.

It seemed petty—why should he shave?—and she almost enjoyed the minor annoyance that accompanied, but didn't detract from, the little pleasure she was experiencing. (After the kids were born their arguments invariably concerned sex, since for a period of time she didn't feel like making love, and Joe couldn't understand why. It was then that he began to see other women, leaving her alone with the two small kids, and not returning—even when he had to go to work early the next day—till late at night.)

On nights when she couldn't sleep she'd get up, put on her nightgown, and go down the hall to check the kids. They were doing fine. Some day they'd know some version of the truth of what their parents' lives had been like. It worried her that they would be adversely affected by all the fighting (not to mention the constant bickering and the obvious lack of affection between their parents) and occasionally, in the middle of a big battle, she would remember they were there and place a finger to her lips as a signal to Joe that they were shouting too loudly. When they were old enough, and if they were interested, and if she were still alive then, she'd tell them everything they wanted to know. Some nights she'd lie awake on the living room couch, a cushion beneath her head, watching old movies on TV (the best movies, lucky for her, came on late at night), or if there was nothing on TV reading lengthy nineteenth century novels that she checked out of the library (George Eliot, Hardy, James, Trollope, and Dickens were her favorites), books she could never discuss with Joe, who rarely read anything but the sports pages of the newspaper. When Joe left for work and the kids for school, she'd return upstairs, with a cup of tea, and sleep till noon.

Mel put his arm around Irene's shoulders and they walked down the gravel path to the street where her car was parked. A distant police car siren shattered the illusion of peacefulness—there was no getting away from the fact that every minute or two something horrible was happening to somebody—and a dog chained to the tree outside a nearby house howled in response, continuing for a full minute after the sound of the siren subsided. As he walked Mel kicked out at the pebbles, sending them spiraling a few feet ahead of him, as if there was something on his mind he wanted to say but didn't dare. He'd had a few lovers, nothing serious, since he'd been married, but most of the time he was happy with his wife, at least he wasn't as unhappy as most of the other men he knew who complained bitterly about how their lives were "just passing," placing the blame on the shoulders of the person they lived with (it's easier to blame someone else for your problems than deal with yourself) as if they'd had no choice in the matter but had just married the first person they met. Maybe I should have stayed in Oregon? He'd had a girlfriend there and for awhile they'd contemplated marriage but after he returned east they'd lost touch with one another; now she was married, or so he heard, with kids of her own. Being settled with one other person obviously wasn't a normal state—not if so many people were miserable, or claimed to be. But living alone wasn't the answer either, though some people didn't seem to mind.

The streetlight on the corner ("maybe we'll see each other again?") turned from red to green, but there was no traffic, then back to red again, still nothing. Then a big truck pulled up at the intersection, wheezing under its load, and the driver, cap pulled forward over his eyes, bare elbow on window ledge, flicked his cigarette into the night. She kissed Mel one last time, but gently—there was no going back now—and for a moment rested her head on the front of his shirt before disentangling herself and fitting the key into the door of the car, swinging the door open and folding her body in half behind the wheel. Mel bent forward and she lowered the window, reached out and touched his cheek with her hand. "Thank you"— it was all she could think to say, as she turned the key in the ignition, brushed a leaf from her hair, and drove off.

Gina sat at the dining-room table drinking a cup of black tea and turning the coated pages of a book of reproductions of French painting, ignoring the commentary but occasionally checking for the name of the painter, when she heard the car pull into the driveway. It was eight in the evening, cooler than it had been in a week, and she'd spent most of the afternoon indoors cleaning house: vacuuming the microscopic specks of lint and ash from the living room rug, washing dishes, changing the sheets of the bed in the bedroom upstairs, scraping the leftovers from the sides of bowls and the surfaces of plates that had accumulated on the bottom shelf of the refrigerator (it was hard to remember that most of the time she was cooking for one person, herself, and invariably she prepared more food than she alone could eat) into the trash, scouring the sink and tub and mopping the floor of the bathroom. As she worked around the house she played records (turning the volume as loud as it could go so she could hear the music upstairs): Sarah Vaughan, Billie Holliday, and the record by Dinah Washington which she'd bought after hearing it at Eric's. (It was "their" record, and "I'll Never Stop Loving You" was "their" song, but listening to the record didn't make her feel sentimental, no sudden pangs of regret about whether or not she should have stayed.) It was soothing to let the words of the song and the music fill her head—she could listen to it, now, without stopping what she was doing and swooning—and occasionally she pretended that she was the person who was singing she was performing on stage in a smoky nightclub, a drummer and a bass player keeping time behind her, and all her friends from high school—all her rivals as well, and the boys who'd taunted her—were in the audience. She'd bought the book about French painting also because of Eric—it was a requirement for the course he was teaching, the person who'd written it "an old friend," or so Eric had said—but looking through it now, the overhead light casting a sheen over the surface of each page, didn't bring back any memories either.

She was meditating on a full-page reproduction of a painting called *The Slave Market* by a nineteenth-century painter named Jean-Leon Gerome. A naked young woman, with small breasts and no pubic hair, her arms hanging limply at her sides, stood in the center of a marketplace surrounded by men in kaftans and turbans. One of the men had placed his hand on the woman's head, tilting it toward him and prying open her mouth with his fingers so he could inspect her teeth and gums. In the background, other men and women went about their murky business. Gina was wondering if she'd ever get to Europe to see any of the paintings in the book in person—an odd thought, since most days she could barely get herself out of the house and down the street—when she heard the car, the sound of footsteps on the path, and holding her breath—the key in the front lock. Usually hy this time of day she was already upstairs, and though she knew it was time she and Frank had a talk about their plans ("if you want a divorce you can have it, no questions asked") the last thing she wanted was some kind of ultimate confrontation, another big scene.

If he were in a bad mood or chose to ignore her she'd fix herself a drink, take her book, and retire upstairs to the bedroom, or "her" room as she'd begun to think of it. Her thoughts raced ahead and she began rehearsing in her mind what she'd say if he began shouting at her—"I don't want to talk about it Frank, leave me alone"—when the door opened and she looked up from her book, thinking maybe she'd been wrong and it wasn't Frank at all but some other person who was also her husband. In the old days, when he returned home late, she'd be sitting on the couch reading, and Frank—as she took his hands and drew him down beside her—would blush and look moon-eyed, as if he couldn't believe she was really there. They'd share a beer, passing it back and forth as they talked, and tell each other what they'd done that day; even if it was "nothing," or nothing earth-shattering had taken place, they could always pinpoint some minor event and make it seem like it was important. At the first lull in the conversation she would take his hand and draw a circle with her index finger in his palm and ask him whether he was hungry, "you must be hungry," she would say, and he would follow her into the kitchen like a sheepdog, lean back against the icebox, and watch in amazement as she prepared the food.

She flashed a look from the man in the doorway to the body of the woman in the painting. Then back again at Frank as he passed through the narrow hallway between living room and dining room, pausing to sling his jacket over the arm of a chair. He was carrying a bouquet of flowers tilted up against his chest and as he approached the table he smiled—it was the first time he'd smiled at her in weeks—inclining his head to one side like an embarrassed suitor or a person who'd entered the wrong house by mistake. He dropped the flowers—a dozen tea roses, a rubber band twisted around their narrow stems—on the table, pulled back the green wrapping paper, and without saying a word, not even "hello," he left the room.

It had been awhile since he'd brought her flowers, or anything else for that matter. There'd been flowers on her birthday, and on their anniversary, that was expected. A bowl of dead flowers over morning coffee. She'd always thought dead flowers might be interesting to paint, but she'd never tried. She could hear Frank moving around in the kitchen, could smell the flowers spread out on the sheet of wrapping paper at the end of the table. Back in highschool she used to take the subway downtown to the Met and sit with a sketchpad on her knees in front of the paintings (her art teacher had told her that imitating the great painters of the past was one way to learn how to do it), avoiding eye contact with the women and mostly the men who tried to look over her shoulder and distract her ("if you don't stop bothering me I'll call the guard").

Frank took the flowers and spread them out on the table top. He slid the knife along the bottom of each stem, slicing them diagonally the way the florist had instructed, before arranging them all in the copper pitcher he'd carried in from the kitchen. While he performed these minor operations Gina stared at his hands, from the woman in the painting back to his hands, not wanting to look directly into his eyes for fear she might learn something that would contradict what she felt was happening. He seemed to be concentrating very hard, in a way that made Gina wonder if he wasn't secretly thinking of something else. She was tempted to say, "if you're not careful, you'll cut yourself," the same way a mother might caution her son, but was too confused by the silence to say anything. She lifted the cup of tea to her lips and realized her own hands were trembling, and that she wanted a drink.

"You must be hungry."

He displayed the flowers to her ("do you like them?") and their eyes connected for the first time. He was hungry, but if they wanted to eat—if she were to fix something for them to eat—that would come later. If he were truly desperately starving he could always return to the kitchen and fix himself a sandwich, which is what he'd been doing (on nights when he didn't eat out) for most of the last month, Gina asleep upstairs, Gina lying awake, alone, in her bed upstairs, in their bed, listening to the sounds he made stumbling around the kitchen. No matter how late he came in she was always awake. In the beginning she'd go downstairs and try to engage him in conversation in the hope that one of them might say something to allay the hideous tension that permeated every corner of the house. It wasn't long before she realized merely saying "I'm sorry" wasn't enough. Nor could she do something to make it up to him in some way—"it," the horrible sin of sleeping with another man.

He carried the wrapping paper with the stems back into the kitchen and when he returned to the dining-room he stood behind her chair.

"I quit," he said, placing his hands on her shoulders, and bending forward so his lips brushed against her hair.

"What did you say?"

"I said 'I quit.'"

"What does that mean?"

"It means I'm not going to be a cop anymore. It means I'm going to turn in my badge. 'I don't think I'm suited for this type of work' is the way I put it."

"Did you tell Joe?"

"No, I haven't seen Joe today. I told Donahue."

"What did he say?"

"He said he thought I was acting strange recently but he didn't realize it was this serious. He didn't pry or ask what was wrong. He told me to reconsider—'Don't do anything you'll regret later,' is the way he put it—and if I wanted to think it over I could take a leave of absence...."

"What did you say?"

"I said I didn't want a leave of absence, I just wanted to leave, period. I have two weeks to clear out my desk."

"Your desk?"

She'd never visited the office Frank and Joe shared in the precinct on Pitt Street and for some reason she never imagined that Frank would have his own desk. Being a detective, in her mind, involved working outdoors. It seemed more apt that he had to give up his car—the car the department gave him to drive around—though one couldn't say "I'm clearing out my car." It was more a matter of tying all the loose ends together (at least she assumed this is what he'd meant) so the person who took over wouldn't have to wade through endless folders just to find out what he was supposed to be doing. All the extraneous material would be filed away forever, and the cases that were still active, like the case of the old woman who'd been murdered on Henry Street, would be circled in red. Of course, Joe would still be around to brief his new partner on what was happening.

"What are you going to do?"

"What are *we* going to do? Isn't that what you mean?"

It frightened her that he'd made such a drastic decision without even consulting her. She knew he'd been unhappy with his job for a long time; long before she ever told him about Eric he'd confessed that he'd rather be doing something else. The problem was that he had no idea what that thing would be. Most people, at one time or another, express unhappiness with what they're doing, as if the image they had of themselves didn't exactly fit the image of the person they'd become. But feeling that one wanted to make a change—they were sitting in silence at the diningroom table, holding hands over the book of paintings and actually doing something about it were two different things.

"They owe me some money," Frank said, squeezing her fingers in a way that made Gina think: he doesn't even know what I'm feeling, it's the same old shit—"we have some money in the bank. We could take a trip some where—you always said we never go anywhere and maybe if we get away for awhile, the further away the better—I don't care where we go—things will be different. We can even sell the house and move somewhere else if you want. I never thought it was a great idea to live so close to your parents, and my parents as well, and there's no reason we have to stay. I can get a job doing something else (don't ask me what), I don't care what my parents think—it's their fault I never even considered being anything but a cop, never had the option to think for myself. I'm sick of just going through the motions, questioning everything I do since the person doing it isn't really me, it's just a part of me that's like an appendage that has to be cut off before it takes over. And there are days when it does take over, and I think: if I keep feeling this way I'm going to get killed—I've been so careless lately, it's like I'm putting myself in situations where anything can happen, it's like I don't care anymore what happens to me but I do care, I want to care, I want to have babies (with you), I want to start over, a clean slate. Before we met I remember thinking for a long time that there was no reason why anyone would ever want to marry me and it wasn't just because I was a cop but it had to do with all the feelings that came about because I was doing something I didn't want to do, and I still have those feelings. Whenever I read in the paper about police brutality I realize I'm a cop too and that being a cop just brings out all these emotions about other people, just looking at someone I'm supposed to tell whether that person fits the profile of someone who might commit a crime—that's what I was trained to do but I don't trust my instincts anymore. Anyone could commit a crime and the people who are least likely when you pass them on the street are the people who will go out and shoot someone the next day. . . ."

So he's forgiven me, Gina thought. That's what these flowers mean. Even though she'd been the one who'd caused him pain by telling him about Eric (not saying Eric's name but that she'd been sleeping with someone else), she couldn't help resenting his anger, as if the only way to resolve a situation was to retaliate, fight back. As far as she could understand, the reconciliation—if that's what was taking place—wasn't even on condition that she never sleep with anyone else again; there was no ultimatum, he wasn't treating her, at any rate, like a schoolgirl who'd been caught cheating (and whose punishment was to stay after school and write "I'll never cheat again" a hundred times) or a spoiled child who'd done something naughty. He'd been the one who was acting like a child: did he realize that now? If his anger could end so abruptly maybe he'd never felt any real anger at all, but was just acting the way he felt he was supposed to, playing to the critics in some imaginary audience. One might say "the way a man was supposed to act," but women aren't immune from feeling jealousy or anger either. (If Frank had been unfaithful to me I don't know what I would have done.) It was a rare couple who, in the course of a long marriage, could agree to sleep with other people and still stay together. One reason for getting married or living with someone was to exempt oneself from all the drama that falling in love involved. But the reasons people do things are often more complex than they appear on the surface (or more simple). A psychiatrist, for instance, might learn more from patients by studying their facial expressions and the way they talked rather than putting so much emphasis on the things they say. When he first began expressing anxiety about being a detective Gina had suggested that he get some help, talk to someone he didn't know, who could be more objective.

"But you're the one I want to talk to," he'd insist.

She was tempted, at that point, to say: "Then why don't you quit?" But he seemed so loyal to his image of himself as a cop she was frightened to say anything. If people don't give policemen (or women) the respect they think they deserve, maybe it's because no one can imagine why anyone would want to become such a person. It's like taking the weight of the world on your shoulders, and for no good reason. Wearing a uniform, a badge and a gun, were all ways of disguising who you were. It was like being a child again, playing with toys that were also extensions of yourself. "Have you ever killed anyone?" Gina had asked; it was the first night they'd slept together and they were lying in bed, watching the ripples of the headlights on the dark ceiling. Living with a cop was different from living with an accountant or a lawyer or school teacher. There was always the possibility that when you said goodbye in the morning you'd never see the person again. Frank wasn't your stereotype cop, Gina had understood that from the beginning. She didn't get married to him because he was a cop, that isn't the way things happen. (The first thing you have to remember is that things don't happen in any "way," they just occur, somewhere amid the interstices of time and space, and even destiny, if you can believe in it, has something to do with it all.) If one finds oneself in "the wrong place at the wrong time" it could be said that maybe everything leading up to that moment was out-of-kilter to begin with. When it first dawned on her that she was actually going to marry Frank she couldn't help laughing to herself, as if the world had played some weird joke. "Never in my wildest dreams did I ever think I'd marry a cop."

The flowers were beautiful and she could forgive him too. He knew as much or as little about how to express his feelings as anyone else, so how could he be blamed? She stood in front of the bathroom mirror and tied the belt of her nightgown—it was Frank's favorite, the one she'd worn every night, practically, since they stopped sleeping together. Now that he'd quit his job maybe they could go to Europe afterall, and she could see all her favorite paintings. If it were up to her, that's what they'd do. Italy, France, Spain, Greece. They could sit at the diningroom table, travel guides and slick brochures piled high around them, and map their itinerary.

She wondered what Joe would think when he found out Frank was quitting. Not that he was planning to quit, but that he'd already done it. Too bad he'd chosen this particular moment to get back together; Joe had stopped by again, early that morning, and this time—they were sitting on the couch in the living room—when he opened the belt of her robe and put his hands between her legs she didn't push him away. The last thing she felt like doing was making love—her whole body felt sore from being with Joe—but there was no way she could deny Frank, if that's what he wanted. Hopefully, it would all happen very quickly, and they'd fall asleep again, side by side, just like old times.

* * *

"Read me a book," Caroline said, "before we go to sleep."

"You sound like a child."

"I am a child."

"What book?"

"Any book you like."

"Why don't you pick one out?"

"I'm too tired."

The young man watched her, admiringly, leaning on his elbow, his long dirty brown hair curling over his right eye, as she crossed the room and knelt in front of the bookcase in the corner. No one had ever asked him to read to them before, not in bed, anyway, and he hoped she picked something he'd understand. His parents had had enough money to send him to a private New England prep school, one that had a special program for kids with "learning disabilities," at least that's the way he overheard people describing his so-called problems, but he'd dropped out in the middle of his junior year; it just wasn't for him. The whole point of coming to California was to experience new things and maybe reading in bed to your lover was one of them. If Caroline had been kind enough to pick him up on the side of the road and take him home with her and feed him, the least he could do to repay her was to read her to sleep.

She returned to the bed and tossed the book, a small paperback with a white cover, on top of the blanket. For a moment he thought of reaching for her again—that was one way of avoiding the problem—but he was tired, and things had gone so well between them he was reluctant to do anything that might annoy her. Only that morning he'd been standing on the dusty road outside Bakersfield, hungry and alone, the straps of his knapsack cutting furrows in the flesh on his shoulders, never dreaming that by nightfall he'd be lying under clean sheets, in the house of a woman practically twice his age. It was easy to forget she was that old, though sometimes when she tilted her face at a certain angle she reminded him of his older sister, or his own mother, or the mother of a friend; it was an expression that indicated no matter what he said or did she would always be one step ahead. (One of his first affairs had been with the mother of his roommate in the private high school to which his parents had sent him; she had come to the room expecting to find her son and had found him instead.)

He opened the book and began flipping through it, starting from the back, mainly to check the size of the type. One reason he didn't enjoy reading was because it made his eyes hurt if he did it too long and the last thing he wanted to do was go to an eye doctor. He was vain about his appearance and thought that glasses were a disability when it came to meeting women. They were all right for some people, but not for him. "You can always get contact lenses," his mother had suggested the last time he visited, implying that she would gladly pay for them, but after a few days at home, sleeping in his old room—with the view of the park and the reservoir where, as a child, he used to sail his toy boat—he was anxious to move on; contact lenses, like everything else, could wait—he had plenty of time. There was a tensor lamp on the small table on the side of the bed and he twisted the neck so the eye of the bulb shone directly onto the page. "Start from the beginning," Caroline instructed, more like a teacher than a lover. He raised his pillow, took a taste of warm beer, cleared his throat, and began.

11

There was no reason why the suitcase should feel so heavy. It was just clothing, afterall, whatever was lying around in the heap on the floor at the foot of the bed or hanging in the closet. As he walked past the monotonous rows of sturdy, two-story brick houses, it banged against the side of his leg, and every half-block he had to stop and change hands. Before getting on the subway he'd felt a rush of exuberance—as if a new phase of life were starting, and who knew what to expect—but after the ride, the time waiting on platforms, all the faces of people he'd never see again, and who seemed to eye him warily as if they could read his mind, he felt more like he was approaching the end of something. It was like waking in a cold sweat from a bad dream and then falling back to sleep, only to be immersed in the same vivid nightmare.

As soon as Rita moved in down the hall Mickey knew there was going to be trouble. She would visit in the afternoon and keep Benny company while he lurked around, feeling awkward and self-conscious in the company of a woman he didn't know. They'd sit at the kitchen table talking in low voices and whenever he entered the room to get something they'd stop what they were saying as if it were too private or personal for him to hear. He could feel her eyes following him as he walked around the room and whenever he looked over at her she caught his eye and held it, blatantly, as if daring him to respond. This afternoon, when she visited and Benny wasn't home, she had lingered for a moment in the kitchen waiting to see what he would do. He'd made the mistake—when it was obvious something was about to happen between them—not to return with her down the hall to her apartment. Foolish not to assume that Benny might come home early, though maybe, as a way of ending it all, he had secretly wanted that to happen. As soon as he heard the front door of the apartment slam shut, and then, moments later, saw her running down the street, he knew she was capable of anything—it was her bed, as well—and that the one way she could get her revenge was by calling the police.

Sandra, his cousin, lived with her husband in the Bronx, and he could stay there a night or two before leaving the city, maybe borrow some money from them—her husband Leo was a foreman for the sanitation department, and they owned their own house, they had money to spare—to add to the little he had. Before leaving the apartment he'd taken fifty dollars, five tens rolled into a neat ball in his pants pocket, but before getting on the subway he stopped in the park and bought some pills. Broke another ten when he bought a token. If he were careful he could stretch what he had for a few more days; maybe Sandra would not only loan him some money but could drive him far enough out of the city that he could hitch a ride somewhere, head south.

It was early in the evening when he arrived at his cousin's house and when she opened the front door he caught a trace of glitter in her eye; no matter what was wrong, she, at least, was happy to see him. When they kissed in the small alcove just inside the door she pressed her body against him and lifted her knee slightly between his legs. He lowered his suitcase and she took his arm and lead him into the living room where Leo, a small heavyset man with dark hair and a thick neatly trimmed moustache twisted downward around his mouth, was watching TV: The two men shook hands, but Leo seemed preoccupied with his show, so Mickey sat down a few feet away from him on the sofa and waited for Sandra, who had gone to the kitchen for beers. "Tell me everything," she said to him, sitting cross-legged on the sofa beside him with her long skirt between her legs. It had been a year since they'd seen each other and Mickey wasn't about to tell her everything that had happened or why he was there, and unless he brought it up he doubted that she'd ask. A place to sleep, some money—she could provide that without any trouble. It was worth it just to see him again, he could tell that by the way she looked at him, batting her black eyelashes ("it's good to see you") and taking his hand.

Leo had to wake at five and go to work, so at ten ("we go to bed early around here") Sandra took Mickey upstairs to his room in the attic. Cyd, Sandra and Leo's six-year-old daughter, was asleep; Mickey could hear her breathing in her sleep as he walked down the hall to wash up. In the bathroom he took the money out of his pocket, counted it again, and checked for his pills. He was tempted to take a shower but he didn't want to impose upon Leo, who seemed anxious to get to sleep and probably wanted to use the bathroom too. Back upstairs, Sandra was arranging a sheet around the edges of the bed. "I'm sorry we can't talk more," she said, lingering at the doorway, "but Leo gets angry if I stay up too late."

The room was L-shaped with a slanted wooden ceiling and contained only the bed, a bureau with a missing drawer, and a number of cartons of dented toys and old clothing. Mickey lay on his back, ankles crossed, and stared at the lightbulb screwed into the socket near the door. He could hear Sandra and Leo talking and wondered if they were fighting about something—Leo hadn't exactly seemed overjoyed to see him, and it made him wonder if Sandra had ever told her husband that she and her cousin had once been lovers. He remembered their wedding and how, during the party afterwards, Sandra had led him into a corner and told him ("I know I'm drunk") that he was the one she wanted to marry. Something about her tone made him think she really meant it, at least it flattered his vanity to imagine what she said was true. His thoughts turned to Benny—maybe she wouldn't go to the police at all but was sitting alone in the apartment trying to figure out where he had gone. She would notice the missing suitcase, the space in the closet where his clothing had been. Maybe Pedro was with her right now, maybe she, Pedro, and Rita were sitting around the kitchen table—just the idea made him laugh—trying to decide what to do next. If she had gone to the police she would no doubt tell them about Sandra—at least, if she were thinking clearly, she would realize it was a place he might go.

He undressed and folded his clothing on top of his suitcase—there was a washer and dryer in the basement, maybe he could do a quick laundry before he left—and lay on his back, smoking, watching the flies and moths, the first of summer, dance around the bulb. There was no ashtray in the room so he flicked the ashes onto the floor and when he finished smoking stubbed the butt out on the window ledge above the bed, tossed it out the window, which was open a few inches from the bottom. He was more exhausted than he thought he could be and couldn't remember the last time he'd gotten into bed at 10 p.m. He closed his eyes and thought of Rita, the way she had jumped when the door slammed and how she had slid out from under him, dressed quickly, and left the apartment. He knew there were going to be problems as soon as she started coming around and part of him wished he'd never invited her in; all he had to say was "Benny isn't home now" and she would have gone away. If Benny had returned from her job interview a few minutes later it was possible that none of this would have happened, she would have found them sitting around the kitchen table, drinking coffee or beer, a picture of innocence. He crossed the room, unscrewed the bulb, waiting till his eyes grew accustomed to the darkness, then returned to bed.

He dreamed that he was leaning on the railing outside Seward Park. Whenever someone walked by he would shout out "Grass! Pills! Smokes for everyone! Sensamilla!" but the only person who stopped was an old woman, not the woman he'd murdered, but a well-dressed woman in a fox-fur collar with a small cocker spaniel at the end of a leash. He could see Benny coming toward him from down the street, just a face in the crowd, carrying a large leather portfolio under her arm and wearing a long bright red dress that swirled out around her ankles. When she passed the place where he was standing she just walked by without noticing him. In his mind, and in the dream, he thought, "Well, she got what she wants." He inaugurated each chapter of the dream by taking a pill, in fact the various parts of the dream were like pills themselves, and the more he took the more he could feel his body expand until for a moment it seemed possible to reach out and embrace everyone. Then the woman who had opened the door of Cousin Essie's apartment appeared, apologizing for not giving him any money the day he came by. "Why don't you come home with me now?" she asked. She was in her mid-forties, with a lot of makeup plastered to her skin and around her eyes, bright red lipstick and stringy dyed blonde hair, a cross between an aging prostitute and Eva Peron. She stood very close to him and tried to take his hand but he pushed her aside; if she recognized him it meant she would be able to identify him to the police as the person who'd appeared at her door the morning the old woman was murdered. "I don't know you," he said. He turned to Pedro, who had been sitting beside him on the railing, but no one was there. The woman kept trying to place her hand on his shoulder and each time he deflected it ("I'm going to hit you if you don't stop") until finally he decided to give in and go with her. Maybe if they slept together he could convince her to lie to the police; then he realized that she was his cousin's lover and if Cousin Essie ever found out they'd slept together he would kill him.

Sandra left the house at eight and took Cyd to school. It wasn't as warm as it had been the previous week and before leaving she put a sweater around her daughter's shoulders, slipping the girl's arms through the sleeves, and then buttoning it up the front. On the way to school she told Cyd about Mickey's visit and Cyd wanted to know whether he would be there when she returned home from school. "He might be," Sandra said, but she doubted it. The last time she and Mickey slept together had been a few months after she met Leo and there was some possibility that Mickey was Cyd's real father—though it wasn't something she'd ever talk about to anyone. If she hadn't met Leo she'd probably still be living in the housing projects on Rutgers Street, sharing a room with one or two siblings, and she wasn't about to jeopardize her marriage, not for Mickey, or anyone.

She returned home, locked the door behind her, and climbed the stairs to the second floor bathroom, undressed, and turned on the shower. The water scalded her shoulders and back, and she closed her eyes, lost in a cloud of steam.

She wondered if Mickey was awake, and if he had any plans for the day. When he called to ask whether he could spend the night she had said "yes," almost involuntarily, without bothering to question why or ask if he were in any trouble. She'd never been unfaithful to her husband all the time they lived together, had never even given him reason to doubt her faithfulness, but it was hard to be alone in the house with Mickey and not imagine being in bed with him. Now that Cyd was in school till three she had the whole day to herself, too much time to sit around and paint her nails, stare out the window languorously waiting for something, she didn't know what, to happen. Whenever she mentioned to Leo the possibility of getting a job or even returning to school to get her high school diploma, he looked at her as if she were crazy ("no wife of mine"—it was the old saying"—"is ever going to work"). The only solution to her restlessness was to have another baby, at least that's what her mother and sisters told her whenever she complained, but she wasn't really sure that's what she wanted, at least not yet.

She dried herself off, first her legs and arms, then her back. From the medicine cabinet above the sink she took a safety razor, removed the old blade and inserted a new one. She covered the lower part of her legs with soap until the bar was just a narrow wafer and kept slipping out of her hands. It was only after she married Leo that she ever bothered to shave her legs at all; her first boyfriends never seemed to mind, but Leo had insisted. "It turns me off," is what he'd said. Once she started doing it she became obsessed. Every time she showered she would study her legs beneath the bathroom light. If there was the slightest trace of hair or if her skin seemed prickly or rough, she'd cover her legs with soap and run the razor over the already smooth surface, as if she were planing a piece of wood.

When she was finished she wound her hair in a yellow towel on top of her head and stared at herself in the mirror. After giving birth to Cyd she'd worked hard, exercising every day, trying to lose the weight she'd gained when shewas pregnant. Because she was so small it had been a difficult birth—the baby had been late and there'd been talk of having to perform a Caesarian—and for almost a year afterwards she hadn't felt much like making love, didn't even want Leo to see her naked till she was back to normal. She thought of the time before she met Leo, and how she used to go to sleep fantasizing about all the men she had seen that day, not her classmates but the older men she passed on the street or who worked in the stores in the neighborhood (her mother always thought her odd for wanting to run errands all the time but it was better to be out in the world, roaming the streets, then cooped up inside her apartment) and how she used to make a detour past the park just so she could see Mickey. He would be standing in a group with his friends or leaning against the railing with his arm around some woman— every time she passed there was a different woman—and sometimes he didn't see her, he was so involved in what he was doing, but whenever he did he would wave or call out her name so that all his friends, and even the woman he was with, would turn and stare, The only other times they ever met were on family occasions, when Mickey's parents and her parents and all their various sisters and brothers and all their children got together in someone's apartment, but there were so many people around and the music was so loud it was hard enough to breathe, much less talk to one another in any intimate way.

She slipped a robe over her shoulders, belted it loosely, and went downstairs. From the landing she could see the door of Mickey's room at the top of the staircase but there was no sound, no indication that he was even there. She went to the kitchen, took three oranges from a bowl on the table, cut them in half and placed them in the electric juicer. She cut a few strips of fresh bacon from the huge slab one of Leo's co-workers had brought him from Vermont and spread the strips across the width of the skillet. She turned on the juicer and reheated the coffee that Leo had made for himself before going to work. When the bacon was ready she removed the shriveled strips with the tip of a fork and laid them out on a yellow paper towel on the side of the stove. She broke four large eggs into the grease on the skillet and while waiting for the eggs to fry she poured the coffee, and made toast. When the eggs were ready she removed them from the pan with a spatula and arranged all the food—juice, toast, bacon, eggs, and coffee—on a tray.

He was sitting up in bed, smoking a cigarette, his body outlined beneath a white sheet, when she entered the room carrying the tray of food. "I thought you might like...." she started to say but she was too nervous to finish her sentence. He looked older than she remembered him and she wondered if she had aged as much in his eyes. She lowered the tray to the floor at the side of the bed and handed him a plate and a glass of juice. She sat at the far end of the bed, watching him eat, trying to make conversation, hoping he would explain what he was doing there without her having to ask. The belt of her robe had come loose and once, as she looked over at him, she caught him staring at her legs, her pristine, cleanly shaven legs. "If he doesn't touch me," she thought, "I'm going to go crazy."

When the doorbell rang they were lying together across the narrow bed and Sandra felt his body tense; he pushed her aside and sat up.

"I'm going to get it," she said, fitting her arms through the sleeves of her robe. "I'll be right back."

He didn't say anything. As soon as she left the room

he turned over onto his stomach and looked out the window. Parked across the street was a green four-door American car, maybe a Plymouth, with a little rust along the side and a dented front fender. He slipped a smoke from the pack on the window ledge and walked across the room to where he'd left his clothing. From the pocket of his trousers he took the small container of pills and shook two green-and-white capsules into his palm. There was some left-over juice in a glass on the tray and he swallowed them down, then returned to the window and waited.

Making love to so many different women—first Rita, the woman down the hall, now Sandra, his cousin, reminded him of the old days, when he'd be with a different woman every night. Living with one person had made him feel older, no doubt about it. Getting involved with Benny had seemed like a good idea at first, but in retrospect it had all been a big mistake. Not only for him, but for her too. He heard the front door slam and turned back to the window and saw two men—one in a blue short-sleeved shirt and dark glasses, the other taller and thinner, carrying a lightweight sports jacket over his arm—weave across the front lawn in the direction of the car. They appeared to be arguing about something, the thin one gesticulating with his arms while the heavyset one with the thick neck pointed his finger at his partner's chest. He could hear their voices but he was too far away to catch what they were saying. The heavyset man with the short hair and sunglasses took a handkerchief from his pants pocket (from the description Benny had given him he assumed these were the same detectives who'd come to the apartment), removed the glasses and wiped the sweat from his forehead. The other one, possibly in a gesture of reconciliation, held his hands in midair with the palms upward, as if whatever was wrong wasn't his problem. Finally, the thin detective opened the door of the car and slipped in behind the wheel, while his partner walked around to the other side, stumbling slightly as if he were drunk.

Sandra had said "I'll be right back" but it seemed like a long time had passed since she'd gone downstairs. He was curious about what she had told the detectives, and wondered if she had been able to convince them that he wasn't here, that he'd never been here, and that she had no idea where he was. A good detective would be able to guess that she was lying, but Sandra, given the circumstances, wasn't a bad actress herself. Her father and her older brother had been arrested for armed robbery when she was a kid, and Mickey knew that there was no love lost between her and the police.

He began thinking that when Sandra came upstairs they would make love one more time and then he would ask her if she wanted to go away with him, He remembered the first time they'd made it together, she was only thirteen and a virgin and had bled on the mattress in the back room of the Cobra clubhouse—the place where all the members took their girlfriends when they had no place else to go and how he had slapped her across the face in anger because it meant he'd have to buy a new mattress and had forced her, though she was in pain ("it's always better the second time") to make love again. He envied Leo, and almost regretted not marrying Sandra himself. If he asked her to go away with him it meant taking the kid as well, and that might present a problem. With a little more cash they could get as far as Miami, and from there, with some luck, hop a boat to San Juan.

1982-85
New York City

LEWIS WARSH is the author of over thirty volumes of poetry, fiction and autobiography, including *Out of the Question: Selected Poems 1963-2003* (Station Hill, 2017), *Alien Abduction* (Ugly Duckling Presse, 2015), *One Foot Out the Door: Collected Stories* (Spuyten Duyvil, 2014), *A Place in the Sun* (Spuyten Duyvil, 2010) and *Inseparable: Poems 1995-2005* (Granary Books, 2008). He was co-founder, with Bernadette Mayer, of *United Artists* Magazine and Books. He has received grants from the National Endowment for the Arts, the New York State Council of the Arts, The Poet's Foundation and The Fund for Poetry. *Mimeo Mimeo #7* (2012) was devoted to his poetry, fiction and collages, and to a bibliography of his work as a writer and publisher. He has taught at Naropa University, The Poetry Project, SUNY Albany, Bowery Poetry and Long Island University, where he was director of the MFA program in creative writing from 2007-2013 and where he currently teaches.